THE PERFECT
WEPON

A *LANCE PRIEST* NOVEL

CHRISTOPHER
METCALF

TT Tree Tunnel Publishing

For Ann
(a few lucky people call her Mom)

We can easily forgive a child who is afraid of the dark; the real tragedy of life is when men are afraid of the light.
— Plato or Socrates
or some other dead Greek philosopher

Heaven has no rage like love to hatred turned Nor hell a fury like a woman scorned
— W. Congreve

ACKNOWLEDGMENTS

Again, too many to thank. Diana is accepting of faults, many, many faults. Kids grow but remain cherished, always. Cathy made me look at words differently. Wendy remains an inspiration. Stephenie's take on forever love influenced these words. Google Maps$^{®}$ is a portal unto the far reaches of the world. Looking down on outdoor basketball courts in Ürümqi, China right now. Did you know that Han (Chinese) is the world's largest ethnic group? Did the author mention faults?

Friday, February 26, 1993

The billowing smoke was evidence of what could have been. The buildings still stood. Was it luck? Did they not put enough explosives in the truck? Whatever the reason, they had completed their mission. Their ultimate goal may not have been realized, but they had succeeded in declaring war on the United States.

Prologue

Lonely was the killer.

Taking a life with the precise slash of a razor sharp blade is a lonesome practice. Solitary. A select few know the feeling, the sensation of holding a writhing body as it gives up its last breaths. Gives up its life.

Looking the subject square in the eyes is a must in those last moments. The killer must accept the responsibility. The severity of the crimes committed by the subject matters not during these final seconds. Hatred, revulsion and loathing must be tamed. Set aside. The professional takes over.

This target had done despicable acts. He earned this death a hundred times over, maybe a thousand. In his lust for power, he had elevated cruelty to unparalleled levels. He'd stolen, blackmailed, threatened, stripped others of their tenuous hold on humanity. He had nearly achieved his malevolent goals. Nearly. The killer was summoned to rid the world of this menace and protect those in immediate danger. But not until negotiations failed. The target was bargained with, pleaded with and had been begged to reconsider his plans. All to no avail. A line had been crossed and there was no recourse. No options. This was a pre-emptive, preventative action. Eliminate one to save the lives of many.

The killer was new to this life, but had all requisite skills. This assignment would be a success because failure was unacceptable. In time, this kill would take its place next to others -- many, many others. But for now, execution was called for.

Silently, the killer followed the target through the frozen night. The destination was clear. He was headed to the abandoned warehouse he considered his secret lair. It was the heart of his evil kingdom. His throne was a crate turned on its side. His loyal subjects were rats and other vermin scurrying into corners. The target would observe their black eyes and find them comforting as he smoked stolen cigarettes while seated on his throne.

The killer stayed 60 feet behind and across the deserted late evening street as the subject trudged through knee-deep, and sometimes waist-deep, snow. The shimmering, yet smothering, blanket of white made the night even quieter. The killer expertly kept close to the houses and apartments on the other side of the street, moving from shadow to shadow. It wasn't much farther now.

The low clouds in the night sky reflected the lights of the dismal inner city. The diffused light from this reflection provided more than enough illumination for the killer to see the rise and fall of the subject's boots; the hunched shoulders and bobbing hooded head. The target was oblivious to his watcher, his hunter. His confidence was evident in the blasé pattern and cadence of his walk. Even struggling through snow this deep, his arrogance was evident.

As expected, the subject turned on the street that led to his castle just a quarter mile ahead. In that quarter mile, the buildings thinned out. Houses were left behind and thick growths of trees with branches reached out on either side of the road, creating a tunnel of sorts, even in the depths of winter. The killer assumed the target fantasized about walking triumphantly across the drawbridge and through the gates of his fantasy walled city. The killer had come to know this subject intimately through days of observation. In actuality, this target was not a stranger. The killer knew more about him than others would, or even could.

The warehouse had been abandoned nearly three decades earlier. Its brick façade had crumbled in many places. Any windows that remained were broken. The floor was dirt, reminiscent of its pre-1900 construction. Sagging metal girders were rusted but still strong enough to support the structure after hundreds of winters and thousands of feet of snow piled on top throughout its history.

Once inside, a match dimly lit the subject's face as he bent to sit on the crate in the center of the empty carcass of a building. A cigarette's orange pinpoint glow followed the match. The expanse of the open space was dark otherwise. The killer stood amid deep shadows just inside the door. Less than 50 feet separated hunter and prey. After 30 seconds, the killer's eyes adjusted to the dark. Death was only moments away.

The killer removed a glove. A bare right hand reached into the right pocket of the thick winter coat. Inside, the knife waited. The pocket kept it warm. It was much easier to handle, more pliable to the grip. The serrated blade measured seven inches in length. During its life, it had cleaned fish, deer, moose and even bear. It was a simple, timeless tool that had been maintained in a respectful manner. A hunter knows to keep the blade sharp at all times.

A silent exhale of frozen breath cleared the killer's mind. Like a ghost, the killer moved toward the kill, circling around behind to come at an angle. The strike could be from above, from a position lateral to the target's neck or from below, rising up through the diaphragm into the chest. With the killer two steps away, the target removed the cigarette from his mouth and brought his right hand down to his knee. The entire target zone was now open. The killer chose the lateral entry.

The blade sliced through the dark of night and into the right side of the target's neck. It was a vicious, violent blow. The entire blade entered the target's throat severing arteries, tendons and esophagus. The blow carried the target backward, off the crate to the dirt floor. The killer placed a gloved left hand over the target's mouth and a knee in his chest.

The deed was done. There would be no recovery from this mortal wound. Just inches separated their two faces. Darkness had taken everything now. The subject sputtered. Blood flowed freely as the killer kept the knife in place, inside the subject's throat. A few moments of life remained. The killer tore the blade free from the ruined neck and rose to a standing position.

The next action was necessary for satisfaction's sake. The killer removed the glove from the left hand and reached into another pocket to retrieve a small flashlight. The bulb lit and the spray of light illuminated the killer's face. The nearly deceased target looked up through death to see his killer. If he had more strength left, he would have raged and roared. But he could only move his mouth to form a scream than would not come, would never come. He recognized his killer instantly. He had seen the face before, but never like this. Never this calm, this confident, this peaceful. A moment later, his eyes lost their weak focus as death consumed him.

The killer pulled a rag from a back pocket and wiped the blade, then moved the beam of light to survey the area around the kill. The footprints around the body were all made by the same size and make of boots. The killer had secured a pair exactly the same as those the deceased wore. The flashlight was extinguished. The killer turned for the open door where the silent night and shimmering snow waited.

Chapter 1

It was an ant.

In the midst of controlled chaos chasing a terrorist bomb maker named Amir Shafiq through the streets of Hamburg, Lance Priest adjusted his footfall to avoid the ant. A single solitary little black one. It was nothing, literally nothing. But it was also something.

In 24 years, he'd stepped on thousands, maybe millions of ants, spiders, roaches, beetles. All variety of frantically scurrying insects had died beneath his feet. He could not recall a single instance in which he avoided stepping on one of these seemingly endless vermin. Killing them was nothing. So why had he just adjusted the descent of his right foot to steer clear of this particular fella? Why?

He knew the answer, but he didn't want to think about it, or her. Yes, it was her.

He'd been changed. No matter how minuscule the transformation, he was different. He'd found compassion, if only a modicum. A microscopic sliver of empathy could now be found alongside his general disdain. And he didn't really like it.

It felt unnatural to care. He smiled to himself and shook his head.

So here, with Shafiq only 25 feet ahead of him barreling through narrow and ancient city streets and a Bruce Springsteen song pounding in his head, Lance noticed an ant. Great. What next, call out to the terrorist and ask him to hold up so he could rescue a kitten from a tree? Should he ask the Pakistani bomb maker to stop traffic and help an elderly woman cross the street? Of course, this was just a phase, right? These new thoughts with their soft, beveled edge of empathy and compassion were a temporary state, right?

No time to think about it now. Shafiq swept to the left around a corner and disappeared for a second. The terrorist knocked a lady to the ground as he rounded the turn onto an even tighter ancient street with bricks and stones beneath their feet laid centuries ago. Lance was around the same corner a moment later. He hurdled the woman sprawled out on the street. Helping her up was out of the question right now.

"Es tut mir leid," he called back to her, apologizing in German. He examined his bodily output and reserves. His lungs were fine, heart rate up but not much, legs fine, not taxed at all. No pain at all in his leg or hip where the bullets fired by Saddam Hussein's personal security guards had ripped through back in Baghdad nearly three months ago. This little impromptu chase was three minutes and 14 seconds old. He knew this because of the permanent clock in his head tuned by years of running. Lance could go like this for another half-hour. He was pretty sure the terrorist didn't have that in him. But he was not underestimating the man. The guy had kept up an impressive pace so far. Springsteen sang and the E Street Band played in his head.

The foot chase started just over three-quarters of a mile to the southeast. Two fellow terrorists from the Hamburg cell were being arrested by police on the street outside a coffee shop when Shafiq rounded a corner four minutes earlier. He was late for their meeting. Lucky dude.

It probably would have been just fine for the Pakistani if he hadn't stopped in his tracks and wheeled around in the opposite direction from the arrest scene. His abrupt movement caught the attention of a certain young CIA operative standing 150 yards to the east. Lance was leaning against a wall taking in the thorough arrest procedure from a safe distance. He had been involved in monitoring the terrorist cell for two weeks with his Hamburg counterparts. The cell had come close to achieving their goal of blowing up the Hamburg Hauptbahnhof, the city's central train station. Lance loved that German word – bahnhof. It sounded much cooler than the English "train station."

It was a four-man cell. The leader and his right-hand man were being arrested without incident. A third was currently being detained at a library three blocks over. The German authorities were expecting Shafiq to be in the coffee shop with the other two. Intel had fallen short yet again. Someone should have had eyes on him every moment this morning.

When Shafiq did his little sidewalk pirouette, he caught Lance's eye. He immediately recognized the bomb maker and started walking casually in Shafiq's direction until the Pakistani turned the corner, at which point Lance took off after him. As Lance expected, Shafiq was in full sprint and already a block ahead as he rounded the corner. The chase was on. Cue the music. It had always been like this. When Lance starts running, whether out for an early morning jog or rounding the corners of the track back in high school, his personal jukebox kicks in. He never knew what song was going to play.

Now, nearly four minutes later, Lance was within five paces of Shafiq. If it had been just a short sprint, the lean Pakistani might have made it. He was obviously in excellent shape and seemed to know the Hamburg urban terrain well. But a chase of any distance gave Lance an advantage over most humans. He excelled at chasing down other runners from behind and crushing their spirits in the last 100 yards or so of a race. He'd done it dozens of times back in junior and high school in Oklahoma. He had sometimes let it string out until the very last few strides before he leaned to take the finish line first. It was nothing personal.

Shafiq slowed for a few paces and then suddenly burst to the right. Lance was within feet of him as he pivoted off his left foot to make the turn onto another street. This avenue was wider, less ancient that the previous street. Several cars were traveling at medium speed. The Pakistani veered left into traffic. A driver slammed on brakes and the car fishtailed into a parked van with a loud crash. Two pedestrians screamed and dove for cover. That did it. This was getting a little ridiculous.

Lance had been watching Shafiq and his motions, his fluid movement, to see if there was a pattern beneath his actions. He was hoping the terrorist was leading him closer to a safe house or perhaps a location the cell had determined to meet at in the case of discovery. But this was not to be. Lance could see that his target's actions were not thought out, there was no predetermination. He was merely fleeing.

As he had in the first minute of the chase, Lance went out of body, up to 2,000 feet to observe the scene below. His natural ability to elevate from his current earthly location to look down on the world around him allowed him to see this small neighborhood of Hamburg. He could see streets and alleyways stretching out in all directions like arteries emanating from an urban heart. This particular view of Hamburg, Germany at longitude 53 33 N and latitude 9 59 E came to him via satellite imagery he had reviewed in the days before coming to this northern German city.

Lance never thought much about having a photographic memory. He didn't really agree with others who said he did. For him, the images he sees on maps and photos come alive. Streets, highways, alleys, parking lots, all have features, characteristics he is able to see in 3-D so that when he is actually in a location he has seen on a map, he can 'see' in all directions. The yellow, red and blue lines on maps come alive to show him which direction to take, which shortcut to trust. Satellite images brought this innate ability to new levels of clarity after he joined the CIA three years ago.

He'll never forget the first time he was escorted into a secure room where satellite imagery was beamed for use by CIA intel operators. The feeling was nothing short of orgasmic. He actually blushed a little. For a kid who devoured maps, with their stagnant images that may have been printed years or decades earlier, seeing satellite images that encompassed entire cities and allowed visual drill-down to individual streets with addresses, license plates, even leaves on trees, was awesome. He said just that - "awesome" standing there in that high tech room with television monitors filled with images captured by satellites just minutes earlier. It was truly kid in a candy store stuff.

Lance looked down briefly from above as Shafiq completed his illegal crossing of the street in front of moving vehicles. In his mind's eye, he could see the intersection up ahead and the heavier traffic crowding the busy thoroughfare. And on the northeast corner of that intersection was a school. Lance couldn't allow children to be placed in danger. Decision made.

It was always in moments like this, with pressure and action and violence expected in the moments ahead, that Lance changed. It was not a conscious act. But he became someone else. He became Preacher, an alter ego given the name by other boys making fun of his last name -- Priest. Since a boy first uttered the name almost 15 years ago, Preacher had simply become part of him. One thing Lance knew that others did not, Preacher is not nice.

Preacher put on a sudden burst of speed on the opposite side of the street from Shafiq. In four seconds, he was even with him and then ahead. The terrorist looked to his right and saw his pursuer across the street and did just what Preacher had hoped. The Pakistani suddenly turned left at the last alley before the busy intersection.

Preacher leapt into traffic to follow the terrorist. A van grazed him and he bounced off into an oncoming Peugeot. He slid across the hood as the car squealed to a stop. He was back on his feet in a flash and increased his pace, tearing down the tight alley at full sprint. Shafiq looked back over his shoulder, which cost him a fraction of his own pace. By the time the terrorist turned his head forward, Preacher was upon him. Game over.

In the next second, Preacher reached out and gave the bomb maker's right shoulder a shove with his left hand. The move knocked Shafiq off balance. The bomber stumbled and then tumbled. Preacher shoved him down to the ground while running past. Shafiq rolled several times on the bricks. Preacher was stopped and waiting for him as Shafiq rolled back onto his feet. They were only a step apart.

The next few seconds would tell Preacher all he needed to know about his opponent. If Shafiq reached for a weapon, Preacher would explode at him and see where the cards and body parts landed. But for the moment he watched and waited. He made it a point to never underestimate his competition. It started back in junior high at a track meet in Bixby, Oklahoma just south of Tulsa. That day, Lance's coach had him run in the 100 and 200-yard dashes, not his strongest races. He lined up next to a somewhat chubby redheaded dude who looked like he couldn't do 50, let alone the 100. Young Lance knew he had the chubster beat and started evaluating the other racers. So he was more than a little surprised when chubby proceeded to blow away everyone else in the race. It wasn't even close at the finish line.

He learned two valuable life lessons in those 12 seconds. First, big boys with big bellies can have big muscles underneath. Second, the book under the cover can definitely be something other than what you expect. Since then, he could count on one hand the times he had underestimated someone. He regretted each.

Two seconds passed as he and Shafiq surveyed each other. Lance was watching the Pakistani's ability to take in details. It was in his eyes. And they didn't leave his. No H2T – head to toe optical vertical sweep; no recognizable cognition of the strengths and weakness of his opponent; no shift to a defensive stance. Lance would need to make the first move.

He did so in Arabic, which surprised the hell out of Shafiq, since Lance's hair was bleached blonde and blue contacts covered his hazel eyes. He was the picture of the Teutonic man, Nordic and white. "My brother, why do you run from me?"

Shafiq, taken back, responded in fluent Arabic, not his native Punjabi. "Why do you chase me?" He heaved and drew in a huge breath.

"Because you ran my brother." Lance smiled.

"I am not your brother." Shafiq did not smile.

"We are all brothers in Allah's eyes. All believers, that is." Lance's smile widened and his wait was over.

Shafiq shifted weight to his right foot and threw a right punch. It was telegraphed by the shift of body weight, clenching of fingers on the right hand and slight gyration of Shafiq's right shoulder. Lance saw the parts of the Pakistani's anatomy at work and recognized the action before the human delivering the punch knew it himself. He knew what was happening under the terrorist's clothing, below his skin. He knew the nerve impulses sent form brain to the gastrocnemius, the major calf muscle, would cause it to contract which flexed toes and brought the man up onto the ball of his right foot. Lance knew the man stood just a hair under 5 feet, 11 inches which allowed him to reach a total of 7 feet, 9 inches when fully extended from toe to outstretched finger. Knowing this allowed Lance to lean back slightly and watch the entire series of motions from 8 feet away.

Preacher moved his head to the left and deflected the blow to the side with an extended open left palm. Shafiq pulled back and launched a left rising punch toward Preacher's throat. Preacher shifted his weight to the right and the shot grazed his shoulder. With the move, Preacher knew what he needed to know about Shafiq's training. He knew the bomb maker had been to training camps in Libya. He knew what type of martial arts training he had been provided. The two opening moves and the recovery stance following the initial punch were karate. His choice of the moves let Preacher know the next two or three moves based upon Shafiq's "kata" or model of moves.

Indeed, Shafiq's offensive barrage included a combination of moves Preacher had seen a number of times. They were delivered with speed and strength, but not nearly as fast or as strong as those delivered by Master Jun at Harvey Point, the CIA training facility Preacher had called home for most of three years. Preacher had initially been beaten and bruised by the brutality of his Master's training, but eventually improved to inflict substantial pain on the martial arts master. Shafiq was good, but he was simply no match for Preacher, who along with karate, had mastered seven other forms of martial art under intensive, painful, inhuman training. He had speed, strength and knowledge on his side. But he still maintained respect for the element of surprise.

Their battle kept them in close contact in the narrow alley. Shafiq attempted multiple punches and added elbow blows along the way. A couple of them made contact with Preacher's arms and one smacked his cheek pretty good. It stung and served to put resolve in Preacher's intentions. In response to

Shafiq's sixth thrust, a double-punch and left kick, Preacher countered with a duck, contraction of his own right gastrocnemius muscle which put pressure on the ball of his right foot for leverage followed by a vicious right-handed open-palm blow to the Pakistani's mid section. Had Shafiq's stomach and other organs below his diaphragm not been in the way, the blow may well have broken the terrorist's spine. Shafiq gasped, groaned and collapsed to one knee. Lance could have finished it, but wanted to see how his opponent responded to such a nasty blow. After two seconds, Shafiq rose and faced Lance. His eyes showed determination as he struggled to bring oxygen into his lungs. He then dipped to attempt a sweeping right leg kick. It was an offensive move born of desperation.

Now, the natural reaction to this move is to step back, jump or bend your knee sideways to absorb the blow. Instead, Preacher pivoted in the direction of the coming kick and dipped down to bring his right knee into the path of Shafiq's swinging shin. The crack was audible. The Pakistani's tibia was broken as moving force met immovable object.

The fight was over. Shafiq fell to the ground and brought his leg up and wrapped his hands around his shattered right leg bone. He moaned for a moment before biting his lip. He might have gotten up and soldiered on, but that was a hopeless endeavor. He would have just been punished more. Instead he looked up at Preacher.

"So you caught me, what now?" He blurted the words through his pain.

Lance looked at him for a few moments. He took in the whole picture from head to toe. What he saw did not surprise him by any means. His brief review of Shafiq's file, along with the other individuals in this Hamburg cell, gave him the basics he needed to know about the Pakistani. He could see those attributes now. Attractive, well educated, well groomed, from a high socio-economic status family. Not a foot soldier of the jihad. Most of all, Lance could see intelligence. This guy was smart, deadly smart. The bombs he had produced were smart as well. They had killed hundreds.

Another thing shot through Lance's head as he looked down as his captive terrorist. He wondered for the briefest moment what she would do now. How would she gather information? How long would she let this cold-blooded killer continue to breath before she put a bullet between his eyes? Or, would she torture him, make him suffer and even beg for death? That sounded more like her.

Those thoughts were fleeting, but they were there. And they pissed Lance off. He shouldn't be thinking about her. Shouldn't care how she would handle this situation. But damn, here he was doing it again. He'd need to get control of this, quick-like.

He smiled and spoke again in Arabic. "Now we pray."

"What?"

"It is time, almost noon. Time for dhuhr." Lance held up his wrist and tapped the watch. It was nearly time for the mid-day prayer. "Will you pray with me brother to remember Allah and seek guidance?"

Shafiq looked at his own watch with his hands still hugging his broken leg. "Don't you need to radio other police and let them know you have me?"

"There's time for that. I know the pillars of law enforcement just as I do the pillars of our faith. And right now, we are called to prayer. Will you join me?" With that, Lance stepped back and reached into a holster underneath his jacket to pull out his standard Hamburg police handgun. He held up the gun to show he did not have a finger on the trigger. Shafiq looked at the gun and shook his head, obviously wondering why this crazy German policeman hadn't pulled the gun before and just shot him. Lance knelt and adjusted his orientation to face southeast toward the Kaaba in Mecca. He then placed the gun on the ground beside him. He looked over his shoulder to the man on the ground, "I'm sorry we don't have water for cleansing or rugs to kneel upon, but we must make do."

Lance waited with his hands on his knees a few feet from Shafiq who was definitely surprised by this turn of events. Slowly, the Pakistani rolled over from his rear end to get on his knees. The movement was clearly painful with his broken leg and all. He also couldn't believe this policeman had turned his back on him. The two men prayed in silence, mouthing the words of the salat, or prayer. Both bowing heads and falling to the ground in supplication to Allah. If the Pakistani thought about attacking, he never acted upon it.

When finished, Lance stayed on his knees but turned to Shafiq to talk at his level. "Thank you for joining me brother. No matter our differences, we must follow the laws of God. Peace be with you."

"I agree. Peace be with you," Shafiq adjusted his weight to his left to take pressure off his right leg. "What do we do now?"

"Can I ask what guidance you prayed for just now?" Lance smiled again.

"Certainly. I prayed for strength for what I will surely face. I prayed that Allah would give me the strength to remain at peace during the coming days. I thanked him for choosing me to fight for his righteousness. For blessing me with truth and wisdom."

"Very good. Do you want to know what I prayed for?"

"Yes, please share with me." Lance's peaceful demeanor had calmed Shafiq.

"I also prayed for strength. I asked for the strength not to kill you now." Lance kept the smile on his face. He was gentle, subdued. His body implied no threat.

"Kill me?" Shafiq was perplexed. "You plan to arrest me and take me in for questioning don't you?"

Lance did not reply, only smiled. A few moments later he answered, "Do you want to know what guidance I prayed for this morning before dawn?"

Shafiq didn't answer this time. He only stared.

"I'll tell you. I prayed for the strength and wisdom to find you and your friends. I prayed for his help to stop you from betraying everything Islam stands for with your murderous actions, your bombs that kill indiscriminately." Lance smiled wider, but his smile was not really for Shafiq.

He would have burst out laughing if it wouldn't have spoiled the moment. He was so totally full of shit. He had basically become a Muslim over the past year leading up to and after the brief Gulf War. But his prayers were anything but pleas for help from Allah. He didn't ask for help this morning or a few minutes ago. Instead, he uses the five-times-a-day prayer to remember song lyrics. Just a minute ago, he tried like hell to recall the second refrain of another Springsteen song he hadn't heard in forever. He couldn't remember the verse and it was killing him. Shafiq didn't need to know this little tidbit. Something like that might make Lance sound crazy. Anyway, Lance was on a roll with the whopper he was telling.

"I don't know what you are talking about. I am not a murderer." Shafiq gave himself away too easily. He was going to plead innocent and profess guilt only by association. Lance was a little disappointed. It was not a good lie, no effort behind it. But he assumed it was part of their terrorist training. Funny how they were so committed to their goal of killing and maiming Western and Jewish infidels, but not man enough to stand up and admit their crimes. They hid behind terror and claimed God was on their side when they killed the innocent. Many even believed what they were saying. A perfect lie.

"Of course not. You don't know anything about assembling bombs or placing them in locations where they can kill innocent people. Or about detonating them remotely from a safe distance but still close enough to admire your work. None of that, correct?" Lance said this last part in English and it did exactly what he'd hoped it would. It shook Shafiq.

Shafiq could only look at Lance. He had no answer.

Lance switched to German. "You wouldn't know anything about growing up on manicured streets in Lahore while others suffered in poverty. You wouldn't know what it's like to get a new bike on your birthday and ride up and down streets lined with pretty houses while others endure poverty-stricken lives, dreaming about one day living a life of privilege and excess. You wouldn't know what it's like to be able to afford a Western education in England and have sex with British girlfriends and enjoy the freedoms of an open society while slowly being sucked into a lie that festers among the supposed righteous. You wouldn't know about that would you, Amir."

Lance had made it all up on the spot, like normal. Shafiq was dumbfounded. He had started this day like he had every other in Hamburg. Sure of the fact that he was doing Allah's work. Certain that he was a vital part of the jihad against the evils of the West. But he was also secure in his anonymity. Lance had just blown that away. The gig was up.

"I see you processing," Lance was back to Arabic. "You are wondering what is happening? Who am I?" Lance closed his eyes. He was cracking up inside, but he did have a job to do. Seibel, his CIA mentor, sent him here to work with the Hamburg police and local CIA operatives to gather whatever information he could about this cell and its connections to al Qaeda, the silent spreading menace. The fact that he had lucked into spotting, chasing and catching the chief bomb maker for the most wanted Hamburg cell was pure chance. But life just worked that way for Lance. He opened his eyes. The smile was gone. "God has spoken to me."

The next seconds were a blur. Preacher was on his feet and then on top of Shafiq. He shoved the terrorist on his stomach and pressed the man's face to the bricks that paved the alley. He reached back to grab Shafiq's right foot below the fractured tibia. He wrenched and twisted the foot. The pain must be excruciating and Shafiq should be screaming. But Preacher dug his knee into the bomb maker's back, which forced out all breath, not allowing him to shriek in pain. After wrenching the foot a second time, Preacher released it and spoke quietly into the weeping man's ear. He chose English for this part.

"Yes Amir, God speaks to the chosen. I am one. It was not by chance that I followed you today. I have been with you for weeks. Watching you and your friends as you blaspheme Islam and Allah with your bombs and terror and murder. I have been told that you are to speak with me now, man-to-man, brother-to-brother. You are to tell me everything. You do not have a choice in the matter, brother. And then, after you tell me your secrets and betray your confidants, I will give you my gun so you can put it in your mouth and end the pain this life has brought you. I'll help you pull the trigger. I understand Amir, it will be difficult for you.

"You will not go to paradise and your virgins like you were hoping, but you will be doing God's will, for he has spoken to me. I am your fire, your flame. I am your welcome mat to hell and oblivion." Because Shafiq was face down on the bricks he couldn't see Preacher's face. If he could, he would see that it was blank. This was nothing. Shafiq was nothing. Preacher saw him as less than the ant he had avoided killing minutes earlier. He wasn't going to kill this terrorist today. He was much more valuable than a single alleyway confession.

It didn't take much more. Shafiq was broken. Turned out, he was not as committed to his cause as Preacher was to his. And Preacher was convincing, always is. Lying there on top of a Pakistani bomb maker on centuries old bricks just blocks from the Elbe River in Hamburg, Germany, Lance Priest was nothing less than the hand and voice of a vindictive god. He was the gifted liar, the lethal, ruthless weapon his government needed to fight a new enemy that had declared war on the United States.

Chapter 2

"Drop your pants."

Marta Illena Sidorova's words were a command. The gun in her hand backed up the words. Lance did as he was told.

He undid his belt and let the pants fall to his boots right there on the freezing front porch of a beautiful and secluded mountain villa with snow on the ground, in the trees and in the air. He also hooked his thumb in the waist of his underwear to pull them down a couple of inches and lifted up his shirt to expose his hip.

It was only the second time he had seen her. He didn't take his eyes from hers. She moved hers from his to look at his right leg and hip. The two new scars were there. Still red and inflamed but significantly healed since the bullets had struck him three weeks and two days ago in Baghdad. She held the gun in her right hand because her more dominant left hand was still wrapped. Healing from the bullet Lance had sent through it three weeks and two days ago. If she were to lower her pants, the bullet wound on her right thigh would also be red and inflamed, but healing nicely after field surgery was performed in the apartment overlooking death and destruction below in Baghdad. Lance had also fired that bullet.

She looked up from his wounds to meet his eyes. "So it is true. You did not come out of your mission unscathed." Her voice was calm, subdued. Lance had expected her to be angry. He expected the gun as well.

"Others weren't as lucky. Some didn't make it home. Two bullets are nothing." His words were honest, but they also carried a code. He should have killed her that day, but didn't. Or, more accurately, he couldn't.

"There are casualties in most missions. We all must die sometime, right?" Her English was perfect. No Russian accent. "It probably should have been my time, I think."

Lance raised the waistband of his underwear and let the shirt fall and bent to pull his pants up. He didn't know what to expect when he knocked on the door. A few minutes earlier, he made a point of making as much noise as possible when he parked the car at the end of the driveway a couple hundred yards away. He had revved the engine several times before he slammed the door, twice. The noise easily carried across the field of snow. His chosen path to the front porch of the villa was out in the open where he could clearly be seen from the wall of windows on the west side of the structure.

He found the place easy enough. Seibel's coordinates were spot on. It was indeed a hidden slice of paradise up several dirt and gravel roads that no casual traveler would trek. It was a secret alpine lair for a secretive person. There were surely alarms that he had triggered. She would have installed these protective devices well before taking up residence.

"Would you like to come in?" She lowered the gun and stepped to the side. Her step back carried with it the tiniest hint of a limp in her right leg. Lance winced slightly, witnessing her pain. A reaction he should not be feeling. Damn.

"Yes. Thank you," Lance nodded like a gentleman before stepping into the foyer. He took his eyes from hers, but not without some difficulty. She was mesmerizing in a way. After removing his snow-covered boots, he stepped past her, turning his back to her. He couldn't know what she would do in this moment. She could raise the gun and put a clean shot through his skull. She could jam the barrel of her Graz Buria into his back and order him to the floor. He was ready for anything. But didn't plan to fight back.

Instead, she simply closed the door behind him, turning her back on him. A wary opponent would have surveyed the yard and forest for signs of others who had come with Lance. She didn't look. She didn't seem concerned about those things. Marta walked past him into a small living room with couches and side chairs and a small fire crackling in the fireplace. She set her gun down on the coffee table and sat on a couch, motioning for him to sit in the sofa facing her. He did so. They simply looked at each other. There was no rush. There were no deadlines, no nuclear weapons to be captured, and no head of state to assassinate. Lance was content to let her lead the conversation. He really hadn't thought much further than seeing her again. And whether she would kill him, of course.

"I guess I should be surprised to see you." She broke the silence.

"He didn't tell you I might stop by for a visit?"

"No. I haven't spoken with him since Baghdad. Not since he left after his doctor stitched me up." She was obviously a little more comfortable. Her English words carried a breath of Russian accent. "We only talk a few times a year anyway."

"But you're not surprised to see me."

"No. I didn't really expect you to come. But I knew we would meet again." The smile that accompanied these words was delightful. Lance could tell by the set of her face that smiling was not something she did often, or even naturally. "Our meeting in Iraq was…" she looked away for the first time. His eyes followed hers to the windows and the forest and mountains beyond them. "Strange, I think that is the word."

"Strange works." He agreed with her and smiled.

"Can I ask why you came here? Why didn't you pick a more public place?" Her question implied that coming here was not the smartest thing he'd done. A public place might offer more security, less chance that she would kill him on the spot. He had shot her, after all.

"I don't know really. I have to get back to the U.S. soon. I guess I just needed to. Sorry, that's not much of an answer." He noticed something else happening. He was telling her the truth. Like Marta's smile, it was not something he did often. Honesty didn't come naturally to him.

"That's fine. I think I understand." Her smile was back. Lance shook his head ever so slightly. She noticed, of course. "What is it?" Her smile even wider.

"You should be mad, pissed. I'd understand if you'd shot me a few minutes ago. I'd be fine if you killed me. But instead you're sitting there smiling at me."

So they just looked at each other for the next few moments. Each smiling. It was surprisingly easy for both. She broke the silence again. "I can't help myself." Now it was her turn to shake her head. She turned again to look out the window, but not before the faintest blush lit her face.

Chapter 3

"Go back. Go back to the last one." She was giggling and speaking Russian, her natural language. Her dialect from Novosibirsk in Siberia.

They were sitting outside on the rear balcony overlooking a snow-covered meadow with snow-covered pines in the near distance and unspeakably gorgeous snow-covered mountain peaks filling up the rest of their view. Their cups of coffee steamed into the frigid air. It was the morning of their second day together. As a gentleman, Lance initially declined and then graciously accepted her invitation to stay, sleeping in the small but charming guest bedroom, of course.

He was putting on a show for her. In the last 11 minutes, he had been no fewer than 60 different characters. The little act started when she asked him to tell her something honestly. He proceeded to tell her honest truth after honest truth, but did so in the guise of different characters. His flawless transition from Bavarian nun to Mexican gardener to California surfer to Saudi carpet salesman was nothing less than flabbergasting. Marta had never seen anything or anyone like it. Lance couldn't help but think of watching Robin Williams on Carson or Letterman running through a dozen or so characters in his frenetic manner.

Lance was a one-man show. The coffee cup in his hands, or placed on the table in front of them, was his only prop. And he had a bunch more characters he could pull out, but Marta finally asked him to stop and go back to the used car salesman from Texas he had just done before switching to an old man in a Jewish deli.

He affected the thick Texas accent again and adjusted an invisible cowboy hat as he greeted her. "Ma'am, I believe I have just the automobile for you. It's a low mileage Pontiac and I do declare, you would look like a million dollars behind the wheel."

Her giggle evolved into full laughter as he tilted his head and put the cheesiest smile ever on his face. It was toothy and anything but sincere. "Ma'am, I'm quite serious when I say, you and this car were made for each other. What do you say, can I put you in this beauty today?"

"That's it. That's the one. What's your name?" She was playful and reached out a hand to touch his forearm. He wished he didn't have the heavy jacket on so her touch would have been on his skin.

"I'm Bart. Bart Radish, but my friends call me Horse." He kept the cheesy smile going.

"Horse? Why do they call you that?"

"On account of my last name, ma'am."

She squinched up her forehead for a moment. "Oh, I get it. Your last name is Radish." And she laughed some more. It was infectious and, lovely, that was the word that came to his mind. She was lovely.

"You got it little lady." He tipped his pretend cowboy hat again.

Marta sat back in her chair and shook her head. She brought her coffee cup to her lips. After looking into the distance for a few quiet moments, she turned back to him and spoke in English. "You are truly something. He did not lie when he told me about you and your various talents." After shaking her head again she smiled a new smile; one he hadn't seen before. "I've never met anyone like you. That's your answer."

He furrowed his brow, "My answer?"

"To your question. You were wondering what he told me about you. He said I've never met anyone like you. He said there was only one person he knew that came close." She looked away. Her breath steamed out and floated away on the silent breeze.

He followed her gaze into the beauty of the winter forest scenery in front of them. "And I think we know who he was talking about."

"Do we?"

"Not too hard to guess. I think it's safe to say that you are that one person."

"You think so?" She brought her eyebrows together.

But the strangest thing happened. Lance did not see her procerus muscle at work. He did not watch his favorite muscle tug at the fascia lying underneath her eyebrows pulling them together and creating a delicate crease in the skin between her eyes. He did not look at the orbicular oculi, the muscles surrounding her eyes creating the squint, or the minute tightening in her sternocleidomastoid, the smooth muscles running from the base of the skull down to the top of the sternum on both sides of the neck.

He did not see Marta as he saw others. She was not a compilation of anatomical parts working in unison to create a functioning human. No, he saw something else when he looked at Marta. Lance saw a person. It was a realization that took a whole second to sink in. Damn, double damn. This was bad.

It was his turn to smile and shake his head. "So the question I have is, do you think he was looking for you in all those candidates over the years? Looking for something he'd only found in his most prized pupil?"

She reached out a hand to him. He took it instinctively without hesitation. Although both cold, there was heat when they touched. She smiled again. It was the new smile. Lance liked it. It warmed him further.

"I don't know." Her response was honest. "Geoffrey does things for reasons only he knows. He doesn't share his motives with others, at least not me."

He hadn't held someone's hand since holding his mother's back in grade school. He couldn't recall holding a girl's, or woman's hand, ever. It was a show of affection he was unfamiliar with.

Holding her hand like this brought feelings of comfort and trust, feelings he had purposely kept separate from his relationships with females. Holding Marta's hand on this winter morning was perhaps the most intimate moment he had ever shared. It surprised him. Yet as he started to wander, to travel somewhere else, or maybe go out of body and look down at this intimate scene, she squeezed his hand. She kept him there in the moment.

"Can I say something?" He was hesitant, unsure.

"Of course. Anything." No hesitation in her response.

"I don't know how to do this."

She just looked at him. "What part?'

"Being here; being with you."

She squeezed his hand again. "You're doing fine. You don't need to do anything else."

"I don't know. That seems too easy."

"Don't make it hard." Her smile lovely again.

Even with her honesty and her transparency, he just couldn't help it. His natural tendencies were too strong for him to control and he dove back into the comfort of a created character. "Well ma'am, I'll do my darndest not to." And he tipped his imaginary hat one last time. He'd have to work on actually being Lance. It was a character, a person, he did not know well.

They sat together holding hands for a while longer, neither wanting to let go. He stayed with her for two more days. He was genuinely surprised by her ability to find comfort in his presence; even more impressed by her domestic talents, especially cooking. He never imagined this cold, calculating and supremely talented killer could prepare such fantastic meals. She absolutely loved to bake. She found real pleasure in making and baking bread, cakes and apple pie. He ate it all.

They took walks through the snow. They played chess beside the fire. They tried to one-up each other in target practice using her silenced Glock handgun. He never stood a chance and could only sigh when she put three successive bullets through the exact center of the hand-painted target. She was definitely scary. Definitely deadly.

On the morning he was to leave, Lance didn't want to. He'd never felt this before. They had held hands a few more times, but not advanced in their display of affection. The attraction between them was obvious. It was powerful, like its own gravity. But the time was not right. Each knew it. To explore deeper feelings and sensations at this early juncture would complicate matters beyond their already convoluted status. She walked with him to his car. He had moved it to a detached garage to hide from prying eyes in the sky. Lance pulled open the heavy garage doors and turned to her. A brisk breeze was blowing, but it was not enough to cause the tears that had formed in her gentle eyes. Sadness produced these tears.

Neither knew when they would see the other again. He was returning to Harvey Point, his CIA home away from home. She would be leaving her hidden villa within days to resume her role as a KGB operative gone rogue. Their paths might not cross for months, possibly longer. Neither liked the thought of that. But neither was naïve enough to believe they could make plans. They did not exchange numbers or addresses or quaint code words only they would recognize. Their lives, their time, were not their own. They moved at opposite ends of a dangerous world. Where or when their orbits would bring them together again was up to the stars.

He took the necessary step to her. It put his face inches from hers, closer than they'd been since their strange, but passionate kiss and embrace in Baghdad. She was the first to throw her arms around him. He responded by doing the same. Finally, he pulled his head back to look into her face. A tear escaped her eye and gently rolled down her cheek. He wiped it away and then he followed the curve of her cheek down to her chin with his finger. She brought her lips up to meet his and their embrace took on an entirely new element. Unlike Baghdad, Marta had not been shot a few minutes earlier and Lance had not thought of killing her in the preceding moments.

No, this time, this embrace and kiss were born of a new passion. This attraction, this thing, was real. Undeniable. She pulled away and rested her head on his shoulder.

"Thank you for coming to see me." She sighed.

He surprised himself by laughing at the simplicity of her words and the underlying sentiment. "Thank you for letting me stay with you." She pulled away from him and took a deep breath and a step back. He realized in that moment that she was indeed stronger than him. He did not have the strength to pull away, to be separated.

"Good bye Lance." She smiled and another tear rolled down.

Lance reached up to tip his invisible cowboy hat. "So long ma'am. I truly appreciate the hospitality. I'll be seeing ya." He stepped into the garage and was about to open the door when he turned back to her. Bart was gone, it was just Lance now. "I'll be seeing you. Count on it." He got into the car and started it. He backed the sedan out and pulled away. Marta waved and smiled.

Chapter 4

She turned away before he could see her cry in his rear view mirror.

Tears hadn't flowed from her eyes like this in years. She hadn't convulsed and bent over in emotional pain for just as long. This is the reason she hadn't given herself to anyone, to any man. This loss of control, no matter how brief, was an affront to her being. Marta despised those unable to stay in control of their emotions. She honestly never expected to be one of them. These feelings were entirely outside her expectations. But they would pass.

As she walked back to the house, she stopped and listened to the sound of the car's engine fading away. When it was gone, there was nothing but silence. Her footfall in the snow, with its gentle crunch underneath, was the only sound. By the time she reached the porch, she was herself again. She was ruthless, determined, uncompromising. She was Marta. One to be respected – to be feared.

The tears were distant memories. In 20 seconds, she had shoved those sensations down deep inside. She purposely looked away from his face in her mind as she entered the door and walked through empty rooms. She closed her ears to his laugh and the amazing variety of languages, dialects and characters he displayed for her. She closed her fist to avoid the feeling, the sensation of him reaching across the chessboard to take her hand as they sat on their knees beside the coffee table.

She had realized in that moment that she was ready, prepared to let him take her. But he did not advance. He didn't cross the chasm between them. He had obviously had his share of women. He was beautiful, so easy to look upon and be with. He would know what to do, where to touch, how to read her thoughts as she lay in his arms. She shook her head and brought a clenched fist to her forehead to push the images out. She needed a clear mind for what she had to do.

Instead of the past three days of comfort and pleasure, she thought of the next dozen steps that lay ahead when she departed today. She left numerous issues hanging, ends untied. Her only trusted team members were dead, thanks to Lance. Stop that. Don't think, or say, his name.

The American CIA agent. That was better. Put a vague nameplate on him. He killed them in Iraq. She would have to rely on others she had been cultivating. She would need to invite them in from the periphery. They would welcome the invitation. Working with Marta, or whatever name she chose to work under, meant action. It meant results. And most of all, it meant money. Her operations had generated millions.

Four weeks of silence was not unheard of for Marta. She did not need regular contact or updates. Those she had left in charge of information drops or blackmail operations or money laundering knew that she would be back. They both looked forward to and feared that day. One never knew what to expect from the brilliant and deadly Russian.

Marta kept her confidants to a select few. She would be contacting these few in the coming days. First though, she needed to visit to her boss. Marta needed to see Gregor

Smelinski to show him she was still in control. Her well-cultivated role as a rogue agent, a KGB pariah, had been created in tandem with him. He considered Marta his greatest weapon. He said it with his eyes every time they met.

Funny how these lions of espionage, these two uncompromising leaders thought they knew her. Smelinski and Seibel were unquestionably brilliant. They were strategists with decades of experience on their side. They were the best in their chosen profession. The fact they both still lived and breathed was proof of their survival skills. But neither knew what drove "their Marta." And she knew, absolutely knew, that neither one could see what was coming. Neither knew they were doomed the moment they met her. For as much as they had invested in her in time, resources and training, she had made a greater investment in creating a façade of acceptance. Both the Russian and the American thought they had control. Neither did. No one ever would.

Marta was so much more than their pawn. She would kill them both soon enough. It was just a matter of time and timing. She straightened her stance; stiffened her bearing. She suddenly had to shove down a thought, an image of Lance. Stop it. Don't think the name again. Why had he invaded her thoughts? She didn't like it and couldn't accept it. For the next half a second she saw a fleeting image of herself pointing a gun at him and pulling the trigger. She shoved that one down quickly as well. It caused her pain.

Chapter 5

No one was waiting for him as he walked up the air bridge from the plane that brought him from London to JFK. That was a good thing.

He fell into line with the other international passengers arriving in America; many were tourists making their first visit to the land of plenty. They all pulled out their papers. Most were still blurry-eyed from sleeping on the uneventful 7-hour 30-minute flight. He was carrying a passport that identified him as a businessman from Kuwait City. They were good papers, not real, but good.

He was calm and collected, no nerves at all as he stepped up to the counter for his turn with the bored but vigilant female customs agent. She greeted him by looking into his eyes per protocol. He smiled slightly and handed over his documents. She spent 40 seconds reviewing the passport and Kuwaiti I.D. card. She typed several bits of data into the aged computer sitting beside her on the counter. After reading the data returned to her screen, she turned back to him.

"Mr. Rashidi."

"Yes."

"Your visit to the U.S., is it business or pleasure?"

"All business this time." He continued to smile, but appeared appropriately tired.

"Where will you be conducting your business?"

"Here in New York and in Philadelphia."

"And what is your home address?" She asked.

He recited the address on the passport and then gestured to the document in her hands. "The information on my passport is current."

"When will you be returning to Kuwait?"

"I will be flying to Jordan at the end of the month and then home to Kuwait."

"Do you have your return tickets with you?"

"Oh, no I will be purchasing them within a week or two when my plans are confirmed."

"Very good," she was just about done with him. "Your visa requires you to check in with the Kuwaiti embassy and provide them your contact information while in the country."

He smiled, a tired and weary, but pleasant smile. "Thank you. I'll be sure to contact them tomorrow. I have the number right here." He held up his briefcase and patted it. The customs agent handed him his documents and he made his way to the baggage claim.

After grabbing his bag, he stepped outside into the New York night. Instead of turning left to get in the line for taxis, he turned right and walked down the sidewalk. A taxi bypassed the waiting line and pulled over to the curb 50 feet in front of the man. It was a breach of protocol, but the taxi did have its "out of service" light lit.

The man opened the door and tossed his luggage in the back seat and closed the door to open the front passenger door to get in. He and the driver did not speak or look at each other. There would be plenty of time to talk later. First, he needed to visit the blind cleric in a secret location. There was news to share from the leaders. News that could only be carried by trusted couriers and shared in person with true believers.

He had been to New York two times before, but he couldn't keep from craning his neck and looking up at the buildings as the taxi rolled down the urban canyons of Manhattan. To think, he was in a remote village in the mountains of Afghanistan just three days ago. He looked, but they were too far away to get a good view of the World Trade Center towers down at the south end of the small island. He'd see them soon enough, he told himself.

The man stepped out of his unadorned sedan onto the late evening sidewalk in front of the apartment building he called home. He also called the building his own. Unlike the millions in Moscow trying to scrape by today, only to face a tougher fight tomorrow, he had figured out the game long before coming to the Russian capitol. Politics was the answer. That is where the power is.

Instead of walking to the front entrance where a guard waited to open the door for him, he stepped back into the street and crossed. On the other side, a street vendor stood beside his pushcart. The man, a king among men, walked up to the vendor. The stooped old man bowed as the great man approached.

"How are your potatoes today?" He asked as he reached and lifted one.

"I believe it is an excellent batch in today sir," the vendor stepped aside, holding his hat in his hands. "Please take your pick. Your wife will be pleased with any of these, I believe."

He chose three potatoes and handed them to the vendor who put them into a paper sack. "Excellent choice sir."

"How much?" He asked.

"No charge. Please consider them a gift." The vendor smiled and bowed his head further.

"No, no. I insist. Name your price."

The vendor looked up, the smile faded from his beaten, battered face. "Three potatoes, three thousand rubles." The vendor did not flinch, did not bow his head this time.

If the man, the king, was insulted by the outlandish price, he did not let it show. Inflation was crazy, but the equivalent of $300 for three potatoes was certainly an insane amount. "Now, that is what I like to hear. Capitalism is here. In a capitalistic society the price is flexible, supply and demand. Excellent." And he stepped in close, his face inches from the vendor. The man's guards took several steps closer as well. He waved them off.

"But capitalism also allows for negotiation. So my counter offer to you, my good potato man, is this, five thousand rubles." The man pulled the bills from his pocket. It was a sum many citizens of the Soviet Union, now the Russian Federation, would not earn in six months. "Here take it. The world gives you nothing. You only get what you work for, or have the balls to take."

He handed the vendor the bills, took the sack of potatoes and turned to walk away. "These better be the best potatoes my wife has ever seen." He laughed.

The wealthy man walked across the street to the apartment building. His guards, who had escorted him across the street, stopped at the front door and turned back in the direction of the street vendor who had began packing up his cart. They proceeded to escort the vendor out of the neighborhood and out of this life.

Like many great men, Kirill Cherzny, had lots of others willing to do his dirty work. A street vendor willing to ask an excessive sum for three potatoes today, could be a business owner willing to withhold his monthly percentage next month if word of this incident spread. It didn't.

Chapter 6

Gregor the Terrible was anxious.

His composed exterior gave no indication of his condition. Sitting across from Victor Provodnov, the regional KGB chief for the Caucasus States, Gregor Smelinski heard words and read body language. This man, his hand-picked manager, was lying to him. Lying to his face right now. But, Smelinski's mind was elsewhere.

Smelinski, the leader of all European KGB, now called the FSK - Russian Federation Counterintelligence Service operations, had asked Provodnov quite directly what was happening in Chechnya. The regional chief should know, or at least have a solid grasp on the facts. Instead, he spoke of black market crime syndicates, illegal human trafficking and drug dealers emboldened by wavering leadership in Moscow. The Soviet empire was dying. And the dying bear was unable to control the smaller cubs, the young bears rising in the hinterlands of the Union.

Smelinski knew things were being pulled apart in all directions. He received reports daily from region and station chiefs in each of the republics detailing actions by local governments no longer fearful of retribution by the KGB. There was simply too much change taking place. But Smelinski still had a job to do. When the dust settles on whatever remains of the Soviet Union, there will be plenty of wrongs to right and scores to settle. But some things were unacceptable. Disruption and chaos in Chechnya was one of those things. The recent violence and instability was driven by something the KGB simply did not have a grasp on. It was undoubtedly the damn Islamic menace.

If his mind wasn't preoccupied with Marta, Smelinski might have had Provodnov killed right in front of him, or maybe done it himself. But she had shaken up his world two days earlier, like she had many times before. Smelinski left Provodnov alive, but with strict orders to get a handle on things, or else.

An hour later, Smelinski was on the outskirts of Grozny. He truly detested Chechnya, its roads, its people, its overall insignificance. But he knew this little piece of shit state would require his attention for some time to come. Losing influence here was not an option. The dominos must not fall. Not yet, at least.

He cleared his mind and let the flood of the headlights on the broken road before him wash away his thoughts. He needed to be fresh for his next appointment. Marta had resurfaced and requested a meeting with him by way of coded communiqué. He had a great many questions for her.

She had succeeded in tracking Korovin and Kusnetsov in their attempt to sell nuclear warheads to Iraq. But the reports from Baghdad were sketchy at best. U.S. forces apparently killed K&K. Seibel had obviously been there. His fingerprints were all over the operation. But details, crucial details, were lacking. Chief among these was Marta's whereabouts in the weeks after the mission.

Smelinski had given her a long and flexible leash with her assignment to "go rogue" and create a syndicate of murder and mayhem. It was a clever and multi-layered ruse designed to draw out corrupt elements within the KGB. It was a house cleaning of sorts that Smelinski devised to put things in order in preparation for whatever revolution was coming.

Marta had excelled in her mischievous role, well beyond his, or his few superiors' expectations. Her assignment was to be a loose cannon, a catastrophe machine that could be pointed at targets requiring eradication. She performed superbly. Sending Marta and her legion of brutal killers to prevent the former KGB agents from selling nukes to third-world crazies was a natural extension of her mission. Her ability to operate outside the law put her on a collision course with K&K.

But something happened in Baghdad. Contact with her and her key players was lost. The firefight in that warehouse district had been something. Satellite images showed hundreds of casualties and then an extraction of U.S. military forces by helicopters, followed by extensive bombing of the site by American air forces. Seibel covered his tracks extremely well. The one post-mission communication Smelinski had with his CIA counterpart confirmed acquisition of the nukes from Korovin and Kusnetsov, as well as confirmation of their deaths. But nothing more. If Seibel knew anything about Marta and her team, he did not mention it, of course. But he was certain Seibel did not know the true motives of her mission. He had kept his contact with her to a minimum and only met with her in private, in locations he selected.

But still, Smelinski was left with a huge blind spot where Marta was concerned. She had gone quiet, "off the grid" as the Americans say. For four weeks, she was silent. She had simply disappeared. Until two days ago, when he received a coded phone call at his home. Only Marta knew both the number and the code. His own call to a number only he knew confirmed it was her. She was short, providing only a day and time to meet. Tomorrow in Belgrade. He wanted to drive part of the route to give him time alone to think. He would drive through the night to Sevastopol, where he would catch a flight to Belgrade. He liked flying in and out of Sevastopol because it was such a popular tourist destination. It was so easy to blend in with vacationers returning to their normal lives after a stay on the Crimean Peninsula. He would be there by mid-day tomorrow, if the damn Chechnyan roads did not destroy his borrowed car.

Chapter 7

Fuchs bumped him sliding past on the right. They were both moving quickly down a pitch-black alley with their silenced M4 assault rifles in firing position. Their movements the epitome of stealth. Their trek over several miles of hilly terrain to get to this sparsely populated village lit only by the dim quarter moon overhead had gone without incident. That would surely change in the coming moments. Lance checked to make sure his rifle's safety was off.

While Lance and Mikel Fuchs, his unofficial mentor, slithered along the walls of their chosen alley, Tarwanah and Jamaani, their Jordanian comrades, prowled the next street over. Radio headsets and microphones connected the two teams. But no one was talking. They each knew their assignment. They were here to kill and capture, and then kill some more.

Up ahead, there was a noise in the darkness. Lance nodded to Fuchs. The mentor took a few more steps to a corner then dropped to the ground and peered around. He raised his right hand up against the wall and held up two fingers. Lance dropped to his stomach and slid across the dirt street into the open. He put the first of the two guards in his crosshairs and then moved gently to put the other in the center of the intersecting lines. He was still a lousy shot, but from 40 yards, this was definitely in his comfort zone.

"Go." Fuchs' whisper was barely audible.

In the next moment, Lance exhaled and pulled the trigger, absorbed the rifle's kick, moved to the next target and gently squeezed the trigger again. Two center forehead hits. Two kills. The silencer transformed the shots into brief hydraulic exhales in the night. Damn, he was getting better.

"Two north." Lance whispered into his microphone. Without hesitation, Lance and Fuchs were back on their feet on either side of the wider street. Up ahead, a generator purred.

If one listened closely, between the pistons firing inside the generator's motor, you could hear two more brief hydraulic spitting sounds. Tarwanah had taken out two more guards on the next street over. Intel told them two more sets of guards now stood between each team and their target.

"Two west." It was Jamaani confirming his partner's kills.

Approximately 120 yards ahead, their target awaited. Lance went out of body. He had to make his mind's eye stop at 500 feet. It wanted to go higher to take in the whole village, but Lance was only interested in the street ahead. Looking down on the dirt streets at night did not give up much information. In his head, he reviewed a memorized satellite image of the streets, doorways, windows ahead. He switched to a daytime image he'd memorized. In the photo, a vehicle bearing the same license plates was evident. Back on the ground, Lance could see that Chevy sedan now. It had been moved, but not far. It was still outside the designated building. Two guards leaned on the trunk smoking cigarettes.

At 60 yards, Fuchs would take the shots, unless he signaled that he wanted Lance to take one of them. If intel held true, two other guards should be stationed on the opposite side of the building and right about now, they should be center-targeted by a couple of Jordanian operatives.

"Two south ready." Tarwanah, this time. They were in position.

"Two north ready." Fuchs lay flat on the street up against a brick wall. Lance took a knee and put his crosshairs on the gentleman on the left. He didn't plan on firing, just being prudent.

"Go." Lance whispered. In the night, four nearly silent rapid breaths could be heard. They sounded like stifled sneezes. Through his scope, Lance watched the guard's head explode out the back. He moved his scope to the right and saw the other guard falling, at first on the trunk, and then to the ground. Two perfect kills.

"Two south."

"Two north."

Four more guards were now dead. That made an even eight. Lance and Fuchs were up and on their feet moving forward in shadows. They reached the Chevy and two dead guards then split up. Lance continued on to a far corner, Fuchs stopped at the nearest corner of the building.

They were at their destination, on time and on target. All team members in place and all guards dismissed from duty and from life. Lance put his hand on the bricks of the building and knew instantaneously they were screwed. It was all wrong. He could sense it. Those tiny, nearly invisible hairs on the back of his neck all stood on end. He instinctively ducked, pivoted and swiveled his head to shout, "Abort."

But before he could take a step or roll to the side, an array of floodlights lit up the night. A low hum turned into the wailing of a siren.

"Boom, you're dead." Geoffrey Seibel's words in their headsets were quiet and calm, like the voice of God. He came walking into the light. Lance thought he looked kind of like God emerging from eternal blackness onto a billowing cloud. The director, the unquestioned leader of his own private army within the Special Activities Division of the CIA, stood and looked at Lance.

"Explosives." Not a question. Lance shook his head and looked from Seibel to Fuchs walking back around the Chevy in the street. "A bomb."

"Indeed." Seibel was close enough now to take off his radio. "A device more than sufficient to blow apart the structure, the four of you and much of the surrounding squalor."

Fuchs walked up with his gun resting on his shoulder. "A nice little trap."

"Ah," Seibel raised his eyebrows and looked over at Tarwanah and Jamaani walking around the corner of the building. "A trap. How could that be?"

The four of them looked at one another. Not surprisingly, the other three all settled on Lance. After meeting the other's eyes, he smiled.

"If I had to guess, I'd say bad intel. Deliberately bad intel."

Seibel stepped into the middle of the group. "That would be an excellent guess. But it doesn't get at the why."

"To kill." Lance was not in a good mood after being killed. Drill or not, he hated to lose. "To kill us. Whoever fed the information, did so with the explicit intention of bringing in a covert ops team and blowing them to kingdom come."

"So where did the intelligence for this operation come from?"

Lance looked at the others. Their faces were blank. They'd been through things like this before with their illustrious leader. So here again, three and a half years into his life of espionage, this operation was yet another test, another lesson for Preacher. He closed his eyes. The others had grown accustomed to this practice. They waited in silence.

Lance rose a thousand feet in the air and looked down again on this fake village situated on a jutting peninsula in North Carolina. Specifically, the village was located at the Harvey

Point training facility -- the CIA's farm away from "the farm" in Langley, Virginia. Looking down on the setting in his mind's eye, Lance examined every detail he had studied in the four days leading up to the excursion. He reviewed their route from landing on the beach, into the village and up to the building. He switched from a daytime view to enhanced night vision view using new heat sensing technology. This review took four whole seconds. He noticed the building did not change in all three shots. There were no open doors or windows. The heat signature showed low levels inside that could be humans or appliances.

He opened his eyes. The answers he was looking for weren't in any satellite photos. He couldn't see bad intel. Couldn't see the bad intentions. He knew the answer already. It was Seibel. The master had played them for fools. None of them had questioned him about the intel for the op. They had taken his words as credible. But he left the door open for them twice during briefings and they missed it.

"I believe we did not press Papa for the source of the operational data. If I recall, he stopped at two separate instances during the build-up and we," he looked around at the blank faces on the other three. "Or better, I, did not raise my hand and ask for the source of said data. I'm sorry for killing you all."

His joke brought smiles from each. Seibel turned to him. "What did I tell you about the source?"

"You mentioned 'inside information' from sources in Beirut and Islamabad." Lance had the details down pat.

"Yes I did. And why would these sources supply us faulty, even deadly information?"

"Plants, double-blinds, it could be any number of factors. The reason would be to monitor our actions after receiving the information to ascertain operational structure as well as inflicting casualties on our side," Lance stopped. He turned to look at the building. He saw it before him and then from a thousand feet in the air.

"The bomb is the key." He took two steps toward the structure and turned back to the group. "It wasn't an ambush, a tripwire or a roadside. This was a sophisticated device designed to be detonated by remote from less than 300 yards, right?"

"Something like that." Seibel rubbed his chin.

"So what did I, we, miss?" Lance looked around, scanning for intricate details now visible because of the flood of lights. The other three joined him looking in all directions.

"What are we looking for?" Tarwanah, the older of the two Jordanians, asked as he squatted down to get a better view under the Chevy. The dummies that had been propped up as guards a few minutes earlier lay on the ground at the rear of the vehicle.

Lance looked up at the roof of the building and took a few steps back. "I don't know. But I suspect there were a few details we missed along the way and in the lead-up. He wouldn't have made it quite so arbitrary." Lance turned to Fuchs. They just looked at each other for the moment. Lance noticed the German wasn't looking around for the missed details. He figured it out.

"Misdirection and a mole." Lance shook his head and smiled at Seibel. "False and misleading intel and a plant in the operation." He pointed to Fuchs but kept his eyes locked on Seibel. "Foxy here just happened to show up two days before mission planning began. You wanted me to think, to question more."

Seibel took his time answering. He took a few steps away from Lance into the center of a floodlight's spill, like walking into a spotlight on stage. "Lance, Lance, Lance. My little Preacher, is it always about you?"

Lance laughed at that. The others joined him. They all knew the answer. They were all part of it, part of Seibel's grand plan. But each knew their place. This, all this, everything really, was for Lance. He was Seibel's chosen one. And indeed, it was always about him. Fuchs, Tarwanah, Jamaani and every other member of the supporting cast had their role. But the big guy had his eyes on some prize only he could see, a grand vision, of which he only shared bits and pieces.

"Isn't everything about me?" Lance played along.

"One might think. But alas, there are more things in heaven and earth, Horatio, than are dreamt of in your philosophy." Seibel made full use of the stage he found himself on and offered up some Shakespeare.

"O day and night dear Hamlet, but this is a wondrous strange." Lance took a little liberty with the line. He knew quite a few of the famous lines from the Bard's repertoire and knew how fond of them Seibel was.

"So where did we go wrong in this operation Mr. Priest?"

Lance looked back over the past six weeks from Baghdad to Harvey Point to Hamburg to examine the pieces he'd missed. For the briefest moment, he saw her face and felt the pinprick and blur of its distraction. The past few days of planning and preparation for this drill had given him much to occupy his mind. He had gone whole hours without thinking of her. A smile curled at the edge of his mouth as he forced her from his mind. He looked at Seibel and wondered if his master knew what he was thinking.

"I think my only mistake was taking you at your word. You provided most of the intel for this operation, including location, target, timeline."

"And where might your reliance on one source of data have cost you and your compatriots their lives?"

"At the beginning, in the middle, and then about five minutes ago." Lance was, for whatever reason, the only one who could match Siebel wit for wit. While others were left in their master's strategic mind's dust, Lance was the only one who could even get close to staying with him for any length of time.

"So for all intents and purposes, everything I told you might have been corrupted or at least wrong."

"Of course not. Not everything, just the important stuff. You gave us many salient and usable facts. The team merely neglected to properly vet your information. It seems that you decided to change your tactics yet again and guide us into a death trap to teach me, teach us, that you and everyone else in this world are untrustworthy."

Seibel smiled. His teeth gleamed under his spotlight. "And why would I do that?"

This little to and fro could have gone on for several more minutes if Lance let it. Seibel was in full "Socrates" mode. But Lance didn't need any more mental poking and prodding. He knew where this was heading.

"Because you are about to launch me out into the big, bad untrustworthy world. I'm going to go live into the three-ring circus without a net. And if I had to guess, it has something to do with bombs."

"Go on."

"That little exercise in Hamburg wasn't a vacation was it? I wasn't just there to watch and learn. I was there explicitly to capture Shafiq," Lance stopped. A light bulb went off. He looked down and shook his head again. When he looked up, it was not at Seibel, but at Fuchs.

"I can't believe I missed that."

"What?" Fuchs was dismissive. His accent was heavy on the German.

"If I asked you where you were two weeks ago would you tell me?"

"Of course not." Fuchs smiled.

Lance turned to Seibel. "You sent him to Hamburg just to delay Shafiq for a few minutes so he would be late arriving to the arrest party at the café."

Seibel gave no response.

"Just to make him late so I could run him down and spend a few quality minutes with him picking his terrorist bomber brain." Lance still had so much to learn from the master. "Damn. You just move the pawns around on the board and voila, the game falls into place. You have me and everyone else figured out, three, four moves in advance."

"And yet, you still walk into a trap set by a bomb maker." Seibel was done with the show. "You took the bait, missed a variety of tells along the way and got yourself and everyone else killed."

"You got everyone killed. You killed us to make a point." Lance wasn't done.

Seibel pointed at the building. "That pretend bomb and the pretend guy who made it are going to be your life for the next year at least. You don't get second chances when you are smack dab in the blast radius."

"So I'm going to hunt bombers?"

Seibel turned back to him. "No. You're going to become one."

Chapter 8

The two of them were in Lance's room at Harvey Point, where they had sat and talked numerous times. Seibel was in no mood for small talk and pulled several files from his leather case as he sat down in the desk chair. Lance looked through the first of three files. He was sitting on his bed and had laid out several sheets of paper and photos.

"And here is number two." Seibel closed up a manila file folder and handed it to Lance. "You'll like him. He's a real bad-ass. More than a dozen confirmed events with over 40 kills in Pakistan and Afghanistan." Lance gathered up the papers from the first file and took the second.

Seibel let Lance digest the second portion. He held the third file in his hands. It was very thin.

"Man. This guy is something. These are confirmed?" Lance asked.

"All confirmed by first-person and secondary sources."

"Damn." Lance leafed through more pages.

Seibel sat forward. "Okay. Here is number three. He is considered significantly more dangerous than the other two. Significantly more dangerous than anyone we are tracking at present." Lance looked up from the second file at that. Seibel handed him the third.

Lance opened it and pulled out the two sheets of paper inside. His brow furrowed. "This is it?"

"That's it." Seibel sat back.

"So we don't know anything about this guy other than he was seen in Pakistan in '89? One sighting."

"Just the one recorded sighting in Pakistan. The other was in Brazzaville in September of that same year."

"Says here a plane exploded in mid-air on its way from the Congo to Libya. So we think this dude had something to do with that little incident?"

"That's what we think, yes." Seibel laced his fingers behind his head.

"So, I've looked all over these two sheets of paper and the tab on the folder and I don't think I see a full name for this guy."

"Correct. We know nothing more about him. Just Anwar."

Lance stared at him. He knew Seibel better than that. There was always something more. "But."

"But this." Seibel reached into his jacket pocket and pulled out two grainy black and white photos and handed one to Lance.

Lance looked at it for a few seconds. "JFK?"

"Very good."

"When?"

"Three weeks ago."

"Damn. Is he still in the US?"

Seibel handed Lance the second photo. "Yesterday."

"Shit. Where'd he fly to?"

"Jordan." Seibel sat back again.

"So, we have a virtual ghost for years who shows up in New York. What else do we know about him? I'll bet everything on his passport turned out to be fake." Lance looked deeper into the grainy image to see any details. They were difficult to discern.

"Looks like that is the deal, at least for now. None of the contact information listed on his passport checked out. All dead locations." Seibel locked his fingers and stretched out his hands. "We are now scouring any databases in New York to see if he shows up. We can't be 100 percent certain, but we may have a hit involving the blind Imam.

"Crap. So looks like I am going to start in New York?"

"Actually no. You're going to the Philippines first."

Chapter 9

Actually, Lance decided to go off mission before heading to the island of Mindanao in the Philippines. Three months and six days after the conversation with Seibel, Lance disappeared.

He had been training for this step for years, his whole life, really. He knew Seibel was counting on his particular set of innate devious skills perhaps more than any other element when he brought Lance into the CIA fold. Lance had been patient along the way, soaking in every lesson, every detail. During the first year of his training at Harvey Point, Preacher wanted to ask Seibel on many occasions when the "spy stuff" was going to start. He learned about munitions, invasive penetration operations, target extraction protocol and any number of special ops skills. He wondered why Seibel didn't just have him join the Green Berets or Rangers or even Delta.

It took him a good two years to figure out that Seibel didn't recruit him to train him to be a spy. Lance had been born one.

He learned to master technology and techniques, but he was hardwired to be disingenuous, manipulative, unscrupulous. He did not need training to lie and pretend to be someone he was not. And instead of putting young Preacher through in-depth training in forgery or surveillance or misdirection, Seibel had

Lance accompany him and Fuchs on a number of trips. On these excursions, Lance learned that instead of the actual process and logistics of preparing false papers, for instance, it was infinitely more important to know others who possessed these skills. It was about relationships. And one thing Seibel had in spades was relationships. All around this little globe.

So after months of intensive training in design, construction, deconstruction, detonation and detection, Lance was well versed in the ways of the bomb. He still had much to learn, but between his ears he now possessed knowledge imparted by the nation's premier bomb experts. He also studied the works of leading mass murderers around the world. He could read through the details of a bus bombing in Tbilisi, Georgia and know what type, amount of accelerant, ignition source and other intricate details of the explosion.

He visited with bombers, both domestic and overseas. In their eyes, he always saw the same look when they spoke about explosions. He catalogued this look under 'orgasmic pleasure.' The Israelis let him interview a Hamas bomb maker who had fitted several suicidal true believers with explosive vests packed with ball bearings and nails that then ended the lives of dozens. The guy took real pride it the deadly, violent, reprehensible blasts "his babies" produced by combining mere chemicals and substances that alone had no relation, no reaction.

Lance read day and night on bomb making, explosive ordnance and munitions, blast physics and simple elements that could be combined in small quantities to produce massive explosions. Scary shit.

He built dozens of "poppers" at Harvey Point and watched from a safe distance as they blew apart buildings, vehicles and dummies playing the roles of innocent bystanders. He learned both basic and highly detailed bomb-making techniques. It was knowledge that made him powerful and dangerous and strangely regretful. He felt the rush of adrenaline in the moments before pushing the button and then rejoiced in the unique sensation produced by the shockwave preceding the sounds of the explosion. He became more than a little fascinated by the shockwave, the temporary redefinition of gravity that expanded out from the initial detonation to cause most of the blast's destruction.

Humans stood no chance should he choose to use this knowledge for evil. It was truly godlike.

Seibel worked from the basic philosophy that it takes one to know one, and therefore catch one. Lance was to become one of them. A terrorist bomber. A weapon of mass destruction. His orders were simple. Catch these extremely dangerous individuals and garner as much information as possible about their organizations and affiliations. And then kill them violently, publicly if possible. He was to teach a lesson to those who believed they could inflict pain and misery and death on others from a casual and comfortable distance.

Lance knew this was not his actual mission. But like always, Seibel kept certain details to himself. Papa's modus operandi was always compartmentalization. Lance had grown to appreciate this frustrating aspect of working with someone so brilliant. He knew he was a tool in Seibel's belt, a brush wielded by a master who could see elements others could not when looking at a blank canvas.

Before departing, Lance was required to visit with Stuart Braden, the CIA psychologist tasked with keeping Seibel and his team of ruthless killers in check, mentally at least. Lance was his favorite patient, for several reasons. The visit with Braden was brief and uneventful. He told the psychologist a variety of creative and emotive lies. He enjoyed his sessions with Braden, but was just not in the mood this time. He left out quite a bit, and that told Braden all he needed to know. Lance was already gone. Not available for evaluation and diagnosis.

The psychologist would have to try to dissect Preacher's mind another time.

Good luck with that. Lance thought to himself looking out the window of a Gulfstream III aircraft into the black night and black Atlantic Ocean below, Lance let his mind wander. Six hours earlier he called in his first "relationship chip" by phoning a navy pilot Seibel had introduced him to two years earlier. This particular pilot, Lt. Stan Meadows, was active Naval Reserve and the preferred pilot for transportation of high-ranking military officers and dignitaries. Meadows flew generals, admirals and even lowly colonels around the world, often with only a few hours notice.

Lance had learned through a little lie-sprinkled digging that Meadows earned his stripes flying F-18's off aircraft carriers. His spotless record earned him recognition. His dedication to confidentiality and secrecy made him a valued commodity for the nation's espionage elite. Meadows was respectful to every passenger as he ducked his 6 foot 6-inch frame and walked the aisle of the 14-passenger jet prior to every flight. He would introduce himself and move on, not waiting for a reciprocal introduction. He was the trusted pilot, that's all. It was "need to know." And that meant he did not ask Seibel or Fuchs or Lance any questions before, during or after the flight.

Lance knew this flight, carrying two generals to Antwerp, Belgium had been scheduled three days earlier. He called the military command control center to add his cover name, rank and serial number to the passenger list. His five-word duty description was sufficiently vague – delivery of decision-support materials. He wore a Lieutenant 's uniform and carried a black briefcase; a chain attached to a cuff on his wrist added to the effect. The disguise said the contents of this particular case were important and would be defended.

For some reason, this combination of officer uniform and chained briefcase was the single most respected image presented by the military. This simple costume spoke of importance, dedication and capability.

It was also complete bullshit. If someone, anyone, carried vital information, the last thing you would do is draw attention to yourself with an official-looking black briefcase chained to your wrist. If one were entrusted with top-secret information, it would be in the form of a hidden microfiche or a disk or even sealed in plastic and ingested to be passed at a later time. Wearing an officer's uniform and carrying a black briefcase often meant the exact opposite. Instead of protecting information, that person was protecting those around him. Your basic security work. And often, the man in uniform was anything but an officer. Look closer and the details give them up for the brutes they often are.

Thus, sitting two rows behind the two generals being transported this evening, anyone who knew the truth behind the costume assumed Lance was aboard to protect the generals. It was a perfect cover.

Six and a half hours after takeoff, the Gulfstream touched down at a private field outside Antwerp. The 3,800-mile distance comfortably inside the jet's maximum distance of 4,200 miles. Customs clearance for three-star and two-star generals and an accompanying lieutenant was way too easy. This is why Seibel preferred this method of travel.

Anyone watching the arrival of these three passengers at oh-six-hundred on a misty Tuesday morning would assume they were on their way from Antwerp up the road to The Hague. It was a short hour and a half drive. Of course, anyone watching closely would have seen the two generals get into their waiting car and the lieutenant carrying a briefcase and a duffle walk the other way into the mist. But no one was watching as Lance Priest disappeared.

Chapter 10

The names were never said. The faces sometimes changed, but the assembled members of Account One were the "who's who" of U.S. intelligence. They were gathered this late morning for a special update from Geoffrey Seibel.

He is this elite group's lifeline to reality. Each of them, the heads of the Central Intelligence Agency, National Security Agency and White House Office of Intelligence, receive any number of reports back from the field each day. These reports were full of assumptions and errors based on guesses, false hypothesis and on flimsy evidence.

From Seibel they received only facts. He never relayed anything to this group when he was not 100 percent certain of its authenticity. Today, Account One expected an update on Iraq and the continuing disintegration of the former Soviet Union. Instead, they heard about something called al Qaeda. They had heard bits and pieces before. But Seibel, sitting there with only two sheets of paper on the table in front of him, told them a story they did not expect.

Each of the members of Account One thought that the war was over. We won. Instead, Seibel informed them that the U.S. was fighting a new enemy. Al Qaeda had declared war on the

United States and other western nations in 1989, but resources were just now learning about the network. Seibel detailed what he knew about Osama bin Laden, a few deputies within the organization and their beginnings in the mountains of Afghanistan.

At the conclusion of his report, he paused for questions from the members of Account One. The looks on their faces resembled that of a principal dealing with a perpetually troublesome student. No one spoke, so Seibel continued.

"I've dealt with a number of small organizations, factions if you will. This is different. This is a movement that supersedes ideology. It is cultural. That is the best way I can describe it. These men, these terrorists, are doing something, setting up something we simply haven't seen before. We could kill them all tomorrow and another head would grow."

CIA was the most informed on al Qaeda and added, "Our analysts are setting up a special task force to evaluate threats like this. We are just beginning."

"They are a couple of years ahead of us," Seibel responded.

NSA spoke up, "What are they planning?"

Seibel looked from him to the others. "Everything. Attacks, killings, subversion, evangelical communication, but most of all, bombs. Everything I've seen tells me they are developing a network, a franchise system of bombers and bomb makers."

The room was silent for a few moments until the director of White House Intelligence spoke. "What are we doing?" He really meant, 'what are you doing?'

Seibel knew what he was asking. So he smiled as he spoke. "Quite a bit, of course. We are deploying agents to the field and initiating new training methods as we continue to reorient resources away from Eastern Europe to the Middle East and points east."

That wasn't the answer they wanted to hear and Seibel knew it, so he gave them what they wanted. "The special team has been given new assignments. They have already begun operations." He could tell they were still waiting. "Yes. All team members have been deployed, including Preacher."

That got pursed lips and nods from the men around the table. Preacher's reputation had already infected this elite group of intelligence professionals. Only CIA knew Preacher's true identity and he wished he didn't. He knew plausible deniability was best where Preacher was concerned.

Seibel put a capstone on the report with a final statement. "Body count will be high with him in the field without a net. They will need to grow their new heads quicker."

The report concluded with a short recital of information coming out of Russia involving the escalating growth and influence of the Mob right alongside that of new oligarchs, the small group of men rolling up businesses and rolling in cash. Organized crime in the former Soviet Bloc had assumed power and influence that threatened to destabilize nations even more than the money and power grab underway by the new class of oligarchs.

Chapter 11

Friday, August 9, 1991 — Budapest, Hungary

People change. Their temperament or demeanor can be dramatically affected by circumstances. Their life's roadmap altered, unveiling new destinations and options. Marta Sidorova was not taking change well.

Her circumstances, feelings and disposition had been altered by her exposure to a young CIA agent. But she fought change, literally fought against it inside her head. Moments after he left her presence, and in the months since she had seen him, she attempted to close off a small portion of her mind that held onto memories of him. If anything, she became more resolute, more dedicated to her mission of bringing pain and destruction to those who stood in her way.

Almost four months after watching Lance drive away from her mountain stronghold, she once again faced change as she placed the smoking, burning hot silencer of a gun to the back of a man's neck.

Why did she do it? Because this man lied to her. His lie was one of omission. She had asked a simple question and his response was slow, calculated. He was given the opportunity to join her, but instead, he left a wife and two small children at home waiting for him.

Marta needed soldiers. She needed unquestioning troops to work on her behalf. This man had been groomed for one of these positions. But when the offer was extended to him a few minutes ago, he fumbled. It turned out he was merely a Budapest puppet watching money for the new oligarchs gobbling up wealth and power in a new Russia. Marta had given him a chance to be a real player, but he refused.

She smiled and excused herself from the table in the small café near the Erzsebet Bridge and walked to the toilet. She didn't need to go, just needed to approach the two men sitting at a table nearby from a different angle. In her peripheral vision, she saw them turn their heads slightly to watch her. The two men were drinking coffee and wearing heavy jackets on a warm night. She had seen them come in 15 minutes earlier and watched them scouting out the location 15 minutes before that. The third man in their team was sitting in car a block over. He was supposed to be watching. But an extra set of holes in his head, courtesy of Marta, relieved him of duty. And life.

When Marta emerged from the toilet, she held her purse in front of her body while taking the six steps to the table occupied by the two coffee drinkers. A step from their table, she moved the handbag to the left and raised the silenced Glock in her healed left hand. Both men's eyes bulged, one started to yank the cup from his lips. He didn't get the cup very far before she put the first bullet through his skull. She turned the gun on the other gentleman and ended his life in a similar fashion. Less than two seconds later she stood behind her dinner date. He didn't turn around. There was no time and no reason to.

He tensed when the burning silencer pressed into the skin of his neck and singed a perfect round circle.

"Do svidaniya." She thanked him in their native tongue and began to apply pressure to the trigger. His death would be nothing, but then again, it would be something. It would mean pain, suffering, emptiness, a black hole for his family, his children. A full second passed. A lifetime.

Marta did not see the man sitting in front of her. She did not hear the screams in the cafe. She did not smell the coffee, the baking breads, or feel the cool gun in her grip. Her senses were momentarily lost. She was back months earlier, with him. Lance.

Try as she might, she could not keep him out. In this moment, she felt the danger, the complications, of this new sensation. She was changed. Marta, the ice-cold killer of dozens, pulled the silencer from the man's neck and turned away.

An amateur might run from the café. Marta knew that to run is to draw attention. She tucked the gun into her purse, eyed every single person in the room, turned slowly to the door and walked out. A woman near the exit, hysterical at the sight of the spattered blood, stifled her screams when Marta's eyes met hers. There was ice there.

She walked out the door, through the crowd on the patio and hung a right at the sidewalk. Behind her, people came out of shock and began moving about and screaming. A man stepped out to give Marta one more look to get a better description for the police. As if on cue, she stopped and looked back at the man. He squinted his eyes and immediately ducked back into the restaurant. When the police showed up, he and everyone else in the room described the same individual. Female, medium height, straight black hair in a bobbed style, square-rimmed glasses, business attire. Her general appearance gave away her ethnicity, even though it was being downplayed. The killer, to everyone's eyes in the café, was an Asian woman. You could tell by her makeup, her hairstyle, the way she moved. She was Asian, maybe Japanese. But she was trying to hide it by appearing Western European.

The deception was perfect. Marta knew it. She'd used this one several times. As she rounded a second corner two blocks away, she removed her black wig, glasses and suit jacket and put them in her purse. She pulled out a blue overcoat and removed the pins holding her hair up. She pulled another bag, a light duffle, and put her purse in it. She was a different person. Hair brown, eyes blue, glasses gone. Behind her, the sounds of wailing sirens began. She didn't worry about others coming after her. She had watched her contact, followed by his two accomplices, enter 20 minutes earlier. She scanned the crowd, walked along the sidewalk, stepped into doorways and alleys and found no one else waiting or trailing them.

As she reached the car she had parked 45 minutes earlier, she opened the door, threw her purse in the passenger seat and drove away. She was alone, and that gave her time to collect her thoughts.

Tonight meant four for four. She had approached a quartet of contacts in the preceding months and found each turned. This was the work of someone in power; someone with the stroke to uncover her associates, invade her network and turn those previously under her spell against her. It had to be Smelinski.

As she accelerated onto a freeway out of central Budapest, she thought back to her last meeting four months ago with her mentor in the waiting room of a basement clinic in Belgrade. It was three days after Lance -- she gripped the steering wheel tighter -- after *he* left. She shook her head and Lance's image ebbed from her mind.

Gregor the Terrible was waiting for her as she walked in. She was purposefully late because she had scouted out the location for the previous half hour and found no hidden or latent resources. She gave Smelinski the location for the meeting only 40 minutes earlier, and had been at a fourth-story window looking down as he arrived 29 minutes ago. After the KGB master entered, she scanned all directions from her vantage point. She saw no patterns, no suspicious movement. From the street six minutes later, she saw nothing out of order. Marta used a small pair of binoculars to scan windows looking down on the clinic entrance. She saw no movement, no slightly parted window drapes or shades. She worked her sightline along the rooftops and saw no black shadows, no radios, no glint of glass from scopes mounted on rifles.

She entered the clinic from a street-level door on the opposite side from the main entrance and took a set of stairs down to the basement. Smelinski greeted her with a nod, genuinely pleased to see her alive and well. They sat down next to each other like strangers waiting their turn to see the doctor. Their muted conversation couldn't be overheard by the half-dozen patients and family members in the waiting room.

"So good to see you are well," Smelinski whispered under his breath, looking away from her.

"And you, sir." She was always deferential with Smelinski. It was a role she mastered before their first meeting nearly a decade ago. Seibel had coached her how to do it. "Thank you for coming."

"Of course. I was beginning to wonder about your status. It appears Baghdad was even more exciting than we expected." Smelinski had a smile in his voice.

"Indeed it was." No smile in hers.

"Tell me. Tell me everything." Smelinski picked up a booklet and leaned on the armrest of his chair to get closer to her. "Everything."

"Perhaps another time sir. I am not here to talk about Iraq." She shut down this direction immediately. She had another agenda. "You know what I know, I'm sure. The Americans took out Korovin and Kusnetsov. They then captured the weapons. They obviously had help from other elements either within the Iraqi Mukbarat or Israeli resources on site."

"And you lost your team but survived, thank God." Smelinski was monotone in his deliver.

"No thanks to God. A Delta team had us all in their sights and took out my men. I did not escape unharmed."

"Which explains your absence these past weeks, correct?"

"Correct. Recovery after surgery." She brought her left hand over to her right armrest to let Smelinski see the raw scar where one of two bullets fired at her by Lance had struck. "It is nothing, though."

"Your first time being shot?" Smelinski was still monotone.

"Yes."

"Then welcome to an even more elite club." Smelinski smiled at this. "We all pay a great price for our work. Physical pain is a given. Death is a certainty."

"I didn't ask you here to discuss wounds," Marta changed the subject for good. "I need your permission to begin the next phase of our project. I have established a new target."

Smelinski put the brochure down and leaned his head back against the wall. "I assumed you were ready to get back into action. And I assumed small talk would be short, as usual."

"I'm pleased you understand my need to proceed without delay."

"Who have you identified?" Smelinski had his eyes closed as he asked. When Marta spoke her next words, he kept his eyes closed, but she couldn't help but see the movement of the eye under the lid.

"Kirill Cherzny."

The name was not well known outside of Russia. Those who knew the name, knew that Cherzny was the very latest and least known oligarch rising to the top in the former Soviet Union. Unlike other oligarchs earning a bad reputation through unmitigated arrogance and excess, Cherzny was amassing a fortune quietly, as an elected official.

Marta knew Cherzny was a huge and moving target - a meteor shooting across the sky gathering others into his orbit. But she didn't know what hearing the name did to Smelinski. He kept his breathing in rhythm and opened his mouth several seconds later.

"Why Cherzny?"

"He is positioned differently than the others. He has diversified his holdings from day one. He has reach into almost every segment of the economy and every sector of the government." Marta had been secretly researching Cherzny's operations for well over a year.

"His reach and influence in various segments can be a problem. Cherzny has many, many friends." Smelinski still had his eyes closed. Hiding them from her.

"Those friends are who we need to reach, correct?" She leaned her own head back against the wall.

"Some of his friends are people we might not want to interfere with, not now."

"Are you telling me not to go after him?" She turned to the KGB veteran of three plus decades. He finally opened his eyes and turned to her. He was different.

"I'm saying no such thing. He is perhaps the greatest example of those we have been working to bring down these past three years. He is corrupt, allied with forces that would destroy our nation, and willing to kill those who stand in his way," Smelinski chose his next words carefully. "I am merely telling you that you must take great care should you proceed down this path. Even my assistance and support may not be sufficient to protect you. Please think about it."

Marta repeated those same words to herself as she drove through the night. She was near the border crossing into Austria, about two hours after the incident in the café in Budapest. Since that meeting months ago, she hadn't spoken with

Smelinski and hadn't shared the details of her plans for the Cherzny operation with anyone still alive.

It had to be Smelinski, her mentor. He turned on her and alerted Cherzny's people. He had aligned KGB resources against her and sentenced Marta to death.

She needed information. She needed to see Anton. He was the only person she could trust to tell her the truth about Smelinski and Cherzny, and any connections between them. At the border stop, she handed the Austrian security worker a passport identifying Marta as a citizen of France, a resident of the town of Saint-Denis, north of Paris. The gentleman knew the town and its notoriously high crime rate. He asked Marta in French why she would live there.

"Ah, home is home. Is it not?" She replied in a flawless suburban Paris accent. He accepted her response with a smile and waved her on. She was on the outskirts of Vienna, and 25 minutes later, she pulled into the short driveway of a townhome in the southern 11th district of the city.

She enjoyed this home most of all. It was secret from her other residences, apartments and hotel rooms. She hid this location from everyone, including Smelinski and Seibel. One could imagine her surprise, the racing of her heart, and the tensing of her hands on the steering wheel as her headlights washed across an individual seated in the chair outside her front door where she drinks the occasional cup of morning coffee.

She completed the swerve into the short driveway and turned off the headlights. It took her a few moments to catch her breath. The individual formerly seated in her chair walked a few steps along the walk from the front door to the driveway. He stopped about 20 feet from the car. Even in the dark she was pleased to see his smile. From inside her car, with hands still gripping the steering wheel, Marta smiled back at Lance.

Chapter 12

"How would you do it?"

Her smile and gentle laughter had him again. She was as delightful as she had been nearly four months ago. But now she was healthy, all healed up from her gunshot wounds. She was strong and sure, and didn't hesitate to reach out with her scarred left hand to touch his arm or take his hand. Her question posed to him was a response to their discussion about their day.

In extremely vague terms, the two killers described how they each had been required to take decisive, life-ending action earlier in the day. Marta just finished describing her extrication from the café. Lance had been impressed. She asked him how he would disentangle himself from a similar situation.

"I think the getting up and going to the bathroom doesn't work for guys. You know, the Godfather and all." He couldn't help but smile.

"The Godfather?"

"The movie. And the book before that."

"Oh yes. I don't believe I've seen it, but know the basics." She leaned in closer. They were sitting on a couch in her tiny living room. "So did someone go to the bathroom in that story?"

"Yes. And he came out with a gun and proceeded to put a couple of bullets in his dinner partners."

"So again, how would you have done it?" She insisted.

"Well, the way you describe it. There were three total. One at one table; two at another. We're sure there were no others?"

"Positive."

"Well then," Lance closed his eyes and envisioned the room. He saw the tables, people seated at them talking and eating, and waiters moving about the room. "We need information from the one guy, correct?"

"Yes, only a little, but yes." She instinctively leaned a little closer to him. She wanted to reach out and touch his face, his lips. They had not kissed yet. She wanted to touch the small gash over his right eye. It was fresh, only hours old. She thought it would make his face even more distinguished as he aged.

Lance continued, "I would have waited for them all to be seated. I would watch all sightlines from outside to be sure they were alone. After confirming this, I would enter quickly and put a shot in each of the two men seated together."

"Where?"

"Between their eyes, from four or five feet. I would then turn to the other gentleman and put one in his knee and then place the smoking silencer under his chin, aimed up through his head. I would ask him for the information, and after he provided it or not, I would pull the trigger and casually walk out while the blood spray is still settling."

"You wouldn't run?"

"Draws too much attention. I assume that I have parked a vehicle or have someone waiting for me a couple of blocks away. I would remove my disguise and put it in a jacket pocket since I don't have a purse to stuff it in."

He opened his eyes and turned to her. The smile was gone. Instead, she tilted her head and squinted her eyes at him.

"What is it?" He turned his whole body toward her.

"Where were you this evening?" Suspicion oozed out with the words. She even pulled back a half an inch.

Lance saw the movement and quickly figured it out. "So, did I get it right? Is that a method you would approve of?"

"You didn't answer me."

"Okay. I was here in Vienna. Been here since yesterday morning." He smiled.

"You have not left the city?" She didn't smile.

"No. I considered it after I ran into a group of your friends who gave me this," he pointed to the wound over his eye. "But I had to come see you after they parted with their information. And their lives."

The smile came back. She didn't necessarily believe him, but she just had to hear the story of how he had found her.

"How long did it take you to find me?"

"Today?"

"No, how long have you been looking? Weeks? Months?" She reached to grab her glass of water on the coffee table. She didn't take her eyes off his. "How long?"

Lance sat back and rubbed his thighs, squeezing the aching muscles that resulted from diving, rolling and sprinting just a hours earlier. He smiled at her as she put the glass down and sat back on the cushions. She brought her left arm up to the back of the cushion and rested her head in her hand and very casually reached out her right hand to his forearm. She wished he didn't have long sleeves on so she could touch his skin.

"Are you going to tell me?" She was insistent on this point.

"Five and a half days." He pulled his right arm back to allow his hand to take hers. They laced their fingers. Both comfortable in this time and place.

"Five days? Really?" She leaned forward to place her head on his shoulder. It was her permission for him to tell her his story. "Go on, please."

Chapter 13

"How much detail do you want?" He asked.

"As much as you are comfortable sharing." She replied. Lance leaned his head on hers. He drifted for the briefest slice of a moment. This, like their last time together, was the most intimate moment he had ever shared. This closeness, this letting down his guard, was foreign to him. He wondered if she felt the same. In the next moment, she moved her forehead to his neck. She brought her hand up to his chest. "Please, go on."

Lance pulled her closer, placing his chin on her head. "You are affecting my concentration."

"I would apologize, but I would not mean it. Please tell me how you found me Lance. And don't spare the good stuff." With that, she slapped his chest gently.

Lance obeyed. He closed his eyes and went out of body to look back over the last five days since landing in Antwerp. He had been something of a violent whirlwind moving through Europe. In his wake, he left death, suffering and people grateful to still be breathing. Short on time, he did not have the luxury of building relationships on this off-assignment tour of duty.

"I started in Belgium. I made it to Paris by the first afternoon and went to visit one of only two contacts related to you that I was able to pry out of Seibel.

"Marshon or Broulet?"

"Marshon."

"Felix is a nag. A good man, but an old nag." She nuzzled into his neck.

Lance then proceeded to tell her about visiting Felix Marshon, a pleasant-looking Frenchman who just happened to be a 40-year KGB plant. Marshon had worked in Paris as a bank manager for so long, he probably couldn't even remember being Russian, let alone a communist spy.

Lance met Marshon as he walked up the stairs of his apartment building in the pricy and trendy Montparnasse district. It was the older gentleman's walk that gave him away as a homosexual. Lance knew within a half-second as he watched the dapper gentleman approach the building three minutes earlier that he was gay. Lance greeted him in such a manner that the old spy barely broke his stride as he continued up the stairs, into the lobby and onto the elevator. They didn't speak on the lift as two other tenants joined them. Once they reached Marshon's floor, Lance and the elder spy stepped off. If he wanted to assault Lance, this was the opportunity. Instead, Lance gripped his arm in a friendly manner. They walked down the hall to his apartment.

Marshon's apartment confirmed Lance's assumption. The man was tasteful in his decorating, fastidious in his home maintenance and protective of his sexuality. Lance got right to the point as the door closed behind him. He spoke in Russian.

"I don't have time to chat or play games Felix. You don't know me, and you do not want to know me. I only need one thing from you."

The old gay gentleman took a step back. Lance had invaded his life and threatened his lifestyle by being here. "What is it that you want?" Marshon's response was in French. Lance knew only phrases of the language.

In Russian again, "I need to find the location of someone that very few know. I already know that you don't, but you can put me in touch with others who do."

"Who is it, my young man?" He responded in Russian this time.

"I'm not going to say the name. But you already know who I'm talking about. You don't need me to say her name." Lance said the key word – "her." He watched the Russian spy closely. The man turned his head, raised his eyebrows and brought a hand to his wrinkled chin. It was delay. He needed to think about his next move.

"Felix, you know at least two people who have the information."

"And who are these people?" Felix was feeling a bit braver. He began to think that he might have the upper hand in this matter. Lance decided to tell a few lies.

"Your name came up several months ago during a sweep of a database being decommissioned at the source. A review of your relationship to the subject provided linkage to several resources both active and inactive." Lance thought to himself that it sounded sufficiently vague. It sounded like bureaucracy, both Soviet and American. To add a little intrigue, Lance switched to Russian accented English. "You are undoubtedly aware, based upon your interaction and dealings with her while she was stationed in Paris, that the subject has gone off the radar for good. She is no longer in direct contact with any approved resources. Her actions have placed several sectors in jeopardy."

Marshon moved from the middle of the room to a bureau with several decanters on it. "I'm afraid this is not something I am aware of. I will need more information to be of any assistance." And then he moved his hand to a drawer.

Lance sprung across the space between them and placed his gloved right thumb beside Marshon's Adam's apple and his gloved fingers behind his neck. He tightened the grip and delivered a quick strike to the old man's stomach with a balled and gloved left hand. The effect of the two moves left the man without oxygen. It also kept him from reaching for the gun in the drawer. Lance knew how this was going to go the moment he mentioned a female. The rest was just for show.

Marshon brought a fist up to Lance's left cheek. The blow glanced off as Lance turned his head. He squeezed Marshon's throat tighter, twisting the man's neck slightly. He leaned close, just inches from the old man's reddening face. "Felix. I tried to be nice. I told you I have no time for delays. You have chosen to make me an enemy so I will give you just a couple of more seconds, and then I will break your neck. You will never walk along the Seine, hold your young gentleman lover's hand or enjoy the taste of that brandy ever again." Lance made all that up, of course. He didn't know much about Marshon, other than that his real name was not Marshon and he had been working for the KGB for decades.

"Please, sil vous plait." Marshon breathed the words, whispered them.

"In Russian." Lance demanded.

"Pozhaluista," the old man pleaded through gritted teeth.

Lance did not enjoy this. He would've rather obtained the information peaceably and moved on. But he could tell, when he had Marshon on the elevator, that the ancient spy was looking for ways to subdue or kill him. He became even more determined when Lance mentioned a "her." It appeared Marta had put the fear of death into the old man. Lance thought to himself that she had likely been here, in this very room, getting her message across. And then a light bulb went off. She killed his lover. At some point in the past few years, Marta made her point to Felix Marshon by having his lover killed. It was likely brutal and done right before his eyes. Marshon's reaction a few minutes earlier was telling. His next few lies were merely cover, and not very good.

Lance continued in Russian. His accent guttural, from the mean streets of Moscow. "I didn't come here to hurt you. I merely have a job to do, and I have very little time," Lance released the man's throat and took a step back to allow him to compose himself. "Now, take in a few breaths and tell me what I need to know."

Marshon bent over and put a supporting hand on the bureau behind him. After a few moments he straightened and resumed his regal bearing. "I truly have no idea where she is. But I know several others she had dealings with since I last encountered her." With that, he reached into a breast pocket and pulled out a handkerchief to dab at his lips and wipe his brow.

"Go on." Lance sagged his shoulders to appear relaxed. He turned away from Marshon to look out a window. He noticed a few moments earlier that the lip of a tray sitting on a table beside the couch provided a nice reflection of the man standing behind him. Lance turned away to allow Marshon to further compose himself and complete the plan the old sleeper agent had hatched in his head. Lance watched the man's movements in the lip of the tray. He reached for the drawer again and silently pulled out the gun and aimed it at Lance.

Preacher sprang again. He grabbed the gun and violently twisted it. He pulled the man close, picked him up and propelled him to the couch. After throwing him onto the sofa, Preacher brought the gun up to the man's chin, not the chin per se, the submaxillary triangle of soft skin between the chin and throat.

"You have served your time and your country. You have decided to take the information you possess between your ears to your grave. I respect that starik." Lance intermingled English and Russian using the Russian term for "old man." "You obviously know my assignment included ending your life.

Samoubiistvo is a proper manner for your sendoff." The Russian word for suicide sounded better than the English version.

"No, please. Nyet. Pozhaluista!" Marshon pleaded for his life. Lance was a little surprised. He thought the old man would prefer to go gracefully into that dark night. "I'll tell you. I'll tell you."

"Please do." Lance bent down to whisper in Marshon's ear. "I'm listening."

"She will kill me when she finds out I told you this." He was near tears.

"She will never learn the source from me. Go on." Lance gently pressed the gun deeper into the man's throat.

"One man is in Munich. The other is in Milan. Her network is extremely sparse. There has been some talk about Vienna. That is all I know."

"You have names and addresses for Munich and Milan?"

"Yes."

"Very good. I'll take that information and be on my way." Lance stood and removed the gun barrel from Marshon's chin. He switched the gun into his left hand and reached into a pocket to pull out a piece of paper and pen. He handed both to the old man. "Please write the information for me. Thank you."

Marshon moved his head left and right and rubbed his throat where the gun had just been. He then wrote down two names and addresses on the crumpled piece of paper. Then he handed it to Lance who had walked around in front of him. "Now, please go."

Lance looked at the paper. "So, you just happen to have this information memorized?"

"I am no fool. If I had this recorded somewhere other than my mind, it could be discovered, and then she would find out I had been less than precise in my actions. She is unforgiving."

Lance looked at the names and addresses and memorized each. He closed his eyes for a few moments standing over the old spy and went out of body up to the height of satellites and then back down to Munich and the street referenced. He descended to street level to look at cross streets near the address. In the next moment he moved to a satellite view of Milan, Italy. He then descended to a couple thousand feet. He had never been to the city and didn't know the streets like he did Munich. He opened his eyes and bent down to Marshon to shove the paper into the man's mouth.

"I would destroy that information and leave no remnant." He turned toward the door, took a few paces and stopped. Lance examined this situation anew. He had met this man 12 minutes earlier, and now he held his life in his hands. The next decision was already made for him. Loose ends could lead to harm for him and for Marta. Lance turned back to the man seated on his sofa. Like dozens of others in the last year, this human was dead the moment he encountered Preacher. This peripheral player in the spy game now possessed information that could not be allowed to be passed to others who would use it to destroy. This man had seen Lance. He knew of the connection with Marta.

Lance spoke his next words in Russian. He said them with remorse. "Comrade. You have failed. This was a test. She sent me here, like she has Munich, Milan, Prague and Amsterdam. Some remained resolute in their duty. Others have not. You have chosen your life over hers. You made your choice." Lance tossed the gun into the man's lap and turned again for the door.

Outside in the corridor, Lance delayed his departure. He stood thinking of how Seibel would react when word of Marshon's passing reached him. He leaned against the wall in the hallway and tapped his foot to the song by Genesis that had started when Marshon first reached for the gun.

The single gunshot from the apartment was not loud. It sounded like a tenant had dropped a book to the floor. Lance looked at the scene in the apartment from above the now deceased spy. In his mind's eye, Lance saw that the power of suggestion had worked on the elderly KGB operative. Back in his head, Lance examined himself for some emotional residue from the encounter. There was none.

This was business. Felix Marshon chose both his life and death. He had provided extensive classified information about France, the West and NATO back to the Soviet Union for decades. The information he passed had killed dozens. He earned this death. This is how spies should die.

"So you did not take his life with your own hand?" Marta broke into his narrative, there in the apartment hallway in Paris.

"No. I used yours." Lance pushed some loose strands of hair behind her ear.

"He made his own choice. It was not a bad way to go." She nodded.

"That's exactly what I thought. I hope I get that choice."

"Don't speak of such things." Marta pulled back to look up at him. He met her eyes. "I don't like to think of that."

In this moment, Lance changed yet again. He had spent the first 24 years of his life in exile from the confusion of human emotions. His subtle separation from other homo sapiens was resolute. He'd often felt more alien than human. Like a scientist watching subjects go about their lives as part of a grand experiment. He was fully aware his view of life was the product of a psychological makeup comprised of various disorders. Among them were narcissism, anti-social disorder and general psychosis. Reading about these mental abnormalities had been akin to reading his biography. But he was comfortable in his solitude. It was simply who he was.

But now, looking into Marta's eyes was like looking into a live, interactive mirror. She was a screwed up reflection of his unique package of psychoses. She was also beautiful and lonely and exposed. He lowered his lips to hers and cradled her head in his hand. She rose to her knees to straddle him. Her lips moved from his lips to his neck, cheek and then she kissed the small gash above his right eyebrow. She ran her hands through his hair. His hands fell from her shoulders to rest on her hips. She pulled back to sit on his lap and look into his eyes.

"How am I doing?" She smiled. She was just a girl.

"Very good, actually."

"You will need to show me what to do. I have never." She was shy and vulnerable and honest.

"You are doing fine." He wove his fingers into her hair falling across her face and moved it behind her shoulders. Now, this was truly the most intimate moment of his life of emotional solitude. "Are you ready?" He had never asked before, just taken charge in the moment.

"Yes." She bent again to kiss him and then abruptly pulled away. "And then you will finish your story. You have four more days to tell me about." She moved off of him and stood. He took her hand and followed her upstairs where they shared the most intimate moments of their lives. Those moments stretched into hours, and were followed by the rarest of things – peaceful sleep.

Chapter 14

Angry is a word. Mad is another. Pissed, ticked, livid, incensed; they all worked to describe Kirill Cherzny's mood. He had not built a vast empire in the past decade to see it threatened by the KGB, or FSB, whatever they called themselves these days. Least of all, a woman, a KGB renegade, was not going to take what he had earned, what he had won.

"This is very quickly moving past an annoyance Gregor Ivanovich." Cherzny stirred his tea and then tapped his cup. He made a performance out of the act and followed it by taking a delicate sip of the steaming beverage. "I had your assurances that you could control this situation, this woman."

Smelinski sat across the table from Cherzny. They'd met maybe a dozen times in this out of the way diner. It was really just four tables in a back room of a store. But it offered the thing Cherzny prized above all else – privacy. He could conduct business here without intrusion, without the fear of detection. Smelinski truly hated coming to the place.

He'd met in far worse places, scarier, dirtier. It wasn't the place; it was the company. He disliked Cherzny more than he detested the room. But his preferences were of little concern to Cherzny.

"I told you from the beginning that she would be challenging. She is not like others. She can't be bought or bribed or bargained with. She doesn't see the world the way you and I do."

"I know, I know. You've said it all before. She is special," Cherzny took another sip of tea. "I can certainly see what you mean. Very strange, she left that fool alive this time. Why do you suppose she did that?"

Smelinski smiled. "Because she knew you would finish the job for her."

Cherzny smiled. "And you are positive, absolutely sure we can not convince her to change her mind, to join my team?"

"If she joined your organization it would only be to get inside so she could kill everyone and take everything. You would soon be a distant memory." Smelinski had a difficult time keeping his mouth shut around this prick. Cherzny's arrogance was such an affront. But if he wasn't careful, Smelinski would end up dead, with his beloved KGB gutted by Cherzny.

His position in the duma, the Russian parliament, and his appointment to the executive committee, with oversight of the former KGB, gave Cherzny power. Add to that his hundreds of millions, maybe billions of dollars, that he had amassed and it was easy to see the writing on the wall. Do what he says, or else.

Cherzny had made it very clear to Smelinski several years ago in their first meeting in this very room that a revolution was coming. Gregor the Terrible, and the other vestiges of a bygone Cold War era, would be swept aside. Smelinski could not allow that to happen. He had fought for too long to protect his homeland to see it dismantled, bought and sold like so many other institutions the oligarchs were collecting. He chose to play along.

He hadn't gone quietly into the night. Marta was his creation, his weapon against the endless corruption. Smelinski, like his counterpart Seibel, always saw the strategy through the forest of tactics. He would never admit it, but Smelinski knew full well, knew it when he gave her the orders to infiltrate, dismantle and assume the resources of those doing harm to Russia. He knew it would lead to Cherzny.

But he was forced to disavow her, to abandon her. All the while hoping, praying that she would complete this mission; that she would do to Cherzny what she had done to others. For Cherzny's prying and omnipresent eyes, Smelinski had thrown Marta to the wolves. He had sent other resources after her, hunted her. If she were killed, all would be lost. Cherzny would win.

Gregor the Terrible had indeed done something terrible to Marta. But he knew deep in his empty soul, if any one human could survive, overcome any obstacle, it was her. Smelinski walked a razor's edge. Death waited on one side and another death, at the hands of a vengeful Marta awaited him on the other side. But that death would mean that Russia, and all he had worked for, would survive. He prayed for that death.

"Then, I guess we shall see won't we," Cherzny downed the remnants of the cup of tea and poured another cup from the small pot on the table.

Chapter 15

The light of morning beyond the drawn curtains breathed life into the room. Unspoken words during the night, and now morning, told of their union, their met needs. This brief moment amid years of dark and lonely lives was a vacation. This was a holiday. Their time together, today and with any luck, in the future, would bring a respite from the demands of their chosen lives. What exactly that future would bring remained a mystery. But this thing between them, whatever it is, it was real. It now carried demands of both of them; demands that would supersede orders and missions. This was a life sentence.

Each of them rose, he after her, to use the bathroom. She was fastidious in brushing her teeth and left a new toothbrush on the sink for him to use. She returned to the bed naked and he used the toilet and brushed his teeth. As he returned to the bed naked, she watched his approach and threw the blankets aside to welcome him back into the warmth. They made love again with renewed exploration.

Afterward, they lay together beneath a sheet. The heat, the sweat between them, was something new and exhilarating, and delightful. That was again the word that came to Lance's mind. Damn.

"I would ask you how you feel, but I have a fairly good idea," Marta's lips moved against the skin of his shoulder as she spoke. Her left finger making circles on his chest.

"Your idea is correct, if it assumes general and specific satisfaction." His arm wrapped around her allowed his hand and fingers to caress her waist and hip.

"Thank you." She moved her leg on top of his. A full-body hug.

"No, thank you."

"But I insist," she smiled and kissed his shoulder.

"Can we both agree on general and specific gratitude?"

"Agreed." She moved her face to his chest. "I'll remind you that you have more story to tell me."

"I remember. Would you like me to continue now or after breakfast?"

"Now please. I am going to need you to perform other duties after breakfast." Her smile was again, delightful.

Lance squeezed her tighter as they laughed together. "Okay then, where was I?"

"Marshon had just shuffled off this mortal coil."

"Indeed." Lance closed his eyes and returned to Paris and his next moves. He told her of his train ride to Milan, and his quick tracking and brief visit with a man known to the art world as a collector and historian. To the world of espionage, he is known as a reducer. His job is to collect data, information and rumors from various disparate sources and compile it into useful facts and figures that add value to data collected from general field sources. His true value is the sheer number of contacts from both sides who trust him to relay information. His life and career had been well-defined during the Cold War. Now, he was basically a mercenary working for all sides, protected by the impartiality he maintains. He was a one-man Switzerland in the heart of Milan.

Because Lance was off mission and several thousand miles away from his assignment in the Philippines, he could not contact resources he would have normally accessed to uncover what he needed to know in advance of meeting with the man in Milan. So he chose to do the next best thing. He lied. Lance drew the man in with a phone call, met him in a darkened smoky room while disguised and left him alive to live the remainder of his life. Lance was somewhat pleased he didn't have to kill him or encourage him to commit a life-ending act. The information he took away from the meeting pointed to Vienna. That was twice the Austrian capitol city had been mentioned in 24 hours.

The next morning, Lance walked into an upscale department store in Munich and asked the woman behind the perfume counter if he could speak with the Geschäftsführer -- the general manager. Because there were cameras mounted on walls and in ceilings, Lance was disguised again. His choice of disguise for this meeting was spur of the moment and the result of a brief shopping trip in a secondhand store on the seedier side of town an hour earlier. The 'woman' who asked to speak to the manager was dressed in a long coat, slacks and flats. Her hair, a deep red, flowed down onto her shoulders. Her eyes hidden behind sunglasses.

The general manager walked up to the woman. His eyes squinted when Lance turned around. It was immediately obvious to the manager that Lance was a man. It was probably the stubble of facial hair. But Lance didn't much care what the general manager thought, he just wanted to fool anyone else looking on. And the cameras watching from above.

Lance took the man's arm in a very professional yet affectionate manner and steered him slowly toward the main entrance. Along the way, he spoke to him in German about duty and respect and responsibility and commitment amid the disintegration of the Union. Their conversation continued as they walked out to the street, across, into and out the back of a café. In the alley behind the small café, Lance released the man's arm and told a few convincing lies about Marta and the need to contact her immediately on behalf of several reigning members of the former KGB leadership. He mentioned a couple of names to cement the lie.

"I know this all comes to you as a surprise, but my time is limited, non-existent really. I must make contact with Ms. Sidorova within a day or two." Lance watched again as the mention of Marta's name brought a physical reaction from this experienced espionage professional, just as it had Marshon in Paris and "Mr. Switzerland" in Milan. He was amazed to see grown men quiver at the mention of Marta and the thought of her retribution. Lance needed to offer superseding levels of punishment for non-compliance.

He continued in flawless St. Petersburg Russian. "My orders are simple. I am to meet with you and three others over the next two days to determine her location or to pass along a message that we must speak with her directly."

"I am truly sorry," the manager replied in German. "I do not know either the woman you mention or her location."

"Of course. I understand that this kind of information would be valuable to those in possession of it. But I must be very truthful with you; your name has been mentioned by three of the four people I have spoken with in the last 36 hours. I have been told that you are indeed a trusted resource for Ms. Sidorova. You and another in Vienna." Lance let the last sentence hang as a lifeline for the scared man. He bit.

"Vienna, yes. Vienna is what I have heard on several occasions. Rumors only, but from reliable sources." He smiled as he said this.

Lance decided to take it to the next level. This required some violence. He spun rapidly away from the man and then back to him, the movement gave the manager time to take a defensive position. Lance lunged with a slow roundhouse punch. The manager, a lean man in his late-fifties who stood 6 foot 2 inches, deflected the punch and spun to deliver a chop to Lance's neck. Lance absorbed the blow but fell to the ground. He got back up, somewhat wobbly, and threw a left punch that was again deflected and followed by a kick that sent Lance sprawling. The manager followed the kick with a knee in Lance's back. Lance gasped and remained on all fours as the manager stood back up preparing for his next attack.

As the man stepped toward him, Lance held up his hands and pleaded in German. "Please, no more. I apologize for my actions. I am under extreme pressure and obviously acted inappropriately."

The manager straightened from the crouch he had assumed the moment before. "You are an amateur and you have placed me in danger with your novice actions. You have no idea how much damage you could cause me and others with your bumbling approach. You are very lucky I do not kill you now. I would be saving you from certain and painful death if you ever did find her."

Lance whimpered. "I'm sorry. I will leave. I am off to Vienna this evening to meet with Alexi. I will not mention your name or that we met."

"Jesus. You don't know what you have done. You don't know the players or the complexity with which she has built her network. Who is this Alexi?"

"He is her primary contact in Vienna. He is at the Hotel Imperial. You must know the place."

The manager shook his head. "Again, you are out of your league. I don't know anyone named Alexi in Vienna." The manager took a step forward. It was his last.

Preacher shot up out of his crouch with such lightning speed, the store manager did not see it coming. The blow Preacher delivered to the man's throat made a sickening sound. Before the man could fall, Preacher grabbed his left arm and delivered a blow with his knee that removed the remaining oxygen in his lungs. Preacher held the man gently and lowered him to the filthy bricks lining the alleyway. He lay there quivering, stunned and sputtering, looking up at Preacher unable to bring in enough oxygen.

"Shh. The next few moments are mine my friend. I need to know the correct name and location for the contact in Vienna. You confirmed Alexi is wrong, so now you will provide me the correct name. I'll remind you, time is of the essence. I understand your fear, but I must convince you that retribution from Ms. Sidorova pales in comparison to the vile, deadly and unrepentant acts I have committed and will commit. You and your life, and that of your family, are nothing to me. I've killed dozens of wives and children. Yours will be forgotten moments after I stop their hearts from beating. Please, now. I can either help you and then leave this alley and travel to Vienna, or I can leave you here to die a slow suffocating death then pay a visit to your home and then to the homes of your grown children and their children. Death comes to us all. The choice is yours."

Lance closed his eyes and drifted out of body to look down on the scene. He was not pleased with himself. He was embarrassed to have resorted to a threat of violence toward a family. It was not him, not his way.

He would never.

But time was collapsing around him. He needed to move faster. He needed results, and this method is very effective. Still, he was embarrassed as he looked down on Preacher and the heaving individual he crouched over.

The store manager was a proud veteran of two-plus decades of clandestine service on behalf of his homeland. This was the closest he had come to death, and the second time in two years that his life and those of his family had been threatened. He looked up into Lance's eyes, but instead he saw another set of eyes. The young woman who sat across from him at a café was so absolute in her conviction that nothing would ever stop her. He could not protect his family from evil like this. So here again, this young man looked down upon him with the same eyes, that same complete absence of empathy. The source of this kind of evil escaped him. He had killed men. Seen others die before his eyes, but he never felt the emptiness this man, dressed as a woman leaning over him, expressed through his words, actions and his eyes.

"Anton." The name was whispered through teeth gritted in pain.

"Where?" Preacher was unmoved by the name.

"Vienna. He is a policeman, a detective."

Lance smiled at the man and reached down and grabbed the lapels of his jacket to pull him up to a seated position. "Thank you. I am sorry to have to put you through this. But you knew what you were signing up for when you took this job back before I was even born."

"Yes, I knew." The Russian spy sputtered and rubbed his neck.

"I know you have to live in doubt after our encounter this morning, but I can tell you without any hesitation, that I will not divulge the source of the information. I was never here. And if we ever meet again, it will be because I need your assistance. I feel the time is near that people like us will have a new and common enemy." Lance got up and rapidly walked out of the alley. He took a bus across town, and then another before boarding a train that took him through Salzburg, then Linz and into Vienna just four hours later. Customs was no problem for a young American tourist backpacking across the heart of Europe. His money was appreciated everywhere it was spent.

"So that brings you to Vienna two days ago right?" Marta was now propped up on her elbow looking down at him. For another moment, Lance was lost again looking at her. She was glorious with her hair falling down over her shoulder. He looked from her face to her shoulders and then down her body to her lovely feet. She lay naked beside him, just for him. He couldn't help but reach for her and trace the silhouette of her body as far as his hand could reach. She let him take his time and smiled at his involuntary smile.

"I'm sorry. What was your question?" He brought his eyes back to hers.

She shook her head and dropped her face to the pillow. "Oh god."

"What? What is it?" He brushed her hair from the side of her face and then rubbed his hand down her lovely back. He brushed his lips down to her left shoulder blade and kissed it. This too, was an involuntary action. He experienced a number of them in her presence. "What is it?"

She turned her head from the pillow. "This is just so crazy. I don't..." she couldn't find the words. Lance didn't respond verbally. Instead he kissed her back below her shoulder blade. "Lance."

"Yes." He was further down, almost to the small of her back.

"You know what I am going to say." She was direct, as always.

Lance was no fool and recognized his cue to break from this round of kissing. He brought his face to the pillow next to hers, keeping a hand on her back, again involuntarily. "Do I?"

"I need to say it." The smile faded from her face. It was replaced by a serious stare that pierced him.

"I'm not stopping you." He smiled just a little. "Would you like me to say it first?"

"Yes. That would be reassuring." She reached and took his hand.

"Okay then," he rose onto his elbow and reached down and pulled the sheet up over them. Then he rolled her from her stomach onto her back. He swept the hair away from her face and behind her ear. He could see her serious look from moments ago was now headed for tears. He caressed her cheek and then her lips with a fingertip and stared into her mesmerizing eyes. "I love you."

The tears came. She used the sheet up to soak up the saltwater. They looked at each other for a few endless moments. This was a first for each of them.

"Are you reassured?" He smiled and she joined him. She pulled him to her and covered him with kisses and more tears.

She broke away and laughed and cried. "I don't think I want to say I love you."

This set Lance back for a shocking moment. "Okay."

She smiled broader and brighter and kissed him again. "No, silly. Love is the wrong word now. I have to say that, more than love you, I need you."

The smile returned to Lance's face. "Really. That's serious."

"Very." Her lovely procerus muscle pulled her beautiful eyebrows together.

"And how long have you felt this way?" Lance took this opportunity to wipe away a tear rolling down Marta's cheek.

"From the first moment. The moment I first saw you in Baghdad."

"Even after I shot you?"

"Twice."

"After I shot you twice." Lance winced at the thought for maybe the 3,000th time in just over five months.

"Yes. Even though you wanted to kill me. My feelings for you have not changed at all, except to feel an even greater need. You have infected me."

"Infected?" Lance furrowed his brow at her choice of words. "And is there a cure for this?"

"No. None. This is a terminal condition."

"And if I were to shoot you again?" He tilted his face away in a wry smile.

"It would hurt, but not as much as losing you." The serious look returned to her face. She was afflicted in this moment.

Lance brought his lips to hers and then traced her chin, cheek and eyes with his lips. The salt of her tears tasted like love. He smiled at that thought. It sounded like a line from a trashy romance novel. "I think we are going to have to get out of this bed in a little while and do some serious talking."

"Yes. In a little while." She kissed him again and pulled him to her. Then she kissed his cheek and neck and spoke into his ear. "And you will have to finish your story. But in a little while." A little while took longer to get to than either expected. But neither minded.

Chapter 16

Morning turned to afternoon. The world and its demands and timelines and dangers passed them by for one day. She was just a girl, and he just a boy in love with her. It was easy. It was anything but reality, but it was nice for a few short hours.

Marta brewed French press coffee. Lance made toast, his specialty. They sat down at the small table and talked about anything but business. She asked him about baseball. He admitted he wasn't much of a fan, but gave her a quick tutorial on football, American-style. She enjoyed sitting there, listening to him talk. Without her asking, he eased into her favorite character, Bart Radish.

"And then, there are them thar touchdown dances. Don't care much for them, but some are downright creative." The fun lasted for a few more minutes until Marta got them back on task with a simple question.

"What do we do now Lance?" She sipped her coffee after asking him.

"I have to admit that, kind of like our last time together, I never thought past seeing you. I honestly haven't considered next steps."

"What is your mission?" It was a direct question like usual. But this one carried baggage and strings. His hesitation didn't concern her in the least. "I understand your need to keep mission particulars secret. I just want to know the basics, like where will you be and how long we will be apart. I am asking for very selfish reasons."

"Like I said, I hadn't considered next steps and how we proceed." He rubbed the back of her hand where the scar from the gunshot marred the beauty of her skin. "Listen, I want to be very clear with you. I am a liar. I lie every day, every hour of every day. But I am not lying in the least when I say that I want you in my life." He gestured to the table and the room. "I want this. I honestly have no idea how we do it, how we can make this happen, but I want it."

"Do you need it?" Seriousness was back in her eyes.

"More than you do."

"You're wrong. You have known this or something like this before. For me it is a revelation. I am not the same person I was six months ago."

"That's funny." He circled his finger around the raised scar on her hand.

"How is it funny?"

"I could say the exact thing, those very words. I am not the same person I was every day of my life before seeing you, meeting you in Baghdad." He sat back and bent his knee to bring his bare foot up onto the chair he sat on. He wrapped his left arm around the leg. Several bruises were obvious. "Meeting you changed me. I was just saying that to myself the other night in that alley in Munich, and before that, several months ago in an alley in Hamburg. I have been changed by this, by you. And you have to know, I have never known anything like this."

She sipped her coffee and took a bite of toast with jelly. "How are you changed? How are you different from before?"

"Lots of ways really. You, the image and thought of you invade my mind at the strangest moments. The thought of you makes me stop, for just the briefest moment, and think about my next step. It's like you're with me in some way. Very strange."

She laughed at this. She grasped his hand in both of hers. "You just took the words out of my mouth. Just yesterday evening in Budapest, I had to shake my head to get you out of there, right in the middle of that café. It is a little frustrating."

"Yes, that's it. It's frustrating to not be able to control it."

"Exactly," she brought his hand to her lips. "I'm infected by you."

"No cure?" He asked.

"No cure." She replied.

They moved from the kitchen table to the living room. They were kneeling at the coffee table. Spread out on the table were three maps. They were slightly more dressed than before, and in full strategic mode.

"From Mindanao, I'll likely head through Indonesia and India to Pakistan. My assumption is, it will be three weeks to a month before I am back in Europe." Lance moved a finger from Pakistan to Vienna.

"A month? That's too long." She went back to Pakistan on a map of Asia. "Perhaps during your stay in Pakistan you can get away for a day or two in Dubai. There are several flights each day from Karachi."

"I'm afraid I'm going to be a ways from Karachi. Maybe Peshawar, possibly Quetta."

"There is nothing in Quetta. I know, don't ask." They had agreed not to ask details or contacts, just locations. "Quetta?"

"I know. Go to hell and hang a left." He cracked a joke.

She laughed. "That's funny. You could say that about a lot of places I've been."

"So what about you? Where will I find you if I need to?" He focused on Europe.

"My plans will take me to Bucharest and Kiev for sure. And then most likely Moscow." She moved her fingers across the map, somewhat tentatively. He noticed.

"You're not sure?"

"No. My plans are changing daily. The generalities are the same, but I have been rebuilding my team since Baghdad."

He sat back on his feet. "Sorry."

"Don't apologize. You were successful in your mission. You were more than successful, you were amazing, from what I heard." She moved to sit against the sofa behind her.

"What else did you hear?"

"No details, must I remind you?" Her smile concealed nothing.

"We are going to have to talk about one detail."

"I think I have a good idea."

"He will find out, if he hasn't already. He'll find out about us and he'll surely feel the need to get involved somehow." Lance brought his hand up to his chin to think.

"We are players on his chessboard are we not?" Her use of chess was ironic. He had thought the very same thing when he realized Seibel was behind just about everything. His is the invisible hand moving pieces on a board game of his own creation.

"I'm sure he's already got people looking for me. He undoubtedly knows about my flight to Antwerp. He wouldn't have to make much of a leap to put two and two together and figure out I was looking for you. Hell, he probably thinks we have seen each other several times since Baghdad."

She looked at the maps for a few moments, lost in thought. "Do you think that is what he wants? This is what he wants?" She gestured to the two of them.

"Do you mean us?"

"Yes, you and me together. Is that what he had planned all along?" She raised her eyebrows. It was not the first time she had thought of this.

"I've thought of that. Wondered if you are the reason I'm in this game." Lance leaned back against the couch.

"Does that change how you feel?"

"About you?"

"Yes."

"You and I both know Seibel is the master manipulator. His little plans and schemes affect us all. My feelings about you have nothing to do with him. He may have had something in mind when he found me, but he never mentioned you in more than a passing manner. You were at the periphery of the Baghdad mission. I was completely surprised to stumble across you there." Lance smiled and then closed his eyes. He went out of body and back to Baghdad above the apartment building he'd entered, supposedly to get a bird's eye view of the action below. But what if?

What if it was all his plan? What if he sent Lance into that building for the sole purpose of running into Marta and her team? Now that would be devious. And so like Seibel.

"Where do you go?"

He opened his eyes. "What?"

"When you close your eyes and sometimes even when they are open. You leave. Where do you go?"

He pursed his lips. Damn. She had him figured out pretty dang well for the few short days and nights they had spent together. "I drift."

"You do it a lot."

"I know."

"I saw it twice in Baghdad and several times at the villa. I wonder what you see when you drift away."

"Do you want to go with me?" He raised his eyebrows and went Cheshire Cat with his grin.

"Yes, take me."

He crawled around the table and sat next to her. He took her hand in his and kissed it, then closed his eyes. "You are from Novosibirsk right?"

"Yes. You turn right at hell."

He laughed at that. "Mother Russia's third largest city, you know. East or west side of the river?"

"I'm sorry?"

"Which side of the river did you live on?"

"East."

"Northwest or southeast of prospect Derzhinskogo?" He referenced a major thoroughfare.

She looked at him, with his eyes closed, and wondered again what he saw. Did he know about her childhood? Did he know about her? "Southeast."

"West or east of Ulitsa Borisa Bogatkova?"

"East."

"North or south of Ulitsa Kirova?"

"Lance. I don't..."

"Almost done. Please."

"South." He didn't know about it. He wouldn't do this if he did. If he knew what it did to her.

From 50,000, then 10,000, and now 2,000-feet over Novosibirsk, Lance peered down on the largest city in Siberia. He was looking now at a satellite image taken probably a year ago. Lance had seen it, and hundreds of other images, on his most recent trip to Langley. He saw rooftops of houses and apartment buildings and warehouses and train tracks. The Ob River cut the city in half. He was enjoying the drill-down until a moment ago when Marta's voice gave up a good bit of emotion he hadn't heard before. He decided to stop.

He opened his eyes and smiled at her. In her eyes, he saw the tinge of emotion evident in her voice. "Sorry. Stupid party trick."

"That's okay. What did you see?"

"Your hometown, from a few miles up."

"Satellite image?"

"Yes."

"Can you see a lot of them?"

"Yep."

"Right now?"

"Yes. Right now."

"Do you need to close your eyes?"

"No. It just helps me get a clearer image."

"Just photography?"

"Photos, maps, people."

"Photographic memory?" She was an inquisitor by nature.

"I don't think so. Maybe."

"See, you are even more special. I knew it. I think you may be the most gifted person I've ever met."

"No way. Nothing special, just weird. I'm anything but special. Strange yes. But not special, not like you."

"Lance. I don't believe for a moment that you haven't known since you were a little boy that you were special, unique. I'll bet you had to work hard just to keep your talents hidden from others. You were probably an average student, average athlete, average everything."

"You got it. Guilty." He smiled and shook his head.

"So how did Geoffrey find you?"

"Foreign Service Officer exam. He ran across my application and questionnaire."

"Oh yes. The questionnaire. I know about that."

"You see, right there. You have a significant advantage over me. You have been exposed to Seibel for 10 or 15 more years than me. You know some trade secrets I don't."

"Not really. He is still a mystery to me. I only know what he wants me to know. Plus a little more I suppose he doesn't know I've learned." She grinned a little at that.

"You'll have to share some of that with me."

"Later. You still owe me the last day and a half of tracking me. Tell me how you discovered my secret hideout and how you got this little scratch." She circled her finger around the cut and bruise she had cleaned extensively and kissed dozens of times. "And I assume these little bruises probably have a story as well." She rubbed her hand from his ribs to his legs. She had examined the extensive bruising the night before and found nothing broken.

Chapter 17

"I'm sorry to have to tell you that Anton is dead."

They had moved up to opposite ends of the couch with their legs entwined. He held her bare foot in his hands massaging it. He had to be careful because she was extremely ticklish.

"Damn, Lance. Who didn't you kill?"

"I didn't kill him."

"Who did then?"

Lance explained to Marta his progress, from arriving in Vienna three days ago, tracing Anton to the police station and arranging to meet him at an out of the way pub four blocks from the polizeirevier -- the police station.

Anton Metzger was a relic. At 61, he should be retired from the Vienna Police and enjoying a fine pension. He should also be dead. Few other Cold Warriors had seen the extent of duty Anton had. He had avoided meeting his demise by being smarter and sharper than those opposing him. As a child, he emigrated from the Ukraine with his parents before the Second World War. He followed his lifelong dream of becoming a police officer. He also followed his father into the family business, as a spy for the Soviet Union.

His development as a resource for the Soviet Bloc included stints as a relay, repository and finally as an active agent, always working behind the scenes to keep Vienna and points west unstable. His position as a police investigator, working narcotics and homicide, gave him a perfect cover. He was allowed to travel in all directions investigating crimes.

For Marta, Anton had become the one reliable information exchange conduit with Gregor Smelinski. For Lance, Anton was the guy several sources had pointed to for reliable information about Marta's location.

Before walking into the bar, or kniepe, Lance surveyed the surrounding blocks twice. He couldn't tell what it was, but something had his hackles up. After making sure it was safe, Lance entered the quaint establishment. He was wearing a blond wig, glasses and a cheap suit that was three sizes too large so it hung on him, adding thirty pounds to his frame. The pub was dark inside. It featured wood paneling, low lights hanging from dirty chains and a bar backed by several hundred bottles.

Anton was at the bar. He did not greet Lance as he took a seat two stools over. Lance spoke German with a Russian accent as he ordered a draft. After several minutes, the bartender stepped over to talk to a waitress. Lance broke the ice with Anton by asking about restaurants in the area. He said he had a yearning for Asian fare. Anton suggested a couple of places a few blocks over. He recommended a Thai restaurant famous for its noodles.

During the next 40 minutes, they talked about food, drink, travel and women. They drank a good deal. The bar filled up with people getting off work, and Lance moved to the stool next to Anton to give a middle-age woman his seat. Now just inches apart, Anton spoke into Lance's ear.

"What do you want, you young punk?"

"I am trying to find someone." Lance replied quickly in a whisper.

"Make it quick."

"If I say her name I will have to kill you Anton, or Antonovich."

"Go screw yourself."

"Will do, right after you share the information between your ears. If you will not part with it voluntarily, I may have to remove it by force."

"Threats? You silly boy, don't make threats you are unable to fulfill. Tell whoever sent you here to send someone with some balls and hair on his chest."

Lance enjoyed this spirited conversation and was about to respond when something in the mirror caught his eye. It was another set of eyes, and they were looking right at him. He lowered his head to take a swig of beer. When he lifted his head, the eyes were still looking at him. Lance realized why he had missed the man on his sweep of the external environment. The guy was already inside when Lance walked in. He was sitting with two other men at the table.

Lance had missed him before now because he couldn't see him in the mirror from his original seat. Damn. Not good. He turned to Anton, "Enough. Four sources west of here identified you as the repository of information identifying her whereabouts. I need nothing more than an address and I will leave."

"If I had that information and gave it to you, she would kill you the moment you got within a kilometer. You would not even get close enough to look in her eyes before her people cut you down. You are a fool to ask and I am not nearly fool enough to let a sliver of information like that into my head, let alone out of it." The alcohol and age worked to let information slip from Anton's mouth. It was clear, he like all the others, dreaded Marta's wrath. She had put the fear of death into dangerous men. She was good.

Lance stood up on wobbly legs. He saw the three men tense at his standing. He faked a stumble and put a hand on Anton's shoulder to lean in close. "You are going to tell me what I need to know my old friend. But right now I need you to concentrate. The three men seated at the corner table, are they yours?"

Lance dropped a few bills to the floor and bent to pick them up. Anton took the opportunity to spin on his stool and have a good laugh at Lance's drunken act. He scanned the room and the men at the corner table. Lance stood back up and took his seat next to Anton.

"They are not with me. I thought they were yours. They were here when I arrived."

"Not with me. I missed them when I came in. I was concentrating on the street."

"Your mistake then. You will learn. I have been watching them. They have taken no action. That's why I thought they were with you." Anton was suddenly the elder statesman spy teaching a young rookie.

"Who are they then?"

"They look Czech, maybe Polish. The clothes, the hair, the teeth."

"KGB?" Lance asked.

"Maybe. Is the KGB, or what is left of it, looking for you?"

"No. I'm not on official mission. I'm freelancing."

"You are CIA." Anton scoffed.

"No, I'm KGB, like you." Lance replied.

"Whatever you say, I don't care. I am going to get up and walk out of here now. We will see how our friends respond. Are you ready?" Anton stood up on shaky legs and dropped a few bills on the bar. He slapped Lance on the shoulder and meandered to the door.

Lance spun around on his stool and made eye contact with each man at the table. Their move. Two stood and began to move toward the door. The one who'd been eyeing Lance remained seated, staring at him. Lance had to make a decision fast. He didn't like the looks of the two men following Anton. Something about the guy seated, and what he was looking at...

The blow came from the right.

Lance had only a microsecond to move his head to the left to avoid the full impact. It was a gun, the butt of a gun handle to be precise, and it hit Lance just above his right eye.

His faint to the left and the accompanying blow sent him off the stool. But before he hit the floor, he was spinning and rolling on his left shoulder. The training kicked in and Preacher took over. The blow to his head stung, but his reflexes had helped him avoid severe injury. He was alert on several levels, taking in hundreds of data points and formulating a plan to kill at least two men in the briefest possible time, and take the show outside and kill one more so he could capture the last remaining member of the team and break him to obtain vital information.

When he rolled back to his feet, he saw who had hit him. It was the bartender and the man was in the process of moving the gun along an arc to take aim at Preacher's head. It was clear in that instant the original blow was meant to incapacitate him. If unsuccessful, a bullet or two would finish the job. The bartender made a mistake though by not coming around the bar.

Preacher didn't need to go out of body to see the bartender was trapped behind the bar. He could not shoot him if he ducked down under the bar's overhanging counter on the customer side. Now, this obstacle would only hold for a second or two as the bartender and the man formerly seated at the corner table converged on him. As Preacher dove for cover, he looked back at the man reaching into his jacket for a gun.

Another thing about the suit Lance had chosen for this meeting, because it was so large and ill-fitting, it provided ample room to hide the gun holstered under his left arm. If Preacher had time in the next second and a half, he would have rejoiced at his spur of the moment decision to secure a firearm through nefarious means earlier that day. After setting the meeting with Anton this morning, he ventured into an area of Vienna tourists and most locals avoided. In a crowded and smelly quadrant of the ancient city, he purchased a Graz Buria handgun and 50 bullets. He bought the holster at a used military equipment store.

None of this crossed his mind as he reached into the jacket, gripped the handle of the gun, pulled, aimed and fired at the remaining gentleman from the three-person corner table. The man had his gun drawn and was a step from firing at Preacher. The guy's chest took a direct shot and he crashed into a table of three women. Screaming and chaos ensued. One down. Preacher dove to the right, to the end of the bar where the bartender would have to exit unless he tried to jump over the bar at the front end.

Preacher aimed the gun at the open walkway and kept his peripheral vision up along the bar. Four seconds passed as people jumped under tables and raced out the door. Preacher decided to take action. He rolled closer to the walkway where the bartenders raise a section of counter to walk behind the bar. He reached the gun around the corner at floor level and shot three rounds in an arc. Two missed, one hit. Damn lucky shot. He rolled onto his back to expand his area of vision. A groan from the bartender was followed by four shots fired through the walk-through space.

Preacher scooted on the floor back past where he had been seated, staying under the protective cover of the bar ledge. He got to a crouch, and then sprang to three-quarter height with the Graz Buria in both hands. The bartender's head was visible. He was looking at the spot Preacher had just been. He saw Preacher pop up from the corner of his eye and turned his head. Preacher is still a horrible shot, worse with a handgun. But this was a little over seven feet. The bullet he put through the bartender's eye shattered a bottle of whiskey behind him after coming out of the back of the man's head. Two down.

Preacher turned for the door and burst out onto the sidewalk. By his cranial clock's count, 28 seconds had passed since Anton had walked out with two men following him. Lance assumed the gunshots from inside the bar changed the men's assignment. If Lance were giving the orders, he would have kept one man on Anton and assigned the other to watch the door. With this in mind, Preacher dove and rolled to the left the split second he kicked the door open, pleased it opened outward.

It was good and dark outside and lighting was poor. As expected, several shots came his way as he rolled behind a vehicle parked on the street. The shots came from behind another car parked about 40 feet away. Jammed against the car and the curb, Lance dropped to the asphalt to look for the man shooting at him. The headlights of an approaching automobile silhouetted a pair of feet and legs. He knew it was the guy because he was the only person not running or cowering on the ground after all the shooting. The Graz held 15 total rounds. He had fired five inside. Ten shots left, that should be enough. Preacher just wished the guy wasn't 40 feet away. This would be a crapshoot.

He lay on his side and took aim at the guy's feet. He fired four shots. Two made sparks on the road as they skittered past their target. One hit a tire on the car the shooter stood behind and one struck the guy in the ankle. Damn that had to hurt. Lance rolled fully into the street to get a clear shot as the man crumpled to the ground on his shattered ankle. Another car coming up the street gave Lance all the lighting he needed. From a prone firing position, the 40-feet were no problem to find center mass. He shot three more bullets and was amazed that all three hit the poor fella. Two in the chest, one in the neck. He had to admit, he was getting better. Three down.

The clock in his head ticked past 46 seconds since Anton walked out. Preacher jumped to his feet and ran down the street. He was taking an educated guess on the direction, but it just felt right.

Two muzzle flashes and two shots rang out from an alley 60 feet ahead on the left. Preacher was almost to the alley when one of the guys who'd been at the table came running around the corner. They ran right into each other. Preacher brought his gun down on the guy's left shoulder. The gentlemen, in return, kicked Preacher just below the left knee. The guy was bringing his gun up to shoot so Preacher head-butted him right smack on the bridge of his nose. It was a crushing, literally crushing blow. The guy's gun dropped to the sidewalk as he fell backwards completely knocked out by the blow. His head struck the sidewalk with a sickening dull thud. Fifty-nine seconds gone. Preacher was a little pissed. He needed information. This guy had just capped Anton and was now out cold, maybe dead. He needed to get the hell out of here without gathering the information he came for.

With time ticking away, Preacher decided to grab the guy by his jacket and pull him into the alley. Once there, he dropped him and ran to Anton. As expected, the old spy had been shot twice, but was still alive. A dim light outside a back door entrance to a candy store provided the only light. It looked bad for the old KGB veteran. Lance bent down over him.

"Anton. Comrade can you hear me?"

"Screw your comrade crap." The old curmudgeon had enough in him to be salty.

"I'm sorry you have to go like this. Here in some dingy alley. Killed by a nobody."

"I'm not dead yet." Lance saw the old investigator had his gun in his hand. "I have a few minutes left."

"Tell me how to find her then. It won't matter to you in a little while."

"It was probably her who did this. Probably because you screwed up and came looking for her."

"No, this is somebody else. This was not her work."

Anton smiled and spit up some blood. "I know. If it was, we'd both be dead and our families would be next."

"So tell me. I am actually here to help her."

"She is beyond help. She has descended to the 7th level of hell with no return. Smelinski has seen to that."

And so Anton Metzger died, but not before giving Lance an address that only he knew. After giving Lance the address, he told him to go screw himself again. God rest his soul.

"Wait, say that again. What were his exact words about descending into hell?" Marta sat up and pulled her feet from Lance's hands to put them on the floor. She was ready to move, to explode. "His exact words Lance."

"He said 'she has descended to the 7th level of hell with no return. Smelinski has seen to that.'"

"That's all?"

"Yes. That's it. What has you so upset? I thought the Smelinski disavow of your services was your cover."

"It is. It was."

"Then why are you so angry, aside from the fact that one of your contacts is dead?"

"My god. I can't believe I missed this. I can't believe it took me this long." Marta stalked across the room to the window. "I've been a fool."

"What is it? What do you mean?" Lance followed her, but stayed several feet away to give her space. She was combustible.

"It is Cherzny. He owns Smelinski. It was Smelinski behind Anton's death. It was not about you. It was me he was after."

"How do you know?"

"How did you contact Anton?"

"I called him from a pay phone. He was at his desk and told me to call him back at another number. I called it and dropped a few secrets that very few know and he agreed to meet me."

"Those secrets, were they about me?"

"Yes, but only someone truly connected to you would know them."

"Only people like Seibel and Smelinski, right?" She asked.

"Correct. So when he had me call him at the second number, I dropped only one of the nuggets. It worked."

"Yes it did. Smelinski must have had the entire station house bugged. He heard your coded information, and sent a team in to snatch you and kill Anton."

"He wouldn't kill Anton. Those two have worked together for what, 30 years?"

"He would and did kill him. Why do you think you were hit on the head instead of shot in the back of your head? They were ordered to take you alive, to find out what else you know about me."

"Marta, wait. Take a step back; tell me what this is about. Isn't Cherzny the billionaire? One of the oligarchs running things now?"

Marta turned from the window. "Yes. But he is not one of them. He is the one running it all. He hides behind his elected office and a facade of working-class values, but he pulls the strings everywhere. He has reach into the government at every level."

"And why is he after you?"

"Because I targeted him."

"For what?" Lance asked.

"My mission. For four years now, my mission has been to take down anyone standing in the way of our government reassuming control after the Union falls apart. Take out anyone stealing from the people to line their own pockets. Annihilate the corrupt."

"So all your chaos and anarchy and murder and mayhem, it has all been about flushing out corruption?"

"Yes."

"Damn. You have done an incredible job. I mean really something." Lance stepped over to the window. "So you think Smelinski, the incorruptible Gregor the Terrible, has been corrupted by Cherzny?"

"I thought it, and now I know it. I saw it in his eyes when I brought this to him in Belgrade. He tried half-heartedly to steer me away from Cherzny, but I told him I had already begun the mission."

"How did you start it?"

"I set up several meetings with attaches and operatives doing Cherzny's dirty work around Europe. When I made them an offer they couldn't refuse, they still refused." Marta continued to look out the window.

"That's what you were doing in Budapest yesterday."

"Yes. He was an accountant laundering Cherzny's money through dozens of banks. He too said no. And, he had two men with him sent to kill me. They were most likely Cherzny's men."

"Damn. This complicates things." Lance turned back to her.

"Not for you. You don't have anything to do with this." Her words had a hard edge to them.

"Six months ago I would have agreed with you. But now, I have a stake in this thing."

"No. Don't do that. Don't do this. I won't let you get involved."

"I'm involved."

"No. Don't make me push you away."

"Okay." Lance walked back over and sat on the couch to defuse the situation. "Marta, will you sit for a moment?"

"No, I'll stand. It helps me think." She was already making plans and completing moves in her head. He could see her formulating strategy and planning deadly action. He had to admit, watching her like this turned him on. She was beautiful and deadly and unique. And, at the moment, she was his.

"Then listen to me for just a minute."

"One minute, and then we need to go. I need to go."

"Okay. I love you."

She stopped her mental calculations, her planning and looked at him. His words diverted her. "I love you." She said in return.

"Good, so we have that straight. I'll say it again. I love you. I told you I am a liar, I'm a killer, I'm a real bastard."

"And I still love you." She took a small step toward the couch and caught herself.

"Good. And I love you even though you are a killer, a world-class murderer. Damn that sounds really screwed up doesn't it?" He laughed.

"A little. But it doesn't change how I feel and what I have to do."

"I understand. I just want you to take into consideration my concerns. As I said, if I had learned about you and Cherzny six months ago, I would have shrugged it off. It would have been nothing. But then I saw you, I met you. I don't know where this is going or how it will end, but I can't let you leave here without telling you. You said something earlier about being shot but it not hurting anything like losing me. I feel exactly the same."

She took another half step. "And because I love you, because I know how you make me feel, I can't let you get involved. I can't let you get caught in this and be hurt or maybe killed."

He smiled. "Don't you see, that's exactly how I feel. I can't let you get hurt or killed. How am I supposed to live after that? This thing, whatever it is, has taken over. I'm different. It's weird."

"I know. I know." She breathed out slowly and then took three more steps to join him on the couch. "What do we do?"

"I think you know what we have to do." He leaned into her.

"I do. But I can't ask you,"

"Don't ask. I'm in. Let's kill them both, Cherzny and Smelinski. That's the only solution, eliminate the greatest threats."

Marta put her head on his shoulder. He took her face in his hand and kissed the top of her head.

"And then when it's done, we'll have to kill one more." He added.

"I know.

Lance reached under her chin with a finger and brought her face up to his. "He won't really mind though. Seibel brought you and me together to see which one of us would kill him."

Chapter 18

The southern island of Mindanao has the highest Muslim population of any of the Philippines island chain. This creates a distinctive atmosphere where Islamic separatists established the Autonomous Region in Muslim Mindanao, ARMM.

With the ARMM, Muslims in the Philippines have provided a model for other parts of the world featuring a strong Islamic presence within the borders of an existing nation. With the ARMM, Islamic fundamentalists have established a wild west training grounds of sorts for all kinds of nefarious goings on. Beginning in the 1980's, terrorists from around the world started converging on Mindanao and surrounding islands because of its notorious lack of governance.

The region does have a Sultan running things, sort of. But tribes, gangs and drug syndicates reign supreme. The western region of Mindanao, and the stretch of Sulu Province islands reaching southwest to Malaysia are reachable only by small aircraft and boat. These sparsely populated islands offer thousands of acres of secluded terrain to build and operate terrorist training facilities.

A boat slid into a small dock on the southern tip of the island municipality of Tapul. Four men on board gathered up their duffle bags and hauled their gear up the dock where three men greeted them. For anyone witnessing this arrival, it was obvious that none of the men were locals. They were certainly not from the Moro tribes that populate most of these small islands. No, these men were Middle Eastern and Persian. The hair, bone structure, eyes and dress differed from locals. They were not the first and wouldn't be the last members of the Mujahedeen, who fought the Soviets in Afghanistan, to travel to Tapul.

One of the four arrivals was the soft-spoken man last seen by Western intelligence sources in New York, traveling under the fake name Rashidi. His actual name, given him by his father at birth, is Fahim Anwar al-Ansari. But he hadn't called himself that for over a decade. His job during the last ten years was to be a ghost, a deadly, killing phantom. He had protected his anonymity by staying off the grid. He lived in remote areas of Afghanistan and western Pakistan and only traveled using non-commercial means. He was required to leave this blissful world of obscurity behind a couple of years ago to begin implementing his grand plan -- the grand plan entrusted to him to carry out.

His Pakistan passport listed his name as Asif Khan Masood, a traditional name. Those who know cricket recognize the name as a Pakistani cricketer from the 60's and 70's.

The attractive gentleman greeting Anwar and the others at the end of the dock went by the name Iqbal. Not his name. But his looks let him easily pass as Indian. The two leaders of the small groups hugged in the sweltering tropical humidity, thousands of miles from their first meeting more than a decade earlier on a hillside in northeastern Afghanistan. Minutes after that first meeting, they were firing on a Soviet convoy making its way up the valley below. Anwar watched as Iqbal stepped several yards away and prepared to fire a surface-to-air SAM rocket at an approaching helicopter. The SAMs were gifts of the U.S. and were already beginning to turn the tide of war against the infidel invaders from the north.

Today, the two acquaintances would spend quality time together training others in the construction, placement and detonation of explosives. And later this evening, Iqbal and Anwar would sit in the dark and update each other on their progress toward the collective goal of bringing death and destruction on a massive scale to the West. They would not say the words al Qaeda during their time together, but each carried the same mission in their heart.

"Peace be with you brother," Iqbal whispered into Anwar's ear on the dock.

"And peace be with you my brother," Anwar whispered back. Iqbal thought for the hundredth time about this man, this strange, quiet and brilliant man. His surprisingly light brown, almost honey-colored eyes, made him stand out. He attracted others to him, even though he worked so very diligently to remain anonymous, just one of the Mujahedeen.

But Iqbal, and hundreds of fighters who stood and bled and died beside the man they knew as Mohamed, Anwar's chosen cover name, learned quickly that he was indeed different. His skills increased rapidly as he learned from another quiet freedom fighter about the intricacies of bomb making. Anwar was trained to assemble seemingly random and disparate items into devices that brought death, devastation and confusion to the invading Soviet enemy. After his mentor from Iraq was killed when one of his explosive devices detonated while he was holding it, Anwar became the senior bomb expert for the region. He eventually became the preeminent bomb builder in the Mujahedeen and one of the Soviet Red Army's most wanted terrorist enemies.

He was ahead of his time in Afghanistan. Even ahead of other bombers fighting the good fight, and killing the innocent along with infidel targets throughout the Middle East. Soon, bombers in training traveled to learn from Anwar at his village hideout. It was those skills he brought to share with others on this small island in the Philippines. From his lessons, others would take deadly skills back to Syria and Lebanon and Bali and Hamburg and then the United States.

In just two weeks on the small island of Tapul, Anwar expected to train a small but dedicated group of bombers who would rain down death on infidels. This all sounded mighty and righteous, and was evidence of his commitment to the cause of Jihad throughout the world. It was also complete bullshit.

Anwar did like the idea of people who deserved death meeting their end through violent means. But his true mission in the Philippines was not simply to train others. He was building a wall of distraction he had planned for years. Exploding bombs in Tel-Aviv and Beirut and Paris and Barcelona and Moscow and Bali would conceal his true intentions. It was all debris on the battlefield, a smokescreen he was sending up to mask his true intentions.

He looked around at the men he had assembled. When he gazed upon others with this look, it commanded silence and respect. Those who knew him knew that Anwar was a man of few words. His lectures were met with undivided attention.

"Brothers, we have a short time here together to perfect our skills and bring justice to the world. What you learn over the next few days will allow you to take our war to the heart of the infidels of the West. We can strike a blow for Allah. Give me your absolute trust and I will give you mine. Allahu Akbar."

This was met by a chorus of "Allahu Akbars." After a meal and sleep, the men gathered the following morning. Mass murder class was in session. Anwar was the teacher. And he was the committed and steady hand of God.

Chapter 19

The steam, smells and crush of nine million people in Manila can overwhelm. These merged elements also provide cover and camouflage for those seeking anonymity amid chaos.

Lance had only been enveloped by Manila's smothering culture for 11 hours, but he was already at home. It was liberating to be exposed in every way, yet hidden in plain sight. All around him, people hustled and bustled and belched and spit and sang. They also talked.

He needed people to talk, to tell him what he needed to know, to help him track a ghost whose sparse trail left tracks that pointed to the Philippines. At least, that is how Seibel read the tracks. And Seibel had a list of four potential contacts he wanted Lance to hunt down to ferret out any tidbits of information about Anwar.

The route Lance had taken to where he now stood in a doorway of a small, leaning house, two streets over from Manila's main drag, was not an itinerary Seibel would have prepared. In fact, Seibel would likely not be aware of the resources Lance had employed to reach this island nation. No, Lance's route over the previous 69 hours would not be the choice of any experienced traveler.

He had flown, ridden trains, buses and a boat. He'd crossed the Asian continent through Russia and Siberia, and stopped over in Japan before arriving in the Philippines this morning. He was tuckered, but no more than normal these days. Sleep consisted of stolen hours on seats, in chairs and on the ground. He'd made his way to the Philippines under the guise of a Russian college senior from Obninsk, the home of the world's first nuclear reactor power plant. To complete the effect, he carried a worn backpack over his shoulder.

He leaned against a wall in the doorway, looking in the direction of a martial arts studio 150 meters down and across the street. Lance was headed there a couple of minutes ago, but he stopped when he recognized someone he knew enter the small building. This particular location was not one of the four Seibel had given him weeks ago during preparations for his "off the grid" mission. So the fact that Mikel Fuchs was now inside the martial arts studio meant one of three things.

Either Siebel was once again babysitting Lance, or the great leader had become concerned by Lance's disappearance and lack of contact over the last nine days and sent in the cavalry. But most likely, Seibel was up to his usual trick of knowing everything and playing his own little chess game. Lance smiled to himself. Damn.

He glanced at the Russian-made Poljot watch on his left wrist and realized he would be spending his birthday in the Philippines this year. Twenty-five wouldn't be a whole lot different than 24, except for the fact that he was in love, way too much in love really.

Keeping his eyes on the front entrance to the studio, Lance's mind wandered. It had been doing a lot of that the past few days. During most of his journey to Manila, he had either closed his eyes and drifted or conversed with others traveling with him.

But most of his time was spent thinking of Marta. He could see her face, brilliant smile, falling hair, proud shoulders, naked body and healing scars. This was bad. He had never been like this and never expected to find himself in this position. While rattling along a stretch of railway in Siberia, he recalled a teacher back in high school asking her students to write down where they expected to be in five years and then put the written assignment in a safe place to review after those five years passed.

Lance finished the assignment first. He wrote one word and folded the paper into thirds like a letter ready to be stuffed in an envelope and mailed. The teacher walked around the room and came to Lance. Like she did often, the teacher squatted down beside him and put her elbow on his desk. She did this to get at her students' level instead of looking down on them.

"Lance, done already?" she asked with inquisitive eyes.

"Done." A seventeen year-old version of Preacher answered with innocence aplenty in his eyes.

"Happy with what you wrote?" she persisted.

"Enough, I suppose."

"Would you like to share?"

"Sure." He handed her the folded piece of paper.

She read the one word he had written, refolded the paper and placed it back on his desk. "You think?"

"Didn't really plan on making it this far. Five years is forever."

He opened his eyes and looked out at a bleak landscape passing by the window of the train and thought back to where he'd actually been five years after writing the word "dead" on that sheet of paper back in Oklahoma at age 17. He was at Harvey Point. Not dead, yet.

Now, if he was given that same five-year assignment, he'd have to give it some thought. In five years he'd be almost 30. Where would he be? Who would he be? Who would she be in his life? Would she be in his life? Damn, there she was again.

None of these thoughts had crossed his mind in the previous 25 years. When he thought of the future, it was an exercise in envisioning a succession of characters and scenarios created to give him a variety of challenges. The future, like the past and present, was a game for Lance.

That wasn't true anymore.

Lance closed his eyes on that train and went back to Vienna, back to her. After they made their decision to find a way to make this screwy relationship work, Lance and Marta spent the next 36 hours making plans, making love and putting things in motion. She introduced him to people he would have never met and helped him create several new covers. A forger in a dreary Soviet-style apartment building in Bratislava, Romania, just across the border from Vienna, produced three new passports that were quite simply works of art. They were better than the real thing.

Marta provided Lance with his transportation itinerary. Again, without her, he would have never discovered the route and unsavory characters both utilizing and providing the transportation.

She was a treasure trove of illicit behavior. She was so full of useful information that he stepped back at one point and just laughed. She reached out to him and put her hand flat against his stomach and stepped into him while he continued to laugh. The moment, shared in a shabby hallway outside a freight forwarding office, was another of those intimate moments they had together during those four days. Their last night together in her townhome was passionate, but tinged with sadness. They weren't like another young couple that had to pry themselves apart for a day or a week. When Lance left the following morning, each knew they might not see each other for months. Or maybe ever.

They lay next to each other. They shared thoughts, fears and even a few hopes in the midst of an uncertain and unknowable future. With her back pressed against his front and her fingers laced between his, she held the back of his hand to her lips and whispered to him in Russian, "did I hear you say that you think you love me?"

"Something like that." He whispered back in Russian.

"Tomorrow will be difficult."

"Just the goodbye will be tough. The rest will merely be torture." He smiled into the back of her head.

"That's what I wanted to tell you earlier." She said.

"Earlier?"

"Yes. Before you looked at me with your eyes and forced me into this bed."

"I think I recall a slightly different version, but nonetheless, I'm sorry if I forced you into doing something you didn't want to by looking at you that way."

"Please. Find another way to look at me or we'll never get out of the bedroom, wherever we are." She moved his hand to her cheek.

He rolled her over to him. "I'm afraid you'll just have to get used to me looking at you like this. Can't help it. I'm afflicted." He stole her line. "And you'll have to find a way to control yourself, and not pull me into the nearest bed every time I lay my eyes upon you."

"That will be impossible, I'm afraid." She kissed him and they could have easily moved from the kiss to making love again. But Lance stopped and put a finger to her lips.

"You wanted to tell me something earlier?" He asked her in English.

She kissed his finger and then shook her head. "I did."

"Well?"

"About tomorrow," she hesitated, "about tomorrow morning."

"Yes?"

"I don't want to say goodbye. I don't want to kiss you and then turn away and cry." She rolled onto her back and looked at the ceiling. "I can't do that." She fell back into Russian so the words came out, "YA ne mogu etogo sdelat."

"Then what do we do?" Lance opened his eyes on the train a day and a half after asking her that question. "Chto my delaem?" He asked the question aloud in Russian – "what do we do?" No one around him heard. The rattle of the train was all anyone could hear. He knew what she had meant. He knew what she needed. He had held her close as they slept. He got up before sunrise and left.

She stayed in bed, not sleeping of course. But she simply couldn't look into his eyes and say goodbye. He fought every urge and avoided kissing her. He didn't linger beside her. He found the strength to pull away and get back to his mission. He couldn't see the assignment in the same light he had back at Harvey Point. Spending time with her, sifting through the debris Seibel had strewn along the path, he had filtered out the unnecessary. The first two culprits presented by Seibel were minor players. They were wannabes. They have killed and will kill others, but they simply weren't worth the effort Seibel was putting forth. The third bomber, Anwar, or whatever he called himself. He was the target.

Lance pulled himself back into his head in Manila. He looked at his watch even though he didn't need to. He knew Fuchs had been inside the martial arts studio for 11 minutes. Before stepping out into the street, Lance scanned both ends of the boulevard. He looked up at windows, into parked and passing cars. He found no patterns and even better, no obvious broken patterns. It was nearing dusk. The light in the clouded sky was fading; the humidity beyond oppressive. He stepped out and walked across the street toward the studio.

This location was not on the list of four contacts in Manila Seibel had given Lance to visit. Fuchs being here at the very time Lance showed up was either serious coincidence or no coincidence at all. With Seibel in any way associated with the equation, it was likely the latter.

He stepped into the establishment and into a small reception area. No one was there to greet him. After absorbing the sounds and smells, he stepped forward into the training room. Once inside, he saw five people. Four were kneeling, one stood. The gentleman standing was the man Lance came to see. He had met him three years earlier at Harvey Point. Lance only heard the instructor's name once. It was Bakunawa. During three weeks of martial arts training, with emphasis on Filipino eskrima and Chinese kuntao, Lance had learned dozens of methods to subdue and kill others. The instructor had been very quiet in his methods, choosing to show rather than tell. Lance appreciated that.

Standing in the doorway, Lance could see Bakunawa was showing his students the proper defense method for a knife thrust, how to seize the weapon and return the knife to its owner blade first. Lance could also see that Fuchs was one of the students kneeling in front of the instructor. When their eyes met, there was no recognition, no dilation or constriction of pupils, nothing. Another student turned to Lance and the instructor saw the distraction and looked toward to him.

Bakunawa, which means dragon or sea serpent, simply motioned to a few hanging uniforms on the wall and turned back to his pupils. Lance walked over and grabbed the first white uniform with an accompanying white belt and walked through a curtain to a locker room. He decided to put his clothes into the tattered backpack and brought it with him back to the training room. He tossed the pack under a bench and walked over to kneel with the others.

He was plum worn out from nearly three days of travel and a full day of wandering the teeming streets of Manila, the world's most jam-packed city. But none of that weighed on him as he fell upon his knees. He found freedom, exhilaration and structure in his endless hours of martial arts training at Harvey Point, in Brazil, in Japan and other locales. To tell the truth, and he didn't often, martial arts training was the closest thing to religion he had found. Probably due to the "centering" that takes place during preparation.

He centered himself and let Bakunawa's lesson wash over him. He didn't need to look at the other students to know they were all advanced. He could sense it. There were no distracted eyes. No scratching or throat-clearing. This late evening class was meant for experts. Coincidence? Who knows? Lance didn't care at the moment. He cleared his mind and focused on the lesson.

After 20 minutes of simple demonstrations of five moves, the instructor invited each student to stand and defend themselves from a knife attack. Each did fine. Fuchs was the best. Lance was okay, nothing special. Bakunawa paired them up. The instructor chose to work with Lance. There was the slightest hint of a grin on his lips as they bowed before sparring. Lance had gotten the best of the master on the last day of his training at the Point.

Eskrima is a Filipino martial arts method that features sticks or blades. The specialty brings together hand-to-hand with joint destruction techniques. It is a brutal form of combat that can be taught to the masses in a short time, giving farmers and fishermen defensive skills to fight an invasion. Kuntao is a southern Chinese school of martial arts that combines strikes, throws and hand-to-hand combat.

Lance stood and bowed to the instructor, then assumed a defensive position. Bakunawa raised a thin rattan stick in his right hand and began stepping left to circle Lance. The instructor adjusted his stance and balance, and lowered his center of gravity another half inch. Lance fought off the urge to go out of body to look down on the two of them. The instructor was lightning fast with a thrusting, chopping motion that sliced the air on its way toward Lance's neck. He saw three options and chose the second. He rose up from a crouch while raising his left hand to intercept the attack and block it. Bakunawa knew Lance's options much better than the student. While his right hand was being blocked away from Lance's neck, he continued his forward momentum and spun his left elbow around to meet Lance in the chest, neck or chin. It was an aggressive move.

Lance saw the continuation of his old instructor's motion and thought it out of character. It was too early for him to turn his head away from Lance. Options again. Absorb the elbow blow. Continue to move up and to the left away from the elbow. Third was best. Apply maximum pressure to his right foot and explode forward with a palm blow into center mass while the master's head was turned away.

The action took six tenths of a second. When his palm met Bakunawa's back, it knocked the master out of centrifugal alignment, causing him to fall to the left as his body and gravity worked to complete the spin he had started. Instead of watching the fall and admire his initial moves, Lance dropped a knee onto the falling man's back which allowed him to reach down with both hands and grasp the bald man's head and chin to wrench the neck, snapping vertebrae, nerves and ligaments. This final action lasted another eight tenths of a second, if Lance had completed the move, of course. He didn't break the neck. Instead he stood up and stepped back to again take his knees while the instructor got to his feet.

The other two pairs had barely begun their sparring and stopped to watch as Bakunawa stood and then took his knees about four feet in front of Lance. The look on his face had not changed since Lance had walked in.

"You have continued your training Preacher."

"Yes master. I am pleased you remember my name." Lance kept all emotion out of his voice.

"Of course I do. It was not so long ago that I taught you and you taught me."

"What could I possibly teach you?" Lance was humble.

The instructor finally broke the slightest smile. "You taught me what I'm sure you have taught others. Always be ready to die. Always be prepared to take a life."

"I can't teach you about life and death. You have it backwards." Lance bowed.

"Ah, but you can. You teach through your actions. There is no hesitation in you. You live and die each moment. You just showed me again, here. You're reaction was utterly unique, unexpected and deadly. One has to be at peace when they are with you, because at any moment you may explode."

Their conversation was quiet, but the others could overhear some of Bakunawa's words. Lance kept his eyes on the instructor. He knew what was next.

Bakunawa stood and turned to the others. "I know what you are thinking. You wonder how a young stranger can walk in and best me in no time at all. How can this happen?" He took two paces toward the others and turned back to Lance. "Your next question is not for me. It is for him. Ask." He gestured to Lance.

The first to speak was a short, stout man, thick neck and barrel chest in a 5-foot 2-inch frame. "Master Bakunawa, may I work with this stranger?"

The instructor kept his eyes on Lance. "Your question is for him, not me."

The stout man adjusted his posture to address Lance. "May I spar with you next?"

Lance had not broken eye contact with Bakunawa. "This is your school master. I would not assume to exercise with others without your permission."

Bakunawa laughed. "You have my permission." He moved to the side. Fuchs kneeled down a few feet from the instructor to watch. His demeanor calm, almost bored.

The stout man, who appeared more Asian than island, moved to face Lance. After rising and bowing. The two men adjusted their stances to defensive postures. The man held a stick in his right hand as Bakunawa had a few moments earlier. He took less than a second to initiate his first move. It was a fast, compact action to match the compact man. But the thing is, he waited almost a second.

Lance had his first move mapped out before this new sparring partner walked over. With reflexes far superior to most humans, Lance once again exploded at his opponent, delivering an elbow. Instead of spinning, he bulled forward before his opponent could execute his knife thrust. With extreme force, Preacher planted his elbow in the man's upper chest near his left clavicle. Everyone in the room heard the muffled snap.

Lance stepped behind the man as he recovered from the blow. The guy spun to launch an attack with his still working right arm. Lance was ready for this move. In fact, he had just seen it in his mind from 15 feet in the air looking down on the two men. Lance didn't know this gentleman and didn't want him to incur excessive hospital bills, so he completed his planned move – a dropping, spinning kick that swept the guy's feet out from under him and sent him flailing onto his back. Lance was on him in the next half second in a position to grip his throat, rip away cartilage and crush the trachea. This short battle was over.

Lance kneeled to allow the wounded man to get to his feet and move to the side. The stout man had too much pride to leave for the hospital now. There wasn't much they could do for him but set the bone and put his arm in a sling.

In succession, Lance accepted challenges from the others. He took a pretty serious kick to the side from the next and then a fist to his still bruised right temple from the third gentleman. But they both suffered more severe and, if the battle were real, mortal wounds. Finally it came time to face off with Fuchs.

Lance had intentionally kept the other sparring sessions short because he knew Fuchs would likely drag out their two-step. After all, Fuchs knew Lance, had sparred with him numerous times at Harvey Point, whipping him on several occasions. Fuchs had stayed on his knees, relaxed and watching the proceedings as Lance took out the instructor and the other three students. He showed no emotion as he stood and walked to the center of the room and dropped to his knees about 10 feet in front of Lance.

The two of them looked at each other for over a minute. No rush, no need to hurry into this. In their previous meetings, Fuchs had always been able to counter pretty much every move Lance attempted. Lance had speed on his side, but Fuchs was always in position and prepared. It forced Lance to be extra creative in his attacks, which in turn, left his defenses open, vulnerable.

Lance had gone out of body one time last year to watch the fighting below and thought he had figured it out. It was Fuchs' feet. They moved in tiny fractions of inches. Lance watched how Fuchs' feet glided across the floor. His feet were often hidden inside boots so one couldn't see the miniscule movements as his toes and heels adjusted to his center of gravity. It was poetry of sorts, and Lance saw the beauty in the motion.

It was just one more thing Lance had come to respect about his quiet compatriot. He couldn't ever get much out of Fuchs. Hell, he still didn't know where the guy was from. He was either German and screwed up, or American and too damn smart. Lance didn't really care, as long as Fuchs was on his side when bullets started flying. He nearly smiled thinking about how things had lined up to bring them both to this room approximately 8,500 miles from their adopted home in the marshlands of North Carolina. But he didn't smile. It would have been wasted on Fuchs anyway.

They stood, bowed and assumed their positions about eight feet apart. They didn't move for another half minute. The stout gent with a broken collarbone winced and moved his shoulder. He wanted them to get the show on the road so he could get on his way to the hospital. Lance took a step to the left and then exploded at Fuchs with a flying kick. It was just for show. The older man stepped back and to the right to avoid the blow. But he was not quick enough for the next move. Lance threw a spinning back fist before his feet even touched the floor. The blow caught Fuchs smack dab in the gut. He brought up his left arm to block Lance's next blow. Problem was, it wasn't a blow. It was a roll that gathered Fuchs' left leg and flung him to the ground.

Fuchs brought around an elbow that caught Lance in the center of this back. It stung like hell, but Lance had a lock on Fuchs' ankle that allowed him to wrench it mercilessly if he saw fit. But he didn't want an injured senior operative backing him up. Lance gave it a little twist and then rolled to the side and back to his feet. Fuchs was right after him, throwing a left lead punch and then elbow that hit Lance in the left shoulder as he ducked down and locked his right arm behind Fuchs' left leg. He raised his mentor up and brought his hand up to Fuchs' throat to throw him violently to the floor. The move should have frozen him for a moment, but Fuchs was already rolling onto his side and swinging his right elbow to connect with Lance's right knee. It was a debatable tactic and that told Lance it was not the actual move.

Preacher jumped to his right, which forced Fuchs to change the direction of his swinging elbow as he rose off the floor. From this new vantage point, Preacher could see what he needed – Fuchs' feet. They were up on the balls with toes splayed out. He was preparing to explode off the floor. Preacher didn't need to go out of body. He retraced the series of movements that brought them to this point to see the pattern. He knew what was coming and watched Fuchs' toes for the cue.

It came, and Preacher knew right away he had misjudged. Fuchs rose off the floor like an alligator shooting up out of the water to snatch a bird or zebra. Lance stepped back and bent into it, but the force exerted by Fuchs was too much. Preacher was bowled over and in the next moment he was on the floor with Fuchs on top of him. His only chance now was Einstein's theory. He needed Fuchs' body to stay in motion, so he continued the roll created by Fuchs crashing into him. Fuchs felt it and tried to stop, but Einstein won and Fuchs couldn't stop the momentum from propelling him into another roll with Preacher gripping his uniform.

With Fuchs again on his back, Preacher made three moves before the older operative could react. He put a knee in Fuchs' groin, a forearm to his neck and delivered a short, powerful and painful punch with his right palm to Fuchs' left ribcage. The blow created the half-second of hesitation Preacher needed to complete the kill. He stood, stomped Fuchs' left knee, kicked the exposed neckline and swung a right elbow in a trajectory to crush all cartilage in Fuchs' nose, rendering him incapacitated for at least six minutes.

These last moves were not actually performed. He acted them out, pulling up on each. As he stood up and reached a hand down to pull Fuchs from the floor, the other men watching huffed with disapproval. They felt cheated. Each had been hurt by Preacher's ferociousness, and were not pleased that he did not deliver full blows to this other stranger.

Lance didn't need to see their faces to know they were pissed. One of the men got to his feet and took a step toward Lance before Bakunawa spoke up. "Very good, students, I believe each of you have demonstrated excellent skills. You have honored me and my school today with your work and dedication." Lance and Fuchs kneeled at the periphery. "I want to thank our young student here for demonstrating excellent technique. He is very skilled, and has improved immensely." Bakunawa bowed to Lance and then joined them all in kneeling.

The gent who had stood to protest returned to his knees. The group observed silence for several minutes with no eye contact. Lance used the opportunity to finish piecing together the lyrics to a punk rock classic from The Clash. The song had been playing in his head since he walked into the studio.

Chapter 20

"He figured it was just time." Fuchs spoke between spooning mouthfuls of steaming miso soup into his mouth. They had walked several blocks to a café and were enjoying the soup before their noodles came.

"So was the studio your idea or his?" Lance finished slurping his soup.

"Mine. I knew you'd avoid your assigned contacts for awhile." Fuchs answered.

"So how many days had you been going there to wait for me?"

"Four. It was like a vacation, spending all that time training," Fuchs smiled at Lance for the next part. "For all the good it did me. You son of a bitch, you figured out my moves before I started them."

"Only some of them." Lance had no intention of telling him the secret was in his feet. "I got lucky and you know it."

"No, you just keep every little thing chronicled in that computer brain of yours and pull it out when you need it. That, and you still want to kill everyone." Fuchs pushed the empty soup bowl to the side.

"Not everyone." Lance picked up his bowl to get the last drops.

Fuchs leaned back. "Should I ask where you've been the past 10 days?"

"You can ask, but I don't think you'll get an answer."

"There are a number of theories, you can imagine." The smile was back on Fuchs' face.

"I can imagine. I'm sure he's a little ticked. But he sent me out with a fairly loose timeline."

Fuchs leaned on his elbows to get close. "He can't help himself when it comes to you. You know that. He doesn't appreciate being in the dark."

"Can you share any of these theories of where I've been and what I've been doing?" Lance leaned back now.

"After you got off the plane in Antwerp?" Fuchs asked.

"After that." No surprise they tracked him that far.

"There is a whole continent for you to cover. But a suicide in Paris the next evening caught his attention."

"Suicide?" Lance's eyebrows rose.

"Yes, a long-term KGB player. Not an active player in bomb-making, to our knowledge."

"Anything else?"

"A 30-year KGB mole policeman in Vienna shot dead in an alley a couple of days later really raised some eyebrows."

"Vienna? That's one place I still need to visit. Old Europe with significant Eastern European influence. Such history there." Lance had leaned close so they could speak just above a whisper.

"He's definitely afraid someone is off mission."

"But here I am, a couple of days late. No problem, right?" Lance met Fuchs' smile with his own.

"Its not my job to follow you or babysit, as you all call it," Fuchs leaned in closer. "I'm not here because I want to be. You understand that, right?" All traces of German gone from his voice, Fuchs seemed a little pissed off.

"You don't need to be here." Lance replied.

"Too late for that. I'm to work with you. We are to follow through with your original mission. Maybe I can help shorten the cycle."

Lance hadn't worked with Fuchs on an extended mission. They had only participated in sweeps in Jeddah, Baghdad and Oman. Working together to gather intelligence, work it into strategy, and initiate tactics would be new. Lance knew there was more to Fuchs, but he still couldn't get past the physical aspects the man embodied. Fuchs was like a lion moving through a jungle catching and killing everything he wanted or needed.

"Why did you let me win back there?" Lance tried a change of subject, to lighten the mood.

"I didn't." Fuchs replied.

"You did."

"When?"

"During the roll, after you came off the floor. You tensed but didn't move. You could have done about 12 different moves, but did none." Lance added.

"Nope. You were too fast this time. I gave nothing away." Fuchs took a drink of water and leaned on his elbows. "I don't want to delve into your personal life and certainly not your labyrinth of a mind, but you are different from the last time we were together at the Point."

Lance furrowed his brows appropriately. "From a month ago? How so?"

"Your economy of movements. You are lacking the flourish with which you usually act." Fuchs smiled.

"Flourish?"

"You know what I mean."

"Not sure I do. Enlighten me please." Lance leaned in on his elbows.

Fuchs smiled for a moment and glanced around the room. It was obvious he knew every detail, every person, every action taking place. Just as Lance did. "The closest way I can describe it is that you are like a cat with a mouse trapped under your paw. You play with people, like a cat plays with its food before killing it."

Lance snickered at that.

"You laugh, but you know. I've seen you in action enough. You're some kind of freak of nature living among us, but not one of us."

"Damn. I've known you for three years, and this is more than you've said to me in all that time."

"You can diffuse it and turn it into whatever you will. I knew from the first time we trained at the Point you were not normal. He thinks he picked you, he found you. He's got it backwards. You found him. You would have found him eventually."

"Geez. You're going a little deep." It was Lance's turn to smile.

"I'm just trying to make my point." Fuchs nodded.

"And that is?"

"You are simply not the same person. I watched you in that studio. Where you used to push and prod and evaluate your options, you simply stripped your motions to a bare minimum and destroyed anything in front of you, me included. It was really marvelous to watch."

"I was just tired and didn't want to waste energy before I got to you."

"No. You never miss an opportunity to put on a show, never. You are different. I can see it right now."

"Okay, so people appear different. Especially someone who's traveled non-stop for days. You are seeing things that aren't there."

Fuchs snickered this time. "As I said, it is not for me to delve into your personal life. I just know he is going to have a few questions when he sees you."

"Okay Mikey," Lance turned his head to look out into the night. "I'm guessing you have some new information for us to act upon."

"Just a few pieces. We need to jump on down to Mindanao."

"That was going to be my fourth stop."

"Let's skip a couple and see if we can't find this son of a bitch."

As if on cue, a single beep emanated from Fuchs' bag lying on the floor. He reached down and pulled out a pager and looked at the readout. "Let's go."

"New orders?" Lance was grabbing his things and putting money on the table to pay for the meal.

Fuchs stood and picked up the bag and put the strap over his shoulder. "No. Just a go ahead."

Chapter 21

Turns out, Geoffrey Seibel had about 70 men under various forms of detailed and satellite surveillance at any one time. One of these men just happened to be on the tiny island of Tapul. He had arrived on the boat with Anwar.

The man, who was noticeably bald, was somewhat easy for cameras to spot from 150 miles above in low earth orbit. He had traveled from Bahrain to Pakistan to Brunei under visual surveillance by agents, but contact was lost there. Seibel put the satellites to work and a small boat traveling from the large island up the chain of small islands reaching down from the Philippines caught one analyst's eye. Further satellite images showed the boat hugging coastlines and docking on Tapul, a tiny municipality island.

Seibel liked the looks of it. Detailed imagery of the island pointed out a few interesting looking compounds. Near one facility on the southeast end of the small island, there were several craters. These craters featured the telltale signs of explosions, with debris in defined hub and spoke patterns; like maybe bombs had been detonated. It was the kind of needle in a haystack break that comes every few decades. Ensuing satellite imaging showed activity at the compound. People were there, including a bald man.

And wouldn't you know it, Geoffrey Seibel had his lead field infiltration operative just a few hundred miles away. The coded page Fuchs received in the restaurant ordered him to call a secure line, which would then be transferred several times and connected with Seibel. Papa was surprised to learn his senior operative just happened to have the junior member of the team standing beside him.

"Put him on." Seibel was short with Fuchs. No patience right now. Fuchs handed the phone to Lance. They were using a payphone in a laundromat.

"Yello'" Lance smirked to Fuchs as he spoke.

"Was she in Belgrade or Prague?"

The smirk slipped from Lance's face. "Who would that be?"

"She has her hideout somewhere in eastern Europe. She's been able to keep it secret from me and my minions. But I'm willing to bet my little hound dog was able to track her down." Seibel seemed downright jovial.

"Track who boss?" There was a tiny trace of venom in Lance's voice.

"Our mutual friend, of course."

"What do you need from us?" Lance wasn't biting.

Seibel hesitated. "Ah yes. Business. You'll have to fill me in later on your visit. Please tell Foxy to expect a message in the next eight minutes. Get to the airport now. You're flying." Seibel hung up.

Lance hung up the phone and turned away from the booth. "He seemed a little tweaked with me for some reason. Don't know why. I made it here, just a little late."

"I don't think he liked being out of contact with you. You were not at any of your designated locations and had not checked with a single contact provided." Fuchs added, "Are we off to the airport?"

"Yep. You'll be getting another page in a few minutes with instructions. Do you like having that thing on you all the time?" Lance pointed to the pager clipped to Fuchs' belt.

"Not really. Keeps him too close. What was he asking you about? "

"Nothing really. Just chatting."

"Seemed like he was grilling you pretty good about her." Fuchs insisted.

Lance stopped and looked at him. "Just like I said to him, who is this 'her'?"

"Where was she? Prague or Munich?" Fuchs smiled.

"Who?"

"How long are you going to keep this up?"

"You guys keep talking in this code and I'll catch up some time. Right now you have lost me." He gave nothing away. A consummate liar.

"Like I said, your personal life is your own. But there are lines we can't cross without jeopardizing everyone else. She is one of those lines."

Lance looked off into the distance and the hustling of passersby. He wiped sweat from his brow. The heat and humidity of the Philippines were oppressive, even at night. "Mikel, all I know how to do is cross lines that get me in trouble. You brought me on board to cross as many lines as possible. And you all put your lives in jeopardy the day you roped me in back in Dallas."

"You need to think about this. Be honest with yourself." Fuchs responded, leaving the Dallas thing alone.

"Shit. Honesty? When did you start getting all touchy feely? You've been lecturing me for hours now."

They continued walking down the street to a major thoroughfare to catch a cab. Just before they hailed one, Fuchs answered his question. "I don't mean to lecture you. Its just that I can see a razor's edge here, a line that you are walking." The cab pulled to the curb, but Fuchs stepped in front of Lance. "You are playing with fire and there is no doubt you're going to get burned."

Lance didn't miss a beat, "No doubt."

Four hours later, Lance, Fuchs and a pilot named Horatio touched down at Zamboanga International Airport at the southwestern tip of Mindanao Island. They had found a pilot willing to fly them late at night by asking the right questions and offering cash. Forty-eight minutes after landing, they boarded a boat Seibel had arranged for them. His contact had stocked the speedboat with maps of the Philippines southwest island chain, food, water, assorted guns and grenades. The boat also had a satellite-linked radio, for any changes in plans.

Fuchs took the wheel and Lance immediately passed out, after memorizing a detailed map of Tapul. He could dream about the island from 10,000 feet and swoop in for a closer view when he reached REM sleep. The trip would take about three and a half hours.

Two hours later, Fuchs woke Lance. It was still dark at 4 a.m. The engine and the pounding of steady waves had put Lance into another world and he didn't wake easily.

"Time to rise," Fuchs shoved him a little harder than necessary. "We are about an hour out. Papa wants us to check in at 4:15."

Lance rolled to a sitting position to orient himself. He'd never been all that great on boats and was surprised how well he'd slept. Fuchs pointed to a built-in cooler where he'd find a Coke. He took a few swigs and stepped up beside Fuchs at the wheel. Mist splashed up every few seconds. It helped him wake up.

"Anything new?" They had to yell to be heard over the roaring engine.

"No. We'll see in a few minutes when we check in."

"So let's recap." Lance went through the details as Seibel had relayed them to Fuchs at the tiny Zamboanga airport. High-res satellite images pointed to at least a dozen individuals at the camp. Best guess put at least one known terrorist there. Bomb craters near the compound indicated explosives training. And best of all, Anwar was a known associate of the Omani terrorist who'd led them here.

"You think we'll actually get that lucky? A ghost we know next to nothing about might just be there, on this tiny speck on the this big ol' round sphere?" Lance turned away from the steady burst of mist from the front of the boat and leaned against the dashboard next to Fuchs.

"We've gotten lucky before."

"This lucky?"

"No. This is one in a million." Fuchs wiped his face with a rag he had found on the boat.

"So data like this is likely not the result of luck. My guess is Papa is more than a little sure about this."

"More than likely. Yes."

"Still just you and me, right?" Lance's question was more of a statement.

"Yes. Two-man op. At sun-up."

"Eyes left open?"

"None." Fuchs replied. They were here to kill not capture.

Fuchs powered the engine down then killed it. They opened a channel on the radio and called in.

"Morning gentlemen," Seibel was chipper, for late afternoon. Twelve time zones separated them.

"Good evening," Lance replied in Russian.

"Gentlemen, this is potentially an open line so let's be brief. There are no alterations to report. Last round of images provided no additional information. Number is unchanged. Goal is unchanged."

"Number in our party the same?" Fuchs asked.

"No change. Only you are dining."

"No take out?" Lance this time.

"No." Seibel wanted this short.

"Confirmed." Fuchs was ready to sign off.

"Was it Milan?" Seibel apparently couldn't resist.

"Signing off. Sleep well." Lance cut the transmission.

"Persistent isn't he?" Fuchs smiled as he started the engine.

Lance looked to the east. The faintest glow in the sky gave the first hint of daybreak about an hour away.

Chapter 22

Sunday, August 19, 1991 — Island of Tapul, Philippines
The first bullet hit him just to the left of his right shoulder socket -- the glenohumeral joint. It passed through without breaking any bone. The next one was lower and definitely broke bone as it struck a rib. Felt like the seventh rib, costae verae numeral VII, from his study of the human anatomy as a nine-year-old. Didn't feel like it punctured the lung or any other organ in the thoracic cavity. He owed Seibel an ass-kicking, if he ever saw him again.

The compound had proven not to be very secure as the two of them converged from 45-degree angles. Problem was, the estimate of 12 targets in the facility was about 100 percent low.

Lance silently took out the lone guard on the beach with his knife. There were five buildings in the camp. He and Fuchs identified the two likely to have the most terrorists sleeping inside. They moved in on the two buildings, nodded to each other and threw two grenades through windows. This was not silent kill strategy. The explosions blew the morning wide open, and were followed by screams from inside and then as a few men exited doors only to be mowed down by automatic rifle fire. Lance moved on to the next building and tossed a grenade through an open window. The explosion was furious. The roof on the small outbuilding blew off at the corners.

The bullets started flying as Fuchs moved up on his next building. It seemed the fourth and fifth buildings had at least a half dozen men, based on the number of muzzle flashes. Lance fired back from his vantage point behind a tree stump. Two men exited the building Lance had just blown. They were staggering, trying to run away. At 45 feet, they were easy for his bad aim. They fell immediately. But his shots gave away his position. That's when he was hit.

Damn. This was bad and getting worse. They didn't have a body count, didn't know how many more men were in the compound. The moving formation he saw exiting the fifth building about 75 feet from his location brought a new realization. The men who flowed out of the building did so in formation. One glance was all Lance needed to see what that meant. He also knew right away that one of these men had shot him.

All five men were Mujahedeen, veterans of the Afghanistan war with the Soviet Union. It was easy to see their training, their skill, their experience. The second man out the door, now moving away from Lance with three others covering his flank, was Anwar, their ghost.

Lance had to try for the kill. He fired two dozen rounds at the retreating group. Two men fell. Not bad, but Anwar wasn't one of them. Lance got up to a knee and brought the weapon on top of the stump to steady his aim when the remaining man covering Anwar's flank fired off a salvo that sprayed the stump, barely missing Lance's neck. He returned fire and put the man down.

Sixty feet away, Fuchs was moving on the fourth building in slow, expert fashion. Lance glanced over and knew right away the men shooting back at Fuchs were not Mujahedeen. They were not disciplined in their firing or formation. They shot from windows, which made them sitting ducks as Fuchs got closer, close enough to lob a couple of hand grenades.

Lance looked back to see Anwar and another man reach the tree line approximately 150 feet away. Damn. He was about to take a chance with a few more rounds in their direction when pain ripped into his right thigh. He was hit with a third bullet, this time from behind.

He looked down and was thrilled to see the bullet had missed his femoral artery. He rolled to his left to see a muzzle flash from the corner of the first building he had blown apart with grenades. One of the men had evidently crawled outside to join the firefight. Lance fired a dozen rounds in that direction. They hit the ground and the building but not the man. Lance was safe for the moment behind a small hill, but he couldn't help but look back in the direction Anwar had fled. This close to completing the mission and embarking on the new mission he and Marta now shared.

Thinking of her for the first time in about five hours sent something of a chill down his spine. He surveyed his wounded shoulder, chest and leg and cursed. This was going to seriously affect his productivity for the next few weeks. The process of surgery, wound care and rehab flashed through his mind. But just as he finished this thought, the next took over. He might not be productive, might not be anything at all if he didn't get the bleeding stopped and a round of antibiotics coursing through his body within hours. Shit, he could be dead in a little while.

It was the first time he'd thought about dying since meeting Marta. He saw her face, a tear slipping from her eye, a slow motion collapse to the ground. He went out of body in the next moment and looked down on himself, over at the guy shooting at him and then over at Fuchs. There was no time. He needed this thing over now.

Something strange happened next.

Standard procedure for Lance is going out of body to survey the situation, uncover details missed, and then jumping back into his head to take action. This time, instead of going back inside his head, he watched as Preacher rolled onto his back and pulled out his two remaining grenades. From the prone position, Preacher lobbed one in the direction of the first building, and then rolled back on to his front to rise up on a knee as the explosion erupted about 15 feet from the shooter. From up there, Lance thought it was an excellent throw.

He watched as Preacher got up from one knee to his feet and ran perpendicular to the building, taking him out of the shooter's view. He continued running, limping really, around the building. Lance rose higher into the sky to watch Preacher round the back corner of the building and find the shooter lying there shaking off the effects of the explosion. Preacher put two bullets through the back of the man's head. He then stepped into the blown-out building to make sure no other men were inside recovering. Nope. The six men inside were dead.

Lance looked over at Fuchs attacking building four. He realized something in this moment. He shouldn't be able to see Fuchs. He couldn't see him from the building Preacher stood inside, so how could he be watching the scene unfolding a couple hundred feet below him like this?

The next thing that happened was also a first. The disembodied Lance stopped what he was doing and talked to himself, talked to Preacher. A third set of eyes watched this floating Lance come to a slow realization.

He was dying. Death was looking at him. Damn. Not now. Not with all this work to do, all these new first-time things happening. But Death didn't care about plans or agendas or love or missions. Lance and Death, watching from on high, heard the explosions as Fuchs tossed two grenades into building four. At the same time, Preacher came limping out of building one. He looked bad, blood-soaked and weak. Didn't look like he had long, but he kept going toward Fuchs to help mop up any remaining terrorists in training.

One final exchange of fire ended quickly as Preacher joined Fuchs. An eerie silence took over. Lance and his new friend Death moved down closer now that the shooting was over. They saw the look on Fuchs' face when he turned to see Preacher.

The older CIA killer rushed over to Preacher and helped him to the ground. The spirits descended to just a few feet over their heads. Fuchs' emergency medical skills took over. He tore off Preacher's field jacket and ripped the shirt to get a look at the injuries. He then tore the shirt into strips and tied one around the shoulder entry and exit wounds and then he stuck his finger in the hole near Preacher's ribs to stop that bleeding and feel for the bullet. It was too deep to pull out with fingers. He tied another strip of shirt around Preacher's right thigh.

During all of this, Preacher lay there on the dirt. The early morning light now filled the sky. The oppressive heat had already kicked in. But Preacher wasn't looking at the sky, or Fuchs, or his wounds. No, he was busy starring up at Lance Priest and someone he didn't know. The two of them were floating right there over Fuchs's shoulder as he worked to staunch the flow of blood from Preacher's many wounds.

"Doesn't look good, does it?" Preacher spoke to Lance.

Fuchs thought he was talking to him, of course. "Not that bad, not any worse than Baghdad."

Preacher ignored him. "What do you think bro?" He asked Lance.

"No problem." Fuchs responded.

"No, not you Foxy. I'm asking Lance up there."

Lance smiled at Preacher. "You look like shit, like one of those GI Joe's you tore the hell out of when we lived in Florida."

Preacher laughed at the memory. He turned to the other guy next to Lance and spoke in Russian, "How bout you? What do you think buddy?"

The ghost, who looked equal parts Seibel, Marta and Max von Sydow, smiled as well. "I can't lie to you."

"Oh, c'mon. Go ahead and lie. It's what we do." Preacher's vision began to go fuzzy.

"Okay, okay. You are dead. No chance to pull through this time." The spirit seemed to move into Lance and come out the other side.

"Crap. Lousy time to die, and not where I planned."

"You never..." Lance responded.

"I know. I never had a plan. Never cared much about it before now either. Before her."

Lance came down near the ground on the opposite side of Preacher from Fuchs. "Not much you can do about it bro."

Preacher reached up to Lance. "No worries, right? She'll be fine. She's done fine without us up till now anyway."

"Yep." Lance the ghost took Preacher's hand. "She'll be fine. I think she really likes you though."

"You or me?" Preacher laughed at the inside joke. He coughed and spat a little blood. Not good.

"Me. I'm better looking." Lance cracked up as he said this.

"That will have to work for now my friend." Fuchs butted into the conversation and brought his head down in between Preacher and Lance. "Let's go."

"No, that's okay. We're fine. Get out of here and go see if you can't find our ghost bomber out there in the jungle."

"Nope. Let's go." Fuchs straddled Preacher and pulled him up to a sitting position, then pulled him to his unsteady feet. He bent over and let Preacher fall onto his shoulder and then he proceeded to carry him to the beach and north the quarter mile or so to where their boat was waiting. Preacher was in and out of consciousness for the shoulder carry. But he did remember looking back at Lance and the other fella and wondered if he'd see them again.

Once on the boat, Fuchs put Lance on the floorboards and broke out the first aid kit. Minutes later he was on the sat radio talking with Seibel who had been busy arranging for Special Forces to mop up, and a forensics team for onsite evidence collection.

Seibel wasn't thrilled to hear Lance had been shot multiple times but was happy Fuchs had a good grip on him this time. They arranged for a helicopter pickup in the village of Parang, on the western tip of Jolo Island. The helicopter would get Lance to the hospital in Zamboanga in about 50 minutes. He might just make it.

Lance, floating overhead, didn't think Preacher had a chance.

Chapter 23

Tuesday, October 1, 1991 — Yugoslavia, Egypt, Chechnya
Three explosions, one massive, two medium, ripped through a train station in Zagreb, Yugoslavia, a crowded open market in Cairo, Egypt and on a bus outside Grozny, Chechnya.

The October morning was six weeks and two days after the morning raid on the terrorist training compound. It was a well-planned and executed operation. The combined explosions killed 211 humans. Very effective terror events.

He watched the images on the screen and knew each of the explosions were sufficient to achieve their goals. The bus in Chechnya was just a husk on melted wheels. The Cairo market's stone and dirt floors were stained red. The train station could only be seen from a quarter mile away. It was the largest of the bombs. He could tell by the spray of glass, brick and metal that the explosion ripped off a third of the north side of the building. It was indeed massive. Amazing that a common travel trunk sitting on a loading dock could hold enough explosive material achieve such results.

Anwar personally constructed each bomb and traveled to every destination to work with separate teams. But he was nowhere near any of them when they detonated. He was in Syria, surrounded by hundreds of miles of desert. A television antenna brought him news of the carnage. He took no pleasure. But he was satisfied with the results, the message delivered. That message was simple – change is coming. Freedom from oppression will be born from ashes.

Anwar prayed at noon and then again at 2 pm. He thanked Allah for the skills, the patience and the commitment to follow through with the plans he and others devised in mountain villages in Afghanistan. He was truly a soldier for jihad. He was a vessel through which Allah will bring justice to the world.

He was doing his duty, his job. And he had much to do. This was only the beginning. This was war.

Watching a television screen in his office thousands of miles away in Moscow, Gregor Smelinski saw the pattern in the separate incidents. He didn't need to work hard to see it. He was frustrated by the lack of his, or anyone else's, ability to detect and derail these terrorist acts. He was especially disappointed that one of the acts occurred in his backyard, albeit an ugly backyard in Chechnya. Again, without any advance warning. None.

Smelinski needed to act quickly, decisively. He had already placed half a dozen calls to resources in or near Grozny. Nobody had anything. The perpetrators were a complete mystery. He had a few ideas. If this had been the bus in Grozny only, he would have assumed, along with everyone else, it was Chechnyan separatists. But explosions in three separate cities, all taking place within the same hour made this an international event. It would undoubtedly bring together international law enforcement and intelligence forces.

He had a number of resources he could put on the case. They would do a fine a job. They would undoubtedly find traces, tracks. But he didn't have at his disposal a ruthless hunter and tracker who would stop at nothing to get her man. He turned away from the television at the ringing of the phone on his desk.

Smelinski was lost in thought, seeing her face. He had a tinge of regret in his voice as he picked up the receiver. The person at the other end of the phone likely took his faraway tone to be reflective of the day's tragic events.

Four TV screens played news footage from around the world. Geoffrey Seibel watched each. CNN had the best compilation of all three incidents. The news anchors on the cable news channel were now recognizable in the aftermath of CNN's coverage coup of the brief Gulf War earlier in the year.

Seibel didn't have to ask who could have done this. He knew, maybe more than anyone else. This was Anwar's work. This was precision and patience and payback for the raid on Tapul. Seibel could see the pattern behind all three. He could see the separate events were adapted to new timelines to put them on the same day, the same hour.

The latest footage coming in from Chechnya was as bad as the images of Cairo and Zagreb that had been played dozens of times now. "This is big news," one of the anchors said. Seibel took that as a sign and muted the volume. He had already been on the phone with the Director of the CIA, NSA and the White House. He told them all the same thing – Anwar. The world's elite terrorist bomber announced that he had come down from the mountains of Afghanistan. Al Qaeda was now a force to be reckoned with, everywhere.

He shook his head. They'd almost gotten him. They were so close, closer than they'd likely be again for a long time. Anwar would become a ghost after this. Seibel, like Smelinski, would put resources to work alongside other nations in an attempt to track and kill him. But he, like Smelinski, was without one of his greatest resources. He'd lost Lance more than three weeks ago when he limped out of the military hospital in Hawaii and fell off the face of the earth.

He had disappeared. No doubt he was still pissed about the whole Tapul scene and the bad intel that nearly got him killed. But more than that, Lance was just plain different. He didn't have any passion for finding Anwar anymore. The two times Seibel had visited him in the hospital, Lance had been gracious but empty. He probably should have died on that island, probably would have preferred that to the surgeries and recovery he was working through before he disappeared.

Then there was the matter of Marta. Lance gave nothing away of his involvement with her, but Seibel could see with eyes closed the effect their relationship, regardless of how insane it was, had on Lance. Seibel held that she had changed him more than being shot a second time in eight months. Fuchs had confirmed the changed Preacher he encountered in Manila. Seibel didn't want to use terms like "beyond salvage" and "no longer applicable" that members of Account One were muttering. He had too much invested in Preacher. The kid was just getting started. "Give him some time," he whispered to no one.

Seibel screwed up sending just the two of them into the compound. But hell, they killed all but three of the two dozen men in the small complex. He knew it wouldn't be the last time he'd send them to their death.

Chapter 24

"Damn, you couldn't have picked a Rockefeller or the Sultan of Brunei or maybe even Prince Charles?"

He was reading an in-depth article from *The Economist* about Russian oligarch Kirill Cherzny. And, even though it was written primarily from a financial point of view, the article detailed fairly intimate aspects of this man from Belgorod, near the Ukrainian border, who rose to local and regional power through politics before turning to oil, minerals, transportation and now technology to build incredible wealth.

"His little empire touches everything." Preacher looked up from the magazine to watch her move across the floor with the beach, waves and palm trees gently waving behind her. Every time he looked at her it was like a dream. Words didn't work to describe what she did to him, what she meant. Love was far too tame a description of his feelings for her.

"I think I've said that a few hundred times." She was wearing a bikini top and khaki shorts -- a mix of beauty and tomboy.

"I know, I know. I'm just restating so it will settle in my brain. I'm like that, you know."

"I'm beginning to see how you are." Marta leaned against the railing of their balcony. A gentle breeze blew through her hair. Lovely, he thought.

"He's basically in charge. The president is his lapdog. It's all right here. He has his hand, or at least his little pinky, in everything. Like a web." Preacher added.

She laughed and came back inside to sit beside him on the rattan sofa. "It is exactly like a web. And that is precisely why Gregor should have wanted him isolated and contained."

"But he was already turned." Preacher reached out a finger to swipe at a small insect that had landed on her lovely shoulder. "I wonder how long ago?"

"Years, at least. The way I see it, Cherzny identified players like Smelinski a decade ago and systematically brought them into his sphere. It is just like everywhere else, everyone is in someone else's pocket. He just happens to have the biggest and deepest pockets."

Preacher snickered. "You are on a tear today, on fire with the metaphors and analogies. I'm loving it."

She moved her hand to rub his chest, the non-bandaged side, of course. "I'm loving you."

"See, right there. You are too quick for me today. On fire." He grasped her hand in his and brought it to his lips. This, all of this, was too easy. Like Vienna, only with more severe injuries this time.

They'd been here 16 days. The island of Yap in the Philippine Sea was their floating fortress of solitude from the world. He didn't know where they were going nearly three weeks ago when she stepped into his hospital room on Oahu. He didn't much care, as long as it was away from the hospital, and somewhere they could be alone.

He'd heard of Yap, but never looked at it on a map because there were so few roads to memorize. The islanders were very respectful of their privacy, believing the two of them were on an extended honeymoon. Which, in certain ways, it was, except for a significant decrease in amorous activity as a result of Preacher's wounds.

Lance held up the magazine again. "Says he lives in the same apartment he moved into when he came to Moscow 13 years ago. He does not surround himself with the trappings of extreme wealth. He and his wife live simply, without extravagance. Downright homey. Sounds like rags to riches."

"Yes, he does keep that apartment. But the rest of the apartment building has been cleared out, except for his flunkies, bodyguards and consorts." She ran her hands through her hair and leaned her head back on the colorful cushion atop the rattan framework of the sofa. She brought her feet up onto the ornately carved wooden table in front of them. "The apartment building, located on Utkeski Prospect, has 88 units on 6 floors, two elevators, which both work – an amazing thing in Moscow. There are three entrances, all secure. The front entrance has a rotating security detail. Access to each floor requires a card key. The codes for these keys change weekly, requiring issuance of new cards to the building's few tenants.

"Cherzny's apartment has been expanded to integrate security applications, including reinforced walls and doors and bulletproof windows. Hidden stairs provide access to units above and below. Backup generators located in the basement of the structure could power it for three months. The roof features a helipad. The perimeters of the building and adjoining properties are under constant video surveillance, with roving teams of security personnel dressed as business people, police and street vendors."

She opened her eyes and leaned forward to rest her elbows on her knees.

"I would say you went somewhere else right there," Preacher put the magazine on the table and he leaned over to rub her back. "And my guess would be Moscow. When were you there last?"

"Nineteen days ago."

He thought that through. "So you went to Hawaii straight from Moscow." He knew she had been busy after they separated six-plus weeks ago, but he wasn't thrilled she had gone right into the lion's den without him. But he stopped that thought immediately. Marta was more comfortable in dangerous situations than anyone he'd ever met.

"I know what you're thinking. You wish I hadn't gone to Moscow on my own," she turned her head to look at him. Her smile was deadly. "You may not believe this, but for the first time ever, I actually debated going there alone. Never once crossed my mind before..." she trailed off.

"Before?" he caressed her arm with the back of his hand. He did it naturally, not aware of his need to touch her as much as possible, constantly was best.

"Before about six weeks ago." Her smile turned into a slight frown.

"Oh. I see." He put his lips to her right shoulder. "I think I know what you mean."

"Lance, you are getting in the way of my work. You are affecting my behavior," her face inches from his.

He smiled and kissed her. She welcomed his lips. He pulled away enough to speak into her ear, "Marta, you are affecting my life, not just my work." She kissed his jaw line and neck. The conversation was over for now. They both would have liked to get messy and sweaty, but his injuries still required some control. She was patient, but it was running low. She needed him back to 100 percent soon.

It was later that evening that Lance was able to get a few more fragments of information out of Marta. She wasn't withholding facts on purpose, they had just avoided talking shop for two weeks. But lying there in the soothing warmth of the tropical night, she laid out the steps she had taken after he had left her still in bed in Vienna.

They had devised a fairly detailed plan with multiple contingencies. She told him about traveling to Belgrade to meet with two contacts, then to Sarajevo to check up on an operation she had placed on autopilot earlier in the year. From there, she flew to Moscow and worked her way through several peripheral resources she had called upon sparingly over the years. She researched security, travel patterns, key team members and potential leverage points in Cherzny's personal and professional lives. It was a nuts and bolts report with just enough detail to make it believable.

But Lance wasn't fooled. Left between the lines and floating around the edges was the real story. He didn't push her on it. She'd share more when she was ready.

If she had been willing to share the details of her weeks away from him, those details would have indeed got his heart racing. Marta did travel to Belgrade, Sarajevo and Moscow. Those were not lies. And she did visit field resources in each city. She just neglected to tell Lance that she killed one contact in Belgrade and wounded another. Was shot at and attacked on the road outside Sarajevo. And some of the information she extracted in her review of security and other details in Moscow was due in large part to her torturing a man who thought he was about to enjoy her intimate company.

Her Belgrade excursion returned her to the heart of downtown, where she set up an appointment with a telecommunications professional she had worked with a dozen times in five years. He was unmatched in his knowledge of wired communications and moving data over phone lines. Turned out, he was also scared to death after receiving the call from Marta, and had placed a call moments later to the number two KGB man in the city. This, in turn, set in motion a plan to ambush Marta, with six men stationed at perimeter sightlines outside the drug store where they were to meet.

Marta, after a several meetings with people lying in wait to kill her, expected the attack. Truth be told, she was hoping to provoke it. She looked down on the street in front of the drug store from a third floor window and counted five men that shouldn't be there. That meant there were likely others. She focused her binoculars on one gentleman situated 150 yards from the store's front door.

The man leaned against a wall in a doorway, lazily holding a radio up to his ear. His eyes aimed at the street. He had no reason to think the glass door to an office building behind him would come into play. Minutes later, Marta moved to the building and stood inside the door for three minutes, watching the man, listening.

He spoke into the radio only once. Before he heard the door behind him open, Marta brought the retractable club down diagonally on his neck and shoulder. The blow caused momentary paralysis. She picked up the radio and put it in a pocket and dragged him back into the building.

"Comrade," she spoke Russian to the KGB operative. "You chose a good day to die. The sun was shining. Only a few clouds in the sky. And tonight you can visit your children using your angel's wings. That is unless you will be stuck down in a fiery pit." She was inches from his face. A silenced gun jammed into his neck.

She smiled pleasantly. "Did they tell you I was dangerous, or maybe just that I'm a girl?" She laughed at that. "I guess I'm both really."

She moved the gun from his neck to his shoulder and fired. The bullet exploded quietly through his body and into the wall behind. Her gloved hand clamped over his mouth muffled his scream.

"Tell me one thing, and I may let you live."

"Anything," he pleaded without hesitation when she moved her hand.

"Your call numbers and pass codes. Now, and don't delay." She reached into her jacket pocket and pulled out a small tape recorder.

The broken and bleeding man recited three phone numbers and six passwords. He did not hesitate in the least.

"Very good. One more thing, how many children do you have?"

"Two." He answered.

"Why?" she raised her eyebrows. It made her think of Lance and his fascination with the procerus muscle.

The man did not grasp the meaning of the one-word question. "What do you mean?"

"Why do you have children and still do this job? Do they, or your wife, know that you might never come home when you leave the house each day?"

"No. They have no idea."

"Then you live a lie, a series of lies."

"Yes." Tears came to his eyes. He knew he was a dead man.

"I don't know you, and I never will. You are a lucky man to have a family. You should have chosen a different profession. This is not a job for a family man."

"I know, I know." He began to cry. He would never see his children again.

"Calm down. I'm not going to kill you." The radio in her pocket burst with static and then a whisper asking where the man was. He had left his post. "Answer them, and then step outside the door for two minutes. At that time, you can fake being shot. You never saw me, of course. And then you have a choice, continue living your lies, or find a new profession. You will have a few weeks of recuperation to think about it."

With that, she stepped away from him and deeper into the dark building. He struggled to his feet and made it painfully out the door, where he stood for two minutes and then cried out in pain, for the others to hear.

Marta watched the scene from the third floor window two buildings over. The KGB operative she had shot was taken away and the others converged on the store to escort her telecommunications expert out to a waiting car. It was well executed.

Later, Marta waited inside the telecommunications expert's apartment. The hours passed. He was not coming home. She sat there in the dark, her gun in hand. She felt somewhat relieved not having to shoot the man. She was alone with her thoughts. They were annoying at first, but she was slowly growing accustomed to having something of a conscience. She thought of Lance, and wondered how his day had gone and, of course, how quickly he could get back to her.

The next afternoon, Marta left a meeting with a contact beyond reproach. The businessman knew little about her and had always been helpful in aiding her development of assets in Sarajevo. She had shown up without notice in his office on the southwest end of the city's downtown. He welcomed her into his office and was receptive to her questions about her crumbling network.

He had heard the talk on the street about the sanctions placed upon her by Moscow. He did not like them, did not think Moscow could call those kinds of shots anymore. Not even Smelinski.

He informed her of two new factions growing in prominence, and confirmed her prediction that Sarajevo would indeed be a flashpoint in the coming racial and ethnic violence between Croats and Serbs. He saw war for Yugoslavia and death for his people, his family and friends.

Marta left his office with a good bit of information. She also left with three tail cars. And she was pretty sure a helicopter overhead was there for her as well.

Within minutes, the tails were in active pursuit, and like a bad American movie, guys leaned out car windows shooting at her. "Zhalkii," she muttered looking at the rearview mirror. She used the Russian word for "pitiful" as she concentrated on the streets ahead. She lost focus for just a moment when she thought of Lance. Not his face or smile or body, she thought of his photographic memory. He would know which turn to take, which highway onramp to choose.

Instead, she had to work with what she knew of Sarajevo. She'd been here many times and knew her way in and out of town. She rounded a corner from a busy thoroughfare onto a two-lane street with cars parked on each side. It was perfect, and she reacted in a perfect fashion. Two of the three cars chasing her came around the corner a moment later. She slammed on the brakes and swung the car sideways to create a roadblock. Before her car was stopped, she was out the door with a gun in each hand, aiming the weapons at the approaching vehicles as she moved around the rear of her car.

Marta knew about windshields and their ability to deflect bullets. The angle of the shatterproof glass could protect the person behind it. The first car pursuing her came screeching to a stop. She could see in the eyes of the two men inside they knew they were in trouble. She burst into a run, and was parallel to the driver's side window a second later. She aimed both guns at the window and fired six shots. Glass exploded and the men inside were dead before broken glass hit the asphalt below.

The second car had also come to a skidding halt. The driver slammed the car into reverse and it started accelerating backwards. Problem was, Marta was already running in their direction. There wouldn't be enough time to get it up to speed.

The passenger in the car recognized this fact and began firing at Marta through the windshield. It was a mistake. When the bullets from his gun exploded through the glass, the shatterproof glass did its job and spread the impacts across the screen creating an impossible mosaic. Neither driver, not passenger could see Marta as she rolled on the street next to the car. She came back up to a knee and fired two shots from the gun in her right hand into the front right tire, and then three shots from the one in her left hand back through the broken windshield. Her shots found their targets. The driver was hit and lost control. The car swerved to the left and into a parked sedan.

Marta crossed in front of the car. She fired three more shots into the passenger side window. The glass didn't explode this time, but the bullets did their job. She didn't stop to admire her work. Instead, she looked up at the helicopter hovering overhead and thought "what the hell." She steadied her aim by placing her right arm atop her bent left arm and fired the remaining six bullets in her gun. All six hit the copter. Two struck the windshield, leaving two distinct holes she could see from 200 feet below.

She sprinted back to her car and saw up ahead that the third vehicle was waiting at the end of the block. The driver had gone ahead in an attempt to cut her off. She hopped into the driver's seat, spun the steering wheel and floored the gas. She was up to 40, then 50 kilometers in seconds. She grabbed the seat belt and strapped it over her, preparing for impact. The driver of the third car put the transmission in reverse and pulled out of the way at the last moment. Marta blew past doing 60.

The car appeared in her rearview mirror a minute later as she took the onramp onto E761. The freeway would take her northeast into the mountains, away from Sarajevo. She kept the pedal down. Marta had driven this road several times before and really enjoyed the twists and turns it offered.

She worked out a plan to slam to a stop around one of those turns and put a hail of bullets into the car chasing her. The helicopter presented another challenge.

After a few minutes of blazing through the mountain road, she slowed a fraction to let the chase car gain on her. Her spot was up ahead. She focused on the road and rearview mirror. The helicopter would have to wait.

She took the hairpin turn at 45. Rubber burned and gravel flew as gravity and momentum tugged at the four wheels holding her vehicle to the earth. She continued to swing the car around onto the shoulder on the inside of the turn. Her vehicle faced the oncoming road, and the car chasing her. She had reloaded both guns a few miles earlier. She calmly stepped out of the car with both guns ready and bent to a knee to steady her aim. Marta fired seven shots at the windshield and front tires of the car as it rounded the hairpin corner. The driver lost control, and the sedan plowed straight ahead into the rocky mountainside to the right of the roadway. Marta was up and running at the vehicle as it crashed to a stop.

Both men in the car were still alert. They opened their doors and spilled out. They came out firing. Marta didn't change her approach in the least, firing from about 50 feet away. With two barrels blazing, like another bad American movie, she placed four holes in the head of the vehicle's driver. Not bad at all considering she was running full speed. The passenger ducked down beside the vehicle and crawled to the rear. Marta could see his next move, so she dove to the ground and skidded to a stop just off the road.

She lay on her side with her guns aimed at the spot she expected his head to appear. When it did, she fired eight shots, hitting him with six. He was a bloody and dead mess before he hit the ground.

That left the helicopter.

Marta was back on her feet and to the wrecked car in a flash. She reached in and grabbed 9 MM and a shotgun in the back seat. She rolled to the ground beside the car just as the helicopter cleared the mountain. It swooped slowly down on the scene. Marta inched her way underneath the vehicle as the copter came in close for a better view. The blades whipped the air, creating tremendous noise and dust as the pressure of pushed air bounced off the tight valley walls. She had chosen the perfect location.

The bird descended for a clear view and clean shot by the shooter hanging out the chopper's door. She waited, covering her face with her arm to protect from dirt and debris blown by the propeller. The pilot maneuvered the helicopter straight over the car, just the mistake she needed. Marta rolled out and lifted the shotgun to take aim at the bird's rear rotor. She fired both shells. The spread of pellets struck the spinning vertical blade causing damage and creating a cacophony of sounds. Pellets sliced through metal and ricochet in every direction. Several struck Marta in the legs, ripping into her jeans.

She dropped the shotgun and aimed the 9 mm into the door of the whirly bird as it spun around, losing control. The shooter hanging out the door was annihilated. She raised another gun and fired through the open door at the pilot. He too was hit. She knew what was coming next and decided to play it safe by diving back under the sedan for protection.

In the next few seconds, the helicopter rose slightly, spun four times and then tipped to it's left side, causing it to pick up speed, accelerating into the side of the mountain. The pilot's dead weight on the stick was all that was needed to send the bird to its fiery death. The explosion was deafening in the tight valley. As the fireball rolled down the hill on the opposite side of the road, Marta emerged to see a VW van approaching. The driver slammed on his breaks 200 meters from the deadly scene.

Marta would have preferred no witnesses. She had a choice. Race toward the van and dispatch the passengers in the vehicle or sprint across the road to her idling car and hightail it out of there. She chose a middle ground. She jump in her car, nailed the gas to spin it around and shoot directly at the van and its terrified occupants. She stopped beside the driver's door, jumped out with gun in hand and pointed it at the man's head through the window. She could see a woman beside him with a look of pure, uncontrollable horror on her face.

Marta tapped on the window and signaled for him to roll it down. He shook his head so she pointed the gun at his forehead. He complied.

"T23N7. That is your license plate number and that tells me your name and address. You did not see me here. Is that clear?" She shouted in English.

"Yes. Please." The gentleman replied.

"Drive away or stick around for authorities, but do not mention me, or I will use that name and address and pay you two a visit. And then I will visit your relatives. Good bye."

She turned and slid back into her driver's seat, closing the door behind her. She was completely calm, already coming down from the adrenalin rush of the chase and shootings. She had killed eight men in 16 minutes. They should never have followed her. She was happy to leave the couple in the van alive. Just months ago, she wouldn't have done that. She was different, changed.

As she sped away from the chaos and death behind her, she thought of the trigger for the attack. Did her contact in Sarajevo give her up? She just couldn't see that happening. More likely, his office was bugged. Maybe it was bugged just to see if she ever showed up, or perhaps it had been wiretapped for years. She considered that the most likely scenario as she drove away, further into the mountains northeast of Sarajevo. She ran back through the preceding minutes and laughed to herself again. It really was like a bad American action movie. Lance would have loved it. He'd never hear about it, but she knew him well enough to know that stuff was right up his alley.

Indeed, she shared none of this, or the gruesome details of her recent Moscow escapades with Lance. He didn't need it right now.

"How did you find me in Hawaii?" Lance broke into her concentration, as he often did nowadays. He had let her drift for a few minutes and watched her little trip into her recent past. It was fun just looking at her lying there with eyes closed.

She opened them, "How do you think?"

"Originally, I thought it was your psychic abilities and our mystic connection. But then I thought it through and had to consider a couple of other options."

"And, what did you come up with?"

He closed his eyes. "I assume that two days after I was to connect with you through the phone message service in Brussels, you began to think something was up. Two days after that, you knew something was amiss and you called the service to be sure my message wasn't misplaced. When you found nothing from me, you considered your very select set of options and then checked for any messages from Papa."

"Papa?" She knew already.

"Seibel." He opened his eyes, smiled and then closed them again, but not before sliding his hand down her arm. "I was off on another one of his missions and if I was missing, it's not much of a leap for you to try that avenue."

"But why would he leave a message for me? I have nothing to do with you, right?" She turned onto her side and propped up on her elbow.

"He works in mysterious ways, you know."

"I know. I know."

"So, am I close?"

"You are correct, as usual. Have I told you how much you are like him?"

"Ooh, that hurts. Really, that's tough."

"Too bad. It's true." She fell on her back, her head on the pillow. "Christ. If I stop and think about it for a minute, it's Freudian. He is my father and you are the image of my father that I seek for assurance and approval."

"Come on. I'm nothing like him." He laughed and snuggled into her, pulling her close. "He's chocolate, I'm vanilla. He's Mercedes, I'm Honda. He's-"

"He's a master manipulator without equal and yet, you are his equal."

"His equal?"

"You are his heir, his disciple and protégé. Except..."

"What?"

She turned away to look out the window. He let her remain silent for these moments. "Except you are no one's equal. That is to say, no one is your equal."

"Man, such praise from one in a billion. I am not your equal, not in your league even."

"I'm not trying to elevate your esteem." He laughed at that. She sometimes messed up her English phrases and chose words that were too formal. "What?"

"Nothing. Please, continue." He said.

She turned back. "You don't need me to tell you anything. You know how he feels about you, how I feel about you. As much as you resemble him, you are much more. Lance, there's no one like you, anywhere. I've been to a great many places and seen and met people of all types and there is truly no one quite like you. That's the only way I can say it."

"You know, you took the words out of my mouth. I've not seen as many things as you and never will, but you are a singular creature. One in a billion, or six billion, like I said."

"You don't have to say that. You don't have to qualify your feelings for me in any way."

"I'm not. Just stating fact, as I see it."

"Then I'll just say I love you." She smiled, her smile. It was a singular smile just for him.

"That's all I need to hear."

"It was love at first sight for me, you know. Never felt anything like it before. I'll never feel that way again, except the next time I see you after being apart." She moved closer and put her head to his chest.

"I can do better than that."

"How do you mean?"

"It wasn't love at first sight for me."

"No? Then what was it?"

He pushed her back so he could see her face. "It was death."

"Death?"

"Death. I was done the moment I saw you. I've already told you how it, how you've changed me. I knew in that moment and in all the others we've been together that I would never change the way I feel about you. It's a life sentence. I'll die knowing it, no matter what happens, even if I never saw you after today."

"Don't talk about dying. I've already asked you that."

"I told you, I died when I first saw you. All the rest of this is extra, like heaven I guess."

"Damn Lance, you are so good at this."

"At what?"

"At making me want you, love you, need you. All of it." She pulled him closer.

"Then my plan is working." He kissed her. Their conversation was over.

Chapter 25

"Lie to me." Her eyes were half closed as she rested her chin on his chest, the left side of his chest; the side not still healing from bullet wounds and surgery. They were lying on a blanket on the beach a few hundred feet from their thatched-roof cabana. The waves in the lagoon were gently lapping. If they were on a honeymoon, this would probably be the moment they would both remember when they pulled out the photo album years from now to show to kids and then grandkids.

They would both be graying, shriveling and yet still share that certain look when Yap and their honeymoon came up.

But there were no photos from this holiday. No bright and shiny gold and diamond rings on fingers. This was a retreat, a reprieve. But it was also the proverbial calm before the storm. They were leaving tomorrow. The previous 19 days of peace, quiet, sand and sun would only be a memory. Nineteen days was a long time though. For many young couples, it could be a relationship killer. But for these two killers, it was just more glue to bond them together.

"You know I can't lie to you." He had his left hand behind his head. His right was still sore, but he gently stroked her hair.

"Come on, just tell me a few lies." She pleaded.

"I just can't. I haven't told you a single lie in weeks."

"But you are so good at it. Try it."

"You always know when I tell you lies. You nail me every time. Maybe when we get off this island, which I am definitely ready to do, I can get back to my old ways."

"I just wanted to be comforted by you and you are most comfortable when prevaricating. It is your natural state."

"Well, I'm not comfortable now." He rolled his eyes.

"Oh, I'm sorry. I was just trying to help you feel better. I thought you were very anxious about leaving tomorrow."

"I am. I'm ready to get back to normalcy and routine. I need to get back to people, lots of people. I have to admit, just a little, that I'm bored. It's not you, it's just this place that I'm ready to leave."

She rose from his chest and sat up with her knees pulled up. "I'm sorry you feel this way."

He burst out laughing and still somewhat painfully sat up to put his chin on her knees. She didn't look happy in this moment.

"This is a side of you I've not seen," she pulled her head back a bit.

"Uh, honey, you asked for it."

"What? I don't understand." She furrowed her brow and he melted inside. It was that quick.

"Marta what did you ask me to do one minute ago?"

"To lie to me, not to become a… jerk is what you say."

"And what did I say?"

She looked back over their brief conversation and then suddenly shoved his forehead. "Not jerk, you're an asshole."

"Sorry." He smiled wider. Marta's anger was a brilliant treat for his eyes. Her eyes lit up, her cheeks blushed.

"Which ones were lies?"

"Which ones do you think?"

"The part about leaving here."

"Wrong."

"Which parts then?"

"All of it. Every word I spoke. I did as you asked."

"Damn you."

"You're welcome."

Chapter 26

Preacher's plans were changed by headlines on a newspaper folded over a chair at the small island's airport. He picked up the paper, read about the triple bombings three days earlier and turned to Marta, who stood in front of a man at a desk confirming their reservations for a chartered plane.

She turned to see his look. His brows furrowed, his procerus muscle hard at work. She walked over and he handed her the paper. He turned away to look out a window onto the runway. After a minute, he turned to her as she finished the article and looked up. Her face said it all. Change of plans.

"That's my friend's handiwork. I'll bet he built each one." Preacher was looking at her, but he was gone, out of body looking down from a satellite view 200 miles in orbit. He peered down at Zagreb, Cairo and Grozny. He was about to zoom in to each location when she brought him back.

"All within three hours of each other. That required teams. Not one man."

"Anwar used some soldiers. My gut tells me Grozny was a suicide bomber. The others were planted."

"This changes things." She was dead on, as usual.

"Definitely does."

"What do you need to do?"

He smiled. "I need to talk to Siebel. I'll bet there are a dozen messages waiting for me at the service."

"We'll have to adjust our plans." She was matter-of-fact, not hurt.

"You'll have to promise to not do anything without me."

Her turn to smile. "I'll wait. A little while, at least."

"You could go with me, help me." He squeezed her arms gently. He was serious.

"No. You will need to concentrate. I would get in the way."

"You already get in the way. Every moment. You know that."

"Lance. You will need to be someone else, move quickly without explanation or baggage."

He exhaled and shook his head. She knew exactly what he was about to do. She had done it herself many times. She kissed him and turned back to the gentleman at the desk.

Preacher watched her, admired her. At least they had the long flights over the next day together. After that, they would go separate ways. It stung, he could feel it. He knew they'd have to part at some point. But he still didn't care for it. Hell, he hated the thought of it. Damn.

Law enforcement officials still had the Zagreb train station roped off six days after the bombing. The damage to the facility was extensive, massive. Preacher squatted on his haunches and took in the destroyed north face of the structure. Twisted metal, burnt walls, fixtures and casings were evidence of a massive explosion. From his vantage point 150 meters away, Lance could make out a good bit of the mess. His vision from on high, allowed him to see down, through the gaping hole. He could see the train cars mangled by the blast. He knew it was a single case, because he had a copy of the preliminary report from Interpol.

He wanted to walk around the site to get a better feel, to smell the remains, the burn. But something told him to stay away. He couldn't see them, but he could feel eyes watching the devastated building. And he had a pretty good idea what those eyes were looking for -- him, or at least someone who looked like him. Someone seen from across a chaotic training compound in the Philippines.

All evidence pointed to a large case or trunk placed on the loading dock. Residue and fragments pointed to ammonium nitrate; lethal and fairly easy to assemble. Forty-one people were killed instantly. Another nine died later that day and the next. And at last count, 72 were still hospitalized. It could have been much worse if the blast had occurred at rush hour.

And that was the fact that perplexed Preacher. Anwar could have killed hundreds, if he had waited until the evening rush hour, instead of late morning. He assumed Anwar wanted to demonstrate his power more than kill. Lance stayed away from the crews still combing the wreckage for evidence. He looked around in all directions to see if anyone looked out of place or appeared to be cataloging the onlookers. He saw no one. He closed his eyes and reviewed the dozens of photos and hours of video collected by Interpol. These gave him the perspective required to go out of body and look down on the scene in the minutes before the explosion.

In his wandering mind's eye, he surveyed the crowd visible in security camera footage. He looked for the case, but couldn't see it. The person or persons who placed it, knew where the cameras were positioned and avoided detection. It was a good job, for a mass murder. Message sent.

Decked out in a comfy tan cotton blend thawb and white ghutrah headdress, Preacher looked enough the part of a desert resident that no one gave him a second look.

He walked through dry, cool streets and alleys in ancient Cairo. The streets were bustling. Hard to believe that a bomb killed dozens a couple of streets over just a week before. When he came around a corner into an open area, he could see the destruction. Even though significant effort had been made to clean up the bloody mess, there was still much to do. Looking around, he saw shattered windows, blood splatters along rooflines, debris blown into the sides of buildings and piles of rubble waiting to be hauled away. One such pile was being loaded onto a dump truck by day laborers. Police stood watch casually around the perimeter. That was normal. A week and a day after a massacre was enough passage of time to allow people to return to habit, normalcy.

Preacher walked slowly to the left to get a better view of the scene. Two things were obvious. This was the work of more than one bomb. And this bombing was punishment. The message was plain to see – "you have sinned against Allah and Islam. You must pay."

He saw an old man sitting on a stoop across from the market and decided to approach him.

"Greetings sir," he said in Arabic.

"And to you my young man." The aged gentleman replied without looking up

"May I sit beside you?"

"Please," he waved his hand in a welcoming gesture.

Preacher squatted and then sat. He looked around for a full minute without speaking. "Such a waste. Such destruction."

"Have you traveled far to come see this destruction?" The old man knew Preacher's accent was not local.

"I am visiting from Jordan and felt the need to see for myself this horror. Useless."

"Not useless. No, very useful for sending a message I think."

Preacher glanced at the old man who continued to look straight ahead.

"And you, where have you traveled from to see this?" Lance placed the man's accent from Syria, maybe Iraq.

"Oh, I live here now. But I am from elsewhere."

"I see." Lance let it end there and silently watched the action before him. He observed the patterns, or remnants of patterns. In his months of bomb training at Harvey Point, he spent weeks on explosive design and blast radius analysis. He was especially intrigued by the destruction wrought by the shockwave blown out, or pushed, by the explosion. It often did extensive damage, but the debris following the blast usually gets the credit.

He could see where two bombs had been placed about 40 feet apart. Distinct craters showed where they had been detonated. The Egyptian Security Service's initial report estimated that each bomb was loaded onto a cart pulled by donkey. The explosive agent this time was apparently acetone peroxide. To add to the misery, the bombs were packed with nails, marbles and ball bearings. Brutally effective.

Thirty-eight were killed immediately. Another 16 died within days and more than 60 people were recovering from injuries. Preacher was about to excuse himself from his companion when something caught his eye. It was a strap, a camera strap. It extended out from underneath the old man's robe. It didn't fit. And then it clicked. Damn.

He had stumbled right onto someone watching the bomb scene, someone being paid to sit here and take photos of anything, or anyone, meeting a certain description.

"What do you have to report old man?" A harsh tone in his voice.

It caught the older man off guard. He began to turn his wrinkled head in Preacher's direction.

"Don't look at me." Preacher was abrupt and dismissive. "Keep your eyes forward and tell me what you have seen today and yesterday. I have not received a report in three days."

The man hesitated. He was not prepared for this.

"Quickly. I've wasted minutes sitting here beside you waiting for you to wise up. Get on with it." Preacher changed his accent to mimic the intonation he heard from a number of Saudi, Jordanian and Omani generals in the build-up to the brief Gulf War in January.

"I'm sorry. I did not expect your visit. I, I have been following my orders. I have delivered my reports and film as ordered." He was all apologies.

"Well then someone else has been lazy and slow. I am to travel to Libya this evening and need the latest information. Now, please." Preacher softened his tone slightly.

"Yes, of course. There is nothing new to report today. They continue the clean up. Investigators from Interpol were here yesterday, but no one today. I'm sorry. That is all."

Preacher didn't respond. He envisioned the process as he could see it unfolding. This man, and likely others, were paid a stipend to watch the bomb site each day and then drop their report and film in a box. From there, a courier would take it to another location where it would be picked up by someone who would then relay information and develop the film.

This was the kind of break that only comes to the lucky. Preacher shook his head at his dumb friggin' luck once again. *Better living through lies and deception.* He turned to the man. "Very good. Now, give me your ID."

"What? I'm sorry?"

"Your identification now, quickly."

The old Syrian reached into his robe and pulled out an ancient leather wallet. He extracted his identification card and hesitantly handed it to Preacher, still not looking him in the face. Preacher took the card, memorized its details and handed it back.

"Isaac, I thank you for your service. Please continue your procedures. I will report our conversation to my associates and commend you for your attention to detail. I will also call upon you at your home within the month for another assignment. Be ready for my visit."

With that, Preacher stood and walked away. It was almost 4 p.m. and Isaac would likely be leaving the bomb site within the hour. He needed to make himself scarce and watch the old man to be sure he was right about the process.

About 50 minutes later, he learned he was wrong. And 30 seconds after that, we was pissed off at himself. A motorcycle came around the corner and Isaac stood up. He pulled out a piece of paper and the film from the camera and extended his hand. The man on the motorcycle reached out and took the items and dropped them into a satchel around his neck.

Preacher was pissed because he had planned to follow Isaac on foot to a drop location and then follow the person who picked it up from there. A motorcycle changed things. As the driver revved the bike's engine while stopped at an intersection, Preacher had to think quickly. He looked around and saw his best, but still lousy, option. He hopped onto the bicycle propped up between two buildings and rode after the motorbike. Luckily traffic was heavy, which kept the man on the motorcycle from taking it up to speed.

Preacher stayed back 40 to 50 feet behind the bike. He didn't look too conspicuous on the bicycle. Many others were traveling in the same manner. At an intersection, the motorcycle turned onto a street with less traffic and accelerated. Preacher followed and pushed his legs hard to keep the motorbike in sight, hoping this didn't last too long, He was mostly healed from the wounds received in the Philippines, but his right leg was still raw and weak. And three weeks resting in paradise had not increased his stamina much. He was sadly out of shape and his lungs complained about it.

The courier on the motorcycle turned left at another intersection about 100 yards ahead. Preacher pounded on the pedals. His right leg screamed at the punishment. He rounded the corner and was glad to see that traffic was a little heavier. But the cycle was nowhere in sight. He pedaled furiously, looking right and left down each alley. Just before he reached the next intersection, he saw the driver getting off the cycle down a tight alley to the right. Preacher skidded to a stop and dropped the bike on the side of the road, walking on weak, shaky legs.

The rider stepped behind the motorbike and into a doorway. Lance looked in all directions and sprinted gingerly down the alley to the doorway. He peeked around and could see that the door led into a small lobby and up a set of stairs. He had no time to plan next moves, just react. He entered the building and snuck up the stairs. When he reached the step fourth from the top, he could see the motorcycle driver at the end of a hallway about 70 feet away. The man knocked on a door, reached into his bag and handed over the items Isaac hand given him.

No words were spoken. The courier then turned and walked toward Preacher. He stepped back down the stairs as quietly as his weak legs allowed. He stepped outside the screen door and into the alley.

Fifteen seconds later, the bike's driver emerged and walked over to his bike where Preacher was waiting for him.

The courier automatically grabbed his bag, protecting it. The bag, or any weapon or any defensive skills he possessed offered him little protection. Preacher had no patience for conversation.

"I know you are just a courier, but you have gotten yourself into something that you will likely not survive." He spoke Arabic, the accent from the desert Bedouins he encountered and lived among in Saudi Arabia.

"What? Excuse me?"

"I have no time for your lies or excuses. Tell me exactly what you know about this job, this courier circuit. Now." Preacher took a threatening step forward. Four feet separated them.

"I don't know- I just pick up things from one place and deliver them to another." The courier inched back.

"Who pays you?"

"I don't know. It is cash in an envelope handed to me through a slot in a door."

"Turn around. You forgot to give them something." Preacher didn't want to hurt him, but time was short. He needed to be back up the stairs and in that room now.

"No, please. I..." the courier pleaded.

Preacher cut him off. "This is simple. What is your name?"

"Kamil."

"This is simple Kamil. You will come with me back up stairs, or I will kill you now and put your jacket on and go back up the stairs. Decide now." Preacher took another step closer. It was menacing. His legs were almost back to normal from the bike ride.

"Please, I have a family, children." Kamil pleaded.

"So did I before they were killed by people you associate with." Preacher lied convincingly, as usual. "Now Kamil, I have no time." He took the last step and reached to grab Kamil's jacket lapel.

"Okay. I will go."

"Good. Now." He spun the courier and shoved him toward the door and reached into his thawb to pull out the gun he had shipped to himself at the Cairo Airport Sheraton. They walked back into the building and up the stairs. Kamil required a couple of pokes in the back to carry on. "Knock and tell them you forgot to give them something. Be convincing brother." Preacher put the gun's barrel to Kamil's neck to help him get this job done.

He knocked. Preacher stepped to the right of the door out of view of the peephole. Footsteps across the floor inside were slow, a heavy person. Someone leaned against the door to get a look.

"What do you want?" A man's voice muffled somewhat by the heavy door.

"I, I forgot something. I have it here for you."

"What is it?"

"A piece of paper. I forgot to give it to you. I am sorry." Kamil was convincing.

Locks on the door turned. The door cracked open a few inches. Preacher shoved Kamil to the side and exploded into the door. It connected with the man's head with a violent crush, a thud. He dropped as the door flew open. Preacher was three steps into the room in a flash. A man sat at a table smoking. Another was watching TV. Preacher was about to take a step toward a hallway to the right when the guy on the couch looked from him to the doorway. It was wrong.

Preacher dove to his left and rolled to look back at the door as Kamil came through with a gun leveled at him. They both fired. One of Preacher's two shots hit Kamil in the left shoulder. Kamil's shots were high, not compensating for Preacher's dive. The bullets struck the couch and the neck of the poor guy sitting there. He was a goner. Kamil stumbled back into the hallway and turned to run back down to the street. Damn. Preacher had read that one wrong. He was more than a courier, probably much more.

Preacher was back on a knee a moment later pointing his gun at the gentleman who had been smoking at the table. The guy was now up and reaching for a gun on the kitchen counter. Preacher had him clearly in his sights, but the hallway and what lay down it were a concern. He took a quick look around in that split second as the guy grasped the gun and began to turn towards him. Newspapers, computer, guns, a vest over a chair – he'd stumbled into a terrorist safe house. He'd been in half a dozen in Jerusalem, Germany and England. They all looked the same.

He made a split second decision. He needed Kamil more than these guys. He rose to his feet as the smoker began arcing the gun towards him. Thirteen feet separated them. Preacher wouldn't miss from this distance, he hoped. And he didn't, putting three successive bullets in the guy's chest, neck and chin. He too was a goner. Preacher stepped over to the heavy man knocked out on the floor and shot him in both knees. That would sting a little when he came to. He turned to the apartment's hallway and however many terrorists that might be cowering in other rooms. "I'm going back out to join the units surrounding this building. They have shoot to kill orders. Do yourself and this fool a favor and put bullets in your heads before we get you in a special room and find out where your families live."

He raced down the hall after Kamil. He could hear the sound of a key turning and a kick-start pedal. Preacher knew the bike wouldn't start. He had ripped off the ignition line in the seconds before Kamil came out. As he reached the stairs, he heard the cycle fall over. Kamil was taking off on foot. Good, well good on most days. We'll see here in a few minutes.

As the terrorist courier approached the end of the alley, he turned and pointed his gun at Preacher just coming out the door. It was about 110 feet. He'd have to be really good to make this shot. Still, Preacher plastered himself to the wall. The four shots were not even close. He thought, "this guy might be as bad as me."

Chase on. Preacher took off after Kamil. As expected, a song started in his head. He recognized the infectious drum beat immediately. The bass line came next. It was that song about addiction and love. Strange choice, but the DJ in his head was anything but predictable. He reached the street seven seconds later and turned in the direction Kamil had gone. He could see him up ahead elbowing his way through pedestrians and street vendors. At an intersection, Kamil stepped into the street and crossed right in front of a van that screeched to a swerving halt. Preacher took the opportunity to cross the street as well.

Doing so, he paid close attention to his right leg. It felt fine, but stiff. There was local pain at the wound sustained in the Philippines, but nothing serious for now. His shoulder felt fine as well. He increased his output and closed the distance. Kamil raced down an alley to the right. It looked dark down there.

Preacher reached the alley's opening and peeked around the corner. Right on cue, three shots were fired at his head as he pulled it back. People passing by dove to the ground. Ladies wearing scarves and burqas screamed. Preacher took in all their faces, or at least the eyes of the women. He smiled to reassure them. After waiting six seconds, he shot around the corner into the alley, zigging across the opening prepared to roll. No shots came. Kamil had moved on.

Preacher peered down the alley as the second verse of the song started. Lance looked down from 2,000 feet at the map of streets and alleys and ancient chaos below. It was basically a beehive. Kamil could go in seventeen, make that eighteen, directions. Which was best? Which one would he choose?

Preacher burst toward the far end of the alley, but stopped suddenly because Lance told him to. Kamil didn't run out the other end of the alley, he'd gone in one of the three doorways up on the right. He was likely crossing through a building to the next street over. Preacher smiled up at the empty sky as he spun on his heel and took off back up the alley to the street and then hung a left and then another. He was on a secondary street looking at the fronts of stores and a dentist's office. He slowed and hugged the building front.

Nine seconds later, Kamil came walking out of a record store about 65 feet in front of Preacher. The chase was back on as the terrorist swung his head to the right and spied his pursuer. Kamil raced to the end of this street and crossed the next intersection, running inside an old warehouse that had been converted to an indoor bazaar. It was going to be crowded in there.

Preacher made the door five seconds after his rabbit. Up ahead, he saw a table being flipped over and knew which direction to go – the other way, of course. He planned to overtake Kamil on the other side of the building as they raced in the general direction of the far end. Preacher came into an open area at the center of the building and knew before his first step that this was where Kamil had hoped to lead him. Sightlines were clear. There was good light from the open atrium. So Preacher dove to the ground and rolled to the right. He counted five shots hitting the wall above him.

Now, if the motorcycle driver/terrorist courier had a Sig Sauer like Preacher thought from the brief flash of black metal, then he had one more bullet in the chamber, unless he had another clip on him. Possible, but not likely in this scenario. Either way, Robert Palmer just kept on singing, telling whomever would listen that they might as well face it. People in the bazaar screamed and ran and screamed some more.

Preacher came up to his haunches behind a thick pillar and stuck his head around to see where the bullets came from. The place had gone apeshit crazy. Running, screaming, trampling, crashing, the place had it all. Preacher turned away from the direction he was expected to run and hightailed it out a door on the east side of the warehouse, along with dozens of shoppers. He raced to the north end of the building. As he rounded the corner onto a loading dock area, he slowed to a stroll and then watched moments later as Kamil ran out one of the bays and jumped to the street below. It was a very athletic move, especially for a guy with a bullet in his shoulder. Problem was, Preacher was now only 20-feet behind as they raced up the street to the next intersection.

From this close, he thought he could hit the guy in the leg with a bullet. But he was running, moving, jostling. No guarantee he'd hit his target. Kamil hung a right at the next alley. He was slowing down, getting tired. Preacher was there a moment later and closing the gap to 15 feet. A delivery truck blocked the way ahead. Kamil dove under it and scooted out the other side. Preacher chose to jump up on the front bumper and climb over. When he jumped down, he was only a few feet behind Kamil. Race over.

Like he'd done to Shafiq in Hamburg a year earlier, Preacher reached out and shoved the guy's shoulder. Except this time, the poor fella had bullet hole and blood soaking the shoulder. Kamil tumbled to the ground. Preacher stopped a few feet ahead and turned back to see something he didn't want to. Kamil had his gun out, but instead of pointing it at Preacher, he was moving it to his own open mouth. Clearly, he wouldn't be taken alive.

Options. Preacher could dive on top of the terrorist to rip the gun away. Probably wouldn't get there quick enough. He could shout out something provocative. Something like, 'I'm a friend of Anwar's' or maybe, 'I'm al Qaeda.' Decent options. But he chose a third. He already had his gun out, so before Kamil could get the barrel into his mouth, Preacher aimed and fired into Kamil's right hand holding the gun. The bullet exploded through skin and bone and tendon, releasing the gun by reflex. Pretty good shot, even though it was only nine feet away.

Kamil screamed in pain and then rolled to get on his feet. He was ticked, seriously pissed. He looked bad, but still came forward. His left shoulder and right hand were useless. So that basically left his legs. And Preacher was very impressed with the sweeping leg move Kamil attempted. But funny thing, it was the exact same move Shafiq tried in the alley in Hamburg. The similarities were striking and therefore not coincidental. They had trained together, or been trained by the same person. Damn. What kind of luck this was. Preacher shook that thought and put a straight arm down to deflect the kick. Kamil threw his good shoulder into Preacher's abdomen. Again, a good move.

Preacher pivoted and lifted the wounded man off his feet and spun him onto his back with a painful thud. Kamil's injuries were simply too serious for him to mount a threat. After getting his breath back, he attempted to get back up.

Preacher didn't want to extend this little episode any longer, so he stepped in to deliver a kick to Kamil's sternum that blew him off his feet. He then bent and punched the man in the injured shoulder. It was a mean, merciless even. The excruciating pain in the man's eyes was really something, so naturally, Preacher punched him there again. Kamil nearly passed out from the pain. That was fine.

Preacher leaned in to whisper in his new friend's ear, "Kamil, or whoever you are, stay with me for just a moment." He slapped his face gently. "Listen to me. You and me, we are going to be good friends. We are going to spend some quality time together and then you are going to tell me all about your friends and their friends and then about your family. And then I am going to kill all of them, every one. You took your chances back in the apartment and missed me. I don't hold that against you. But you have chosen the wrong life, the wrong side; to kill and maim and destroy others. You made the wrong choice brother. And now you are going to pay."

Preacher used the palm of his hand to deliver a vicious strike to the man's temple. Combined with his head striking the brick street below, the blow rendered the terrorist courier unconscious. Up above, Lance approved. First things first, he and Preacher needed to find a phone. They needed to call in transportation for two from Cairo to an undisclosed location. This is war.

Chapter 27

This might be insanity. Maybe just some remnants of his near-death experience. Either way, it was crazy.

The Gulfstream, piloted again by Lt. Meadows, cruised at 32,000 feet. But up there on top of the jet, riding along like he was straddling a horse, was Lance. He was transparent, like a ghost rider. The winds at 600 miles per hour just whipped right through him. Every once in while, he whooped and a hollered, like that guy in that crazy 1960's movie riding that missile.

Meanwhile, Preacher rode comfortably inside the aircraft sitting beside a shackled and bandaged terrorist. He would divulge more information about himself, his family, his friends and especially one Anwar Mohamed. Preacher didn't much care about the guy's background; he just wanted to know about Anwar's operations, his methods, his processes.

Preacher was probably freaking Kamil out just a bit with the conversation he was carrying on with Lance. The other two agents, sitting two rows back, didn't know what to think of it either. All they knew was this kid had clearance from the top for this trip, the very top.

Preacher closed his eyes and drifted back to Yap. He had done an excellent job keeping his new permanent out-of-body situation from Marta. She looked past his eccentricities, chalking them up to his brush with death.

It wasn't that, of course. Nearly being killed had changed him almost as much as she had. Granted, it did give him a new perspective on life – an overhead perspective that was always turned on. But it was not the new outlook on life others refer to after a near-death experience. He didn't find religion or a sense of living in the now. His near-death experience flipped a switch and turned something on in his subconscious. He had two views of the world at all times. Kind of like funky 3-D vision.

It was jarring at first, when he woke up in the hospital bed in Hawaii. The first thing he saw was Lance floating up there and simultaneously Preacher lying in bed. Before, it was one or the other. Seeing both was incongruent. But after several days, he got used to it, came to appreciate it. It was super cool.

The part about actually seeing Lance up there was a bit strange. He didn't know why it wasn't Preacher hovering overhead instead of Lance. The conversations, both verbal and non-verbal, between the two had become normal now seven weeks after nearing the pearly gates. He smiled at his personal insanity and turned to Kamil, who was looking at him from the corner of his eye with a quizzical look. Preacher hunched his shoulder and nudged his terrorist companion. It must have hurt, because Kamil cringed away.

"Where we're going is a very interesting place. It is between countries, outside international law. It is a place outside the jurisdiction of any sovereign nation. Really doesn't exist, not on any map or in any phonebook." He turned away. "In Western religions, it is commensurate with Purgatory, the place between Heaven and Hell. Do you know about Purgatory?"

He waited. Kamil had spoken very little. After knocking him out, Preacher dragged him off the street into a travel agency. He convinced the woman at the front desk not to call the police, because he was Egyptian secret service and his bloody, incapacitated companion was a wanted criminal. He used the lady's phone to call a local number that was relayed to another local number and connected with Cairo CIA operations. He requested immediate ground transportation, and to have air passage arranged for later in the evening. It was 4 a.m. when the plane took off from a private airport outside Cairo. That gave them time to bring in a doctor to dress Kamil's wounds. Overall, a fairly smooth operation.

"Yes. I know of this place, Purgatory." Kamil finally answered.

"Good, then you understand the basic concept. Now, what is interesting about this particular Purgatory, is that it is a black hole. Do you know what that is?"

"In space, a black hole, yes."

"Yes. Well this black hole we are traveling into is notorious for welcoming in humans of all kinds but never letting them leave. It sucks in bad guys, their friends and families and children and grandchildren. Most are never seen again. It is a little like all those people killed in that market last week. They were there one minute, and gone the next."

"It sounds frightening." Kamil smiled while saying this.

"I don't know about being scary. It is just inevitable. People like you made the choice to kill others, not thinking about what it means for families and loved ones. You consider their deaths acceptable in the eyes of Allah. So, in the same vein, the deaths of your family and friends are justified. They are demanded really. I have personally travelled throughout the Holy Land and through Persia and Indonesia, all the way to the Philippines, to gather family members and bring them back to this place so that they can share the same fate as your murdered masses. It is really quite beautiful, especially the children. Their faces, their minds, become so clear in those last moments. You'll enjoy pulling the trigger or slicing their throats with your blade. After the first few times, you realize you are relieving them of the burden of living in an unjust world."

"Pull the trigger? What do you mean?" Kamil asked.

"Oh, I'll hold your hand while you put the barrel of the gun to their heads or put the blade across their neck or hold their head under water. It is always the same, you'll fight at first, and then you'll look forward to it and even begin to exalt Allah as you dispatch those you love. You'll know you are sending them to a better place, a place you will never go, of course." Preacher smiled up at Lance whose hair was whipping every direction.

"You can try to place fear in me. Attempt to force me to confess and give you information about others. It will never work." Kamil was agitated, his fingers gripped into a tight fist.

"You'll talk. You'll tell us everything. You'll do it gladly. It's never failed. You will ask, beg me to kill you. I'll tell you no dozens, maybe hundreds of times. You'll devise very creative ways to kill yourself, including running headfirst into your cell wall or stuffing a towel down your throat. But you'll always pull back just a tiny bit. You won't follow through. Just like you weren't going to pull the trigger and kill yourself back there in the street. You just wanted me to act. I did. You lost."

"I've already won. Our victory is guaranteed by Allah. We are righteous in our actions." Kamil spoke assuredly.

"No. No. Don't confess now," Preacher put his hand on top of Kamil's. "Wait till we get there. You will see righteousness and true commitment to Islam. I forgot to mention, everyone working at this place is Islamic. They are brothers who know the true word. They are pure in their beliefs. And they are sure, 100% positive, that you and people like you, are wrong. Your precious al Qaeda is nothing but a disease, an infection."

Preacher turned away. That was about 10 minutes solid of lying. He'd made up every single thing he'd just told Kamil. But man, it was good stuff. Lance smiled down at him from up on top of the world.

Chapter 28

Account 347A: Message, Jan. 3 – Yodel mountain, rain preemptive.
Account 347A: Message, Jan. 5 – Onlooker rearview.
Account 347A: Message, Jan. 6 – Last bastion. Brick. Roll.

Seibel wanted to see him. It was January, 1992, five and a half months since the debacle on Tapul. He was back to full strength, injuries healed. All that was left were scars. No big deal, everyone has scars.

"Braden is pissed at you." Seibel sat across from him in an Augsburg bierhaus they had frequented over the years. Preacher's boss took another swig of his large mug of a local lager. "Says he hasn't seen you since last April. Has it really been that long?"

It had been all small talk so far. News, politics, even some sports that Preacher had no idea about. He was out of touch when it came to American sports. In the corner, a two-man oompah band started up. The noise was a relief. Lance, ever floating overhead, started nodding his head to the cacophonous beat. Preacher cracked up. Seibel took his laughter to mean general satisfaction with the music and environment. He smiled as well.

The music also meant the small talk was over. Seibel leaned in close. Preacher leaned in to hear him. "She's changed."

Vague, yet direct. The 'she' was Marta, of course. "I know."

"What, no denial?"

"Why bother. You know everything, right?" Preacher's smile was not one Seibel had seen before. It was jaded, well, more jaded than usual.

Seibel sat back and took another drink from his huge beer mug. The waitress took away their plates and offered another round of beers. They accepted. There was no rush. "You're different too."

This brought another burst of laughter from Preacher. "That's what Foxy said."

"He was right. It is obvious that she has had an effect on you. Well, her and spending a little time with the angels." Seibel was gifted at getting to the point without using concrete language. He was referring to Lance's near-death experience.

"Those angels were awful gnarly, wearing dark robes, with black eyes and a fiery smoke trailing behind them."

"Damn. You made some interesting new friends." Seibel could keep up with anything Preacher threw at him. Lance even laughed at that one from Papa.

"So, you were saying…"

"Our mutual friend has changed from the person she used to be, from the person I've known for years." Seibel looked off for a moment, seeing something other than what his eyes took in.

"So you saw her?" Preacher pulled him back with the words.

"Yes. Two days ago in Prague. Just for a few minutes. She was off to another appointment. Didn't have much time for me."

"How was she different?" Preacher asked.

"It was obvious. Didn't take any deep observation to see it." Seibel leaned in even closer; he wanted Lance to join him. He got Preacher instead. "She was not all there, holding something back. She was always so utterly focused, scary focused. The kind of focus that cuts through you." Seibel looked away again, remembering a young girl he met for the first time. "So seeing her now with her focus shattered, her attention somewhere else. It was obvious. It was you."

Preacher had been watching him and listening as best he could with the oompah twosome blaring and Lance up there bopping his head, tapping his foot on nothing. He shook his head to clear it, "So you're sure it's me and not something else, maybe the fun stuff she's dealing with."

"Jesus, you too." Seibel pursed his lips.

"What?" Preacher reached out and jokingly pushed Seibel's shoulder.

"I knew I was playing with fire, mixing up some unstable chemicals in a lab that I might have to pay the price with a shitload of collateral damage, but..." he shook his head again.

"But what?"

"I didn't expect this -- this change, this complete loss of focus. Damn."

It was Preacher's turn to laugh. He did so and slapped the table along with the rhythm of the music and raised his mug to toast and cheer the scene. "Here's to complete loss of focus."

Seibel was not amused.

Preacher finished the beer and brought the mug down to the table with a loud thud. "Let's go." He stood and threw a few bills on the table. Seibel finished his beer and followed.

They walked several blocks through a cold German night and ended up in the basement of a small apartment building. They sat on a bench in the hall outside a small laundry for tenants and continued their conversation from the pub. "What do you know about her current situation?" Preacher asked.

"Not much, other than she got herself into a never-ending shit storm with Cherzny."

"What do you know about him?" Preacher leaned forward, his elbows on his thighs.

"Quite a bit, but I'm sure it's less than you, and a lot less than she knows." Seibel leaned forward also.

Preacher needed more. "What do you know that I don't?"

"Probably not much, except that he is high value and protected."

"Protected? Why?" He raised his eyebrows.

"Interests, Lance. Lots of interests in lots of markets and market segments."

"Money. We want him protected because some people are making money off him?" Preacher shook his head.

"Not some people, everyone. He and his corrupt regime have brought a semblance of stability to Mother Russia and we want that to continue. That is the party line."

Preacher was a little agitated. "That your line?"

"I don't have a line. I follow orders."

"Crap. That's crap. You could turn this, work your magic."

"Nope. This is above my limits. Cherzny touches everything. He's built a web that we don't even have a 20% grasp on. It's everywhere. And you don't have any idea how it affects me to know she's caught in the middle of it." Seibel's head and shoulders drooped.

"You can get her out, you know you can."

"How? Smelinski was her bankroll, her firewall. He has dropped her, even more, he's been active in assisting Cherzny's operatives. Never thought I'd see that happen, but he, like everyone, is caught up in this web. No way out."

"So, he just cuts her loose. That's it, she's done." Preacher already knew all this, just wanted to hear Seibel's reaction.

Seibel was ahead of him, as usual. "Don't go where you are about to go."

"What, where?"

Seibel sat back, crossed his legs and turned to him. "I guess we should get to the point, right?"

"That's why you're here."

"Let it go. Don't continue down this path. You need to step away, convince her to run away, get out of the line of fire. There is no protection I can offer her now." His words were a scalpel cutting skin, exposing organs below.

"You're serious. You won't fight?"

"Can't fight. Not now. This is not one of her compartmentalized operations to take down a business unit or regional office or even a network. She signed her own death warrant the moment she uttered Cherzny's name to Smelinski."

It was Preacher's turn to get serious. Lance even lost the smile on his face sitting up there on a fluorescent light tube. "Then I'll have to."

"Preacher, don't do this. Convince her to stop, and maybe this will die down."

"That's why you're here isn't it? You came to tell me to end this or end up like all the others who've challenged Cherzny." For the next three minutes, Preacher recited the names of no less than 43 people who no longer breathed air or exhaled carbon dioxide because of Cherzny. He detailed types of death and the likely reasons. He did indeed know more about the man than Seibel. "He is mass murderer just as much as Anwar. He's a friggin plague spreading through Europe that will make its way to America before long."

Seibel was not moved by the soliloquy. Impressed, but not moved. "Cherzny is off limits. No more discussion. You need to understand that."

"Cherzny is dead." Preacher didn't miss a beat. "He was dead the moment he assigned resources to terminate her. And you know who is next."

"Smelinski?"

"Da."

"And then me?" Seibel saying this should have been a surprise, a shock. But Preacher wasn't playing games.

"Everyone dies."

They sat in silence for half a minute. Seibel returned to his elbows on thighs position. "It wasn't supposed to go this way."

"What? Your experiment?" Preacher knew exactly what Seibel meant.

"Yes. My little experiment and our government's multi-million dollar investment."

"You always knew that you were playing with fire, with her and me. We are who we are. You can try to repackage and repurpose, but Einstein's theory is difficult to refute."

"I'm not here to debate quantum physics, so let's get to the heart of this little matter and maybe you will open your eyes." Seibel stood for the next part of his speech.

"Please, go on." Preacher sat back. Lance leaned back against a stud in the wall above the ceiling.

"What do you know about her?"

"Come on, don't go with the 'you don't know her' line. That is cheap, so beneath you."

"Shut up, let me speak. You need to hear this." Seibel turned and stepped away to organize his thoughts. "You met someone named Marta Sidorova in Baghdad. You shot her a couple of times. You wanted to kill her, should have killed her. It would have been easier, but you didn't and here we are."

"Here we are." He couldn't help interrupting. Seibel ignored him.

"You went to see her in the mountains and from there, you two have become some kind of team. You've formed an alliance, but that alliance is built on lies, all of it. I'll ask you again, what do you know about her?"

"You know what I know."

"I don't. She is as gifted a liar as you, better in many ways."

Preacher recited the details he knew of Marta. He held back a few particulars, of course.

"Okay, not bad. Not a bad story either. You won't be too surprised to learn that most of it is false."

"Which parts?" Preacher sat forward.

Seibel leaned against the wall. He took a deep breath and began. "How did we find you?"

"The questionnaire. T-12A." Preacher referred to the single page form he filled out when he applied to take the Foreign Service Officer Exam back at the University of Tulsa in 1987.

"That's what we told you. And you believed it."

"How then?"

"You remember, I told you that you were and are still the only person to get a perfect score on that screwy thing"

"Yeah."

"That's true. But I fibbed a little when I said no one else ever came close. A 16-year-old girl completed the questionnaire and got an 87%. The highest score we had ever seen. So we looked into her. It was an amazing story, shocking really. She had killed her brother at the age of 11."

"Come on, this is ridiculous. It's reaching, weak." Preacher interrupted more forcefully.

"Please, let me finish. The girl was institutionalized, where she killed another child, a boy three years older than her. She was moved into a more secure setting where she proceeded to kill two male guards who tried to molest her. She was 15 by then. An instructor who worked with the girl found her to be gifted in a number of areas, but completely cut off emotionally from the world; an introvert in every aspect of the word.

"She was gifted at languages, reading comprehension and intricate math concepts. So the instructor had her take a number of assessments and tests. One of these was the Foreign Service Officer Exam and before that, she completed the questionnaire."

"So, you're saying Marta took the U.S. Foreign Service Officer Exam in Russia, the Soviet Union. Why would they do that?"

"I didn't say the girl took the exam in Russia." Seibel kept his eyes steady. Waiting for it to sink in. He didn't have to wait long with Preacher.

"Where then?"

"The girl was from western New York, right outside Buffalo."

It was Preacher's turn to sit forward with elbows on thighs. "What are you saying? Be clear."

"I don't have to tell you anything. I'm doing this to help you, to protect you from something you can never control. The girl in question, completed the questionnaire, took the exam, and three weeks later killed a seventh person. It was a fellow resident of a youth corrections facility. The killing was the state's last straw. They were set to turn her over to adult corrections. That's where I come in." Seibel adjusted his lean against the wall and crossed his arms. Lance, hovering just a few feet over his head, stared at the guy. This was one amazing story.

"Seibel to the rescue, right?" Preacher kept his eyes on the floor.

"That's right. I stepped in and gained her release into my custody."

"And then you shipped the little murderer off to the Soviet Union to become a double agent in training."

Seibel broke out into a broad smile. "Here's the kicker. You won't believe this, but guess what language the girl's parents and grandparents spoke around the house every day of her life?"

"Grandparents? You didn't mention them."

"They died by the time she was 8."

"And you're going to tell me that her parents and grandparents spoke Russian."

"Indeed. She spoke Russian as naturally as she did English. Maybe better."

"So you decided to drop her off on a street corner in Moscow. The KGB would eventually notice her skills."

"Actually, it's not much different than that. She was up for it; didn't take any convincing. She wanted something and someplace new 5,000 miles from the horror she had enveloped herself within in New York. We built an elaborate, yet sparse backstory for her in Novosibirsk. It wasn't hard to find a family that had been killed or disappeared at the right time. And it wasn't hard to pick orphanages and foster homes that have changed hands or burned down. She basically showed up one morning alone, tired and hungry on the doorstep of a church school that took her in and cleaned her up. Her special abilities soon put her on a fast track and few asked about her background because of her skill level; her potential.

"She showed great promise in language comprehension and strategic concepts, as well as tactical implementation. She was a natural. And the KGB found her by the time she was 18." Seibel smiled again. He was proud of what she had done. His crowning achievement.

The two of them looked at each other for a few moments. The game had changed again.

"A few minutes ago you mentioned finding me. Where were you going with that?"

Seibel pushed off the wall. It was a natural movement. He then turned away from Preacher, rubbing his forehead. This was unnatural for him. Lance was first to notice it and looked down at Preacher with furrowed brow. The ghost's procerus muscle tugged at his eyebrows. Preacher read the look. After all, it was his face up there. "Right after we were introduced to a young girl in western New York, we decided to do a database search into other violent crimes committed by youthful offenders. There were thousands, so we narrowed the search to killings, murders. One such suspicious event that popped up on the radar screen was a questionable suicide by a man in Fort Worth, Texas. The guy was such a prick, that no one looked too closely into the details. Nothing could be proven, because the scene was so clean, but it did raise a couple of eyebrows.

"Frank Wyrick was dispatched to collect data on the minor involved, one Lance Porter Priest, age 12. He came back with some interesting information about the boy."

"Jesus. When I was 12?" Preacher said the words, but Lance was doing the watching.

"So, you can imagine our utter surprise when your name flashed before our eyes again nine years later. Wyrick was dumbfounded when I called him with the news." Seibel smiled as he said the words, but he had turned away from Preacher again. Another unnatural move for Seibel. This time, Preacher didn't know how he did it, because the whole hovering, floating, going out of body thing was supposed to show him only what he could see with his own eyes. But, sure enough, Lance could see Seibel's face as he turned away from Preacher and looked down the hall to the doorway to the street above.

The hovering ghost glanced down the hall as well and saw the flash of movement in the darkness. It was tiny, almost imperceptible, but it happened nonetheless. What happened next took a total of six seconds.

Preacher burst up from the bench and exploded into Seibel, using his forearm to crash into his mentor's neck from behind. The effect of the blow was a violent collision of Seibel's head into the brick wall. He was stunned, but not out. As he started to slump to the floor, Preacher helped him get there quicker by delivering a chop to the right side of Seibel's neck and shoulder. The CIA legend was out cold as he hit the tiled floor. Before the older man completed his descent, Preacher turned and dove for the doorway into the small laundry area. As he did, he heard the tink-tink-tink of three metal objects striking the wall. They were fired from what sounded like an air gun, which meant they were tranquilizer darts. Damn.

Lance wanted to stay there and see who came down the hall. His best guess was Fuchs. But Preacher pulled him into the laundry. You see, the slow walk through Augsburg on mostly deserted winter streets to this destination was not chance. Preacher led Seibel here because he knew two secrets about this basement in this apartment building.

Like his childhood obsession with hide and seek, Lance had prowled the streets of Augsburg two years earlier when he was stationed here listening to radio transmissions emanating from the Soviet Union. He learned about secret places, tunnels and doors, like the one in the laundry leading up a flight of stairs to the main level. Once up the stairs, Preacher used the second secret he had discovered. The office on the main floor had a hidden door behind the wall near the desk that led down a tight spiral staircase to a service tunnel below the street. The stairway was probably built four or five centuries earlier.

Preacher climbed the stairs and closed the door behind him. Stepped into the office and opened the hidden door to the staircase, closing it behind. He was in the sewage level before anyone following him even made it up the small hidden staircase from the laundry.

He felt his way along the low, narrow tunnel for 200 feet and found the set of stairs he sought. It was tight like the others, and at the top he found a door that led into another apartment building. He silently stepped into a hallway, tiptoed down the hall and stepped out a rear door. He'd done this three times before, but usually late at the night or early morning.

Once outside the rear door of the apartment building, he climbed into a Volvo idling at the curb. Marta was behind the wheel. Her smile was delightful.

Chapter 29

Thursday, March 19, 1992 — Moscow, Russia

A brief trilogy of thunderous explosions brought fear and panic and destruction. The first ripped through the center of an apartment building, basically blowing out the core of the structure and slicing the east side of the building off. No one was killed in the blast.

The second explosion blew apart a dozen or so offices on the ground, second and third floors of a government office building approximately six minutes after and four and a half miles from the smoking hull of the first explosion. Again, no one was killed in the empty building.

The third explosion five minutes later was deadly. It occurred on the underside of a parked sedan with two men inside. The amount of material used in the charge was sufficient to blow a crater in the road, send the car 210 feet to the north and incinerate the vehicle's occupants. The buildings surrounding the blast were damaged extensively. However, no one else was killed.

Smoke billowed into the air above each site. Sirens wailed. Police and military were placed on the highest alert. Checkpoints were established in grids around each incident. The city of Moscow was shut down and shut off by this calamitous triple act of terrorism.

Within minutes, the media began talking about the blasts in relation to the three explosions from the year before, which were also separated by only minutes, but were thousands of miles apart in Zagreb, Chechnya and Cairo. Investigators examining the sites would all find traces of the same materials, devices and accelerants used in the bombings from the previous year. It was obvious to anyone that the bombings were related. The methods, the directional shaping of the explosions, the source of detonations, were all similar. They all pointed to one conclusion – this was the work of the same bomber. This was an attack on Moscow, the heart of Russia.

And within hours, video and grainy images surfaced referencing one individual – a bomb maker named Anwar, who fought against Soviet soldiers under the name Mohamed in the mountains of Afghanistan. He was implicated because he had obviously done this. He had finally attacked Russia in retaliation for the Soviet Union's invasion of Afghanistan in 1979. He was a fighter for jihad, a Mujahedeen. He was a known killer of hundreds of Red Army soldiers. He was an expert in explosive devices detonated by remote, by fuse and by radio. He was a murderer.

The media and law enforcement focused on the three Moscow bombings. In doing so, they missed three others in the country. At a private airport 60 miles southeast of the Russian capitol, a Learjet was incinerated from within via an accelerant that raced through and ravaged the aircraft's fuselage as it sat parked in a secure hangar. The hangar was empty. No one was hurt in the flash fire.

They also missed a mountain dacha in the hills outside of Stepantsminda, Georgia that collapsed and avalanched down the side of a mountain when the pylons holding it in place from below were blown out at their metal roots. The multi-million dollar structure was a total loss. Good thing it was empty. No one killed.

The final bomb ignited to create smoke and flames on the shimmering waters of Sevastopol Bay on the Black Sea. The 110-foot sailboat burst into flames and lit up the marina. It was a total loss with crews unable to reach it before it burnt to the water. Good thing no one was on board.

To the casual observer of the evening news, the explosions did indeed appear to be the work of terrorists attacking mother Russia. For the more informed, the attacks could all be directly tied to one individual – Kirill Cherzny. Each of the properties, structures and vehicles destroyed by the bombings were his. Only those very informed about Cherzny's extensive holdings would be able to piece all this together. Marta Sidorova and her partner Lance/Preacher Priest knew more about the Russian oligarch's operations than most, a lot more.

Marta knew she could drive, or better, herd Cherzny to a location of her choosing by eliminating his options. It was a gamble, but she had a secret weapon. This weapon just happened to be an expert at planning, building, placing and detonating bombs.

Preacher wanted desperately to help Marta get out of the mess she found herself in when she set her sights on Cherzny. But he also quite selfishly wanted to put on a public display that could only be traced back to Anwar. Strategically planting his name and image with certain people and specific locations helped implicate the terrorist.

They found a beautiful alliance in their consolidated union. The two of them had still not talked about the 800-pound gorilla in the room. Preacher kept his conversation with Seibel to himself. He didn't care if they withheld a few things from each other. Heck, if she was withholding the fact that she was not born in Russia, he was keeping his little floating other self thing a secret from her. In many ways, they were like any couple in that aspect – they kept parts of themselves secret from their loved one. Nothing strange there.

The fact that they were lovers on the run from the former KGB, the CIA and the tentacles of a Russian kingpin made their relationship a little more interesting than others. But again, life is strange.

Preacher stood exactly 172 feet from the house at the center of a large compound in the northeast section of central Moscow. He hid behind a towering oak tree in a garden area to the east of the house. From his vantage point, he could see both the front and rear entrances to the compound. It should be any minute now. Cherzny's vehicle had pulled in two minutes earlier. The head honcho was inside with security personnel stationed at the front and rear doors. It wouldn't be long until others arrived.

Marta was nowhere in sight. That was because she was inside. This home, beautiful by any standards, was the residence occupied by Cherzny's longtime mistress Anna. He moved her here three years earlier for several reasons. One of the important reasons being the underground infrastructure he was able to construct. The home could be transformed into a base of operations if necessary. After the explosions now 40 minutes old, it was necessary.

Inside, Cherzny composed himself in the front foyer. He looked into the full-length mirror on the wall. He didn't like what he saw. Cherzny was shaken by the events of the last hour. He frowned at himself and exhaled. He was in control and would find out who did this and make them pay. They always paid.

The powerful oligarch walked down the hall to the kitchen that had a small dining room attached. Anna was sitting at the table. She too looked shaken. He looked at her and followed her glance to his right, turning his head to look into the kitchen. Marta leaned against the counter with a gun in her right hand and her left index finger pressing a small earphone to her left ear. She wore a black wig and fake beard. Cherzny opened his mouth to speak, but Marta raised her finger to stop him. She turned her head to listen and then turned back to him.

"Go ahead, please." She was quite polite.

"I was going to say that I assume you killed Ivan."

"Anna's bodyguard?" She asked.

"Yes."

"Yes I did. It was quick and painless. More mercy than he deserved."

Cherzny turned to Anna. "No need to worry my dear. She is not here to harm you. It is me she wants. She is fascinated with me for reasons I can't fathom." He took a step toward the dining table, very confident for someone so close to death. "And your being here certainly confirms my first impression of all this destruction today."

Marta smiled. "You thought it was others, competitors at first. Probably Karlov. After him, you thought of the Kiev gang. I know very well the way you think through a challenge."

Cherzny furrowed his brow at that. The look gave him away. She was correct. "No. I knew it was you. Not acting alone of course." He pointed to the radio headset as evidence of her reliance on a team to put all this in motion.

Marta shrugged, "Regardless, your operations have been dealt a serious blow tonight. You have lost huge amounts of data in your computer warehouse and a good many of the key individuals you rely on to maintain your empire have been compromised or killed."

Cherzny maintained his cool exterior, but his hand trembled as he brought it up to adjust his tie.

Marta looked away as Preacher's voice came over the headset. "Go." Her one-word reply to his request. She pushed away from the counter and let the gun sag at her side. "Prepare for a little noise in a few seconds. And I'd advise ducking." Right on cue, four explosions shook the night. Heavy drapes kept shards of glass from flying across the room. The explosions rocked the house, rattling art on walls and knocking dishes from shelves.

Marta stood and walked over to the table, a couple of feet from Anna. "That last round was my cue to get moving. Anna, before I go, the wire transfers to the locations we discussed are all confirmed. Do you have anything to say to Kirill?"

The attractive women in her early 40s looked from Marta to Cherzny. The surprised look on his face was priceless. Anna raised a gun she had been holding under the table and pointed it at her lover, her keeper. Her hand did not tremble. She pulled the trigger four times, putting four bullets into his chest. He fell to the floor gasping, sputtering. It was an anti-climactic death for a man who had destroyed so many lives. But Marta considered it a fitting end.

Anna jumped to her feet and dropped the gun on the table from her gloved hand, momentarily frantic. Marta stepped to her and took her shoulders.

"You did well. You are free. Now, upstairs to your room, your closet. You are the anguished mistress. You need tears and hysteria. In three days, you can leave. Go anywhere; no one will care about you." Marta picked up the gun from the table as the woman fled the room.

In seven trips to Moscow over the last eight months, Marta had embedded herself in Anna's life after casually bumping into her in a department store one afternoon. In ensuing visits, she had learned of the woman's plight, her fears for her life once she became too old for Cherzny. Marta learned of the mistress' hatred for her captor. So Marta offered her the opportunity to escape. But she needed to take the final step herself. And she had done just that with those bullets in her oppressor's chest.

"Two entering from north. Remaining sentry on south is out." Preacher's voice rang in her ears.

A few minutes earlier, four large all-terrain vehicles had arrived. Preacher knew the vehicles because he had been lying under each early this morning. Underneath each, he had attached an explosive device that required only a brief radio signal to detonate. As they pulled into the courtyards at the front and rear of the compound, Preacher toggled levers on the remote he held in his hands, after he had put plugs in his ears and stepped behind the towering oak, of course.

The explosions were ferocious. The men inside three of the four vehicles were incinerated in moments. The fourth vehicle was blown sideways and toppled over, but its occupants were not killed instantly. Preacher was headed toward the overturned vehicle when two men raced from it to the north door, requiring him to alert Marta over the radio.

"Thank you," she replied and moved down the hall to the foyer, where she slid to the floor and waited. Outside, Preacher approached the one vehicle not in flames to peer inside. The two men in the vehicle were unconscious, piled on top of one another. He turned toward the rear door to the home and raced across the ground in the darkness with only flames lighting the night. He too wore a black wig and beard.

The two Cherzny security members had split up upon entering the home. The one that found his way into the foyer from the rear was met with a silenced bullet an inch above the space between his furry eyebrows. "I'm coming in." Preacher whispered.

"Go to your left." She replied.

He complied and hugged the wall as he followed it to the left. Marta rose from her prone position and moved back down the hall toward the kitchen. She knew the layout of the home well, having been inside several times. The guy had only one way to a back foyer near the kitchen. Marta knew this and slid to the floor again in the kitchen listening for any footfall. She didn't need to remind herself of their need to be out of the house very soon.

The lone remaining Cherzny security operative hugged the wall and aimed his automatic rifle into the kitchen, preparing to enter. The instant he stuck his head around the doorframe, it was hit by three shots. One from Marta and two from Preacher behind. The man crumpled. Marta scrambled to her feet. Preacher stepped to meet her. Even with a beard and bad wig, he wanted to kiss her, to ravage her. Later.

"Let's move." They said in unison, in Russian. They raced back down the hall into the foyer and out through the back door. If they had taken the time to look at themselves in the full-length mirror, they would have seen two Arabic men in beards run by. Kind of funny.

Chapter 30

Once out into the night, they ran across the rear courtyard littered with debris from vehicles blown apart by explosions. Marta diverted to look into the vehicle tipped over on its side. Preacher heard two silenced shots while she was out of view. She did the job he should have done minutes earlier.

Sirens wailed in the distance. They ran out the gate, down and street where they rounded a corner and hopped into a waiting sedan. Marta leapt behind the wheel, since she was the better driver of the two. They were at the end of the block when three police cars came around the corner. She slowed to let their headlights wash across their vehicle. It worked, they were spotted and two of the three police cars fell in behind their car as they fled the smoldering scene behind. A minute and a mile later, another two vehicles joined the chase. They were plain, dark colored sedans, which gave them away as KGB, now renamed the FSB or Federal Counterintelligence Service. Who could keep track these days.

Marta jammed the accelerator to the floor, accelerated into corners, barreled down straight-aways and splattered into other cars entering major thoroughfares. She knew the streets of Moscow, knew them by heart. It was amazing to Preacher, and

Lance sitting atop the vehicle, watching her work behind the wheel. She was simply marvelous, Preacher and Lance agreed on the description. More cars joined the parade as they veered off a major city street into a smaller business district with much tighter roadways.

This chase lasted 11 minutes and it worked to perfection in bringing attention to them. Preacher leaned out the window several times and took some lousy shots at the tires of cars pursuing them. It was a lame attempt to emulate the movies, but one actually hit a tire. Friggin' amazing for him. Marta was enjoying herself and even reached out and smacked his butt one time as he leaned out.

At the 12th minute, Marta changed course and made a u-turn on Tverskaya Ulitsa, back toward the destination they had passed a few minutes earlier. As they approached, she slammed on the gas and got decent separation from the police vehicles close behind. The underground parking structure up ahead was massive. It could hold thousands of cars. Right now, it was mostly empty.

Their vehicle went airborne as they hit the entrance ramp into the structure at 70 miles per hour. As they passed the pylons supporting the structure's main entrance, Preacher toggled a switch on his handy little remote and the blast behind them brought down several tons of concrete onto the entrance ramp, blocking it immediately. They both looked up into the security camera to be sure it caught their bearded faces.

A few moments later, he pushed another lever and the entrance at the far end of the massive structure exploded. A third toggle brought a third and final blast at the remaining entrance.

All vehicle entrances and exits were blocked. But doors were aplenty, so they needed to move quickly. Marta swung the car around a turn and raced down a ramp to a second level underground. The area around the car was deserted.

They jumped out and ran over to a service door. Preacher hit the last lever and a small blast followed by disbursement of a rapid accelerant shook the vehicle and engulfed it in flames in seconds. Everything inside was charred to a blackened crisp.

Marta inserted a key into the service door handle and opened it. Inside, they entered a stairwell that took them down two more levels into a tunnel that lead away to the north. They ran without speaking along the dimly lit route. As they approached a door marked exit, they stopped to catch their breath and looked at each other. They couldn't resist and grabbed the other to pull close. Two Arab-looking dudes kissing in a dim corridor. Funny stuff for Lance to watch from his perch over Preacher's shoulder. His laughter infected Preacher, who began laughing as well seeing what Lance could from up there.

Marta didn't know why he was laughing, but joined in. They were nearly free and a little chuckle was in order. She ripped off his fake beard and the wig from his head. She pulled out a moist towel in her bag and wiped his face. He did the same for her, kissing her several times during the process. They each removed as much makeup as possible and changed clothes. He got into standard western blue jeans, a sweater and coat. She put on black jeans, boots with heels, a sweater and long coat. She took off her wig and let her hair down and became the beauty he loved to look upon.

They placed their dirty clothing, beards and wigs in the bag and stepped to the door. They looked again into each other's eyes and kissed gently. Without a word, they opened the door and climbed the dark stairwell that led to an empty outdoor mall. He turned left, she turned right. They would see each other again.

Chapter 31

Three men watched three separate televisions reporting news from Moscow. One of them was just miles away from the destruction. The other two were in the U.S.

Gregor Smelinski saw images on the screen and heard the inane jabbering of news anchors broadcasting from Moscow television stations, but nothing was sinking in. He'd been on the phone since minutes after the first blast, and made his way into his office in the Lubyanka, the home of the KGB. Reports came in about sightings of several bearded Arab men near the sites of the explosions in the days leading up to the detonations. The chase from a residence to the underground parking facility had produced a great many reports from FSB operatives and local police. They were preparing to enter the structure, with all entrances and exits now secure.

If any of the attackers were in the underground facility, they would be captured or killed. The chatter on the lines increased as heavily armed crews prepared to breach the structure.

They wouldn't find anyone. She was gone, disappeared. Smelinski sat back, turning away from the TV. Gregor the Terrible felt relief. The man who had controlled his life and those of thousands of others for much of the previous decade was gone. If not dead, Cherzny was severely injured, reduced to a pitiful creature. She had planned this well, executed it flawlessly and escaped. She created a massive and intricate deception that implicated Arab and Islamic terrorists. The first security camera images from the bombsites were beginning to show up on news reports, each showed bearded, dark haired and dark skinned men. He smiled at the extent of the production. "Brilliant." He whispered with eyes closed.

He opened his eyes to look at the watch on his wrist. He could stay here in this building for days, weeks even. But one day soon he would die. She would see to that. She was too slick, too sharp. He smiled again at her abilities. "Amazing." He muttered in English for some reason.

The phone on his desk interrupted the jabbering on the television. It was a secure line. Nine people had this number. He spun the chair back around and reached for the receiver. When he brought it to his ear there was only silence at the other end. It was Marta.

"Da." He spoke after 10 seconds.

"Enjoy your freedom Gregor. I'll collect on this debt in the future. Any further action will result in something unpleasant." Her voice was calm, cool and he could feel it, she was close. Maybe watching him right now. He glanced at the window.

"I understand my dear. And I am quite impressed." His relief came through.

Then Marta dropped a bomb. "Major will receive this same call in a few minutes. Goodbye Gregor." The line went dead but Smelinski held the receiver to his ear. The dial tone droned on for 20 seconds as the KGB master of the universe traversed time and space reviewing her career, her time in the KGB and before. She just exploded a significant portion of Smelinski's mind with one word – Major. It was their personal code for Geoffrey Seibel. They were the only two who used this code. If she was calling Seibel next, it could only mean that she had been doing the CIA's bidding as a double agent. She had fooled Smelinski all along.

He felt the muscles in his chest tighten. Marta wanting to kill him was fine, understandable. Her being an operative for Seibel was more than shocking. The American had done it to him yet again. How? Where did he intercept the girl? Damn.

Just under 4,853 miles to the west and south, Geoffrey Seibel watched CNN in his home office. It was just after 1 p.m. in Washington. Eight hours earlier than Moscow. The images coming in were really something. Four massive explosions now reported. A chaotic chase through the streets of the Russian capitol apparently ended with the terrorists cornered in a downtown Moscow parking garage. News of Islamic fundamentalist terrorists behind the plot was already spreading. They even mentioned Anwar by name. This was brilliant. Completely ballsy, and completely, utterly, brilliant. Seibel couldn't help but smile.

He looked at it all behind closed eyes. He could see the structures damaged, the pattern utilized and the strategy behind the plan. The bombings had steered Cherzny toward a defined location where, more than likely, he had met his demise. He would no longer be a stabilizing force for international commerce. Underlings, competing interests and the growing international strength of the Russian mob would carve up his empire. That was unfortunate, but Cherzny's fate was sealed the moment he ordered action against Marta. He was just like all the other men who thought they could control her. All were wrong. Most were dead. One day soon, he would join them.

Seibel had been on the phone with several people during the last two hours. He, like them, did not have much information about the Moscow attacks. It was all educated guesswork. Granted, he did know exactly who had orchestrated and carried out the attacks. But he didn't share this with anyone. He withheld this even from his boss, the CIA Director. He'd tell him later, when he had all the facts.

He closed his eyes and saw both of them. He swelled with pride thinking of the sheer brilliance, the catastrophic brilliance the two of them represented. He had played a part in bringing them both into this life and developing their skills. He knew he could not claim their innate abilities toward mischief, lying and killing, but he had guided Marta, and then Lance. Damn, they were good. She was ruthless and cunning and deadly. He was flexible and dishonest and despicable. They were perfect, perfect for each other. And uniquely dangerous for the rest of the world.

Seibel looked at the phone on his desk and wondered who would call first. He guessed it would be Lance. He was wrong.

The phone rang three minutes later. It was Marta.

"You've seen?" Her question was short. The conversation would be as well.

"Yes. Watching now. Very impressive." His reply was short also.

"I'm signing off for now. Don't look me up." Translation – don't come looking for me and don't send anyone else.

"Understood. How long?"

"Time and tide will tell. Circus received the same message."

Damn.

Seibel gripped the phone tight in his hand. She told Smelinski. Nearly 11 years of deceit revealed. "Understood." He whispered. He just lost his most precious weapon. She was alive, but no longer his secret. The question now -- did Smelinski know about Lance?

"Goodbye." Her voice had a smile to it and then it was gone, replaced by a dial tone.

Geoffrey Seibel, spymaster, ringleader, legend, replaced the receiver on the phone. He couldn't help but smile, even though he'd lost her. She had been a marvel from the beginning and he would undoubtedly see her again. She deserved a break, a vacation from the death and destruction she had wrought on his behalf. She would return to him one day, and likely put a bullet through his brain. That was fine. He deserved it. He couldn't think of a better way to go.

And then he thought of Lance. Dying at his hands would be justice as well. That's what you get for playing both Machiavelli and Pygmalion.

Two hundred and eleven miles to the north and slightly east, Anwar Mohamed Mustafa sat in a Brooklyn diner finishing his lunch and watching the television hanging in the corner of the room. He was clean-shaven, his hair short. He could be Italian, Spanish, Turkish, Greek or any number of ethnicities. When he was apart from his operatives in Manhattan and New Jersey, he left behind his Arab persona. Earlier this morning, he walked block after block on this fine spring day. He smiled at others along the way.

This was one of his favorite places to eat in New York. He loved the mashed potatoes. The secret was leaving the skin on and just the right amount of garlic. He scooped up last a bite of his potatoes and wiped his mouth. A swig of coffee washed down the meal. He kept his eyes on the television screen and CNN's reporting of the Moscow bombings. A very impressive operation.

His eyes squinted slightly when the first grainy image from security cameras showed up on the screen. In the next minute, an image captured seven years earlier on a hillside in Afghanistan filled the screen. Damn. It was him. A lousy photo, but him nonetheless. He'd seen the photo before. An operative who was given the printed photo in Jordan showed it to him. The image was proof they had very little good intelligence on him. He had eluded them for more than a decade now.

The audio on the TV was turned down low so he could only see images and the computer generated text and graphics on the screen. The American anchors were attractive and pleasant to look upon. It was all so childish. The waitress stopped by to take up his plate and pour more coffee. He thanked her in accented English and then looked out the window into the street. He pieced together what he had learned over the last hour. Four explosions for sure. Images of Arabs captured by nearby security cameras. His fuzzy bearded image splashed onto the screen in connection with the bombings and now with the bombings from seven months earlier. People attempting to flush him out orchestrated it. People who did not have much information about him were attempting to force his hand, to force him out into the open. He smiled for a brief moment. He was out in the open right now. He was walking among them. One of them.

So who was behind this? KGB, CIA, Mossad? They were grasping at straws floating in water. Again, it was so childish; so beneath them. It stood no chance of succeeding and they knew it. So why? It certainly raised the level of the game, but it really put them no closer to tracing him. He was a continent away from the action in Moscow. The questions were many. The answers unsatisfying. His operatives in and around New York would certainly be excited and agitated by this news. The blind cleric would see this as another opportunity to inflict pain on this infidel nation.

Anwar put a few bills on the table, got up and walked out. The spring day had warmed even more during the last hour. He decided to walk several more blocks and couldn't help but smile as he did so.

Chapter 32

Wednesday, August 12, 1992 — undisclosed location

Kamil al Ransfri wasn't praying. At least not nearly as habitually as he had been before he was shot, chased and captured by Preacher in Cairo. For whatever reason, and he knew the reason, he had lost faith. He also knew this was a sin that would keep him from a life of eternal bliss, but he was simply changed by the experience. Preacher had changed him.

It started on that plane over the Mediterranean Sea. It continued during conversations in the bleak and dark prison he now called home. The change was cemented by the actions George, a.k.a. Preacher, reported back to him in the months since.

Kamil's family had been destroyed. His younger brothers killed. And his Imam had disavowed him as a heretic, an infidel who faltered when faced with a challenge. Kamil was at a spiritual crossroads. He should have prayed three times today already, but hadn't. He just didn't have it in him.

Even on the occasions George showed up and asked him to join him in prayer on the floor of the tiny cell, he could not do it. Maybe it would come back. Probably not. He had traded his soul for those of the innocent people he had killed in the market in Cairo when he pressed a button. George had shown him photos of the people he had killed, the children. They were innocent and did not deserve their deaths. No amount of devotion could make up for murder. It was wrong, and Allah had punished him accordingly by sending an avenging angel. George was his name. And he was surely the righteous hand of God and the Devil in one. He was truly evil, yet truly loyal to his beliefs. He was a dichotomy, a living example of the battle taking place inside each of us. George was good and evil, life and death.

Kamil was ready when the knock came on his cell door. It was him. He'd been informed this morning that George was coming. He looked forward to these visits because they were so challenging, so informative. The man who'd bested him and placed him in the proverbial chains that bound him, was his sole contact with the outside world. He usually brought unhappy news, but it was news nonetheless.

The door opened and Preacher stood there smiling. He was dressed in simple clothes. His hair dark, eyes brown, skin darkened. "Greetings Kamil, friend." He waved for the prisoner to follow him. A guard stood 12 feet away. He was not necessary. Kamil knew George could kill him in a dozen ways. It would be a fine death, a deserved end.

"Greetings George. You look well." They walked down the corridor to another door that opened as they approached. After walking through it, they turned to enter an interrogation room that had been transformed. Metal chairs and tables were replaced with two soft leather chairs and a cherry wood table. A pitcher of ice tea and two glasses sat on a serving tray on the table.

"Have you been praying?" Preacher asked as they each took a seat.

"Some, not every day." Kamil responded, resigned to his fate.

"You struggle, I can see. I understand."

"Do you?" Kamil was nearly broken.

"I am not comfortable with all that I have done. I know it is wrong to kill, but I also know it is necessary to punish, to avenge. Yet who am I to enforce laws written by men who can only guess at God's intentions? That is my challenge." Preacher was pious, devout. A floating Lance loved the show he was putting on below. Lance also thought for a moment about being an angel. Maybe that's what he was really. Perhaps he had died and left his earthly body behind and now floated on breezes and currents. This made him laugh. Preacher was interrupted by Lance's laughing and glanced up at him with his brow furrowed. Kamil thought is was just another example of George's insanity, his divine inspiration.

"Why have you come to see me today?" Kamil got right to it. "What news do you bring from the world?"

Preacher poured them each a glass of tea and settled back in his chair. "There has been more death at the hands of those you associate with. They attacked the heart of Russia with many bombs. Scores died and many more were injured. Most innocent, of course."

"I am sorry to hear this. I know that Russia is home to a great many infidels, but also many of faith. I will mourn the innocent." Kamil bowed his head.

"It was Anwar. He coordinated a spectacular attack, brilliant really. His choice of explosive device and explosive agent was similar to the one you detonated. Could have been many more deaths, but the toll was still very high." Preacher sat forward and took a drink of tea. He was the image of conviviality, sitting across from a terrorist who'd killed dozens and been trained by Anwar to kill many more.

"I assumed that's what you would tell me. That's why you are here."

"To talk about him?" Preacher replied.

"Yes, to delve into my head again to look for him. I don't know why you keep trying. I don't mind your visits, even enjoy them. But I don't know any more. I have nothing more to add. I've told you everything I know of the man. I owe him nothing. I don't protect him with secrets." Kamil was open today. The news of the Moscow bombings had affected him.

"I'm not here to mine you for more data. You know I enjoy your company. I benefit from just being near you."

"How is that?" Kamil tilted his head, like a puppy.

"What do you mean?" Preacher just smiled.

"How does being here help you? How do you benefit?"

Preacher continued to smile at him. He then sat up, turned away and shook his head as if to clear a thought and turned back. When he did, his face was different. It was sallow, a little haggard. The skin hung as Preacher relaxed his corrugator spercilii muscles above his eyebrows along with his zygomatic major muscles on his cheeks. He adjusted his position and pose until it became obvious to Kamil. The terrorist was looking into a mirror of sorts. His eyes squinted and he moved his left hand to his chin. Preacher did the exact same with his eyes and hand, but it was his right hand to provide a "reflection" of Kamil.

"What are you doing?" Kamil's voice rose slightly with the question.

"What do you mean?" Preacher's reply was in the terrorist's exact vocal tone and quality. The accent perfect.

Kamil continued to squint and then leaned forward. Preacher did the same. It was eerie.

"How, how do you do this?" Kamil tilted his head ever so slightly while asking the question.

Preacher's head tilted, "I'm sorry, have we met? My name is Kamil al Ransfri from Syria. I don't believe I've had the pleasure. It is an honor to make your acquaintance." And Preacher held out a hand, but the way he did so was different, it was Kamil's hand, his movement.

Kamil just sat there. It came to him after a few moments. The realization was sublime and he smiled. "You have been portraying me. Out in the world, you have been acting as me." His smile became a short laugh. Hard to tell if he was scared or impressed.

Preacher mirrored the smile and laughed as he spoke, "I am you. I have been Kamil for months. I have traveled far and been introduced to many, many brothers dedicated to our cause. I have helped in several projects, including the one just completed in Moscow. It was glorious, beautiful really. I was close enough to feel the heat. The wind, pushed by the blast, caressed my face. It was a glorious blow struck against the infidels." Preacher's eyes opened wide and wild. He was a true believer.

After a few moments, Kamil caught his breath and his head cleared. "That is why you have come back to me time after time. You needed a little more of me to put on your show, to become me."

"No, no not at all. I have been you since the first time we parted. I have mingled with others in our cause who have known you for years and have not doubted me in the least. You see, you have the perfect visage for me. I saw it the moment you road past on that motorcycle. Your light skin and subtle western features were ideal. It was just so perfect, don't you think?"

"Quite amazing."

"And Anwar, or Mohamed as he still prefers, has been most welcoming. He is quite pleased with my, our abilities." Preacher turned his hand over as he said this. His open palm signifying openness, humility. It was time for the gamble. "I have been on the periphery mainly to this point. He had not invited me into his closest company, he allows only a few to know his plans, as you know. But he has seen fit to give me more responsibility in each mission. I believe I have earned his trust, his respect. He is truly Allah's hand. He brings justice to the earth through Allah's wrath." Now, to see if it worked.

Kamil sat motionless. He was confused, shocked. That was good. A confused man can be coerced to act, to make mistakes. Preacher waited patiently. "He, he welcomed you?" It was a good start.

"Yes. I did not push in the least. I waited for his call, and when he beckoned with a small assignment, I delivered a solid performance. Very professional." Preacher was modest, respectful in his demeanor. His head bowed.

"Did he ask you about my father?" Bingo. Kamil was bare, open.

"He mentioned our father, spoke in reverence of his memory." Preacher's head still bowed.

"He was a great man and Anwar knew of his piety, his commitment to Islam and freedom." Kamil looked away. He looked at his father in his mind. It was time.

"He finally welcomed me into a meeting, a gathering of leaders over tea."

"He did?" Kamil was proud.

"Yes. He shared only the framework, the outline of his master plan that only a select few have been blessed to hear. He gave no time frame, and only mentioned that it would be on a scale not seen before. It will shake the world, bring the infidels to their knees."

"It will. It will. More than anything before, it will strike fear into their souls and make them question their support of Israel." Kamil let slip more than he intended. Preacher gave no notice of this information, only agreeing with a nod. He smiled back at Kamil with the terrorist's own smile, the same fire in his eyes. It was a magical moment.

"The American Devil. He will pay with blood, with death." Preacher whispered.

"Yes. Glorious death." Done. He had what he needed.

Preacher wanted to explode, to rise up and rain pain and misery and more pain down on this speck of humanity. But Lance stopped him. Just as Preacher was readying his attack, Lance came down from the ceiling and sat cross-legged in the middle of the table. It calmed Preacher down. The two of them just looked at each other. Lance spoke first.

"Looks like you did it buddy." He smiled as he said it.

"You think?" Preacher smiled back.

"I think we are going home."

"To the American Devil?"

"The Devil!" Lance brought up a fist and raised his pinky and forefinger to make horns as he whispered the words menacingly. Preacher couldn't help but crack up.

In the meantime, Kamil had recovered a portion of his senses and wondered just why his friend George was laughing. "What is so funny?" He asked.

Preacher couldn't see Kamil with Lance in the way so he leaned into and through the ghost. He was no longer a reflection of the terrorist. He was just himself, a ruthless killer. "I was just talking with my angel and he said I have to let you live, at least for another day." And with the smile gone, he reached out and grabbed Kamil's shirt to pull him close. "I was going to kill you a few moments ago. It would have been a slow, painful death with my smiling face the last thing you would ever see. But my angel talked me out of it. He said you have more value on earth than in hell. I don't know, but he is usually better than me at judging people."

Chapter 33

"Here to babysit me again?"

Preacher was not surprised in the least to see Fuchs waiting for him outside. He leaned against a railing outside the small, unadorned and unobtrusive building that functioned as a black site, a prison that did not exist. Fuchs was bearded for the first time Preacher could recall. He hadn't seen him since the Philippines, where Fuchs saved his life.

And Preacher couldn't stop the song by Three Dog Night that started up in his personal cranial radio station. His right foot tapped the song's beat as he stopped a few feet in front of Fuchs.

"No, I was just stopping by. I'm surprised to see you here." It was a lousy lie. It was supposed to be.

"Where did you fly in from? Couldn't have been too far for you to get here so quickly. I've only been here for a couple of hours." Preacher had taken his chances coming to visit Kamil over the past few months. He didn't know if Seibel had a kill or capture order posted for him. Fuchs being here was only slightly alarming.

"Not too far, northern Italy when I got the call." Fuchs looked tired.

"Been looking for me?" Preacher walked over to lean against the same railing.

"Not for a couple of months. He had me track you to the Philippines and through Indonesia and India. But you were never there. It was all false evidence, very clever. I figured it had to be her."

"It was. She is much better than I am at leaving those digital and electronic footprints that lead you to the wrong conclusion." Preacher smiled at Marta's seemingly limitless abilities.

"You look well. Fully recovered I assume." Fuchs waved from Preacher's shoulder to his leg.

"All better. I didn't have the opportunity to thank you back then. You had to run off on another mission. Someplace fun I hope."

"Always." Fuchs lied again. Another lousy one. "Did you find Anwar?"

"Got close, but no. My friend in there just confirmed what I've been thinking for a while."

"And what's that?"

"He's planning a little tour de force in America." Preacher looked up at Lance. He was busy looking down at Fuchs, reading every detail, evaluating every move, or lack there of. Something had Lance on edge. The visual data being fed into Preacher's brain by looking around was being processed by his very active subconscious. The result was a hovering ghost on high alert status. Something was definitely wrong.

"America is a big place. Do we know where? Or maybe when?" Fuchs didn't know he was being spied on from above.

Lance saw it. A miniscule jetting of Fuchs' eyes to the right. He looked in the direction and Preacher followed his ghost's sightline. It was a van, a black van. And something inside it moved. Lance then looked to the east. Parked over there was another van. This one was dark blue.

"Foxy, are you here to take me in?" Preacher's question got no reply. So he stepped closer to Fuchs. "Can I ask you something?"

"Sure." Fuchs gave nothing away.

"Were you there when he trained her? I assume it was at the Point. And I assume that you, and maybe one other person in the world, knew about her. Probably Wyrick, maybe Braden. Were you there?"

Fuchs kept his eyes on Preacher but nodded.

Preacher's mind was racing, expanding. He was looking into Fuchs' eyes, watching the van to the north and the one to the east all at once. He worked through options one by one and chose the seventh after moving through 16 he could see.

"She is a much better shot than me." Preacher smiled as he said it.

Fuchs replied with another nod. "Yes, she is. Even better than me I think. A natural."

"Maybe." Preacher pursed his lips. "I owe you my life. I don't owe him anything."

"This isn't about debts owed or debts to be collected. This is simply work, our job. And you have chosen to go off mission one too many times."

"How's that?" Preacher remained right in front of Fuchs.

"That was quite a show in Moscow last week.."

"Was it?"

"It got everyone's attention, as you knew it would. Anwar is a household name from Moscow to Los Angeles. He is one of the world's most wanted terrorists and no one even knew his name eight days ago."

"How 'bout that." Preacher kept his eyes on Fuchs. Lance pivoted his head in all directions. In one of the vans, he saw a radio come up to a man's face and looked at the other van to see a response. Preacher leaned his head to the left to get a look at Fuchs' right ear and the radio earpiece in it. Fuchs heard the radio conversation but gave nothing away with his eyes. Preacher was impressed with him, like he always is. "Mikey, I really hope Tarwanah and Jamaani aren't in either of those vans. That seems so beneath them."

"Too bad about Cherzny, of course." Fuchs ignored the comment.

"Of course. A great loss."

They just looked at each other. Fuchs' lack of movement became clear. Anything more than a fidget would result in a half-dozen or so men filing out of the vans with guns trained on Preacher.

So Preacher played his hand. "When you and Seibel trained her, did you know she would kill you?"

The question caught Fuchs a little off guard. He hadn't considered it, at least for many years. "No. I knew she would kill many, she already had. But she would never turn on him or me. There is no reason."

"Sometimes there is no reason when we die. I should have died on that tiny island or in an alley in Baghdad before that. You should have been killed dozens of times, yet here we stand. Me alive and you dead."

Fuchs' eyebrows tugged at that one. "Dead?"

"I said it before and I meant it. Thank you for saving my life. I'm sorry you have to go, but this death is as good as any. To die at the hands, or at least the finger, of someone so gifted at death is an honor, I think, at least."

Fuchs' got it. "So you are going to kill me? Right here?"

"No. Not me, her." Preacher raised his eyebrows somewhat in resignation. "Please don't move. You have a beautiful little set of crosshairs on your forehead right now. I know you scouted the area when you and the teams arrived. You checked all surrounding buildings at a cursory level. She watched it all and relayed it all back to me. Do you mind?" Preacher pointed to his jacket pocket.

"Go ahead." Fuchs couldn't help but look over Preacher's shoulder and the buildings a quarter mile away. Lance, watching from above, laughed. That damn Preacher is such a good liar.

Preacher pulled a headset out of his pocket to show Fuchs. "This was all her idea. She comes up with the good ones. Coming here is a little stupid, but you and he would think me just crazy enough to keep doing it, to pay this particular resource another visit. Her only frustration at the moment, from what I can tell, is that Seibel is not with you. Or at least is not willing to show his face."

Fuchs laughed. "You and your b.s. You had me going for just a second."

"I know. It's good isn't it? Can't help it. So what do we do?"

"What do you mean?"

"Do we let you die, or do I save your life?"

"Enough. Cut the shit."

"Fine." Preacher raised his left hand just an inch. It worked. Fuchs didn't want to die here, for little or nothing. Not today.

"Wait." Fuchs nodded and leaned forward just an inch.

"Call them off. Send the vans away." Preacher wasn't playing games. The two of them stared for a few moments.

"Leave." One word from Fuchs got two engines started. The vans pulled away slowly.

"I think you were supposed to bring me in, not kill me. Then why is that guy up there on the roof still pointing a rifle at my head?" Lance had risen a couple hundred feet into the air and spotted the sniper's rifle on the rooftop. Preacher could see the barrel protruding over the edge of the building's roof ledge. "It makes me think that maybe you were sent to eliminate a threat if I did not come peacefully. Not very nice."

"He is not supposed to kill you. Strict orders. Just hit you in the leg, maybe both." Fuchs' matter of fact response sufficed.

"Wouldn't be the first time I got shot in these damn legs would it?" Preacher fake-punched Fuchs in the gut. "Well okay then. I guess we need to say goodbye."

Fuchs just shook his head.

"What?"

"I always knew you would be too wild, too unpredictable. Your value was always limited by your erratic behavior. But he was always so sure."

"Okay. To put a capstone on this touching little farewell, I'm going home to hunt a terrorist who wants to blow up Americans. If that is off mission then so be it. Tell him to come and get me himself. When I find and kill Anwar, you can come and give me hell for being too wild and unpredictable. And you're welcome for saving your life today Foxy."

Preacher turned away and walked toward where the blue van had been a minute earlier. Fuchs stood there for a moment and scanned the horizon. He then did something a little funny. He waved and nodded his head as if to thank Marta for not putting a bullet through his skull. Lance was being tugged along by Preacher, but he cracked up at Fuchs standing there waving.

He and Marta had been tracking, researching, investigating anything and everything about Anwar. They had been to nine European, Middle East and Asian countries and spoken with hundreds of humans offering varying quality of information. Most of it led nowhere. Anwar was indeed a magician.

But, a few of the leads uncovered pointed across the Atlantic Ocean to America. Kamil's confirmation a little while ago was all they needed. It took a few months to soften Kamil up and get him to slip up.

Preacher was headed back home. Marta was returning to the country of her birth for the first time more than a decade. If Anwar was there, they would find him and stop him. They would kill him.

Chapter 34

Tuesday, September 22, 1992 — Fairfax, Virginia
They would just sit there. This was routine for the two of them. One would remain stoic, eyes closed. The other would watch him, waiting patiently. But this time was different. A third person sat there, well not really sat; he floated up in the corner of the room.

"Do you believe in angels?" Preacher ended the silence, opened his eyes and looked up at Lance. The question was for Stuart Braden, CIA psychologist and resident Lance Priest psycho-agent expert. Braden sat across from Preacher.

"We've talked about my religious beliefs several times. I don't think we need to revisit that." The psychologist was patient. He was also extremely pleased to have Lance, or at least the person he believed to be Lance Priest, with him. It had been more than 18 months since their last session. Lance, or Preacher, had been around the world several times since then. He'd found Marta, nearly been killed in the Philippines, disappeared, and most likely blew up a good portion of Russia back in April. He returned to the U.S. several months ago to track Anwar.

"No Stu, I don't want to discuss your religious or philosophical paradigms. I just want to know your thoughts on angels, ghosts maybe." Preacher turned from a ghostly smiling Lance to an unsmiling and very pale Braden. "Just your opinion."

"I don't really have one. I've not thought much about it. Can I ask why you want to know?" Braden had a hundred or so questions for Preacher but was willing to bide his time. This session would stretch well past an hour. Seibel had ordered Lance to come in, now that Papa and Lance were talking at least.

"No opinion at all?"

"Nope. None."

"Okay. What about just ghosts, forget angels." Preacher insisted.

"I don't believe in ghosts, but I know the foundation for belief in apparitions lies in trauma, stress, fear. There has been extensive research into belief in afterlife beings. I have not read much on it, but I did have a patient who believed his deceased mother had come to live with him and his wife. It led to divorce. I think it might have been a scheme to bring about a desired result."

"You said trauma, stress and fear. What about death?" Preacher kept at it.

"What about death?"

"Couldn't it be the foundation for belief in apparitions?"

"No. Death is only the foundation for being dead. You know, gone, passed away, shuffled off this mortal coil and all." Braden smiled.

"Did you hear about my little incident last year?"

"In the Philippines?"

"Yes, that one."

"Yes, I heard it was serious. You were lucky."

"No, you were lucky," Preacher nodded. "You got to keep me around. I just have to be the freak show for the circus."

"So am I to understand from your line of questioning, that you believe you may have had some form of extra-perceptual experience after nearly dying?" Braden smiled as he asked this.

"Something like that." Preacher closed his eyes again and went back to Tapul and being shot, and Fuchs carrying him and Lance just floating up there looking down at him. Maybe that was it. Maybe Lance did die that day. Maybe this was all an afterlife, a screwed-up afterlife. No, that was crazy. He opened his eyes to look at Lance. The ghost just shrugged his shoulders. He didn't know anything more than Preacher did. "Something happened out there. It changed me, no doubt about it."

Braden let that sit and simmer for a few moments. He was waiting for this opportunity. "From what I hear from the field, it wasn't just nearly being killed that changed you. Some people are under the impression that a significant relationship changed you before that. It changed your priorities. Your actions took on a significantly different element, a different direction. That's all he'll tell me."

Preacher was waiting for this as well. "So you want to talk about Marta?"

Braden was surprised, but stayed calm, professional at the mention of her name. "Only if you do."

"As you know, and as you mentioned, I came here because he ordered me to. He's nagged me for months. Being here takes me off task. I'm kind of tracking a terrorist bomber, you know." Preacher smiled at that. "I didn't come to talk about her, but I know that's what he wants you to get out of me. But before we do, I want you to put your hand behind your back and hold up some fingers."

"What? Why?"

"Please, just do it and then we'll talk about Marta and me, and whatever else turns you on."

"Fine." Braden put his right arm behind his chair and held up two fingers. Lance moved over into the corner over Braden's shoulder to look.

"Two. Do it again." Preacher commanded.

Braden furrowed his brow and held out his forefinger and pinky, commonly known in Oklahoma as the dreaded Hookem' Horns symbol.

"Two again. Go Texas." Preacher smiled at him with eyes closed. "One more time, please."

Braden shook his head, as he often did in Preacher or Lance's presence. He opened his hand behind his chair to hold out all fingers and thumb.

"Gimme five baby."

Now Braden was freaked out. Not only was Preacher getting the numbers right, he was doing it as soon as he flashed them and with eyes closed. "How the hell are you doing that?" Braden sat up in his chair and looked around the room for a camera or other device allowing this little show to take place.

Preacher opened his eyes. The smile was gone from his face. "Ghosts, I guess." He looked away and then up into the corner. Lance wasn't smiling either. Neither of them had an answer for how they were doing this. He hadn't planned on freaking Braden out with a parlor trick. It just came to him in the moments of clarity being with the psychologist brought. Instead of perfecting his lying with Braden, his screwed up mind and extrasensory angel chose to take over. He was a little embarrassed by it all and decided to sit up and treat the man with the respect he deserved. That meant nothing but the very best, most detailed lies.

But, just for a moment, Preacher and Lance looked at each other and shared a sensation they had felt every time with Braden. For some undetectable reason, the whole situation – the room, the air, the quiet – it all felt Asian. Maybe oriental. It was nothing either of them could pinpoint, but this sensation always came to Lance or Preacher when sitting in Braden's office. Maybe it was the feng shui of the room. For some reason, maybe because there were two of them with Braden this time, it was more acute, more obvious somehow. Strange.

Hours after their session in Braden's Fairfax, Virginia office, the two of them walked along a trail beside a small lake not far from the office building. It was pleasant and peaceful. Preacher was cryptic in his description of details, feelings, emotions. He glanced around constantly, feeding data to his angel. Lance was doing the same from about 500 feet. They spotted two surveillance operatives, one with a directional mic pointed out the window of a Chevy Blazer.

"… And she told me about her extensive covert operations, very extensive." Preacher said.

"What kind of details did she share?" Braden asked.

"Everything. She told me everything from the beginning through last week."

"Last week? You were in touch with her last week?" Braden was either very good or simply unaware that Seibel listened to every word spoken between him and Preacher.

"I spoke with her this morning. We update each other almost every day on progress."

"How do you keep these communications secret? It drives Seibel crazy, as you surely know." Braden smiled at the thought of frustrating the unshakable Seibel.

"I can't give you any details, of course. We have worked out a nice system, very efficient." Preacher smiled as well. He could see Seibel's face as he listened to this from some hidden location. "Technology just keeps advancing every day."

"Indeed." Braden stopped and reached out a hand to halt Preacher. "I need to ask you one thing. I still have a thousand things to ask you, but one aspect for sure I need to address."

"Shoot." Preacher stopped and turned to face Braden.

"Are you planning to kill Seibel?" Braden was serious. His face was a little ashen, like he didn't really want to talk about this.

"Why would I answer a question like that?" He didn't miss a beat.

"It is a simple question. I'm not asking it as a professional. It's really more personal in nature."

"And what led you to this simple question?" Preacher tilted his head slightly.

"Things I've heard from him and others. Your evasiveness this past year. Your involvement with this Marta, and her history with Seibel. And I can completely understand it."

Preacher broadened his smile. He enjoyed this, really enjoyed this stuff. "No. I'm not planning on killing Papa." Then he leaned in close to Braden's ear, close enough to kiss him, and whispered. "But she is." He put an arm around Braden's shoulder and took things to another level. He whispered with no trace of emotion in the words. "Everything is in motion now. It is amazing what can happen in five months. One can learn about a man, his wife Eileen, their three children Peter, Lou and Cinda. Bank account numbers at four institutions, investment property in Rhode Island, bankruptcy filings by a brother-in-law in Maryland. It is amazing how all this comes together."

He kept the lock on Braden's shoulders and kept them walking forward. He continued to tick off detail after detail of Stuart Braden's personal life. It was surreal and unpleasant. When he finished, Braden had moved well past simmer to boiling. But the painful squeeze Preacher kept on the psychologist's upper body kept him tethered.

"Are you done?" Braden exhaled as he spoke. "Will you let me go?"

"Unfortunately, I am just getting started." Preacher again brought his lips to within a whisker of Braden's ear. "It is challenging keeping up with her."

"She is really something. She has changed you, made you stranger than you were. How did she do it?" Braden was still pissed at Preacher's in-depth knowledge of his family.

Preacher suddenly released his grasp. Braden breathed in deeply. "Ask her yourself." They had walked from beside the lake over to a parking area. A red Chevy sedan pulled up and the passenger door opened. Marta smiled at Braden from behind the wheel. "Stuart, I hope he hasn't been scaring you with his stories. Let's go for a ride. Come on."

Preacher gently shoved Braden into the car and closed the door behind him. Marta peeled out and pulled away. Preacher turned back to look at the Blazer about 300 yards away. It started up and pulled out into traffic. Lance noticed another car starting up 250 yards away to the east. Both Preacher and Lance laughed. The drivers of those vehicles stood no chance keeping up with her. No chance.

Preacher turned back toward the building where Braden's office sits on the second floor. Something had caught Lance's eye, so he zoomed down from 1,000 feet to look in the window of Braden's office. Tough to make him out, but it had to be Seibel.

On the other side of the tinted glass, Seibel stood looking right through Lance at Preacher 250 yards away. A radio on the desk beside him was mostly quiet now. The primary noise coming across was the fountain in the center of the small lake Preacher stood next to. Seibel took a tiny step forward and more light from outside illuminated his face. Lance laughed and turned back to Preacher.

"How long is this going to go on?" The spirit asked the one on the ground.

"Don't know. It's getting old. Seems like real paranoia." Preacher's response was to his alternate self, but the words reached Seibel in the office. "At some point he is either going to need to kill me or drop this crap. We've got a friggin terrorist to catch."

Lance turned back to Seibel. He pressed up against the glass. He would have liked to go through it and see what Seibel was doing, what he was feeling. But since Preacher couldn't see past the glass from this far, Lance was limited. "You know what I'd really like to do?"

"What?" Preacher answered Lance.

"I'd like to float in there and pee on him so he'd think it was raining inside."

Preacher laughed at that image. Seibel didn't laugh. He just watched and wondered if Lance had lost it.

"Does he have a gun on me?" Preacher looked around for evidence. Lance shot back up to 800 feet and used the visual data Preacher supplied to look around.

"Two."

"Where?"

"Top of the building he's in and fifth floor of the office building to the east. It's the only window that's cracked."

"What about a mic? See anything?" Preacher continued peering around. He knew that Lance would see things he missed, but he needed to supply the data.

"One left to chase Marta, but another one is in a van in the lot south of the building."

"Is he listening?" Preacher asked himself.

"Can't say. But I would say it's likely." Lance came down to about 150 feet. Preacher looked up at him. Seibel glanced up to see what Lance was looking at.

Preacher brought his sightline back to Braden's window where Seibel stood. "I just told you last week you need to drop the Spanish Inquisition. You're looking for something that's not there. Anwar is very likely right here, less than 20 miles from us and you keep watching me. Why old man?"

Most people would be surprised being found out like this and probably take a step back into the room to become obscured. Seibel stayed where he was and answered, even though his young prize couldn't hear him. "Because I didn't bring you this far just to track a killer. I need you to become the killer. Become the terrorist, so you can think like him, act like him. Be him, then kill him." He didn't add what he'd been thinking for sometime. He needed her to help Lance become the killer Seibel knew he could be. Seibel's heart had nearly jumped out of his chest a minute earlier when the car swung up next to Lance and Braden. He knew it was her. She was back in her native land. She wasn't here for a visit. Marta never made any unnecessary movements. More than likely, she wanted to kill him. No telling what she would do with a kidnapped Braden. They had quite a bit to talk about.

Preacher turned away and walked across the grass. It was a cool fall day. He crunched leaves beneath his shoes as he made his way. Lance provided him a beautiful view of the changing leaves of the urban forest of trees as he walked.

Chapter 35

Marta Illena Sidorova was reborn in October 1992.

For her, it was a fourth birth. She was born the first time in Cheektowaga, New York, just outside Buffalo. Her second birth occurred when Seibel left her alone near Moscow just outside an orphanage. Her third beginning was 18months ago in Baghdad when a young man walked into her life and shot her. Twice.

A month earlier, Preacher shoved Stuart Braden in the car ostensibly to kidnap and interrogate the psychologist. There was no interrogation. No torture. No threats against Braden or his wife and children. Preacher just wanted to bring Braden and Marta together. He knew fate would do the rest. Driving at a ferocious speed, leaving the park next to Braden's office, Marta smiled at the psychologist gripping the armrest built into the door beside him. Speed and frenetic activity were second nature for her. Driving a little fast to evade three cars was nothing, literally.

"How do you do?" She had to shout over the car's radio that blared a new tune from U2. Marta didn't have the benefit of a built-in cranial soundtrack like Lance and Preacher.

Braden looked at her and then back over his shoulder at the chase vehicles being left rapidly behind. "I don't know."

"Do you know who I am?" She glanced at him as she made an unannounced left turn just inches from the bumper of an oncoming pickup truck.

"Yes. I think so."

"Good." She smiled and patted his left leg. "I'm Marta."

"I guessed that. I'm Stuart, Stuart Braden."

"Nice to meet you Stu. I've heard quite a bit about you." Only Lance and Preacher called him Stu.

"From Lance or from Seibel?" He turned to watch her reaction.

"Preacher, I mean Lance. He enjoys his time with you, his relationship with you. He feels really bad about the little threat to your family he implied a few minutes ago. He would never hurt them, never hurt you. Unless you betrayed him, of course."

"Of course." Braden turned back to look at the road. "He's always made that clear. He is very seldom transparent. But he was very clear on the subject of betraying him. And you don't have to apologize for his threats. Nothing he does really surprises me."

Marta laughed at that and turned the radio volume down. "Then it wouldn't surprise you to learn he told me to put a gun to your head and see what you were willing to say to keep me from pulling the trigger?"

Braden was silent. He shook his head. "That doesn't sound like Lance."

"He's changed. Not the same as he used to be." She was matter of fact.

"I could see that earlier. He's different. Like something is missing. I guess I attributed it to his being shot."

"I thought that may have been it initially, but I don't really have the background with him that you and Seibel do. So the change in him was not as easy for me to see." With that, their first session had begun.

Braden turned to look at Marta as she checked the rearview and side-view mirrors and expertly maneuvered the vehicle. He knew next to nothing about this human, but he knew he wasn't put in this car with her to be her prisoner. Lance had brought them together. He had lied to both. That was evident, and only natural for Preacher.

During the next four weeks, Marta Sidorova opened up to a stranger, a trained professional of a stranger who was mesmerized by her stories, her life. At least three times per week, Braden left his office and walked or drove to an appointed location where a different person met him each time. These different people were Preacher decked out in all variety of disguises. He was practicing roles and stayed in character as he "met" Braden on street corners, in restaurants, behind stores, in waiting rooms and on train cars. Braden tried to keep a straight face, but sometimes couldn't help himself. Especially when Preacher sat down next to him on a bar stool dressed as a hooker, a damn good-looking transvestite hooker, named Sharyce, with a "y."

Preacher would escort the psychologist to another location where he would sit and talk with a changing, evolving Marta. It was like his first sessions with Lance Priest four years earlier. Marta was a living, breathing, hurting, hating, fire-breathing chameleon. She was a killer in the truest sense. He had seen it before, with Lance and with Fuchs and Seibel.

In 12 sessions, Marta had gone from distant and aloof, to engaged and laser-focused. She was on the verge of a breakthrough. Braden was skilled at unraveling the trickiest wrinkled human maps. And he had a secret weapon when it came to Marta.

Preacher was coaching him. He never stepped into details, but Preacher gave Braden little hints he should be on the lookout for during his sessions with Marta. This exercise in self-exploration was indeed something of a gift Preacher gave to Marta. It was something that could help her, if she let it. She fought against discussing herself at first; wanting only to mine Braden for details about Lance or anything about Seibel he would give up. But gradually, Braden was able to massage their conversations to include her life, her childhood, her young adult territory and her adult life as a professional killer, blackmailer and provocateur.

Marta's rebirth, her phoenix-like rising, her emergence from darkness that had surrounded her every moment into the world of light and possibility came during a session in a motel on the Pennsylvania-New Jersey state line just south of Philadelphia.

The two of them had spoken about Lance during each session. Sometimes it was just a few comments. Other times, they spent hours on the topic. Marta offered fertile, unplowed fields on the subject. She brought a view, a perspective that neither Braden nor Seibel could ever know.

When Marta spoke of Lance, she referred to a loving, generous, appreciative, warm and surprisingly kind individual. He was the love of her staggeringly bleak and despairing life.

The psychologist could see in her sometimes brilliant, occasionally lifeless eyes, that Marta's consideration of the future and living in that future was conjoined with Lance. She held the idea, the sliver of hope, in trembling hands. For a brutal, pitiless killer with black ice in her soul and lethal venom in her veins, she was at least tenuously willing to embrace the possibility of happiness.

Driving to this particular session from Braden's office took the standard two and a half hours it takes Braden to drive home. It took even longer because Preacher stopped in a parking garage to change cars. It was habit and Braden just had to deal with it.

Two and a half hours was a long time with Lance, even longer with Preacher. Braden didn't know he'd get this time until Preacher surprised him in the parking lot. A somewhat rough frisking was a little uncalled for, but Preacher knew the games Seibel liked to play.

"So where are we going tonight?" Braden was casual.

"North. Just outside Philadelphia."

Braden's reaction was not good, not happy.

"Relax. We're not going to your house. Not too far from there, but no need for alarm. Geez, you'd think I'd have earned a little trust."

"Don't give me any of your trust b.s. You've neither earned nor desired any trust. It's not in you." Braden was still smarting from the thought of them going to his house, or anywhere near it. "Why there?"

"Just because." Preacher was always stingy with details.

Their conversation over the next couple of hours was in-depth and illuminating. Preacher hadn't given him much since returning to the country several months back. They did go pretty deep into the subject of Geoffrey Seibel. Braden didn't reveal anything too sensitive, but he did divulge a variety of views Seibel had shared with him over the last two decades.

A portion of their trip was also spent discussing Seibel's introduction to Lance nearly fifteen years earlier. Braden obviously wasn't thrilled to learn he had been kept in the dark about Marta. He did confirm his help in creating the questionnaire and the evaluation of youthful violent offenders as a sub-category.

As they neared their destination, Preacher abruptly changed the subject from Lance to Marta. In the preceding weeks, he had been sprinkling tidbits and hints for Braden to explore in his sessions with her. For the meeting this evening, Preacher wanted to arm Braden with a little more.

"So, you know about her childhood, her brother, her parents, right?"

"Correct. I have the basics on all that."

"And you know about her time in state homes and foster care and the abuse she suffered."

"Yes. She faced significant challenges, and responded in a most violent manner to each instance." Braden was very cordial, very professional.

"So that's my question for her, for you."

"What's that, what's your question?"

"Why. Why did she keep going? Why didn't she take another way out? Why not end her life a long time ago? After her brother, after the foster homes, after Seibel abandoned her in Russia. Why not just take a step off a building or put a gun in her mouth?" Preacher looked from Braden to Lance outside the window doing a superhero pose flying through the air beside the car.

Braden let that sink in for a few moments before responding. "So what you really want to know is motivation. What is her motivation for both living and doing what she does?" It was a question he had asked Lance no less than a dozen times.

Preacher heard it in Braden's voice. "No, don't go there. That is completely different. I didn't go through anything like she did. My life doesn't even come close."

"But yet, it is a mystery. What could possibly drive someone to do the things she does, the things you do?"

"Her. Not me."

"I'm sorry, but it is almost one and the same. You and her." Braden was adamant.

"No. I told you, she went through so much more than I did. She suffered; she was basically held captive and then was a prisoner of the state. She has seen and lived through things I'll never know, never comprehend."

Braden let that sink in for a moment. "So you are left with a quandary. What makes someone else tick? It is indeed life's greatest mystery. And I believe it is as unique as we are. Most people never explore their true motivations in life. Others know from an early age what they want, what they need to do, to attain it."

"So what is your hypothesis for her?" Preacher was anxious.

"I don't have one yet. I don't know."

"Come on. You have an idea. You've got to have something in mind after a dozen sessions."

"This is really important to you isn't it?" Braden liked seeing Preacher concerned for someone else.

"Don't try that on me Stu. Don't put me under your little microscope and look for amoebas of truth and bacterium of lies. I don't work that way. You know there is no there, there."

Braden smiled at his repeating this line for a fourth or fifth time with him. "I know you like to think that, believe that. But it is physically, mentally and clinically impossible. All humans have a 'there' at their core, a reason for every action. Be it survival, or revenge or anger or hunger or desire for detachment."

It was Preacher's turn to smile. Lance, riding on the roof of the car, grinned at that one as well. "Desire for detachment. Geez Stu, how long have you been working on that? I'll bet you even said that line into a mirror. It's not bad, but a little bit cheesy."

"You think so?" Braden's smile transitioned to furrowed brow.

Preacher laughed up at Lance, who was now standing on the roof of the Toyota shouting the words "desire for detachment" through cupped hands. Braden didn't laugh along with Preacher.

He should have known better than to try to share his clinical and diagnostic ideas with Lance.

"Sorry. Sorry Stu, really. It's just that is really good. I mean you nailed it."

"Shut up. You never change. I think you are growing, evolving even, and then you let your guard down and you're the same as five years ago."

"I said sorry. You were the one who tried that shit on me. But like I said, this is not about me. I asked you for your ideas on Marta." He slowed down and turned off the highway onto a two-lane road. "We're getting close. Look, I don't believe for a moment that you don't have a better handle on her motives, her reason for still being."

Braden stewed in it for a few moments. "Okay. I was sandbagging, but I think you can see from your previous outburst why I hold some things back from you. You frustrate the hell out of me. I used to find it challenging, stimulating to try to pin you down. But I've learned the sad truth, you are incapable of being genuine, being real, even for a moment."

"No there, there."

"Bullshit. No framework for honesty there. No infrastructure for truth. You keep it all hidden. You have your reasons, just like she does."

Preacher turned into a parking lot of a small motel and killed the lights. "She's watching us right now, so finish up. What are her reasons in your estimation?"

"Marta has been searching her entire life for a challenge, for someone to offer her a real competition. She was literally searching for you every day of her life. Besides me, she has let nine people into her life to see if they could indeed challenge her abilities. Six of the nine are dead. Still alive are Seibel, Smelinski and you. She has not been bested, and each of you have a limited number of days left."

Preacher digested Braden's professional take on patient Marta. "So in your professional opinion, she has been searching her whole life for someone to kill her, because that's the only way she can truly be bested."

Braden nodded then shook his head. "You already considered this hypothesis, of course. I'm two steps behind you, as usual."

"Three steps really." Preacher smiled and slapped Braden's shoulder. "Just to be clear, you fully expect her to dispatch Seibel and Smelinski from this earthly realm. They failed in their duties of besting or beating her so now they have to be eliminated. And then it's up to me."

"I have no doubt that she loves you. She's more in love than anyone I've ever met. But..."

"But love is not enough. Not for her."

"For you to be the true love of her life, the one man deserving of her blind affection, you must kill her."

Preacher shook his head and looked in the direction of the room Marta stood waiting. She was undoubtedly looking out the window at the two of them. "That is messed up Stu, really."

"You asked."

"So to encapsulate your theory, Marta is totally messed up, needs me to kill her to prove my love or will take care of me like she has done so many others."

"That about covers it."

Seven minutes later, Preacher was gone on foot into the dark. Braden sat across a small table from Marta. She had procured a ham sandwich, chips and a Coke for him, since he was missing dinner with his family.

"So I suppose you and Lance spoke about a great many things on that long drive up here."

"Too many." Braden was enjoying the sandwich and the soda would give him the little pick-me-up he needed after two-plus hours with Preacher.

"He is very distracted these days. He can only concentrate when he is deep into one of his trances, looking for any clues left by Anwar." Marta was basically talking to fill the space as Braden ate. He already knew most of what she was saying. Anwar was top-secret public enemy number one for Seibel and company, and the number one target for Preacher.

"He talked quite a bit about Anwar on the drive. Fixated is the word I would use. If the guy is in the U.S., Lance will find him." He took another swig of Coke. "He's fixated on him almost as much as he is on you."

She smiled and huffed a bit at that. She liked it, but it made her uncomfortable to think of the two of them talking about her. This psychologist, that she had only known for a few weeks, was now a repository of information others had killed and died for. Marta looked away from Braden. She hadn't thought of killing him since that first day. It was somewhat alarming to her that she had not evaluated him as a threat and assessed his weaknesses to capitalize upon, and kill him. "He likes to think he knows a thing or two about me."

Stuart Braden realized something right there, right then. He had been given an opportunity to change the world. Sitting in front of him was the only person he had met in the past five years who stood even the slightest chance of getting through to Lance Priest.

She was, plain and simple, the only person with any power over the one human he had encountered who possessed the ability to change the world. It was a circular argument in his head, but it was clear that Marta was Lance's tether to reality. She was an anchor he had dropped into a sea of utter nothingness that he had been skittering across. But Lance was also a human time bomb, and Marta was the fuse.

"Marta, I'm going to tell you something that he never would. Something he would be very upset about if he learns I have told you." Braden bowed his head slightly, an act of contrition.

She tilted her head sideways. It was a minute, but measurable action. She was waiting.

"Lance loves you. But he is not Lance anymore. He has changed, something has changed him. He is an alternate personality. I noticed it immediately, within minutes of seeing him after more than a year and a half. I don't know if it was meeting you, nearly being killed or a combination of both. But he is not Lance."

"Go on." Marta was prepared for more.

"He is suicidal. I have no doubt that he would put a gun under his chin right now if it weren't for you. He is looking for any reason to end his life. His fascination with Anwar is superficial. It is light and fog. He is hyper-focused on you. You are, without a modicum of doubt, his reason for living. But here's the thing," Braden sat back. He took a breath and swallowed. "He is certain that he cannot save you."

"Save me? What do you mean?"

Braden let it sink in for a moment, let her think it through. "What do you want from him?"

She stiffened. He had hit the exact chord he'd hoped for. "I don't want anything from him."

"Do you want him to save you or kill you?"

She tilted her head a little more. "You're serious."

"Most people never meet their soul mate. I didn't even believe in the idea until he shoved me in the car a few weeks ago. You two truly, in every sense of the word, were meant for each other. Every word you have told me these past weeks could have come from his mouth and his comments five years ago were line for line your words today.

"But the way I see it, you have all the power. You are the one who will decide where this goes and how it ends. You have the power to love and live or to kill. But this time, if you decide to kill, you will succeed in besting the one person in the world who could give you happiness." Braden pushed back from the table. Now to see if anything he'd just said had any effect on Marta. He ran his hands through his graying hair.

Marta just looked at him, watched him. She was off somewhere else. She was in an apartment in Baghdad. It was a room like many others she had been in before. It was nothing. She expected to complete the mission, secure the nuclear warheads, and ensure that two former KGB agents were eliminated. She did not expect him.

She heard the silenced shots from the front room. There were three of them. Before she could get up from the chair positioned next to the window, Lance was there, in the doorway. The feelings that washed over her then, did so again now.

One moment in his eyes was a lifetime. He could kill her and it would be fine. She had at least seen him one time in her life. He was glorious, like a fallen angel, a hero without an ounce of remorse or pity. He shot her in the leg and she felt nothing. Truly, she felt no pain, just pressure and gravity.

He motioned her to step back and sit against the wall and then shot her again, this time in the hand. She felt a tinge of pain, but no more than a paper cut. But then he was with her. He was within inches of her, giving her the chance to grab and crush and claw. But she didn't. No, instead they kissed.

Sitting there, just outside of Philadelphia nearly two years later, she flushed as she had in Baghdad. That was her first kiss. One or two boys had tried before, but they paid dearly.

Lance's lips were like an angel breathing light, the devil spewing fire into her soul. It was life-changing. She was changed. Marta was wrong. She was not the cold, lifeless, doomed person she thought she was destined to be. Damn.

She came back to the motel room and Braden running his hands through his hair across from her. Marta simply exhaled. With the breath expelled from her lungs went years of pain and anger and hatred. When she breathed in, it was as though she were welcoming oxygen into virgin lungs. It was new and different.

She smiled. Braden smiled back at her. She reached out a hand to him and he took it. Just as she had welcomed fresh air, she welcomed the human touch. Marta was reborn. She was hopeful, instead of cold and calculating and lonely, ever lonely. This was a rebirth, a realization, that welcomed her into a new life.

She simply smiled and didn't think about the next minute or how to kill with bare hands the person across from her and escape through the plumbing access panel into a vacant unit on the other side of the wall.

She just sat and held Stuart Braden's hand and waited for Lance to return to her.

Chapter 36

Monday, January 18, 1993 — Detroit, Michigan
For the third time in two years, he was chasing a fleeing terrorist. This was full speed on foot through dirty streets of a rundown and fallen Detroit neighborhood. This time, there was deep snow on the ground. And this time, she was helping him.

It wasn't Anwar. But it was the closest thing anyone hunting the ghost had found. And Preacher and Marta had uncovered this direct link to Anwar the old fashioned way – threats, torture and detective work. He had discovered a lead in London months ago that connected the dots right to Detroit and the terrorist cell they had just raided, along with an FBI counterterrorism team.

Running full steam like this with Lance bouncing around up at the building tops and a power pop song from the 80's by the British band The Outfield playing in his ears, Preacher considered his career. He had the choice to leave, to quit a couple of years ago. Could have walked away six months ago after that incident with Fuchs. He didn't need to develop into what he had become. He had become what Seibel wanted him to be. Preacher ate, drank, slept and dreamed bombs. He was a friggin' terrorist.

But looking back, he never doubted the choice. He knew soon after meeting Geoffrey Seibel that there is a necessary place for people who do bad deeds. Necessary bad deeds.

The means by which he performed his professional duties, that was the thing that caused him to take note on certain occasions. He was a killer. Lance was a killer. Marta, Fuchs and Seibel were killers. All of them had taken lives. But the inverse result of taking, ending lives, was giving others the right, freedom and peace to live theirs. Hell of a trade off.

Preacher smiled at this little philosophical soliloquy taking place in his messed up brain while sloshing through snow on the mean streets of Detroit on this bitterly cold January day. Lance smiled down as well. He enjoyed the debate, not the song so much, but the conversation going on in his earthly body's brain was interesting, fun even. Lance decided to move up to about 1,000 feet so he could see the streets moving out in all directions. From up there, Detroit didn't look so tough.

This guy they were chasing was a member of a cell that had come together in Detroit over the last three years. Three of the five members of the group had, a one point, worked in some capacity with Anwar. Two of them trained with him. Preacher had just seen a coded bomb-making manual written by Anwar lying on a bedside table in the apartment. Preacher shot two men in the legs. Marta put two others down with shots to the extremities. They left seven FBI agents in the apartment to clean up, cuff and transport the men. The runner, who got away by jumping out of a second-story window into a snow bank, was now about 70 yards in front of Preacher. The dude was keeping up a very impressive pace for the wet, slushy conditions.

Marta had stepped out the front of the building and taken another route to head him off. The two of them worked together like a team that had been side-by-side for years. They didn't need to talk into their radio headsets to communicate next moves. He knew she was two streets over to the north running perpendicular to the route he was on. She assumed the rabbit would jog that way instead of to the south when he reached the next major intersection.

Traffic was light. A few cars and trucks, almost all of them American-made gas guzzlers, slogged along six-inch deep snow-covered boulevards. Up ahead, Marta's assumption came to pass. The runner turned right and left Preacher's view for a few seconds. When he came around the corner, he slowed to a walk. In the snow, face down and now a little bloody, the man lay, a hand held to his head. Marta stood a few feet away holding her gun. The two of them looked at each other. He loved this ruthless killing machine, and for some reason, she loved him. They only had a few minutes before FBI anti-terrorist operatives caught up with them.

Preacher bent down and lifted the man to his feet and pushed him into an alley. Marta looked back and then in all directions to see if they were being watched. They weren't. It seemed people running through the streets was nothing too exciting in this neighborhood.

A few steps into the alleyway, Preacher pushed the man up against the wall and stepped back. He recognized him right away. It was Abu Jamal Nosar. He was one of the two who had trained with Anwar in the high mountains of Afghanistan six years earlier. He was allegedly one of the bombers from a Malaysian blast that killed 16 four years ago. This man was in America to kill, plain and simple.

"Brother, do you recognize me?" Preacher asked the winded and bloodied man. Marta had evidently wrapped him on the head as he ran past her. A gash on his forehead had blood running down into his right eye.

"No, I do not." Nosar had an accent from the Emirates. He wasn't from Syria as his records indicated. Preacher guessed Kuwait, maybe Yemen.

"I have been looking for you for some time. It is good to finally meet you."

"Who are you?" Nosar was matter of fact in between breaths. He looked from Preacher to Marta, standing at the mouth of the alley 20 feet away.

"Are you sure you don't recognize me?" Preacher smiled.

"No. I've never seen you before."

"Ah, but you have. You were on a small island in the Philippines a year and a half ago. I missed you by that much." Preacher stepped closer. He was sure now that Nosar was one of the three who escaped that morning. He had those three faces locked in his mind. Problem was, they all operated under other names out in the world and it took seeing them to recognize them. "You were very lucky that morning. You and Anwar and one other."

"I don't know what you're talking about. I've never been to the Philippines."

Preacher stepped in close and grabbed Nosar's hands and brought them up. He sniffed the fingers and closely examined them. "Burns." He turned to Marta. "His fingers are burned by chemicals. I can smell nitrate just like in the apartment. He has been working on a little fun today even." Preacher stepped back again and brought his hands down to his sides and turned to Marta, very calm, unthreatening. "Go get the car please."

He returned to Nosar. "So our little detective work proved effective. You were getting ready to place a bomb here in Detroit. Such a strange choice, but the home of America's beloved auto industry. Home of several large bridges and Motown Records. I'll bet you don't want to tell me what you were planning to blow up do you?" He got no reply. Time was running out. An FBI sedan would come down the street in a minute.

"I am supposed to hand you over to the authorities, but now I think I need to spend a little more time with you."

"I don't know anything. I don't know what you are talking about." The terrorist was committed to his façade. But then he dropped his head and reached down to his belt.

"Don't." Preacher whispered. Both he and Lance could see the simple physiology in the man's movement. The rise of the right shoulder by a quarter inch, the bending of the right elbow. Even with the layers of clothing, Preacher and his ghost watched in slow motion the man's human anatomy at work. The cognition evident in the eyes, the command sent from brain through the nervous system to arm, hand. The nostrils flared to allow the intake of oxygen before an explosive movement. Humans are so interesting.

Nosar pulled out a knife. He undoubtedly thought with Marta's departure to bring the car around, he could take this opportunity and kill this one FBI agent standing in front of him.

Preacher just shook his head. One thing he had learned about himself in his 26 years was a severe dislike of having a knife pulled on him. It had happened three times before. The first was at a lakeside party in Oklahoma. A drunken young man pulled out the blade when someone insulted him. The second was a ticked off Australian secret agent training at Harvey Point. The third was al Bakr back in Jeddah. All three men paid dearly for bringing a knife to a fight with Lance Priest. A broken collarbone, shattered femur and amputation by way of white-hot flame were the results.

His reaction to Nosar pulling the blade from a holster on his belt was immediate and nasty. Before the blade could be brought up for an initial thrust, Preacher stepped in and fired a vicious punch into the terrorist's throat, his Adam's apple. The look on the guy's face made Lance crack up from 15 feet in the air. The knife dropped to the snow below. Nosar collapsed to his knees.

But the thing was, Preacher wasn't done. Knives just get him going. He bent and picked up the blade. "Very well. The question then, do you want your nose or your ears cut off? I'll give you five seconds to choose. One, two,"

"No." Nosar sputtered. It was all he got out.

"Three, four,"

"No. Don't." He whispered.

"Five. Quickly now. There is no time. Or do I choose for you?"

"No, please."

Preacher moved in. His actions were cat-like, lightning fast and smooth, even in the snow.

"No, please. I'll tell you."

"Too late." Preacher brought the blade up and sliced off the man's left ear. The blow to his throat kept him from screaming in pain. Nosar brought his hand up to where his left ear had been. In the next moment, Preacher brought the blade down and sliced off the man's right ear. The brutal, barbaric act took four seconds. Treatment one might expect in the Middle East or maybe the mountains of Afghanistan.

He stepped back as the man grabbed his head on both sides and crumbled to the snow below. Blood mixed with the white crystals to make a pink hue. Preacher bent and wiped the knife through the snow to clean it. This war, that most Americans didn't know was even being fought, was not between good and evil. It was a war between life and death. This killer, who had placed a bomb under a walkway in a pedestrian mall in Kuala Lumpur, meant to kill many more here in the U.S.

Brutality was the language of this war. Terror was its currency. Most people, most Americans, would find what Preacher had just done reprehensible. Most Americans had not seen the remnants of human beings splattered on walls and trains and hillsides. Preacher looked over at the FBI team pulling up in their Ford. They would be pissed at the mess Preacher had created. But they also knew that only certain people could do what he'd done. It was his gift. A gift he shared with select others. Preacher turned back to Nosar struggling for breath on the bloody snow. Killing this bastard would have been a reward. He'd be a martyr, a glorious servant. No, he needed to pay.

Preacher is unpredictable, much more so than Lance. So even Lance was surprised by what his alter ego did next. Preacher shot down to his knees in front of Nosar and pulled the blade back up. He reached down to the red and pink snow to pick up two bloody items. He then put the blade to the bomb maker's mouth and pried his teeth open. Into the hole he stuffed the man's bloody ears.

"Don't make a sound. Think about running, and think about losing all your toes, one by one."

"Damn. That was sick, really sick." Lance shook his head from about 20 feet in the air. "Gross stuff, man."

"Be quiet. I'm working." Preacher said to himself up there.

Preacher walked to the alley's opening to greet the two men who jumped out of their car. Each had their hand on a holstered weapon. Preacher stepped up to stop both of them from entering. His positioning was slightly menacing and the two men noticed right away.

"Holman, what did you do?" It was Ayers. Preacher, using the fake FBI identification of Matt Holman, had worked with Ayers twice before. He gestured at the crumpled, bleeding mass of humanity down the alley.

"Damn." Scarfino added after seeing what Ayers had spied. Preacher had only been with Scarfino once before, in Philadelphia.

Preacher looked from one man to the other. One thing both these men knew was that this guy was not quite right. They, of course, had no idea. "Gentlemen, I am going to have to ask for a favor." He was calm, in supreme control.

Ayers took his hand off his gun. "What?"

"I need both of you to forget about perp number five here. Your report needs to mention only the four men in the apartment. They are good collars, quality intel will come from them. But number five is going to disappear in a couple of minutes, and will never be seen again."

"You're serious." Scarfino half-smiled but kept his hand on his gun holstered under his left armpit. "What are you saying? We just walk away. That's not going to happen." Scarfino was thick, with powerful legs. He looked like the wrestler he had been in college, the decorated Marine he was after that. He turned to capture Ayers's reaction.

Preacher continued. "We only have a minute. I need to be very clear. Listen carefully. This piece of human trash has vital information that cannot be extracted through legal means. He will be removed from this location, and within 12 minutes, he will be out of this country and on a plane to a secret location within hours. Before he steps on that plane, he will tell me where the bomb he has constructed can be found. Ayers, please have that hulking mass of a cell phone ready and I'll call you with the location." Preacher turned, Marta had entered the other end of the alley driving their vehicle.

"This is crazy. No way, no friggin' way you take that individual away from here." Scarfino moved to spread his legs to strengthen his first move.

"Why are you doing this? You know we can't allow you to take him." Ayers was definitely the more calm of the two. "We need to turn him over to proper authorities for debriefing. He has valuable information for the taskforce."

Marta pulled up beside Nosar. Both Ayers and Scarfino were on edge. Preacher needed to go, now.

He looked at both men, from his eyes and Lance's about 12 feet up. He could see the tension in their jaws, Scarfino's twitching left foot, his hand gripped tightly on the handle of his FBI-issue sidearm.

"I'm sorry to do this to you, both of you. Steve, you don't want to try to stop me. I don't want anything to happen to you that would keep you from going home to Patricia and Shelley and Bryan." He turned to Scarfino, "Richard, I know this is hard for you. But you can't stop me. Again, I don't want anything to keep you from returning home tomorrow to Allie and Rog and Brittany."

"What the f-." Scarfino was ready to pounce. Preacher's knowledge of their family makeup was unsettling.

"Let me be clear about the next eight seconds. If you pull that gun, I am going kick your right forearm and then dip and sweep your left leg and bring my right elbow down on the bridge of your nose. And before Steve can reach and pull his gun, I'm going to deliver an open-palm blow to his sternum and follow that with a left elbow to his right temple. If I need to turn back to you, I am going to drop my knee into your chest cracking several ribs and then finish you with a blow to your trachea that will leave you struggling for breath and most likely lead to your incapacitation for up to 12 minutes."

The words and processing them caused Scarfino to hesitate. He loosened the grip on his gun. Lance had come down to eight feet and was watching every twitch, every breath Scarfino breathed, every flutter of his pupils.

"Gentlemen. Your government has entrusted you with protecting the nation and assigned you to the anti-terrorism taskforce. Likewise, your government has chosen to create several extra-legal organizations that function outside the rule and law. The people who work for these entities are chosen for their abilities, both physical and mental, as well as their ability to process and manipulate situations. Basically to lie.

"If you will look over my shoulder, you will see that my little speech lasting 14 seconds brought your attention to my eyes and took your eyes off of the car and its driver. You can see now the driver has the barrel of her weapon aimed at one of your heads. My guess is it is you Richard. The time it would take her to pull the trigger and move from your forehead to Steve's would be less than a second. You would both fall to the ground with little splatters of blood and brain and bone spread out behind you.

"My job is not to please or satisfy people like you or the people you work for. I am in this game to hunt and kill those who would kill Americans by the hundreds or thousands. Your deaths would be regrettable, but excusable, if this individual provides us with information that leads to the kill or capture of Anwar."

Scarfino released his grip on his gun. He was done protesting. Ayers dropped his hands to his sides and shook his head a little.

"You'd kill us, really?" Ayers was shaken by this whole thing.

"I wouldn't be happy about it. But killing is what I was hired to do. Keep that in mind if you ever run up against someone or something that the law doesn't properly address. I'm on your side, but only as long as you stay out of my way. Be ready for that call within two hours."

He turned from them and walked back to Nosar to put him in the back of the car. Marta kept her gun pointed at the two men at the end of the alley.

The two FBI agents just stood there. Scarfino's leg had stopped twitching. Ayers just stared. They turned to each other with no expressions. That said it all. That was scary stuff.

Once Preacher and Nosar were in the back seat, Marta got in and put the small assault rifle next to her on the seat. She closed the door. "I don't know what you said, but you sure scared the hell out of them. I could see it in their eyes."

"I just told them that lovely woman in the car was going to put a beautiful round hole between their eyes." Preacher smiled at the joke.

"Lance, I mean Preacher, that's awful. You know I was only going to put one in their legs. They're nice guys. I'm not a ruthless killer, you know." She smiled the smile only for him. She glanced at Nosar in the rearview mirror. The terrorist was scared shitless by their lover's banter.

"No, not you." Preacher smiled back.

Marta put the car in reverse. But before she backed up, she looked up through the windshield at the sky. It was the fourth time Preacher had seen her do it today.

"He's not over there." Preacher gestured in the direction she had glanced. "He's right up there." He pointed back over his left shoulder out the rear window and Lance floating about 80 feet in the air."

He had finally told her about Lance, about his ghost. It was a Saturday morning a couple weeks back as they lay in bed. She had taken the news without a bit of surprise. She knew something was up for quite awhile and was actually relieved to learn it was just mild psychosis at work. Marta totally understood insanity.

She looked up out her side window in the direction Preacher pointed. She saw nothing. One of these times though, she just knew she was going to catch a glimpse of Lance up there. She loved that hovering ghost.

Chapter 37

It was hurry up and wait. And the members of Account One were none too happy about it. In turn, they each shared their frustration and that of their people. In the case of the White House Intelligence Director, that meant the President. And he took no time at all to drop the big guy's name.

"At some point, you are going to have to produce on this one," White House directed at Seibel. "You have basically said the same thing for months. 'Investigations are underway. Surveillance is providing solid leads. Our man is getting closer.' When are you going to catch him?"

Seibel didn't mind the aggressive line of questioning. In fact, he preferred it. It meant they were engaged. "You all know this is needle in the haystack stuff here. We have leads and evidence that point to multiple efforts underway by terrorist elements within the borders of the country. We are uncovering new information every day. But I never mislead you. And I have been clear for months that Anwar is still at large. He has proven to be a master at avoiding direct contact with other terrorist elements. He is our primary focus now, and will be until he is captured or killed."

NSA weighed in with a new take. "All the evidence I have seen points to nothing. We are not convinced he is in the country, and several members of our analysis team are not sure he exists at all. He may be something of a myth or legend created by the Mujahedeen to scare the Russians. There is little or no proof he is in the country."

Seibel nodded his head. "I understand your reservations. I can tell you we now have firm evidence he is in the country and has been in contact with other terrorists." He looked around the room and pulled three sheets of paper out of the single manila folder on the table before him. He pushed a sheet to each member. "Of course, I will collect these before we leave this room. This man was captured two days ago in Detroit." He paused to let them each read the information about Nosar.

"Who is he?" It was CIA, his boss. He wasn't happy to be getting this info the same time as the others.

"He is a terrorist bomber from Yemen who has fought and trained with Anwar."

"You are certain?" White House asked.

"We are now. I received this information this morning, less than three hours ago."

"Where did this information come from? Who apprehended him?" White House again.

"Preacher."

They all reviewed the page again and then looked at each other. Their looks said it all. If Preacher was involved, this was high-value information.

"Where is this Nosar now?" NSA this time.

"He is outside the country."

"But he was captured in Detroit?" CIA's turn.

"Yes." Seibel looked at each of them individually before he continued. "There is no record of his capture and all evidence linking him to the scene has been eliminated. He disappeared."

Seibel's vague words told the story that hard facts never would. Nosar was redacted from existence. He was no more. Gone.

Seibel continued with the bombshell, "Preacher relayed information obtained from the terrorist to the FBI giving precise detail about a bomb that had been constructed and was in the early stages of being deployed."

All three members of Account One just stared at Seibel. Speechless, for the moment.

The White House broke the silence. "Where was this bomb found and where was it going to be deployed?"

"Detroit. The target was Ford headquarters. The bomb was large enough, that when the truck it was loaded onto drove into the Ford complex, it would have done significant and massive damage." Seibel gave details in an emotionless fashion, slow and deliberate.

"It was on a truck? Jesus." NSA shook his head and then rubbed his temple. "It could have been delivered anywhere. Why Detroit."

"The captured terrorist simply said that is where he was told to place the bomb." These words were haunting for what was not said. If he was told to place the bomb at that location, then someone gave him the orders. And if he was in Detroit, there were likely others in Chicago, New York, LA, Washington, DC.

"Do we know who gave him his orders?"

"Anwar. Preacher has determined Nosar was a longtime associate of Anwar's. He identified him as one of the three who escaped the raid on the terrorist training facility on Tapul."

"That was where Preacher was shot, right?" CIA this time.

"Correct. He was nearly killed. But his intel is reliable on this. He is sure Nosar was one of them. Information garnered from the suspect has proven reliable in two instances already."

The CIA Director was first to respond, "I assume the device in Detroit was the first instance. What was the second?"

"Actually, the bomb was the second piece of information. The first was confirmation that Anwar is in the US." Seibel was matter of fact with this second bombshell.

"Confirmation? How did we get this? Is it reliable?" White House again.

"Information on the potential location was relayed to the FBI field office in Baltimore. They found the place empty, but after obtaining video from businesses in the area, this image was captured." Seibel pulled out a second set of single sheets of paper and handed one each around the table. On the sheet was a fairly clear image of a man walking into a FedEx office. "We have three previous photos of Anwar. While each is of different quality, they all feature the same composite. This image was fed into our computers and analysis confirms it is the same person in all four photos."

"When was this taken?" The President's man again.

"Four days ago at 10:15 in the morning."

There was silence for a few moments as this data was processed. The top man at the NSA was first, "Do we feel this Nosar can provide additional information?"

"That process is underway at present. Expectations are that additional intel on other U.S. cells will come out. Initial information proves our theory that these cells are independent of one another. Not integrated, by design. They all know that knowledge of other operations can be obtained through various means. To protect their flanks, they keep each cell small, compartmentalized."

White House responded, "Can I ask how you obtained and verified this information."

Seibel did not immediately respond, just stared. "It was obtained through various means."

"And these means are less than legal, hence the transportation of the subject outside our borders." He was grandstanding now.

"You have asked that we protect our nation and our interests. The details of the means and methods employed to offer that protection are not always pleasant." Seibel held the stare.

"I assume these methods would not hold up in court. So their reliability must be called into question." The lawyer in the man came out again.

The Director of the CIA butted in. "Information gathered by Seibel and his team has always been reliable. Intel garnered by his operative Preacher has been 100% accurate in all instances. This is not the time to question methods. We need to further empower our resources to stop or interdict these terrorist cells as soon as possible."

"I agree completely, but my concern is our ability to prosecute these individuals once they are apprehended. Information obtained through illegal methods will not hold up in civil or military courts."

Seibel transferred his stare to each member of Account One and waited an appropriate period before responding. He loved dramatic build-up. "Criminals, murderers and terrorists possessing vital information pertaining to the safety and security of this nation are not afforded the same rights as the rest of us. They have made their choice and will pay accordingly. You don't need to worry about this information passing muster in a court of law. It won't. This man, and many others, will never see the light of day again. They will never be a threat to us or anyone else, ever."

Chapter 38

Anwar Mohamed Mustafa made very few mistakes. Few people in this world are as careful as he. Walking into a FedEx office to send a package was no misstep. It was a message for anyone watching. His message was simple – the time for America to pay is near.

He looked up from the map spread out on the rest stop picnic table. It was another beautiful day. Not too cold, for New Jersey in February. The sun was out. The hum of the highway with an endless stream of vehicles was peaceful.

"Not long now." He said to no one, to everyone. His plans, their plans, were in motion. Teams were in place. Dates and times were set. Each cell had its orders and knew nothing of the others. Each team had been trained and trained again. The bombs they would produce will shake this vapid and morally empty country to its foundations. Nothing would ever be the same. It would be Pearl Harbor, but on the mainland this time.

Looking at the map, he knew where every piece in this chess game sat. He never marked anything. Never left any evidence. That was his signature, as much as the methods he employed in perfecting his craft for the glory of Allah, for Islam.

Glancing at Michigan, and Detroit specifically, caused him to pause. He'd heard nothing from them. Even though it was only one communication sent through an indistinct channel, they had not replied for six days now. Tomorrow or the next day, he would contact them again. Nosar was one of his finest students, a true disciple of the art of death and justice. Anwar had known him for years and knew he would not fail.

One hundred and nineteen miles to the south and west of Anwar, Preacher, with Lance looking over his shoulder, surveyed a satellite image on a large monitor screen. This was nirvana for both of them. Looking down on the world from heaven and zooming into the details that only the highest power camera lens could capture was bliss. Preacher was focusing on Philadelphia at present. He was moving fluidly along streets. He didn't know what he was looking for, but something in the pattern caught his eye.

He zoomed out again to a view of the entire nation. His eyes flitted from Detroit to Chicago to Boston to New York to Washington, D.C. to Atlanta, Dallas, Los Angeles and San Francisco. He repeated the pattern, and then repeated it again. He took Atlanta out. It didn't feel right. Lance was looking at the same pattern, but going in reverse, and then random.

"Zoom in on Dallas. Go downtown next to that spirit center." Lance spoke into Preacher's ear. Preacher didn't have to think about how strange it was listening to himself talking from above. He knew this sort of thing happened more when he was tired, like now. And it always happened while he was asleep. That's when Lance chose to have most of his conversations.

Preacher, who had gotten extremely adept at working the joystick and buttons controlling the satellite imagery software, flew down at a thousand miles an hour to downtown Dallas. He moved in a concentric fashion around the downtown he knew better than all the rest he was watching.

"Not enough time for us to cover all these cities. We'll need help." Lance was ready to move on to Chicago. He didn't have to say it. Preacher knew what he was thinking, because he was thinking it as well, of course.

The two of them had good reason to be viewing these particular cities. Nosar had mentioned each of the locations the week before. He did not have much information about the cells, but he was convincing.

They did not have much time if Nosar could be believed. The clock was running and deadlines were set for the next couple of weeks. Preacher could feel in his bones that, like the triple bombings in Eastern Europe and Egypt, Anwar had called for each of these cities to be hit on the same day. Now Preacher just needed to determine the day, the time, the location of each cell in each city and then Anwar's hiding place. No problem. He had two weeks.

Here's the thing. Seibel had it wrong. He told Account One that Preacher used his special methods to extract vital information from Nosar. The methods employed were indeed special, but Preacher didn't administer them in this instance.

Marta had worked her special brand of magic on Nosar. Preacher did weigh in several times to play good cop to her bad, very bad, despicable, ruthless, loathing, murderous cop. Just as he had told Ayers and Scarfino he would, Preacher called in the location of a bomb loaded onto a rented truck in a warehouse in a dilapidated industrial district a mile or so outside downtown Detroit.

He did not tell the FBI anti-terrorism taskforce agents how he, or Marta, extracted the information. They would not have the proper appreciation for it.

After shoving Nosar in to the trunk, Marta drove them just a few miles to the Ambassador Bridge, connecting Detroit to Windsor, Ontario. They passed through the checkpoint with ease and cruised 15 miles to an exit, which allowed them to venture into a clearing with a heavily wooded area fronting it, creating an ideal location to interrogate a suspect.

Preacher took a little walk into the woods. Marta asked him to give her a few minutes with Nosar. "And please ask Lance to go with you." Marta motioned to the sky above them. "He doesn't need to be snooping down on me."

"Got it," Preacher turned and meandered into the thick of trees. Marta opened the trunk and pulled Nosar out. He was in bad shape. Most of the bleeding had stopped where his ears had been, but he'd lost a decent amount of blood.

"Walk over there," Marta motioned with the gun. He complied and took several steps away from the vehicle. "You have information my associate needs to relay to the FBI."

"I have nothing to say." Nosar was arrogant and dismissive of the woman daring to speak to him in such a manner.

"I understand your perception and misunderstanding of this situation. You see a woman before you. Just a woman, nothing more. But what you don't see is the woman I see shaking in front of me."

He squinted at the remark. "What do you mean?"

"Where do you think we are taking you?"

"I don't know. I thought you would arrest me and take me to a jail, a prison."

"Where nothing would be done for days, weeks maybe. No, we are not taking you to U.S. authorities. You are going somewhere you will likely never return from. You are going to a special place that only welcomes homosexual offenders. A unique prison for the extremely socially unfit." Marta stayed matter of fact.

"I, I am not a homosexual."

"Please. I could tell the moment you started running that you were light in your loafers. You are much less than a man. Certainly no one I would ever consider."

This line so completely caught Nosar off guard that he huffed, exhaled in surprise. "You have the wrong man. I am not a homosexual, I would never."

"That's why I said I wish you could see the woman standing in front of me. You are more of a woman than I. If you could see what I see, you'd notice the little things that are going to make you so attractive to the people waiting for you. Not only are you fairly pretty, you're a fake Muslim. That guarantees your position, which will be bent over, most of the time.

Nosar laughed. "You go ahead and play your games. I know you are all talk. You will not take me to such a place. You will follow that laws of your pitiful nation."

"Which nation?"

"America. The U.S.A."

"Didn't you hear the steady beat of a bridge under the tires a half hour ago? We left America. We are in Canada. You will never set foot in the U.S. again. You are going to be taken about 400 miles north of here to a hole in the ground that only the worst kind go. It is very secret, but very useful. Men are taken there and given to others for safekeeping. You will be quite a prize. I can see from here that you will make an excellent warm blanket for one or more of them."

"Talk."

"Why do you think he cut your ears off?" The question caught Nosar off guard.

"He is insane, a bastard." Nosar brought his hands up to his missing ears again. The look on his face told Marta he still didn't believe it had happened.

"He's that, yes. But he took your ears to mark you. Where you are going, people who have lost an ear are known to others as narcs, snitches. Do you know what that word? With both ears gone, everyone will know you are the worst kind of snitch. You will be treated as less than a woman; like an animal, maybe a goat that a herder lies down with in the mountains. You're life will be pure hell. And here's the best part. You will get to go to hell when it's all over. You certainly won't be welcomed into heaven after bedding down with men, many men."

That was it. In a few minutes, she evaluated the subject, zeroed in on the most vulnerable spot in his ego and exploited his greatest fear. It took all of another 35 seconds for Nosar to beg Marta not to send him to this place. Three minutes later, he was trading on his associates and even Anwar. By the time Preacher came back from his walk in the woods, the terrorist hugged and begged him to convince "this evil woman" not to send him to hell.

Less than 20 minutes later, Preacher pulled into a gas station and called Ayers' enormous cell phone to give him the location of the truck in the warehouse. He also told him about a package Nosar received a couple of days earlier sent from a Baltimore FedEx location. Baltimore field agents obtained the videotape from that location three hours later.

The biggest break in stopping Anwar's far-flung operation to bring terrorism to American shores came from Preacher recognizing a man he last saw on the island of Tapul, and Marta putting the fear of eternal afterlife in hell into the terrorist. They were quite a pair.

Chapter 39

"You know, all this domestic action is outside my area of expertise," Seibel was across the table from Preacher and Marta. They were at a Denny's in Irving, Texas, just a couple of miles from Dallas/Fort Worth International Airport. Seibel had to catch a flight. Preacher and Marta were traveling by car, minivan actually. It was her first chance to see a good bit of the country.

In the past two weeks, they had traveled from Detroit to Chicago to Philadelphia to Boston to New York and Dallas. Los Angeles was next and San Francisco after that. Seibel asked to meet with them in Dallas to go over the latest from the mountains of intelligence coming in from around the country.

"You are doing fine from what I can tell." Preacher smiled and drank some more coffee. He smiled again at the image Lance was looking down on. To anyone in the restaurant, this looked like a young couple and a father. Marta caught his smile and he quickly glanced upward to let her in on the joke.

"Just a little frustrating working through the FBI's bureaucracy. Even with highest level clearance coming after your work in Detroit."

"Still nothing in Philadelphia?" Preacher interrupted.

"Nothing concrete. But the four men you identified are under surveillance." Seibel took a sip of coffee and looked up this time to see what they had been smiling at. He missed nothing. They ate in silence for a few moments. It was kind of nice, and to be truthful, it was kind of like a family gathering. He couldn't help but be something of a father figure in their lives.

"And New York?" Marta asked.

"The focus is actually moving to New Jersey, where one group was taken in for questioning just yesterday."

"Anything good?" Preacher asked.

"Nothing I've heard yet." Seibel was obviously frustrated having to work through the FBI's counterterrorism task force. "They can reach me anywhere nowadays, well in cities at least." He held of a behemoth of a cell phone. He didn't like it any more than Preacher or Lance did. It felt like a ball and chain.

"Where are you off to next?" Marta again.

"Back to D.C. tonight. Coordination with inter-agency operations. And then to New York."

"Where is Foxy?" Preacher had a mouthful of pancake. He loved to eat breakfast for dinner. He had learned from his travels that it was an American trait.

"Foxy, Tarwanah and Jamaani are set to leave the Point tomorrow for Boston. I may need them to deviate to New York or New Jersey, but we'll see." This was an amazingly open and direct conversation. There simply wasn't the time for Seibel to challenge them with his mind games. He needed Lance, or Preacher, to keep up his bomb maker trance. His work in each city had uncovered details and leads that others could never see. Marta gave him an extra set of eyes along the way.

"We should be back in D.C. in four days max. Do you need my latest to brief the taskforce again or do you have that covered?" Preacher couldn't address the taskforce himself. None of them even knew he existed.

"We'll see. I'm sure taskforce leaders will want your report." Seibel drank more coffee and pushed his cup to the edge of the table as the waitress approached with a coffee pot in hand. She refilled all their cups. Marta glanced at her watch. It was nearly time to go. The three of them had already looked over the information, maps, photos and lead sheets in the motel room across the street. Dinner was just chat time, which was something Marta was never comfortable with. Especially with Seibel.

She glanced up where Lance was hovering. She couldn't see him, but he could see her and looked into her eyes to see the discomfort she felt sitting this close to Seibel. If Preacher wasn't with her, the two of them would surely not be sitting in a diner talking about the weather. She was less enraged than she had been in months, but she still wanted and planned to kill the man across the table from her. She wondered if he knew his days were numbered, or if he even cared.

Seibel caught her glance upward again and furrowed his brows. Once or twice was one thing, looking up to the same spot six times now was downright strange. What was she looking at? What was she thinking? He broke the silence.

"So, who are you?" He asked Marta.

"Felicia Brownfield, Springfield, Illinois." She sipped at the steaming coffee.

"High school?"

"Westmoore. College at Mizzou. Majored in journalism. Work for the Wichita Eagle as a business reporter."

"Excellent." Seibel liked the cover. "Are you sleeping?"

The question was a left-fielder and out of bounds. He shouldn't be asking about her personal life. She didn't work for him anymore and did not have to answer his little inquisitions. Lance, from above, was quick to notice the tightening of her mouth. It only lasted a microsecond, but it was the first step toward the onramp to anger. And that was obviously why Seibel had asked. He couldn't help being a prick, a controlling, ice-cold prick.

"Okay, time to roll." Preacher sat forward and pushed his plate and cup a couple of inches into the middle of the table. He tapped the table twice to be sure he had both their eyes. He looked at each of them. "We can talk in a couple of days. We have your enormous cell phone number in case we need to reach you before then. Does Foxy have the same pager number?"

"Yes. And he's carrying one of these as well."

"Crap. That definitely makes me think less of him. What about Tarwanah and Jamaani? Are they packing those things?"

"Yes. It is now standard procedure. You'll get one soon."

"Nah, it will be awhile." He turned to Marta. She was calm. "Ready?"

"Yes, let's go."

They got up from the table. Both Preacher and Seibel pulled out wads of cash. "Let me, please." Seibel insisted and dropped a few bills on the table. A man paying was customary, but Marta was the only multi-millionaire at the table. She had made strategic deposits and opened several safe deposit boxes. Preacher had no idea where it all was stashed, only that she had an endless supply of cash.

The three of them walked out of the restaurant. On the sidewalk under bad neon, Seibel tried to make up for his behavior. "Thanks both of you for your work." He turned to Marta. "Especially your volunteer work. It is greatly appreciated by me and those at the highest levels of your government."

"Which government is that?" She couldn't help herself. And she did have every right to call him on his sanctimonious b.s."

"The government of the United States of America, of course." Seibel bowed as he said this. He spun on his heel and walked to his car.

They turned the opposite direction to walk to theirs.

"That was fun, we need to do it again sometime." Preacher put an arm around Marta. She pressed herself into his body as they walked, needing the touch, the affection.

"I'm going to need a full report on what he, you saw from up there." Marta had already come to appreciate the additional set of eyes they had working for them. She understood the basic idea that Lance, the ghost, couldn't really see anything more than Preacher could, but in the weeks since he had told her about this set up, she had witnessed on many occasions the magic that was at work here. Lance simply saw things that others missed, even her.

"I'll give it to you on the road. Some of it is pretty interesting."

"I'll bet." She smiled and squeezed his arm.

Preacher opened her door for her and she got in. He walked around and got in the driver's side of the minivan. They were the image of a happy young couple. Seibel watched from across the parking lot and was pleased, really pleased, even happy. He knew from direct experience, from Braden and from Fuchs and others, that these two people were a couple of truly messed up human beings. The simple fact that they could find pleasure or happiness together was heart-warming.

His mood changed to sadness when he thought of what he was going to have to do to them within weeks, maybe days.

Interstate 40 holds a special place in Preacher and Lance's heart. He drove out of the way on their route to Los Angeles, just so he could share I-40 with Marta, all the way from Oklahoma City to Barstow, California where the highway ends and you have to take I-15 the rest of the way into L.A.

They stopped in Albuquerque to sleep and eat good Mexican food. They diverted into the Petrified National Forest and the Meteor Crater so Marta could see and touch what Preacher wanted to share with her. Along the route, they listened to an entire 'Learn to Speak Turkish' set of cassette tapes. It ticked Preacher off that he didn't know the language at all. Marta had learned a little from Josef, her number three, who Lance killed back in Baghdad.

Their time together crossing the country in the mini-van bonded the two of them, like a young couple traveling cross-country to begin a new job and new life.

"Seni seviyorum," Preacher squeezed Marta's hand and told her he loved her in Turkish as they descended from the mountains dropping down into the valley. Behind the smog, Los Angeles was spread out before them.

Chapter 40

Maybe it was the water. Or maybe it was those letters up there on that hillside. Or perhaps it was just the traffic.

Whatever it was, Lance noticed it first from up there at 10,000 feet. Preacher was right behind him in seeing it. The "it" in this instance, was the complete absence of anything he felt like blowing up. Sure, there were targets, like Disneyland and Sunset Strip and Grauman's Chinese Theater, but they weren't the heart. They weren't at the heart of America. It was wrong.

Preacher and Marta stepped into a phone booth and deposited all the change he had in his pocket to call the coded number on the card Seibel had handed him.

"Nosar lied, or at least told us a lie, whether he knew it or not." He blurted when Seibel answered on the second ring.

"What?"

"He told some truths, but he lied by pointing us out west. Dallas was never in play. There is nothing here in California. I think the whole scene in Detroit was a setup to take us off target." Preacher looked from Marta's face up to Lance who was now sitting on top of the phone booth watching high-priced sports cars drive by.

"Slow down. You found evidence, traces and players in every city so far. You've uncovered a gold mine of potential cells." Seibel was walking somewhere as he talked. His breath was forced.

"Listen. Stop walking and listen." Preacher waited two seconds and continued, "It was all a set-up to lure us, to lure me away from the real target. We moved teams into the field away from real targets. I can feel it." Marta was hearing this for the first time as well. She closed her eyes and moved through the last couple of weeks since Detroit.

"Where, how did you come to this conclusion? What is your source on this?" Seibel was stopped and listening now.

"No source, just patterns and recognition and process. It was brilliant, friggin' brilliant. He played us all in order to get it all set up. It is going to happen within days, maybe two days."

"Where?" Seibel had his eyes closed 3,000 miles away.

Preacher took the phone from his ear and pressed it against his chest. "Do we tell him? He could put a bunch of people in our way." He asked Marta. She was his only partner now.

"You're talking New York and Washington, right?" She was with him, already looking at what they'd missed in tracking all these fake, planted leads.

"Yes."

"Tell him Washington."

He brought the phone back up to his mouth. "Washington."

"You're sure?" Seibel asked. If we pull teams from other cities and those places go boom, we will pay. You and me."

"Move anyone available to Washington, now. It is where I would hit to make the largest impact. No doubt."

"What about New York?" Seibel was no amateur. Not easily buffaloed.

"Have to keep looking, working there. But primary needs to be D.C. We are getting on the first flight. See you in the morning."

"Okay, thanks."

"Use that big-ass cell phone and make some calls. Get people moving."

Preacher hung up the phone and leaned into Marta, putting his forehead on her shoulder. He was thinking, searching for things he'd missed. She stopped him.

"No time to doubt yourself. Nosar didn't lie. He told us Anwar's plans. But Anwar planted them in him and others. He has always been a master at deception, right? Whether letting a Russian convoy through one day and blowing the next one up the following day. Or setting five cans of soda beside the road only to have the sixth trigger the explosion when picked up. He played all of us." Marta pushed his forehead back with her own to bring his head back up. "Let's go. LAX is 15 minutes away."

She pushed him out of the booth and took the keys to drive. Funny thing, right when she was getting into the car she looked up right where Lance was hovering and shook her head. Marta had learned Preacher's patterns and knew where his out of body alter ego could be found. She was disappointed in him for missing the signs. But not as disappointed as she was in herself for not seeing them.

Anwar turned off the street into a driveway. It was a home like any other on the block. A car was parked in the drive already. He cut the engine and got out to grab a package from the back seat. He walked to the side door and entered, just like he had done hundreds of times before.

Inside, three men sat at the kitchen table. They were all Middle Eastern, like him. And they were all trained in building large destructive bombs. He had taught each of them. Anwar took a seat at the table and looked at each.

"Brothers, it is time. Our plans have brought us together one last time. Word reached me that others have been captured, arrested in Detroit, Chicago and other cities. None of us are under surveillance. The other teams have successfully lured the FBI away from us. We must take advantage of this window and fulfill our destinies."

His statement was followed by a round of "Allahu Akbar" from the others.

"You have your missions. You know your targets as well as you know your own homes. Your devices are assembled. We are ready."

He pulled four items from the package he had brought in from the car. He handed each man an envelope and kept one for himself. They opened the envelopes at the same time. Inside, each found a personal letter written by their leader, written by hand in a script that spoke of education and philosophy and dedication to cause. Each letter was signed the same – Osama bin Mohammed bin Awad bin Laden.

The letters had been written the month before in Sudan, where bin Laden, the leader of al Qaeda, hid in exile. The words were private, but could be shared with others if Anwar was successful in bringing his audacious plan to fruition. He looked around the table at the other three men and knew he had done it. Years of planning, putting people and pieces in place, building lie upon lie to mislead the Americans. His plan, their plan, was in its final days of preparation.

The faces around the table represented the locations Anwar had placed them up to two years earlier. Each held jobs, kept up relationships, played active roles in the community. To his left sat New Jersey. Next to him was Philadelphia. And on the right, was Washington. D.C. This meeting wasn't necessary from an operational standpoint. They each had their explosive devices assembled and loaded. He had personally visited each and helped in the assembly. The bombs were powerful, and would be glorious in their destructiveness.

This short meeting was merely to look them in the eyes and give them their personal letters from al Qaeda's leader. He could see the confidence each man held in their heart after reading the message written exclusively for them. "Brothers, we are ready. We will strike this evil nation with vengeance and retribution for their years of oppression and undying support for the illegal Jewish state. Your years of work and dedication will be repaid with the respect of your brothers around the world. We will surely all be welcomed as heroes by Allah when we pass from this life."

He reached out his hands onto the table. The others joined his hands. "Allahu Akbar, Allahu Akbar." Their chorus of chants lasted for another minute. It was followed by hugs and kisses. Anwar bid them all farewell at the door and watched them drive away. In two days, this country – this world, would never be the same.

Both Preacher and Lance were in a trance as they flew five miles above the earth from Los Angeles to New York. Most people on the red-eye overnight flight were asleep. A few passengers were reading. Marta watched Preacher from the seat beside him, holding his hand.

Preacher had his eyes open but was a world away. Lance was lying on the wing of the 747 looking down at the pinpricks of light in the blanket of darkness below but not really seeing anything. They were reaping the benefits of two brains thinking in one head. Conscious and subconscious. Lance knew it was all just him, but he could distinctly feel each personality working through the problem. Preacher was focusing on Washington, D.C. Lance was caught up on Philadelphia for some reason. He was supposed to be thinking about New York, but Philadelphia kept creeping into view.

They ran through people, faces, names, locations. And then Lance sat up suddenly out there on the wing. Preacher broke from his stare and looked out at him. Marta did the same. She didn't see anything, of course. But she knew what Preacher was looking at.

"Geez, you think?" Preacher said to Lance. He knew what the ghost was thinking, of course.

"Got to be. Look at the pattern. After Nosar and Detroit, there were arrests in Philly, New York and DC. Players are in custody, people let their guard down, a little at least. Only natural."

"Damn." Preacher shook his head.

"What is it?" Marta wanted in on the conversation going on in Preacher's head.

"What do New York, Philadelphia and Washington D.C. all have in common in the last two weeks, according to Seibel?" He asked her while leaning his head back.

She thought for a few moments and got it. "People have been arrested, taken in for questioning."

"Cells were broken up. Players were taken off the board." He added.

"So what does it mean?"

"I didn't see it until a minute ago. Actually, he figured it out." Preacher gestured out the window.

"What did he figure out?" Marta asked as she looked out the window at the lights flashing on the plane's wing.

"Counterterrorism resources have been reduced somewhat in each market after the arrests. Efforts have been doubled in other cities. It is plain and simple a classic dodge. What if they let us have those cells so others could complete their missions?" Preacher shook his head.

"Like doubling back to a place after it has already been searched and cleared. That's how the Mujahedeen did it time and time again in Afghanistan after the Russians moved them out of a location." Marta knew her history well. Especially Russian history.

"Exactly. It goes against logic to think someone would go right back to the same place and do the same thing they were doing. Except, here's the thing, I think they upped the game by making us think we have the players in custody. Brilliant. That takes time and planning."

Marta was with him and moving ahead. "Years of planning. I'll bet the members of the cells that were arrested have all been in the U.S. less than six months, a year max. And I'll bet Anwar has been planning this for two, maybe three years. He will have had the real players in place for years. That means jobs, families, mortgages. They would appear to be on their way to becoming citizens."

Preacher could see it for what it was now. Lance turned back to look down over the wing of the jet. "This is really deep-cover ops stuff. These are spies as much as bombers. These men are most likely not transients. That will make them very difficult to find."

Marta reached up and turned her light on. The guy in the seat behind her wasn't happy about it and huffed. She pulled the tray down and got out the sleeve of her ticket envelope along with a pen. She wrote down three things quickly. 'New York, Phil. and DC'. Then she wrote 'in U.S. 18 month min'. 'From Middle East region'. And then 'work visas'. And finally, 'applications for citizenship'. She circled each set of words. "The minute we land, we contact your computer friend at NSA and have him start pounding his databases to narrow the list down to males in the U.S. who meet these parameters."

Preacher leaned forward and tapped her tray a couple of times. "Think for a minute. What kind of jobs will these men have? They won't be taxi drivers. They are educated. Can the type and kind of work they do help narrow it down even more?"

"Sure. We'll eliminate menial labor such as taxis, retail, clerical. That will eliminated even more possibilities. I'll bet we can get the list down to a few hundred, maybe fewer."

"Then what? Do we send out field agents to interview them? We don't have time for that. It would take a week or more." Preacher sighed.

"No. We don't need interviews. Once we get these men I.D.'d, we'll let another computer go to work on the them – a supercomputer."

"How's that? Where is this computer?" Preacher raised his eyebrows.

Marta just smiled. Then she raised her hand and tapped Preacher on the forehead a couple of times. "Right here. I'm willing to bet once the photos of these guys are put in front of you," then she gestured out toward the wing. It was strange, but natural. "And him. I'm sure you will recognize them from somewhere in Anwar's records. Some of the faces are going to jump off the page or computer screen for you. And then, we'll go get them."

Preacher dug into his pocket and again pulled out the card Seibel had given him with the four coded numbers on it. "We'll need help to get to them in time. While I'm talking to my contact at NSA, you call Fuchs and have him, Tarwanah and Jamaani move toward Philadelphia and D.C. We'll handle New York."

"What about Seibel?" Marta didn't like the taste of the name in her mouth.

"I'll call him and tell him to assemble his top secret group. That will keep him out of our way, for a little while at least."

Chapter 41

There were actually 311 names on the list. Now he needed to see their faces. Preacher walked into the New York Public Library and went downstairs to a room full of computers and monitors. He didn't really care for computers, but they served an ever-growing purpose. And today he benefited from this new thing, the Internet, and something called the World Wide Web.

His computer nerd contact at NSA gave Preacher a user name and password over the phone. When he fired up the computer, the date on the screen read February 25, 1993. He typed in the strange http://www address into the machine and was taken to a secure system where a list of 311 names was on the screen. He started with the first since they were alphabetical. Marta sat beside him just as fascinated by computer technology.

Names 46, 129 and 287 were three individuals Preacher recognized after viewing all the driver's license and ID photos. Several others registered in some capacity, but not in the same way. These three were associated with Anwar and al Qaeda over the last decade. He had seen their images before. And number 287 he had even seen in person on the Philippines island of Tapul. He was the third man who had escaped that morning.

The computer listed his name as Ramzi Ahmed Yousef. He left the image up on the screen and shook his head.

"You know him." A statement, not a question from Marta. "You've seen him before."

Preacher laughed quietly and smiled at her. "Guess where?"

"No. Not on the island."

"On Tapul. He got away." Preacher laughed.

"He was the third one with Nosar and Anwar." She knew the scene well having been through it many times with him as he tried to work out what went wrong, other than being dumb.

"Yes. He has so many damn aliases that I didn't know who I was looking for." Preacher stared at the image, the eyes.

"Don't blame yourself. Others have missed him for years." She put a hand on his arm. "Now we can get him."

Preacher reviewed the information available on last known address and hit print. He did the same for the other two men. It just happened that Yousef lived in the New York area, right across the river in New Jersey. The second man was last known to be in Camden, New Jersey – a stone's through from Philadelphia. And number three kept a residence in Arlington, Virginia.

"Just like we thought. Damn," but she said the word in Russian - proklinat' - like she usually does when upset. The two of them would often wander through three or four different languages during the course of a conversation. They did it seamlessly. Each preferred the sound of certain words in Russian or German or Arabic.

Preacher answered her in Russian. "I know. Crazy being right every once in awhile. We'll need to get with Fuchs and Tarwanah and fax them this information so they can move on Camden and Arlington." Preacher clicked to close the computer program he had been using and turned the computer off.

Twenty-three minutes later, Seibel hung up the huge cell phone in his hand. "Damn. He did it. They did it." He turned from the window he'd been looking out of while talking to Fuchs on the phone. Alan Kleinfeller, Seibel's one boss in the world and the appointed executive of the Central Intelligence Agency sat behind his desk.

"Preacher?"

"And his partner." Seibel sat in a chair facing Kleinfeller. "I don't know if they will share their methods, but it appears they found three individuals planning to blow up freedom-loving Americans here on our own soil."

The CIA Director had heard Seibel's end of the conversation with Fuchs. "So New York, Philadelphia and DC. Do we have anything more specific on targets?" He was ready to move, to call other resources into action. He would never tell Seibel this, but he was now, like he was often, in awe of the man's ability to bring things together. The borderline insane CIA spymaster had struck gold with his discovery of Lance Priest. Friggin' amazing. "Do we have resources en route?"

"Fuchs and the Jordanians are on their way to Philly and D.C. We will need to enlist field agents." Seibel sat back and exhaled. "I'm going to New York."

"Why New York? I could use you here."

"It's where they are. It's where Anwar is."

"How do you know?" Kleinfeller sat back in his chair and locked his fingers behind his head. A couple of minutes of relaxation before kicking literally everything at his disposal into overdrive.

Seibel closed his eyes. "It's only natural. He would be aiming for the biggest, most audacious target. Nothing is more American than New York. It is the heart, the beating heart of America. Anwar knows that. Preacher knows it as well. He is thinking like a terrorist."

"How's that?"

"I told you I needed him to think like a terrorist, a bomber. He is not acting, not pretending. I've seen it in him since his near-death experience. He's single minded. He is a terrorist, a radical, a true believer in his cause."

Kleinfeller sat forward. He was ready to go, needed Seibel to get going. "And what is that cause?"

"As far as I can tell. He wants to die. He wants to go up in a fireball with Anwar."

The terrorist drove across the Brooklyn Bridge. Not because he needed to, just because he wanted to. He liked the structure, the sheer size and strength of the link between two New Yorks. The bridge was actually his first target. He considered it a natural five years earlier when he first visited this country. After riding across it in a taxi, he walked it the following day looking at the construction, the fabrication, assembly, weaknesses and strengths. He saw that it would take numerous immense explosives placed in strategic positions to do the job. Several trucks driven to ideal locations across the span might do the job as well, but they probably wouldn't take the entire monument down. He needed to completely destroy his target.

He already knew what it needed to be back then, what his targets were. It had to be the collapse, the complete destruction of a towering edifice. Two of them stood at the southern end of Manhattan. The other symbol of American ingenuity and prosperity stood at the corner of 5th Avenue and West 34th Street. When the twin towers of the World Trade Center and the Empire State Building came down, America's strength, American might and American credibility would come crashing down with them. It will be glorious.

His brightest pupil will place the bomb in the underground parking garage of the WTC – a much simpler mission requiring only one vehicle. The explosions necessary to bring down the Empire State Building required greater planning, placement and skill. Anwar would handle this project personally. It was a grand and audacious plan. And it will change the world forever.

The terrorist bomber walked out of the New York Public Library onto 5th Avenue. He had a permanent street map of New York City basically tattooed into his brain. He hung a right on the sidewalk and reached down to take his partner's hand. It was reassuring. They walked a half block until they could see the tip of the radio tower spire. He looked from the tippy top of the tower on the top of the Empire State Building. His look told her all she needed to know. Her terrorist lover knew his target. The only question was how would he blow it up.

"I need a detailed tourist guide book or access to blueprints. A guide book is probably easier to come by." He pulled her forward. They walked the seven blocks to 34th Street to see what he could find. It was almost noon. Lance was up at about 1,500 feet looking down diagonally at the one-time tallest building in the world. He imagined how scary that would have been to be hanging from the grasp of a big ol' gorilla up there. He was also humming a catchy tune about the Big Apple sung by Frank Sinatra.

The wannabe terrorist and two associates he had gathered for the assignment jumped down from the back of the rented Ryder truck parked in Yousef's driveway. They had been loading material into the back of the truck for several days and had it nearly ready. All totaled, the assembled explosive device weighed over 1,300 pounds. The main charge consisted primarily of urea nitrate with other metals, including aluminum and ferric oxide surrounding the charge. To ignite this behemoth of deadly destruction, a combination of nitroglycerine, ammonium nitrate, smokeless powder and dynamite would be used. The whole thing would go off with a bang when a 20-foot fuse was lit. Yousef and his associates had studied well the manuals supplied by Anwar.

The three men closed the roll-down door on the truck and went inside the house whispering a chorus of "Allahu Akbars."

Six hours later, a Chevy sedan pulled to a curb. Out of the back of the car stepped Mikel Fuchs holding the faxed sheet he'd received from Preacher this morning. He also held another sheet of paper with a recent driver's license photo photocopied for him and 17 other FBI agents from the Philadelphia field office who were setting up a perimeter of the location.

Fuchs leaned into the front window to talk to the agent in the passenger seat. "I'll go on foot from here. I'll signal and you bring in the cavalry." He held up the small radio before tucking it into his jacket pocket. His clothes were dirty, torn. He looked the part for this area of Camden. He brought the field agents together an hour ago to go over the operation. A few of them had raised their eyebrows at this stranger coming in from nowhere and issuing orders, but the commander in charge had received orders from Washington to listen and to obey without question this guy's commands. Within 30 seconds of starting, Fuchs had every man and woman's respect. His plan, details and structure of deployment were more than solid.

They were all impressed with him. It would have been quite a surprise for them to learn it was all a bit of bluster. Fuchs did want the FBI to come in, but only after he had interfaced with the Philadelphia suspect himself. That likely meant dispatching several men to paradise. He assumed it was a small group, three or four at most, to keep a tight lid on the operation. It was just Fuchs walking toward the warehouse. The bad guys were outnumbered.

Three hours later, 140 miles to the south and west, two Middle Eastern men approached a small group of men. The group of a half dozen men sat on benches near the laundry room of a rundown apartment complex. The men were speaking Arabic and smoking. The conversation was pleasant, but heated, as these things usually are.

The two men that joined the group were not regulars. They were new to the area. Within minutes, they joined the conversation and took seats opposite each other on the benches. The topic of conversation was Turkey and the problem of secularism in a Muslim nation. None of the six men noticed when one of the two new members of the group glanced over at three men coming out of an apartment unit across the parking lot from the laundry.

Passenger Geoffrey Seibel walked up the air bridge after his short Continental flight from Washington National to JFK. Two FBI agents met him at the gate and walked behind him, trying to keep up.

One of the agents handed Seibel a folder with the latest intel. He scanned it while walking. A tiny old lady in front of him walking at a fit snail's pace brought a silent snarl to his face. He smiled as he stepped around her. He always knew why he did the things he did. It was for people like her, just wanting to live their lives in freedom, no matter how slow they walked.

Outside, once in the front passenger seat of the car Seibel pulled out his gargantuan cell phone and dialed. He got no answer to either call he made. He wished like hell he'd made Preacher carry one of those damn phones.

Chapter 42

Mikel Fuchs stood about 6 feet, one inch and weighed 198 pounds. He carried himself much lighter, moving like a lightweight, even a featherweight prizefighter. But as he walked along a broken and dirty street in the roughest part of Camden, New Jersey, he carried himself like a bag of rocks. He was slow, plodding. A man with nowhere to be and no one to see. He caused no eyebrows to raise as he approached a warehouse set about 80 feet back from the street between two other buildings that fronted the road. There was an eight-foot chain link fence and gate topped with barbed wire across the front of the property.

Fuchs peered into the space as he sauntered by. There was no activity visible from the front. No dogs either. That was good. As he got past the warehouse, he quickened his pace, rounded the corner of the next building.

He jogged down a dark alley and found what he needed. It was a drainpipe. He grabbed it and shimmied up the side of the abandoned two-story brick building to the roof. Once up there, he moved across the rooftop to the other side where he could see down into the warehouse next door. There were lights on inside, but he could see no movement. He turned his head for a few moments to listen. He heard two voices, one higher than the other, followed by a laugh.

It was near dusk. His dark jacket, jeans and black cap helped him blend into the dark as he descended down the building to a window ledge below and then a 12-foot drop to blacktop. He crouched and moved over against the warehouse, below the one window not blacked out. He looked to his left then to his right. No activity on the exterior. He peeked in and could see a light was on in a larger room past the small office he could see into. Thirty seconds later, a man walked through the larger space carrying something. He saw no one else, but knew from the laughter minutes earlier, there were more inside.

He turned and made his way to the back of the building and looked around the corner. Not much there. One door, no unpainted windows. He slid over to the door to try it. No go, locked. He continued to the other corner of the building and looked around. As expected, there was not much. He walked the 70 or so feet back to the front of the building and stopped at the corner, leaning to spy around to the front. No one around. The double bay doors were closed. He scooted by both to the front door. It was unlocked. After putting his ear to it for several seconds, he turned the rusty handle and cracked the door. He could hear noises, but couldn't distinguish their source.

He silently pulled the door open and slid inside, then climbed eight stairs into a small reception room with an empty desk and a door behind it to a hallway. Fuchs stepped over to the wall beside the entry to the hall and listened. He pulled out the radio in his pocket and made sure he had turned it off. He then set it on the desk. Didn't want it weighing him down. He pulled out two silenced Glocks and rolled his head and neck in a few rotations as he always did before going into action.

Three steps down the hall was a doorway to the right into the open warehouse area. The door was propped open by a small box on the floor. He walked to the door and pressed himself to the wall to listen. He heard footsteps, two sets at least. A short conversation between two men and then a third voice. He heard two exhales as two men lifted something heavy. He dropped to the floor and brought his head into the doorway at foot level. He saw two cars and a large van in the middle of an open space approximately 80 by 60 feet. The men were loading large bags into the van. He could read the words on the side of the bags – fertilizer, and knew right away that he had found his target. The two men loading the van stepped back to grab another large bag of fertilizer. Ten seconds later, the man pictured in the INS photo on a folded sheet of paper in his pocket jumped out of the back of the van.

Fuchs eased his head back and got to his feet. He made sure the safety was off on both Glocks and casually stepped around the doorframe into the open area. He approach was silent. None of the men spotted him until he was just 15 feet from the man he came to see. The terrorist spun around and gasped. Fuchs put a silenced bullet in the man's knee. The guy screamed, howled really. Fuchs turned to face the other two, 20 feet away next to a pallet of fertilizer bags. They held one between them. Their hands were full, their legs exposed. Fuchs put four bullets in them, one for each of their knees. They dropped the 100-pound bag and collapsed, writhing in pain.

He turned back to his target, who was now looking to his right, at the doorway Fuchs had come through. Damn. Through the doorway, came another man. This one was armed with a handgun of his own and started firing immediately. Fuchs dove to his right behind one of the cars. The guy with the gun fired off the remainder of the bullets in his first clip and then dropped the empty clip to insert another. He was good, well-trained. Fuchs had no time to be impressed or pissed off for not checking down the hall for a bathroom before stepping into the warehouse.

He rolled further to the right rear of the Chrysler. He lowered himself to look for the man's feet. They did not come into view. He had stepped around the front of the van. The wanted terrorist with a bullet in his knee took this opportunity to hobble around the van as well. The two men were about 25 feet away on the other side of the van, standing behind tires so he couldn't see their feet. For a fraction of a moment, he peered into the open back of the van. Fuchs was no explosives expert, but what he saw sent a shiver down his spine. The back of the oversized van was jammed with fertilizer bags. Two large barrels stood in the middle with other materials packed around them. This thing would take out half a block at least. It also meant he needed to be careful with his shots.

Thinking of the shots sent another shiver down his spine. The gunshots were likely heard by FBI agents outside, around the perimeter. If they came in for support, they could go up with the van if it were to be detonated. He needed to move, to act. Behind him, the two fertilizer carriers struggled and screamed. One was crawling toward him. He brought one of his guns around and put a quiet bullet in his forehead. The other one saw this and decided to stay where he was. Fuchs then rolled to a crouched position behind the Chrysler and raised up where he could see both the van's front and rear. The shooter popped his head up momentarily and looked through the vehicle's window to spot Fuchs. He immediately ducked back down. He could hear them whisper to each other in Arabic. One told the other to open the door. "I'll do it." Fuchs had a pretty good idea what was going on. He stood to three-quarters height and moved forward until he could see into the driver side window of the van. The shooter was waiting and fired three shots at him. He ducked and was about to return fire when another shot rang out. He had both guns pointed at the window of the van when he stepped back into the shooter's view.

Instead of pointing the gun at Fuchs, the shooter held his gun to his own temple. A quick glance showed Fuchs his target was sitting in the passenger seat. Fuchs took three steps closer and saw what he expected. His assigned subject for today's somewhat important mission had two bloody holes in his head where a bullet had entered and exited. He then saw something that made him shake his head. The terrorist had lit a fuse that looked like it was going to end up in the rear of the van. Damn.

He looked back to the shooter and said, "Go ahead." The man smiled but didn't pull his trigger so Fuchs did. He needed to move, quickly. Before the shooter hit the floor, Fuchs was walking briskly back to the wounded but still living fertilizer carrier. He grabbed the man's left wrist and dragged him toward the bay door. He pushed the button and the ancient door started to rise. When it was three feet up, Fuchs dragged the man behind him out into the dark of night.

He yelled out, "If anyone is close, get back or get down. This place is going to blow in seconds." He heard movement and footsteps out in the street.

Fuchs and his new friend were across the lot and to the chain link fence when the sound behind him changed. He recognized the distinct signature of chemical accelerant as the fuse reached the bomb, which meant it would blow within a second or two. They were about 70 feet from the building with warehouses on each side of them. Not far enough. The blast would hit him hard. Fuchs lifted the bloody man and held him up between himself and the soon to be rubble of a building. He pressed his back against the fence gate and ducked his head.

The explosion was thunderous, massive. The shockwave was painful, followed by heat, fire, then debris. The poor guy being used as a human shield didn't make it. Fuchs and the deceased terrorist were blown away with the fence. They traveled 15 feet backward from the fireball out into the middle of the street.

Fuchs was relatively unhurt. But his ears were ringing something fierce.

His little mission was a failure on the intel front. But he had stopped a terrorist from driving his bomb into a building or mall or football stadium or school. That was a marginal success, but Fuchs knew well that Seibel would be pissed off by the missed opportunity to mine these resources for information.

The third man to walk out of the door carried a box. He was the one both the strangers had come to see. No, more than see, they were here to capture or kill him.

Tarwanah rose slowly, as if to stretch his legs. Jamaani did the same and excused the two of them from the others. Tarwanah, the older of the two Jordanian CIA operatives, walked to the northeast, to the left of the three men preparing to get into a Jeep Cherokee. Jamaani, walked just to the right of the vehicle. When they were each approximately 25 fee from the vehicle, they both spun and sprinted toward open doors with guns drawn. The driver saw Tarwanah at about 12 feet away. He began to scream, but three bullets ripped through his neck. On the passenger side, Jamaani reached the open door and put the silencer to the man's head. He spoke very calmly. "Don't move. Be still."

Tarwanah had turned his aim upon their target now seated in the back seat with the door closed. The man, a native of Yemen, merely looked at Tarwanah. About nine feet separated the two of them.

It was the set of his eyes. Tarwanah had seen the look before. He'd seen suicide bombers several times in person and in videos. They were always the same. This man had that undeniable look. There was no time. "Dive Ja!" He shouted and dove behind a Ford Taurus parked next to the Jeep. He continued to roll away to gain precious feet before the explosion.

Jamaani was looking through the vehicle at Tarwanah when the look of recognition came across the older Jordanian's face. Jamaani knew that look well and started forward to try to reach a low wall about 15 feet in front of the Jeep.

He was in the air, diving over the wall when the vehicle exploded. In the second and a half of elapsed time the two experienced field operatives had before the tremendous blast, they had placed a precariously small bit of distance between them and the Jeep. Each was thrown, blown outward from the explosion emanating from the back seat of the Cherokee. The Taurus absorbed enough of the blast to divert some of the energy and concussive shockwave away from Tarwanah. Jamaani's legs took the brunt of the blast as his head and chest were already over the wall. His body did something of a violent cartwheel and his feet slammed down onto the dirt and sparse mulch in the garden area.

Both would live. They were bloodied and bruised, but knew they'd make it as the smoke and flames rose into the air. Around them, vehicles burned, windows were all blown out. Debris was blown into the brick and windows and doors of the surrounding apartment units. The men gathered for smoking and arguing were all dazed, some were struck by debris.

The Jeep was no more. The burnt and bent frame sat 22 feet from where it had been. The bodies inside were gone. FBI agents approached with caution from all sides. They stayed back a couple hundred yards just in case there were more explosives waiting for them. It was just after dark on February 25, 1993.

Chapter 43

Friday, February 26, 1993 — New York, USA
Information was scarce until after midnight. Seibel paced the office in the CIA's mid-town New York City location waiting for updates. His phone rang at 12:02. It was Fuchs with the latest news from Camden. Half an hour later, Tarwanah called with details of his and Jamaani's evening in Arlington. And at 1:15 a.m. Marta called his mammoth cell phone.

"Where is he?" Seibel demanded.

Marta remained silent until Seibel changed his tone.

"I'm sorry. Is he with you?" Seibel said it slowly, smiling.

"Yes. He is sleeping. I made him take a shot of cold medicine an hour ago. He hasn't slept in three days."

"What do you have?" Seibel tried to keep the smile in his voice.

"He identified several targets in the city. He wants to go back for another look first thing tomorrow." Marta was looking out the window of their way-too-expensive-for-the-size hotel room just off Park Avenue. Preacher was asleep in bed. She couldn't see him, but she knew Lance was hovering, watching her. She smiled up at him. She couldn't see it, but he smiled back. He was pleasant when Preacher slept. The cold medicine gave him a little buzz, so he was extra nice tonight.

"I am going to need more than that very soon." The smile was fading from Seibel's voice.

"What happened?" Marta could tell from the tone, the rushed delivery, that something had changed.

"They, we, got the other two. Just like he guessed. They were preparing to deliver the bombs. We believe they were planning to do it tomorrow." Seibel was matter of fact, cold.

"Did we take anyone alive?"

"No. Both bombs went off. Fuchs, Tarwanah and Jamaani were all injured, but not seriously. They'll make it."

Marta didn't really care about them. People die all the time. She knew Fuchs all too well, and had heard from Lance and Preacher that the Jordanians were good men, but she was only concerned about him. Everyone else could die. They were all going to someday anyway. She needed Lance in her life and didn't at all like the idea of him being caught up in a bomb blast. "What kind of devices were they?"

"A small scale suicide device packed with scary stuff. And a large nitrogen package in a van. It would have done serious damage to whatever building it was near. The suicide device was likely meant for a strategic target, most likely an office in D.C. It appeared the target was wearing a delivery uniform."

"So, not much similarity. Our assumption has to be the third device will fall outside the parameters of the other two. It will most likely be a different design and delivery method." Marta jumped ahead to look at the coming day. Lance was thinking as well. He would have to wake Preacher in a few minutes. A couple of hours of sleep were all he was going to get.

"That is my assumption as well. Details are still coming in."

"Where are you?" Marta changed subjects abruptly.

"New York. CIA offices." He didn't have the energy to lie.

"We'll call you again in a few hours." She hung up and turned to look at Preacher. She needed to act. Needed to protect him. She didn't know what was going through her lover's head, but Braden had given her his inside view. If the psychologist was right, Lance, or Preacher, or whoever he was to her, was going to put himself right next to Anwar when the bomb went off. Braden was positive Lance wanted to die. His strange love for Marta wasn't even enough to sway him from his death wish.

Marta didn't know if Braden was right or not. She simply could not take the chance. Truth be told, she had not given Preacher just cold medicine. Into the little plastic cup, she added several drops of a sedative she had seen keep a subject down for 18 hours. She climbed into bed and lay next to Preacher, tucking her head into the back of his neck. She stayed there for a couple of minutes. He didn't react like usual and press himself against her. He was out cold.

This thing, this life together, living on the road, sleeping in lousy motel rooms, but sleeping together, waking up next to each other every morning, was the best her life had ever been. She'd found a home. She smiled, her lips touching his neck. His screwed up mind, with its endless creativity and infinite ability to surprise, was her home now. All the rest — his smile, his touch, his love — that was the icing. Marta never expected happiness or any place to call home. She could not lose this.

In the few days of downtime they could carve out, they had discovered a cabin next to a babbling brook in a beautiful valley. She purchased it with cash. The four times they'd been there were marvelous. She cooked, he ate. They took walks along the stream, holding hands, of course. Moments like these spoke of a possible future, an impossible life. Maybe.

Marta was not just along for the ride. She was in this game, invested in the outcome. And unlike others who support from the sidelines, she had the skills, the capabilities to play and win. She knew what she had to do. It involved creative problem solving, manipulation of the human psyche and killing, probably lots of killing.

Marta kissed Preacher on the cheek, got up, gathered several things into her bag and looked back at the clock on the bedside table. She was about to close the door, when she stepped back in and looked up into the corner of the room. "Please don't wake him. I know he'll understand later."

Lance looked at her and smiled. He thought Marta was heading out to pick up supplies. After she closed the door, he thought to himself how nice it would be to be able to lie down for a little while and sleep like Preacher.

Since being shot on Tapul, Preacher had read up on his condition, his friendly ghost. He read everything on the subconscious he could find.

But in researching the subconscious in full, Preacher learned what some experts knew – humans are just not aware of the world around them. Unfortunately, most humans only know what their conscious mind tells them. And it is pretty much a linear process, one thought after the other.

But some lucky people, those like Lance, were in touch with their other side, their subconscious. It is really what's in control when humans drive a car, walk, eat, sleep, live. Behind the curtains, the subconscious controls everything. And Lance knew it. He saw everything, literally everything. Nearly being killed pulled back the curtains even more.

While Preacher was looking at an object and figuring out his next move, Lance was analyzing a thousand data elements up in Preacher's head. And unlike most humans, who are only vaguely familiar with their subconscious, Preacher was in constant contact with his.

Lance was always turned on. Always. He felt a little cheated, always having to float around and stay awake 24/7. Such is the life of a ghost, or angel, or whatever the hell he is.

Chapter 44

The taxi driver chose to take the Lincoln Tunnel. He could just as well have chosen the Holland Tunnel further south. Not much difference really. Jersey City, New Jersey was just across the Hudson River and a world away from Manhattan. At 2 a.m., Marta was heading back to Jersey City for the second time in eight hours. She had seen something the previous afternoon when she, Preacher and a team of FBI anti-terrorism taskforce members from the New York office, visited two locations where Ramzi Yousef had been known to reside.

They did not find him or any direct associates at either location. They took three men in for questioning, but neither Preacher nor Marta thought they'd get much. Yousef had done a tidy job of keeping to himself and a close-knit group of friends that lived and worked regular jobs in the community. Nothing out of the ordinary, except his absence. His phone had changed several times. He was known to carry a cell phone as well, which made it more difficult to track his communications.

There was no time for any of that anyway. This thing was going down tomorrow. Marta could feel it. When the team was packing up to leave the second row house they had invaded yesterday afternoon, Marta stood in the middle of the street in front of the home. Preacher was around back. She looked to her left and then to her right. Out of the corner of her eye she saw a curtain fall back to vertical. It could have been any neighbor looking out at the mini-chaos on their street. But something about the action didn't look or feel right.

As they got into the back of an FBI Ford, Marta glanced over at the window. The drapes were open just a fraction. Someone was watching.

At 2:14 a.m., the taxi rounded the corner a few hundred yards away from the row house across from Yousef's former residence. Marta handed the driver two $50s. She got out and disappeared into the dark.

Three minutes later, she was at the back door of the house. Time was short. There wasn't the luxury of entering the house clean and quiet. She put the silenced Berretta that Preacher had procured for her from a black market resource to the lock below to the door handle and fired twice. The shot was fairly quiet. The exploding wood and metal was not. She held up a flashlight and moved into the two-story structure like a compact hurricane. She glided upstairs and down a hallway where she found three bedrooms with two men in one, and one each in the other two. The noise had awakened one of them. The others were still asleep. The one that stirred, sat up in bed. She shined the light in his eyes and said calmly in Arabic, "If your feet touch the floor, you die."

She stepped back into the hall and decided to bring the two singles into the room with the other two. Marta stepped into the first room and turned the light on. The man in bed opened his eyes and she whacked him with the butt of the flashlight. "Keep your eyes shut. Get up." The man stumbled out of the bed. She pushed him with a silencer in his back down the hall to the first room where the light was still off. "Keep your eyes closed. Move, and we kill you."

She went back down the hall where the fourth man was up and out of his bed reaching into a bedside dresser drawer. She put a quiet bullet in the back of his knee. He collapsed and started to wail. "If you scream, I put the next one through your throat. Move, down the hall." She kicked the man as he limped, whimpering and bleeding, to the first bedroom to join the others. Once the last of the four was in the room, Marta stepped in behind him and turned the light on.

They all looked at her and then each other. Each looked past her into the hall to see who was with her. A lone woman could not have done this. She saw the looks on their faces and wanted to smile but didn't. Instead, she squatted down on her haunches to get a better look at them. She needed to see into their eyes from their level. When she got to the third man, the one who had sat up in bed, she knew she had him. He was different than the rest; less nervous, not looking at the gun in her hand. He was not afraid to die, or at least thought he wasn't.

She had no time for games, for delays, for macho facades. She lifted the gun and shot the man in his left shoulder. From about 10 feet, the bullet passed through him and lodged in the wall amid a splatter of blood. He was about to scream when she tilted her head and said, "Do not scream. Do not cry out." The other men cowered. The one she'd shot in the knee pulled his damaged leg up and squeezed it.

"Where can I find him?" She addressed the one she just shot.

"Who? Why are you doing this?"

"I will ask one more time and then I will shoot you again. Where is he?"

"I don't know." He stammered.

Marta lowered the gun and shot him in the ankle. The explosion of the bones in the joint followed the puff of the gun. He screamed this time. She moved her aim and was about to pull the trigger a third time when the fourth man, the one who slept in the room with the other, held up his hands.

"Stop. No more, please."

She didn't look at him, only adjusted her aim to the injured man's right knee.

"Please, no more. I will tell you where he is." Marta was right. The third man was related to the fourth. Her guess was he is a younger brother. The older brother could not take seeing his younger sibling tortured in such a manner.

"Quickly." She turned her eyes to him.

He looked at her for a few moments and reconsidered. But the steel of her gaze told him his brother would not be alive in a few minutes. She was not done. "They moved to another house."

"No, Yasin." It was the second man of the three. Marta moved her aim and put a bullet through the man's head. A mist of blood droplets hung in the air after his body fell. The other men in the small bedroom gasped and cringed. She returned to the fourth man.

"Quickly now Yasin. The location." She said in Arabic.

The first man she'd shot started rocking back and forth and whispering a prayer. Yasin's younger brother, shot in the shoulder and ankle, fell back on the bed grabbing his leg. It was a messy, bloody scene. Marta had definite advantages in a situation like this. Besides the fact that she held the gun, she had been in this very position before – standing, or squatting, in the midst of a group of bad people. Her third advantage was her ability to end lives. She had no problem, either morally or legally, being judge, jury and executioner to those who would harm others. This small group with her this early morning in Jersey City comprised four men, now three, that had direct knowledge of a plot to kill others.

She raised her eyebrows. Marta was sure. "You were saying about a house?" She waited an entire second, then moved her aim from him back to his brother. "Okay, then."

"No, wait please. The house is less than a mile away. I don't know the address. I can show you, take you."

"Good. Let's go, all of us." She stood up and signaled for him to help the other two to their feet. "Now."

"But, they're injured. They can't walk." He protested.

"Then I'll put them out of their misery."

"No. I..."

"You bastards will all either be dead or in custody within the hour. I don't particularly care which. Dead is my preference. You would sit here or sleep or take tea, and then celebrate when you see on the news that hundreds or more are killed. You are each as guilty as those planting the bombs." She stepped menacingly toward them and pointed at their friend on the floor who had began to leak all of his bodily fluids as his muscles relaxed forever. "He's the lucky one in your little family here. He went quickly. You should all pay for what you have done and what you are planning to do. You should pay with pain and suffering and the pain and suffering of your families. You are despicable in your cowardice and hypocrisy. You claim the moral high ground of religious fealty when you are all just Pharisees, murderers, prostitutes. You should not be allowed to breath the same air as the rest of us. Now, we leave here, now. Up." She stepped out into the hall.

The remaining healthy man helped the other two to their feet and then painfully into the hall, down the stairs and to the front door. Marta followed behind silently the entire way. She picked up a large cell phone off the kitchen table as they passed it. "Out to your car. You drive, they get in the back."

The group exited the row house. It was dark and silent outside. No remnants of the FBI invasion of the house across the street the evening before. They made their way to a Toyota Corolla parked a few cars down. The two injured men got in back and Yasin got in the driver's seat. Marta stepped in and jammed the silencer on the end of her gun into his temple, which shoved his head sideways. "Anything, anything at all and you find out very soon if you are going to heaven or hell." She moved the gun from his temple to jam it into his privates. "Drive. Slowly." She looked at the two in the back to make sure they got her message. They were busy bleeding and whimpering.

Yasin drove the car into the street and to the corner where he turned right. As Yasin said, they traveled less than a mile to the south and west.

"It is just ahead on the right."

"Drive past, slowly." She peered out into the night at the house. There was a light on behind curtains. A glance at her watch; it was 2:30 a.m. "Park up ahead. You and I will walk back."

"Why me?"

"Do you have something better to do?" She pushed a little harder on his crotch. He didn't say anything. She turned to the two bleeding in the back seat. "I suppose I don't need to tell you both not to move." She motioned for the driver to get out.

He came around the car and joined her on the sidewalk. "Yasin, I'll bet you only know certain things about Yousef. I'm sure you know that he is planning to set off a bomb, but you are probably not aware of where or when. My guess is you have been used to procure certain items and communicate with various contacts on his behalf. Your location, just across the street from his old house, tells me you were probably used as a pick up and drop off and as a lookout. All of this points to you having pieces of information that hold varying levels of value. One of the primary elements within your mental inventory is a phone number." She pulled out the cell phone she had taken off Yasin's kitchen table. "Dial his number and tell him they found you. Tell him to run. Nothing more. Do that and I will leave you, your brother and the other gentleman alive. You can take them to the hospital and then leave this country. If I ever find you again, I will kill all of you.

"Or, if you don't want to call him because of your dedication to this unfortunate cause, then I will shoot you in both knees, both shoulders and drag you back over to the car where I will put you and your brother at each other's crotch and see which one wants to live by biting the other man's penis off. Gross and disgusting, I know. But I've seen it before, the survival instinct always kicks in and one of you will do it."

"You are evil." He smoldered.

"Oh, evil like blowing up innocent people in the name of Allah? That kind of evil?" She stepped in close to whisper into his ear. "No, I'm a different kind of evil. I am here on this earth to make hypocrites like you and your friends pay. And the payment is not just your life. I take souls. Yours is mine." She waited there just inches from him to see if he had it in him to attack her. After a couple of seconds she stepped away. He didn't have it. He was a coward at heart, just like most.

She handed him the phone. "Dial and say what I told you."

He took the phone reluctantly and dialed a number. He exhaled and drew in a huge breath as the phone rang. Marta watched the house for any activity. At the other end of the line, someone answered. "They found us. Run." And Yasin hung up. He too watched the house. There was no activity, no movement. They waited 30 seconds, and then a minute. Still nothing.

"Let's go, to the front door." She motioned him with the gun and then planted it firmly in his back to move him along. On the front porch, she stepped to the side, "Knock."

Yasin did as he was told. He knocked and stepped back. Deep inside the house, someone stirred. Two people talked to each other. Twenty seconds later, someone looked out the front window at Yasin. Marta was plastered to the brick and could not be seen from the window.

A moment later, the door started to open. Marta jumped around behind Yasin. As the door opened, she shoved him in, knocking him into the man at the door. Marta shot Yasin in the leg and the other man in the knee and ran passed them into the house. Another man stood in the kitchen holding a gun. She put one between his eyes and continued to the back door. No one else was there. She rushed back into the front room where both men were writhing on the floor.

This other guy was not cowed. "You fool. You brought her here. Fool." He yelled at Yasin in Arabic.

"Take it easy on Yasin. He is trying to remedy his failings." She spoke in Arabic and stepped back to the door and shut it. "Get up." She pointed the gun at the man's head. It was immediately apparent he was different than Yasin. He was much more dedicated to his cause, and had never in his life been spoken to like this by a woman. Marta had seen it all before. They only way to break it was immediacy. So she shot him in the other knee and then through the hand and knee again as he reached for the wound. She then bent down to him and placed the hot barrel of the silencer to his stomach and pulled the trigger again. It was brutal indeed.

"There. You now have wounds sufficient to kill you within three hours as blood loss and sepsis set in. It will be a painful death. I can see just by looking at you that you are not going to tell me anything, so I will grab some wire or tape and tie you up and stuff your mouth so you can die here." She stepped away, but he stopped her.

"No please. Don't."

"Why?" She shrugged.

"Please."

"So are you dedicated to your mission or not? Are you not willing to stay silent and stay true to your cause?" She shook her head as she said this. "I am fine with that. I would not expect any less from a true Mujahedeen, a warrior for jihad. Are you going to disappoint me by talking?"

He looked at her through pain and shock. He said nothing.

"Good, let me find that wire. Yasin and I need to leave."

"No, please. I will tell you what you want. Then you can call an ambulance for me, yes?"

She stepped back in front of him. "Tell me where to find your friend Ramzi Yousef now and I will get you help." She looked to Yasin sitting on the floor holding his bleeding knee. She spoke to him, "I'm thinking maybe you knew he wasn't here."

"No, I swear."

"He left last night after the FBI raided the house by Yasin." The other man spoke through pain. "They said they needed to move to a new location. One safer than this."

"Where? Where did they go?" She looked back at the other man.

"They didn't say for sure, but I think I can find out. I will need to make a call. It will take maybe a few calls. I can help. I will need my phone. It is over there."

And Marta knew this was wrong. The seven seconds it took him to say the words were too long. The way his eyes did not follow his gesture toward the kitchen but instead looked at the front door was wrong. In the time it took her head to turn, to spin on the axis connected through her neck and spine, was enough time for the front door to burst open. She was already applying pressure to the ball of her left foot to push her center of gravity to the right. At the same time, she brought the gun up to meet whoever came through the door. She just hoped like hell it wasn't Lance.

It wasn't. There were two of them, and they came in firing Uzis. Even though she was moving out of their main target area, the spray of bullets from those crazy Israeli killing machines caught her in the left abdomen and shoulder. She was still able to fire and put two bullets into the second man and three into the first man coming in. By the time she hit the floor from her initial dive to the right, both men were falling. One with two shots to his chest. The other received three bullets in his face. Both Uzis skittered across the floor.

She hit the floor hard and had to absorb the pain of being shot. She got back to her knee to cover the door in case anyone else came in. Right then, she heard the back door frame splinter as it was kicked open. No time. Marta got up, picked up one of the Uzis and took four painful steps toward the back. She crouched on the floor against the wall. Two seconds later, two men rushed out of the kitchen firing into the living room. She was below and to the left of their arc of fire. She easily took aim and put something like 15 to 20 bullets into each man. They flailed through the air as they fell. She gathered up one of their guns and headed back toward the front door. Yasin was gone. The other guy was crawling toward the other Uzi. Marta did as promised a few minutes earlier and ended his pain by putting a clean shot through his head as she walked past.

Outside, she burst down the front stairs onto the front yard and to the right. Yasin was almost to the Toyota, limping badly. "Yasin. I'm not mad at you. I understand everything you just did." He stopped and put his hands on his thighs as he bent over.

"Then you know I'm ready to die." He gasped as he said it.

"Yes. I respect that commitment. I'm not happy about your choice in causes, but I can't question your commitment." She raised her gun and looked past Yasin to the Corolla. The two men in the backseat were turned, looking at her. Strange. But what really caught her eye was a faint red glow in the back seat. She'd seen it before, twice actually. Both times were when Lance, or Preacher, was showing her how to detonate bombs using a basic long fuse. The dancing, flickering red light meant the fuse was lit and getting close. She put pressure on the ball of her right foot this time, but it was too late.

The car exploded in a ferocious fireball. The shockwave blew her through the air, all the way back to the house. Her head bounced off brick. She was out cold. Luckily, she was on the ground, right at the base of the foundation of the front brick wall of the house. Seventeen seconds later, the house exploded. The blast blew out walls, windows, doors and most of the insides of the small house. The fierce explosion was followed by an accelerant that consumed everything in flames. The fireball bursting skyward was brief, but enormous.

Marta missed the explosion, the fire and the chaos that ensued. She was gone away, unconscious, oblivious to it all. Bricks, stone, plywood, drywall, two-by-fours, dust and ash covered her.

Two hundred yards down the street, a rented Ryder truck pulled out of a driveway. Ramzi Yousef looked down the street at the aftermath of the bombs he had just detonated. He shook his head at it all. His mentor would not be happy with a change of plans this close to going live.

Chapter 45

Word of the Jersey City explosions started coming in just after 3 a.m. Seibel was asleep on a couch in the office of the New York CIA field director. He had been asleep almost a full hour when a technologist monitoring regional police channels stepped in to wake him. That hour would be all he'd get today.

He showed up on scene 49 minutes later. He wanted to see for himself. Seibel flashed his credentials to get access. He and a field agent walked up the street to just in front of the house. Firefighters had put out the flames. The wreckage was still smoldering. This location had not shown up on any recent database searches for Yousef or associates. Seibel rubbed his chin and moved in for a closer look. A police officer was about to give him a hard time, but one look from him was all it took to keep the guy quiet. Seibel maneuvered up the walk, littered with debris, to about 15 feet from the front steps. Rubble was everywhere. He knew the general size of the explosive by the debris field. It was decent size, but not huge; not over the top.

He squatted down to take a look from a lower angle. Why had they blown this place? What were they covering up? He looked over at the wrecked car. It was a carcass of a Toyota. He could see several markers for bodies, in the car, on the ground.

He turned back to the house. There were five or so yellow markers in there. Damn, this looked like something Preacher and Marta would leave behind.

That thought was interrupted by something that caught his eye. It was a hand, over at the base of the house. That body wasn't marked, but had to be a deceased. He stood and took a couple of steps toward the body. It was buried under a mound of rubble. He could barely see the hand. He turned to the police officer that had eyed him a minute before. "You got a flashlight?"

The guy walked over and pulled the flashlight from his belt and handed it to Seibel. "Looks like we have another one over here." Seibel said, turning back to the body.

"Damn, what a mess." The patrolman answered and followed Seibel up to the house.

Seibel shined the light on the hand. It looked like a woman's hand. That didn't fit. He hiked deeper into the wreckage.

"I don't know about that. Let's let the fire and rescue guys extract that body." The patrolman called to him.

Seibel ignored him and reached down to move several bricks and a sheet of drywall. When he moved it, he saw maybe the one face in the entire world he didn't want to see right there. Under the focus of his flashlight, Marta appeared, for all intents and purposes, to be a goner. There was no life in her face.

"Damn. God damn it." He bent to her and put his fingers to her neck and waited. It was faint, but it was there. "She's alive. Help me, she's alive." His call brought men running from all directions. Fire fighters lifted bricks and debris, two paramedics standing in the street were there 20 seconds later. Seibel stepped back. He had to face his next fear.

"Everyone stop. Listen to me." The chaotic crew froze in their places. Some people in this world just have authority. Seibel was born that way. "I am the representative for national security for this sector and this woman is an agent under my direction. I need every one except the medics to turn away from her right now. Now."

Everyone was surprised, but complied. "You two, cover her face now. Do it. Get her onto a stretcher and into the back of the ambulance now. You can stabilize her inside the unit. The rest of you, stay where you are. I need to examine each of the bodies inside to see if any are our agents or if any are the terrorist we have been hunting. Nobody move, except you two." He pointed back at the paramedics and then climbed up the front stairs to where the door had been.

He looked at the first charred body. It was not Lance. The next two were burnt to a crisp, but weren't Lance. The next two were charred on their backs, so he lifted each to see that they weren't him. He continued through the kitchen to the back door, that body wasn't him either. No Lance. Why would she be here without him? They were never apart. He did not recognize any of the bodies as Yousef. Couldn't assume he was dead.

He stopped where he was and pulled out his cell phone and scrolled down to the fourth number. It was the phone number Marta had called from two hours earlier. He dialed the number. A tired clerk at a hotel front desk answered. No time. Marta and Lance would not be listed under any recognizable name. Damn. He hung up and walked back out of the smoldering house to follow the paramedics who had Marta loaded in the ambulance. He got in the back with the medic. The EMT got into the cab to drive. "Let's go, lights and sirens on. Move it."

"Yes sir."

"Wake up! Damn it, wake up! You piece of crap, wake your ass up!" Across the Hudson River and to the north, Lance was screaming for all he was worth. He was pounding on him, kicking him. He jumped on him. But to no avail; Preacher was out cold. He was off on another planet, not dreaming, not aware.

Marta had slipped him a dose of something that put him in la la land.

Two and a half hours later, Preacher heard something. It was Lance, himself. And by god, he was singing their single most hated song. It was the worst piece of crap ever made. And Lance knew it. By singing a tune by Culture Club for the 18th time, he had finally reached into Preacher's brain and caused him to stir. A few minutes later, Preacher was sitting up in bed, still not with it, but he at least had his feet on the floor.

"What did I miss?" He asked Lance hovering there really pissed. "Don't look at me like that."

"Take a look around. Who's missing?" Lance responded.

"Where is she? Where did she go?"

"I don't know. I'm stuck here with you, you know."

"Did she say anything? How could I have slept through it?" he finally looked at the alarm clock on the bedside table. "Man, is it 6:15? How could that happen? Damn medicine. Stuff really works."

"She left just after one." Lance said.

"One? She should be back by now. Where did she go?" Preacher was up. He stumbled to the tiny bathroom and turned on the cold water to splash his face. He drank a few handfuls as well. "I need to go. We need to go. We'll call the service in a bit."

"You need to stop jerking around and get cell phones. This is ridiculous not being able to reach her." Lance was still pissed.

"I know, I know. Maybe we'll start with pagers and see how that works."

"Such a jerk." Lance wouldn't let it go.

"What's up with you?" Preacher was into his pants and throwing a shirt on.

"I tried to wake you up for three hours. Where the hell did you go?"

"Just asleep. I was out, man. Like a friggin' hardheaded baby. Cut the crap, we need to go." Preacher put on his shoes, put on his gun holster, the knife on his belt clip and his coat. He was on the tiny elevator two minutes later.

New York was still fairly quiet on a cold February morning just after 6:20 a.m. He walked along the sidewalk with Lance up at about 300 feet. Preacher stepped into a convenience store for a cup of so-so coffee to get his juices flowing. Two blocks later, he was on the southwest corner of the intersection of 5th Avenue and West 34th Street. The Empire State Building towered over him. He casually looked in all directions and took in details of the hundred or so people he could currently see. Nothing stood out. He decided to do what he'd done the evening before when they came back from Jersey City. He took a walk around the blocks the building occupied. He walked 34th to 6th and hung a left. At 33rd, he turned left again and back at 5th, another left. It took him 14 minutes. He didn't see anything of merit. But the details were different in the early morning light. He still had an unnatural desire to blow this building up. Bring it down. That told him more than anything.

He chose to walk back north on 5th Avenue to get a wider view. No science behind his action. He just wanted to see what he'd see.

Walking across 35th Street, he saw several people about. Up ahead, a man who looked to be in his early 60's exited an eight-story building on the southwest corner of the intersection. The man was carrying a box, like a storage box. It was old school file folder stuff. He was dressed nice, classy. He looked Italian, maybe Greek. Lance walked passed him in the middle of the street and started taking in others. But something made him turn around when he reached the sidewalk.

He looked back at the older man carrying the box. His salt and pepper hair was as well kept from the back as it was in the front. His shoes were shined, again classy, expensive, but not too. Preacher was about to turn and watch the other New Yorkers starting their day when he lowered his eyes to the man's legs. They took step after step in a slow deliberate manner. But as the man reached the sidewalk on the other side of the street, he jumped up onto the curb with the strength, life and bounce of someone much younger than 60, or even 50. It was wrong. His knowledge of human anatomy, muscle flex parameters, physics and gravitational pull all combined to tell him it was wrong.

Lance came down from 300 feet to about 20. He looked down on the man, examining every detail. He turned back to Preacher and smiled. The ghost waved at Preacher to follow — to follow this man.

He did so. Preacher stayed 50 feet back and sipped his coffee as he walked. The man stopped at the corner at 5th Avenue and 34th and waited for the light to turn red to allow him to cross 5th. Preacher stayed back and watched him and a couple of others cross. Once on the corner across the street, the older man waited again for the light to cross 34th. Preacher crossed illegally with another guy as the older pedestrian reached the south side of 34th where he turned right toward the front entrance to the Empire State Building. Preacher tracked him step for step from the other side of the street. At the front entrance, the man opened the door and walked down that famous corridor to the security desk at the end and then walked to the left, to the elevators.

Preacher stayed there across the street watching, thinking. The chances of seeing anything were slim, but still. A minute later, a light came on in an office on the 6th floor. He could barely see it with the tower of the building set back from the larger base of the structure. He wanted Lance to go up there and see what he could see, but his ghost had limitations, as much as he hated to admit it.

Forty seconds later, he had a plan worked out. It involved a few lies and a good bit of acting, the usual. He crossed 34th Street illegally and walked up to the door to the iconic building. It was just after 7:10 a.m.

He strolled that corridor famous from countless movies and stopped at the security desk. Two guards were seated behind it. They were not looking for conversation.

"Gentlemen."

"Yes sir?" The guard on the left answered.

"I know it's early, but I need you both to listen and listen clearly." He leaned over the counter. "Do I have your attention?"

They both looked at him now. "I am with the FBI." He pulled out an I.D. he'd been given by the Bureau a months earlier. "A man just entered this building two minutes ago carrying a box. You know this gentleman, yes?"

"Yes sir. That's Mr. Arizzati."

"What is Mr. Arizzati's first name?"

"I believe it's Frank." The guard on the right answered.

The other agreed. "That's right. Frank. We hardly ever call any of the tenants by their first name, you understand."

"Yes. I understand. I have just come from a stakeout several blocks away and this man you know as Frank Arizzati just left a meeting with individuals we have been monitoring for several months. I am going to need to speak with him in private. I don't expect anything to come of it, but please write this number down. If I am not back down here in 15 minutes, call the number and tell Agent Papas who you are and that agent Landover is here meeting with Mr. Arizzati on the Mohamed case. He will likely send over a few additional agents."

"Agent Landover, we don't want any incidents here. I think we need to call our supervisor and maybe the police on this."

"I understand your trepidation. This is a rush job, nothing I planned. This matter does involve several jurisdictions, including national security. You understand, correct?"

"Yes, but-"

"I'm afraid I must insist you keep this matter local for the next," he pulled his wrist up, "14 minutes. I insist. Which floor?"

"Sixth floor. Suite 612." The guard on the left was quick to respond. He wanted no problems, and for this to be over quickly.

"Thank you. I'll see you back here in a few minutes."

Preacher turned toward the elevator lobby. Because it was still early, one of the elevators stood open waiting for him. He stepped in and pushed 8.

He stepped off on the eighth floor and rounded the corner to find the stairwell. He opened the door and made his way down two flights to the sixth floor. The stairwell door opened quietly and he stepped out onto tile floor. His shoes were silent on the surface. He hugged the wall as up ahead about 45 feet, Arizzatti, or whatever his name was, came out of an office door carrying the box. He walked around the corner. Lance listened to the footsteps, elevator bell ring and the doors open and close. He walked to suite 612.

The lettering on the door read Castle Trading and Imports. Very nondescript, he thought to himself. The glass beside the door was opaque so he could not see clearly inside, but the light was on. He'd seen it come on from street below. He turned the handle but the door was locked. He wished he had his lock-picking gear on him, but alas, there was no time. He took out his gun barrel and punched a hole through the glass beside the door and reached in to unlock the handle.

Once inside, he closed the door behind him silently, but that broken glass was going to be hard to miss. He heard no noise from the offices. To his left was a hall with several offices on the right only. To the right was a similar hall with offices on both sides. A small waiting area with a reception desk was directly in front of him. He chose to go to the right. In the first office on the left, he found an empty desk, but 20 or 25 storage boxes like Arizzati had been carrying. They were stacked against the wall. The next office was the same, only with more boxes stacked higher. The third office on the right was jam-packed with storage boxes, floor to ceiling.

When he got to the last door at the end of the hall, he was surprised when he opened it. Behind the door was an open and unfinished space that measured maybe 70 feet by 50 feet, with more space around the corner. The walls were bare sheetrock and the floor concrete. Support pillars were spaced about 30 feet apart. All that was fine, no big deal. The funny thing was all the storage boxes, hundreds of them. They lined the wall on the right and stood six and seven boxes high. But even stranger, the boxes were stacked eight-high and two-deep around each of the pillars in the open space. Alarm bell city.

Preacher walked a dozen paces into the space to see around the corner. And there he saw the same thing. More boxes lining the wall and boxes stacked around the pillars. Four-alarm fire bells.

He stepped to the wall and pulled a box down. It was heavy, but not too. He set it on the floor and unfolded the lid tucked into itself. His mind was racing, but when he opened the box and took out a stack of papers on top, even Lance up above him gasped at what he found underneath.

Sealed into a plastic bag was a container that contained a variety of chemicals that, when combined with a heat source, would combust and combust with a fury. The little bomb he saw in this one box could blow out the walls and roof a 1,500-square-foot house. He looked left and right. Simple multiplication told him there were more than 250 of these boxes in this open room.

"Damn." He whispered to himself and Lance. He didn't have to finish the thought. Lance knew it already. Preacher's dumb luck had allowed him to stumble on the bad guys once again. When was this luck going to run out?

Maybe now.

At the end of the room, he heard footsteps. It was Arizzati and he was holding a gun. He was about 50, no exactly 52 feet, from Preacher.

"Stop right there." Preacher spun and had his gun out and pointed at the man standing partially in the doorway.

"I was right." Arizzati said.

"About?" Preacher tilted his head. Lance had already flown over to just above Arizzati's shoulder. It didn't take him a second to see what he'd missed on the street. The hair was died white. The skin was wrinkled with makeup. It was Anwar.

He was the ghost that Preacher, Seibel and half the world had been hunting. He continued, "On the street, when you passed me, I recognized you, but couldn't remember from where. It's this city. You see people you have seen before. So many faces"

"We weren't that close on that tiny island." Preacher stepped to the right.

"Close enough. I remember your face. You are so young." Anwar smiled a little and took a step back.

"You were young once too. Before those pesky Soviets invaded Afghanistan, right?"

"Yes. But that was long ago now." Anwar shook his head. "So, you've come to try to stop me. I would love to hear how you found me. I know you have been pecking away at my network around your country, but I thought I had insulation, disconnects." His language was that of a bomb maker. He spoke of connections, wiring, combinations.

"We're pretty smart. It came into focus after awhile. Your other teams have been stopped by the way, in Philadelphia and

Washington. They're all dead." Preacher wanted to take his shot now. Fifty feet was at the far end of his reliable range with a handgun. But what the hell. Problem was, how could he be sure he could stop these damn bombs from going off. And he realized something else, "You left the office when I came in. You took the elevator. That means you've got more boxes on other floors."

"All over the building actually. On this level and others, yes. Ideally positioned to cause the greatest destruction." The smile remained on his face.

"So I can't do anything to stop it."

"Correct. You could shoot me now and could not stop it. This building, this American icon, will come down shortly and everyone inside will die, including you and me." He held up a remote control panel. It was Lance hovering right next to Anwar who caught his lie. The terrorist had just told a little fib. It was the word "shortly." He wasn't going to blow the building now. Lance knew Anwar had no intention of dying, that's why he stayed in the doorway, ready to bolt.

"Then blow it. Get on with it." Preacher played it out, taking a step forward.

"Not just yet. We need a few more people at this party." Anwar stepped back as he said this. He was almost behind the first stack of boxes by the door.

"You lying coward." Preacher brought his gun up as Anwar was closing the door. He fired three shots. All hit the heavy wood door made of oak. He aimed high to avoid hitting any of the boxes.

As he raced toward the door, he heard a small thud-like noise that was repeated a dozen more times. He reached for the doorknob, but nothing happened. It didn't work.

"A little trick I've put in place for my offices," he heard the arrogant words from behind the door. "All of the door assemblies and hinges have been blown. These doors won't open without a battering ram They are solid oak. Very thick and strong. Goodbye my friend."

Preacher raced back around the corner to a door at the other end, it was blown as well. This little maneuver was obviously designed to allow Anwar to shut down the offices and slow down entry by anyone else. It was a delay tactic and it showed Preacher what he needed to know. It was designed to give the terrorist just long enough to get out of the building before blowing it. He kicked at the door. Nothing. Solid friggin' oak indeed, with real metal locks and hinges that were all now disabled, making it a solid wall.

He thought maybe he could shoot through the wood, blast it away. But that would likely not work and if it did, it would use all his ammunition.

Lance got the idea first. The windows.

Preacher ran over to the window. Anwar had not thought of everything. Yes, this is the 6th floor and 80 or so feet off the street, but the extended foundation portion of the building came up to the fifth floor making it only a 25-foot drop. That would hurt, but hopefully not break anything. Lance ghosted through the window outside to take a look. Preacher used his gun to break out the glass. A quick glance around showed nothing to hang on to out there. He would just have to jump for it.

He scooted into the windowsill, turned around and grabbed the ledge to lower his feet as far as he could. No time. He let go, pushed off and spun around in mid-air to prepare for landing. He tucked and rolled as his shoes made contact. Upon impact, he rolled to the right and came back to his feet with minimal pain. Cool move.

He ran to the 5th Avenue side of the building and looked down. Nothing. He ran to the corner of the structure and watched and waited. Fifteen seconds later, Anwar emerged from a different entrance than he had entered earlier. The bomber stepped into 34th Street and had to step back to avoid a taxi that didn't care if he was the world's most wanted terrorist. The streets were busier than 15 minutes ago.

The terrorist ran into and across the street, down to the corner of 34th and 5th. Lance shot up to about 500 feet. They looked in the direction Anwar had come from half an hour earlier and knew exactly where he was going. The top floor of the building on the corner of 35th and 5th that Anwar had stepped out of was a perfect location to see the Empire State Building. The 8-story building was also just far enough away to avoid the debris field from the explosion and falling, collapsing, cascading steel and concrete from 102 stories above. The top floor of the building had a clear view of most of the tower and the 5th Avenue side of the Empire State building's base. Lance could see Anwar from up there. He was near the end of the block crossing 35th Street. He did indeed step into the building.

Preacher looked for his next step. Looking down, he saw a permanent awning was built over the sidewalk on the 5th Avenue side. It was about 30 feet down. Great. No time. He swung his legs over the edge and saw he could drop down to the windowsill about eight feet down. From there he could maybe do the same with the one below.

He lowered his feet to the ledge below and then leaned down to grab hold of the sill, no go. He fell off the edge and couldn't grab to stop his fall so he turned to see if he could control the remaining 20 or so feet of the freefall. Like the minute prior, he hit the surface and rolled. His landing made a hell of a noise, even in obnoxiously loud New York.

Back on his feet, he limped to the end of the awning, swung his legs over and dropped to the sidewalk below, landing next to a surprised group of tourists. He smiled at them. He had another decision. If he ran back into the security desk, he could tell them there was a bomb in the building. In five minutes, they could maybe get a couple of hundred people out while causing real panic. Preacher realized right then that Anwar had not planned to detonate his bombs this early in the morning. He most likely planned to blow the thing closer to lunchtime when it would be full of tenants and tourists. There would likely be five, maybe ten thousand people inside. And all the pedestrians around the structure would be pulverized. There was no time. Anwar was already to his building. He could blow it in minutes.

Preacher burst across the street in the direction Anwar had jogged. He sprinted across 34th and then jaywalked, ran really, across 5th. He was about a minute behind Anwar. But he was moving much faster.

He reached the 8-story building at 5th and 35th half a minute later. A catchy tune by the Cure had started up there on the awning. It was now into its second chorus. Inside the building, a doorman sat behind his desk reading the paper. "Sir, may I help you?" He put the paper down.

"I have no time. The man who just came in, Arizzati..." Preacher pulled out his gun and badge.

"Jesus. What do you want?"

"FBI. Arizzati, top floor I know. Which suite? Now." Preacher had moved past the man to the elevators where he pushed the button. "Now."

"807. Do I call the police?" The doorman moved out from behind his desk.

"Call them now. For what it's worth, call in a bomb threat at the Empire State Building. This is real." The door started to open, slowly. "If I can't stop him, the whole thing is coming down in minutes."

A woman stood in the elevator as the door opened. She saw Preacher's gun and screamed. He pulled her out and pushed the button for 8. The door closed slower than a snail in molasses. He shut his eyes and rotated his head like Fuchs does. He wished Marta were here. Another gun and set of eyes, especially hers, would be helpful. He opened his eyes and looked at Lance sitting cross-legged up in the corner. Life and death shit here and he was up there joking around, doing meditation.

"Funny." Preacher whispered.

"Just getting centered." Lance smiled and moved his head in all directions. Like a ghost needed to be flexible. The elevator moved past 7. Preacher took in a deep breath and prepared to explode.

A bell dinged and the doors snailed open. Preacher burst through them with a spinning roll. He knew from the elevator's position in the building that Anwar's suite would be to the left, at the corner of the building. No one was in the hall. But a video camera was mounted above the door with a quaint little 807 plaque beside it. He was on camera, so he waved.

The camera could not see the ghostly character shooting through the halls, bouncing off walls and taking in every detail as Preacher glanced around during the next half second. The wood grain of the walls, the doors, doorknobs and hinges, the door casings. Lance saw right away the door to 807 was no good. It was more solid than those in the Empire State Building. Lance focused on the wall two feet from the door. Preacher saw what he was seeing and fired 8 shots into the wall in a square pattern 16 and 32 inches away from the door casing. If they were right, this space would be between two studs in the wall. He backed up then he threw himself from the wall across the narrow hall and kicked the wall where he had placed the shots. The drywall within the square pattern he shot exploded with his kick. He did it again, and there was a hole in the wall into suite 807. He shoved his head and torso through the hole, gun first.

Preacher getting his head, his eyes, through the hole allowed Lance to enter the room. Preacher's eyes supplied the data. Lance moved around the room in a whirlwind as time slowed, froze really. Anwar was over in the corner of the unit next to the windows. He did not look up at Preacher's loud entrance. His attention was totally focused on the table full of remotes he was working over. Lance saw right away that he and Preacher had caught the world's premier terrorist bomber off guard. His plans, his procedures were not complete. The bombs weren't ready.

Precious seconds, microscopic moments in the span of lives, were now available for the world's most dangerous terrorist to take action. Not Anwar, Preacher.

Lance Priest, also known as Preacher, wanted to kill right now. He was trained and talented and deadly. And more than that, he needed to kill. This was not desire. It was necessity.

Preacher, with his body halfway into the apartment, took aim dead center at Anwar's back. It was 24 feet. He hit him with all three shots. The terrorist fell forward onto the table, but incredibly, kept working. The Pakistani bomber was in somewhat of a trance, focused on completing his mission, his years of planning.

Preacher broke out more drywall and shimmied through into the apartment. He rolled onto his back and up to his feet with the gun pointed again at the bomber. Anwar rose and turned to face him. He held a remote unit in his hands. And he smiled. He was ready.

So, how much life and death and anything in-between can someone experience in a second, a moment? Lance had lived a lifetime two years earlier when he looked into Marta's eyes for the first time. It was life-changing. He had something, someone, to live for now.

In this moment, looking into Anwar's evil-genius, terrorist bomber's eyes, Preacher had the added advantage of another set of eyes. He and Lance looked at Anwar from two perspectives. They, the two of them, body and spirit, conscious and insanity, Lance and Preacher, could see past the man's dyed hair, the makeup on his skin, the contacts lightening the dark brown of his eyes. Lance saw the burns on Anwar's fingers as he moved his forefinger to the trigger button of the unit in his hand. How many times had this man burnt his fingers assembling bombs?

Lance saw in the wrinkle, the twitch in Anwar's left eye that indicated he was not quite all there. He was obviously in great pain with three bullets in him. Anwar was brilliant in his methods, his planning, his attention to details. But he was missing something. He was lacking that connection that makes someone decent, makes them human. Preacher recognized it immediately, because hell, he lacked the same thing.

While Preacher kept eye contact with Anwar, Lance examined everything else around the guy. On the table, an elaborate network of six remotes was wired together with a large set of batteries on the floor underneath. On the left side of the table was a monitor showing four separate views of the Empire State Building. Anwar had set up video cameras to capture the cataclysmic event. One of the cameras stood on a tripod to the right of Anwar. It's positioning was obvious. He planned to step in front of the camera with the building collapsing over his shoulder to claim the act, to proclaim it for Allah and freedom and Islam and vengeance for the injustice perpetrated around the globe by the great Satan — America.

Lance moved in-between microseconds and came back to the unit Anwar held in his hand. It was wired to the rest. He followed the line to a central unit that was then connected to six others. That likely meant six detonation devices just over 350 yards away inside the Empire State Building. No time. Anwar's finger was moving toward the button. He was not much of a talker and didn't look like the kind who'd planned a long glorious speech. A second and a half had passed.

Options were limited. A shot to the forehead would not prevent a finger from pressing a button. He could shoot the unit, but again, Anwar would likely constrict his grip and press the button. Not much to work with here. It was Lance who came up with another option. He moved down and stood next to Anwar and returned to the network of boxes and remotes on the table. The secret was the main hub. It was a box that measured eight inches by eight and stood about five inches high. It would receive the signal from the wired remote Anwar held in his shaking hand and send it to all the remotes.

Lance turned back to Preacher and made a circle with his thumb and forefinger. He moved it directly in front of what appeared to be the main processor on the simple hub unit. "Hit the bull's eye, Preacher. Don't miss."

Preacher adjusted his aim from Anwar's forehead to the unit on the table. Anwar saw the gun's aim shift and followed it to the table as well. The time it took Anwar to process this change made the difference between one person, himself mainly, and thousands of casualties. When his eyes reached the hub unit, recognition flashed inside his brain and sent a signal to his right forefinger to press the button.

Problem was, this recognition came just as Preacher fired two shots right through the target Lance made for him. The central unit exploded as the first and then second bullet struck it. Anwar's pressure on the button sent an electronic signal down through the wire, but it too was too late. The speed of the bullets had won. The message to the other remotes did not make it through. Nothing happened.

So that was that. Except for the troubling fact that the other individual remotes were all still live. They just weren't centrally connected. Anwar knew this and began to reach for the closest one. Lance saw this a microsecond before Preacher did and brought his other hand up to make another bull's eye for Preacher to hit. This time, it was right at the terrorist's temple, which led to his brain, and his body's central processing unit.

The particular gun Preacher was holding, a Smith and Wesson 9-millimeter, holds 17 rounds. He had fired 16. Three in the Empire State Building, eight shot into the wall allowed him to enter the apartment. Three more were in Anwar's back. The previous two had just destroyed the central remote hub. The last one really had to count.

This was quite a bit of pressure on a guy who failed on the range time after time. Thinking about that now, he recalled feeling that there was just too much time back in basic training and time after time at Harvey Point. He had too much time before, in-between and after each shot. Too much time to think. But he could think about that later. Right now he needed to put a precisely placed nine-millimeter round through the brain of a terrorist bomber standing 17 feet in front of him.

He liked that time was tight. He preferred the pressure. It left no time to think, to over-think. He brought his aim up to the target a smiling Lance was holding next to Anwar's head and fired. The bullet was an inch off target. Not bad at all. It hit Anwar in the head, passed through bone and brain matter and more skull and out the other side where it continued through a pane of window glass out into Manhattan.

Anwar's head tilted left with the blow and his whole body followed, collapsing to the floor against the wall. He was literally dead before he hit the floor. Everything looked good, except that Anwar's outstretched left arm caught one of the remotes on the table. It skidded and then fell off the edge of the table headed for the floor with the trigger button facing down.

From 17 feet away, Preacher simply could not get there in time. Physics wouldn't allow it. It would take him at least a second and a half to get there. Damn. All this work, excellent execution and incredibly accurate shooting for naught. The remote continued its plunge to the floor in super slow-motion. People were going to die; innocent people who never did anything to Anwar. Inside the Empire State Building were thousands of freedom-loving Americans, and visitors from around the world who came to New York to see what all this freedom and capitalism and craziness was about. But again, no time to think about all that, he needed to move. But it was hopeless. There simply wasn't enough time.

Chapter 46

Lance Priest had been born with several quirks. Lying, noticing details, unnatural physical fitness; call them quirks or god-given abilities or even phenomena. He had them. But his main quirk was this little out-of-body view of the world. His near-death experience on the microscopically small island of Tapul in the Philippines morphed his unique quirk into something more. The result was Lance hovering around all the time above Preacher.

A few seconds ago, Preacher realized that Lance came down to the floor for the first time. He stood right next to Anwar and made those handy targets for Preacher to aim at.

But what happened next was more than a quirk. It was definitely phenomenon.

As the remote neared the polished wood floor, where the button would be depressed sending a signal to a detonator a few hundred yards away, it stopped just inches off the floor. It did not send the detonation signal. The Empire State Building remained intact and thousands of people were not killed.

Now, Lance, and Preacher for that matter, never much believed in magic. But this was just that. Because, what had stopped the remote from hitting the floor was Lance.

Yes. Lance, standing there as a transparent ghost one moment, dove to catch the remote four inches before it hit the ground in the next. It was impossible. A ghost could not grasp something real, something tangible, right? Yet here he was.

But here's the thing, Lance wasn't a ghost anymore. It was him in flesh and bone. It was Lance, not Preacher lying outstretched on the floor holding the remote and breathing a huge sigh of relief. He furrowed his brow and then looked over at Preacher in the middle of the room.

But he wasn't there. He was gone.

Lance was confused and rolled over on his back to look around to see if Lance was floating overhead. Then it hit him – he was Lance, is Lance. He wasn't Preacher.

Damn. He set the remote on his chest and lowered his head to the floor. Turning to his left, he saw the blood spreading from the holes in Anwar's head and back. But he was still confused, disoriented.

He'd been Preacher for a year and a half and didn't know how to think as Lance. How did this happen? How did he get across the room in literally no time and stop the remote's fall?

Lance had to face it. He'd gone from one physical location to another without time elapsing. "Man, that's freaky." He said it out loud and expected Lance to answer. But Lance was gone, well not gone really. Just back inside him. But where was Preacher?

Below, on the street, he heard the sirens and tires screeching as the first police cars arrived on scene. The doorman had made the 911 call and the cavalry had arrived. Lance got up gently and placed the remote on the floor beside him. He didn't want to bump anything and kill a bunch of people. He stood up and looked north at the Empire State Building still standing. Huge relief cascaded over him.

He stepped back from the window and looked around the room. On the kitchen counter sat Anwar's cell phone. He picked it up and dialed Seibel.

His boss picked it up on the second ring. "Seibel."

"Anwar is gone."

"What? How, where are you?" he spat it all out as one word.

"Anwar's cozy little Manhattan apartment. Two blocks from Empire State."

"He's dead? You got him?" Seibel was anxious, and then some.

"Yes. Dead. He has the whole damn building wired to blow. We need everyone out and the surrounding blocks cleared in case I missed something."

"Jesus. Let me get people moving."

"Okay." Lance exhaled again. "Have you heard from Marta?" He rubbed his knee where he'd kicked the sheetrock with it.

"Yes. I'll call you back in a couple of minutes. Is this the number to call?"

"Yeah. It's his cell phone."

"Wish we had that a while ago." Seibel hung up.

Lance hung up. He dialed the phone message service he and Marta shared. There were none. He set the phone back on the counter. The police would be up here in a couple of minutes. He needed to see what he could find before they arrived. He was disoriented looking around the room. The disorientation came from the fact that he only saw what his own eyes could see. He didn't have the second set of eyes looking around the room with him. It kind of sucked.

The apartment was classy, with modern urban furnishings. Nothing much in the drawers. Nothing in the cabinets that gave any hints. Aside from the array of remotes on the table, Anwar left nothing of his plans in this apartment. This was his office, not where he lived. Lance stepped into the center of the main room again and relaxed his mind and eyes. He took it all in. He heard the elevator bell ring through the hole he'd shot and kicked through the wall. He had just a few seconds alone.

A framed photo on the wall above the couch caught his eye. It was New York, Manhattan really. Taken from an angle that showed the skyline in panorama. Two things stood out. First was the Empire State Building. The other was two things really, the World Trade Center towers. Out in the hall he heard the jangle of NYPD patrolmen's belts. He called out to them, "Hold up guys, I'm coming out. FBI."

He walked over to the door and opened it and held up his FBI I.D., but asked them to stay out, at least until a bomb squad could be brought in to dismantle the remotes. He confirmed the Empire State Building was being evacuated as well as surrounding buildings. Lance walked back over to the windows to look at the chaos down the street as people ran in all directions. Below, police were stopping and diverting traffic around the area. He felt good for the moment. Disaster averted.

Anwar, dead at his feet, had chosen secrecy and personal control over all aspects of the bombing, instead of bringing team members into this, his ultimate operation. This had allowed the terrorist mastermind to plan and prepare it all, but it also required him to detonate all the bombs himself instead of using timers or others to press buttons. Dumb luck won the day once again.

He stepped back over to the door and spoke to the four officers in the hallway. They told him that investigators and bomb squad were on the way. He waited 20 minutes for police investigators, a bomb technician and the FBI to arrive. He explained the basics to the group in a matter of fact manner. They, and the officers standing nearby, took it all in, staying fairly quiet until one of them, obviously from Brooklyn, couldn't help himself.

"You jumped off the friggin' Empire State Building?"

Lance nodded. "Just a few floors though. That ape lying in the street broke my fall." After he described the number of bombs he saw on the sixth floor alone, the investigators called out additional bomb squads and called over to hasten the evacuation of the building.

A half an hour later, Lance walked with a limp on the sidewalk heading south on 7th Avenue. Everything else was closed off. Anwar's cell phone rang in his jacket. Lance had to admit as he pulled it out, that he liked being able to answer the phone while walking down the street. He hoped it was Marta. Maybe Seibel had given her this number. "Hello."

"Don't quite know where to start. Everything is in motion. The evacuation, FBI and CIA teams are onsite and no one is dead at this point." Seibel was sitting down now. Lance could tell by his voice.

"And you were going to tell me about Marta?" Lance had his priorities straight.

Geoffrey Seibel, for all his brilliance and vision and imagination, is a liar. He chose this moment in time, and in the life of his still very young protégé, to tell a whopper. He knew he was about to change the course of Lance's life and possibly history. Hell, the guy had just single-handedly, literally single-damn-handedly, stopped a terrorist bombing that would have killed thousands and brought down much more than the Empire State Building. It would have changed America forever.

A weapon, a tool this sublime, needed to be unleashed on the nation's enemies in a cruel and unusual manner. Seibel chose now to reorient Lance Priest from solitary recluse who really trusted only one person, to wild animal that trusted no one and wanted most people dead for spite alone. It was dangerous, but Seibel had been planning this next phase for some time. Events had transpired to advance his timeline. The pendulum had swung. It would swing back with chaos in its wake.

"She's dead Lance."

The words silenced the cacophony that made New York unique in all the world. Lance did not hear sirens and voices and tires and horns and steam and engines and echoes and whistles and music and life and love and hope. He heard only the silence surrounding the words uttered by Geoffrey Seibel. He stepped into a doorway.

"Repeat what you just said." He sounded calm to anyone walking past.

"I'm sorry Lance. She went to Jersey City this morning sometime after 1:30. The house she visited was blown up. It was a bomb. Most likely set by Yousef. She was on his trail."

He heard the words, but they didn't register. He was numb, cold. His head twitched to the left. It had never done that before. "She was there, in Jersey City, when the bomb went off?"

"Yes. We have controlled the situation this morning. Officially it was an explosion caused by a gas leak. Yousef was not there. He escaped."

Lance went colder. His head twitched again. "You saw her? Confirmed it was Marta?"

"I did. I went to the hospital in the ambulance with her. She never regained consciousness. She was too far gone. Lance, I'm sorry." He spoke the words to a dial tone. Lance had hung up.

Chapter 47

He needed to run. He sprinted south for blocks on 7th and then east on 18th, then south on 6th. He didn't stop, couldn't stop for miles. He only slowed down when he reached Canal Street, where he went east again until he came to Broadway. He turned south again. Instead of continuing on aimlessly, he stopped and leaned against a building, next to a doorstep. He sat on the step and put his forearms on his thighs, his lungs heaving, sweat dripping, hate seething. He was alone in the city; alone in the world. They both knew they lived on borrowed time from the start. It could never last. It was just that he was sure, positively sure, he would go first. He had not imagined life or the world without her because it had simply never crossed his mind.

But something did cross his mind just then. Words.

He could see words with white 3D letters and solid black behind them. They were the words Seibel had said 30 minutes earlier. The words from his last sentence before Lance hung up. "She never regained consciousness. She was too far gone." Lance closed his eyes and examined the words. He saw them from the front, from the side and the rolled around behind them. He saw something that others never would, never could. The words were lies. They weren't real. Seibel would never have said these words. They weren't his. They were forced, fabricated, made up.

Lance opened his eyes and shot up to 10,000 feet. He looked over at Jersey City and the general location of where he and Marta and the FBI team had been last evening. Then he looked down at the streets and roads to the hospitals in Manhattan. That meant one of the two tunnels. He looked down at the exits of each tunnel and the surrounding blocks to find hospitals on the map in his head. Within 11 seconds, he had narrowed it down to four hospitals on the west side of town.

He stood and stepped into the office behind him. A secretary sat behind a desk. He walked around behind her desk and grabbed her phone and flashed his FBI I.D.

"I need to use your phone. Thank you for your cooperation." He didn't want to use Anwar's cell phone.

He dialed 411. "Jersey City police please." He smiled at the secretary as he waited for the number. "Thank you." He hung up and dialed the number. "Yes, I need two things, please. I need to speak with the chief investigator on the explosion last night, and I need to know the name of the emergency medical service that responded and transported from the scene."

The woman at the other end of the line came back with a couple of questions that Lance easily batted away and then unloaded with several lies to convince her to be cooperative. He hung up with two more numbers to call.

"Thanks again for the use of your phone. Your government really appreciates it." He smiled again at the secretary. He dialed Jersey City Emergency Medical Services. A woman answered.

"Yes, this is agent Randolph with the FBI. I am following up on the incident last night. Where did the unit transport the patient?"

The clerk at the other end of the line looked over this morning's log and found a unit had transported from Jersey City to St. Vincent's. But no information about the patient was available. She could not confirm if it was a male or female or any patient status information. Lance knew it was her. And damn, he'd run right past the hospital 15 minutes earlier.

He hung up and dialed Jersey City Police. A man answered on the third ring. "Detective Hernandez."

"Detective, this is agent Rudolph with the FBI anti-terrorism taskforce."

"Yes, what can I do for you?" The man was tired.

"Just one question detective. Can you tell me if any of the bodies from last night have been I.D.'d?"

"Just one." He ruffled through some papers. "Mordari, Joaquin. He's the only one so far."

"And the female?"

"No female."

"What about the one they took from the scene?"

"No female. There was no female among the casualties or injured on scene."

"Thank you."

"Who's this again?" Lance had already hung up and was headed out the door, after thanking the secretary again.

He walked at first. Needed to get clear in his head what he was thinking. If Seibel told him Marta was dead, the next obvious question was why. Why had he done it? What did he gain by doing it?

It didn't take Lance 30 more steps to figure it out. Seibel was trying to manipulate the situation for his gain once again. His gain was usually the government's benefit, but still, he was a selfish creature at heart. Seibel was trying to manipulate Lance. That was clear. But how long did he think he could keep the lie about Marta's death a secret? He'd have to hide her away somewhere and keep her hidden for months, maybe longer. It was devious. Or, and Lance didn't like this thought at all, maybe Seibel did plan on killing Marta to make some insane point.

Lance needed to pick up the pace. He stepped into the street and hailed a taxi. Traffic was heavy, but it would be faster than walking, or running 20 blocks, and he'd be a whole lot fresher when he got there.

During the taxi ride, he worked through his plan of attack once he reached the hospital. It involved deception and probably a god bit of killing. Maybe a lot of killing, if need be.

The first familiar face Lance saw when the taxi came around the corner from 13th Street onto 7th was Fuchs. He was standing on the corner talking on his huge cell phone. Lance told the driver to keep going another block. He kept his head down while passing Fuchs. He had the taxi drop him off a block past the hospital on Greenwich and started back on foot toward a side entrance. Once inside, he stopped a nice elderly volunteer and asked for assistance locating a patient, or at least the ICU. The woman was most helpful and happy to hear that Lance was able to make it here from Au Claire, Wisconsin.

She told Lance where to find the ICU, the best elevator to take and who to ask for once he was up there. He asked her for a hospital map before heading out. He memorized it while walking to the second bank of elevators.

On the 9th floor, he stepped off and turned right. At the end of the hall he saw two CIA agents doing a lousy job of not looking like CIA agents. They missed him as he crossed the hall and stepped into a break room. He found a couple of lab coats hanging on a rack and took off his jacket to put one on. He put the cell phone in a pocket. Through another door in the break room was a doctor's lounge. A third-year resident was sleeping on a couch. He plucked the I.D. off the guy's scrubs.

He stepped back into the hall and walked toward the two men and then stopped to grab two footies from a box to put over his shoes. He took a surgical mask and put it on over his head but let it hang around his neck. He walked right past the two CIA guards with nothing more than a nod. Inside the ICU, he looked right then left and saw Seibel through several panes of glass. He was sitting in a chair beside a bed. Lance couldn't see who was in the bed, but he had a good idea.

Lance stepped to the right and into a washroom where doctors and nurses scrub up before visiting patients. Inside, he closed the glass door behind him and pulled the dead terrorist's cell phone from the lab coat's pocket. He could see Seibel about 40 feet away.

He dialed and waited. On the fourth ring Seibel picked up. Lance could see the phone come to Seibel's ear. "Lance. I know this is difficult."

"I need to see you, now." Lance was short.

"I understand."

"Now. I'll meet you on the corner of 7th and 16th in 15 minutes."

"Lance, I can't get away. There is too much action here."

"15 minutes. Be there. Tell Fuchs to come as well. He's with you, right?" And Lance hung up. He watched Seibel sit there for a moment. Twenty seconds later, he stood and walked out of the glass room and out of the Intensive Care Unit.

Lance waited another 30 seconds and then stepped into the unit and down to the small glass room. From outside the glass, he could see her, see her injuries. She was bandaged and bruised and bandaged some more. She had an I.V. and an oxygen line. It looked like she had surgery not too long ago. Lance stepped in.

He held her hand. It was just over a year and a half ago that she had stuck her head into his hospital room in Hawaii. Difference was, he was awake and conscious and able to stand on his own two feet. Following her out of the building to freedom was easy. Marta was in no shape to be moved. He couldn't pick her up and carry her out. She truly needed intensive care. She was barely alive. But she was alive.

She looked like hell, but he was just so relieved to see her. Pleased beyond belief to see her still breathing. Marta would pull through. She had to. He kneeled and put her hand to his lips and kissed it. He sang a couple of lines from one of her favorite Russian songs with his lips pressed to her skin.

He stayed with her for an hour. He didn't notice or look up to see Seibel and Fuchs standing out in the main area. They didn't invade his privacy. Additional CIA guards had been stationed at the entrances and exits to the unit. A group of nurses had been herded into the nurse's station. They were all looking at him. Lance didn't care. She was alive.

Finally, just after noon, he pulled away from her. He kissed her on the forehead and stepped out of the glass box. He walked over to Seibel and Fuchs. They said nothing. Nobody wanted a scene in the ICU, so they all walked slowly out of the unit. Out in the hall, Seibel gestured toward the waiting room. Inside were two more CIA agents. All waiting family members had been ushered out. As Lance, Seibel and Fuchs took a seat, sirens could be heard racing by on the streets below. Lance looked in that direction instinctively. Seibel did not. Fuchs was indifferent. Lance noticed his German mentor had a number of scratches and bruises on his face and neck. They looked like the result of an explosion.

A Peter Gabriel song, one of Lance's favorites, started playing in his head. The DJ in his brain only played this one when Lance, or Preacher, was in the mood to do bad, often very bad things.

"She is hanging on." Seibel nodded.

"Barely."

"The doctors say it will be touch and go over the next 24 hours. Her injuries are life-threatening, very severe. She probably won't make it."

"Obviously." Lance was not amused with his small talk. "So you have some explaining to do."

"I suppose this looks pretty bad to you. Like maybe I am playing with you and your life."

"Yep, just like Dallas all over again."

"Looks can be deceiving Lance."

"How so?"

"As usual, I have my reasons and they are 'need to know.' Which means I need to know and nobody else does."

Lance laughed. It was an empty laugh. "That's fine. I don't give a crap about your little geo-political games. Why did you tell me she was dead? What do you gain? How does it help national security?"

Seibel turned to Fuchs for a moment and then back to Lance. "Preacher, nothing is ever as it seems. Nothing. Marta is the person you know, and she is also someone completely different, something totally alien to you."

"How's that?"

"She is loyal Lance. Loyal to her mission above all else. And she has never, and I mean not ever, failed." Seibel nodded.

Lance analyzed the words. He knew of her activities since Baghdad right up until today. She had only failed twice, in Baghdad and yesterday, when she was nearly blown up. "Never?"

It was Fuchs who answered this time, "Never. Better percentage than you or me or anyone else. She may not have your unique skills, but she makes up for it in tenacity and commitment. I would never want to go up against her."

Seibel continued, "She has completed every mission given her. Including you." Those were the words Lance was waiting to hear. The words he had been looking at from front and back and still did not want to hear. In his heart, he was fine with Marta playing a part, a role. But he did not want to think, want to admit that she had never been changed by him. It was naïve, he knew.

"So, she completed her mission with me?" Lance asked.

"Lance. I'm sorry. Yes, she did." Seibel was somber.

"Can I ask what that mission was?"

"Look around you. Where are you? What have you done?"

"She was supposed to make sure I came to New York? That I track Anwar?" It seemed more than a little weak.

"She did it. You did what no one has been able to do. You found him, killed him. I wasn't sure you could do it, but she was. And so was he." Seibel pointed a thumb at Fuchs. "And what do you know? You end up saving thousands and a national landmark. You are the most amazing thing I've ever seen."

"After her." Lance corrected him.

"No, she is excellent and trustworthy and remarkably dependable. You, on the other hand, are utterly unique in your approach to life and death. You are like nothing any of us have seen before in your creative ability to solve our problems."

Lance was back to Marta's two failures. But then another round of multiple sirens sounded on the streets below and then an alarm sounded throughout the building. 'Code Yellow. Code Yellow. All mass casualty personnel report to stations. This is not a drill. Repeat, this is not a drill.'

Lance sat up. He noticed Seibel and Fuchs did not. They heard the same alarm and message, yet they were unmoved by it. His first thought was that the bombs in the Empire State Building had gone off. But then he stood and looked to the south. A pillar of smoke rose from the World Trade Center a mile and a half away. It was too dark to be steam, definitely smoke.

He turned back to them. "You said she has never failed. But she failed badly in Baghdad when I nearly killed her. And she was almost killed last night. She's barely alive in there. I'd say those were two very definite failures." Lance looked back at the World Trade Center.

Seibel sighed, "Lance, that is what I meant when I said 'nothing is ever what it seems.' You see Marta nearly being killed by you and then again early this morning as failures. I see a true professional at work. She is a marvel when it comes to succeeding in her missions."

"Missions?"

"Yes Lance. You were her mission. She was to fall in love with you, but most of all, make you fall in love with her. She succeeded in ways I never expected." Lance didn't want to believe it. But both he and Preacher always felt Marta was too good to be true. She was simply too special for him. His time with her, the love they shared, might have been a dream, a perfect dream. Maybe it wasn't real. Damn.

No. Seibel was lying. His words hurt, whether or not they were lies. But, Lance always expected such treatment from life, from a cruel universe.

"So, what about this morning in Jersey City and the bomb that nearly killed her? How was that a success? She went there to stop Yousef. He got away, right?"

And Lance suddenly felt really dense. He had not put two and two together to make five. He spun back around and looked at the smoke from the twin towers. "Jesus, they bombed the towers. They bombed the World Trade Center didn't they?" He stepped to the window. Seibel sat forward in his seat and rubbed his face. Fuchs remained back in his.

And it hit him, right between the eyes, like a bullet from her gun. She never missed. "You're going to tell me that she didn't fail, aren't you?"

Seibel dropped the hands from his face to look at him. "No, she didn't fail."

"I'm supposed to believe she made sure Yousef got away. Made sure he delivered his bomb." He turned from the window and looked up at the corner of the room expecting to see himself floating there. But no one was there. It was just him, stuck in his head with no Preacher, and now, no Marta. It really sucked.

He turned to face Seibel and Fuchs again. But instead of being seated, they both stood. Fuchs had a strange gun pointed at him. And in the doorway, three agents held the same guns. He was pissed, really pissed and ready to explode.

"You knew he was going to bomb the World Trade Center. You let him do it." His voice was measured, but his body was tense, like a leopard ready to leap at its prey. Ready to rip it to pieces.

"Lance. Don't be absurd. I would never allow a bomb to kill innocent people. But we can't stop every attack."

Lance exploded before the last syllable was spoken. Fuchs, and the three agents, fired at the same time. Lance was hit by four tranquilizer darts. The sedative was fast acting, but not fast enough to stop Preacher from jumping the row of chairs between him and Seibel and landing a swinging blow to Seibel's neck that nearly separated the man's head from the rest of his body. He was delivering a knee to his boss's sternum when he was viciously kicked in the head. It was Fuchs, and it should have knocked him out, but it didn't. Lance was unstoppable in this mission. He grabbed Seibel's throat with the intention of ripping out trachea and arteries and veins and tendons and the old man's life. But the problem was his hand. It wouldn't grip, wouldn't squeeze like it needed to. It wouldn't respond. Another blow caught him in the head and then another tranquilizer hit him in the neck.

Then there were bodies on him. Blows rained down. He kept fighting, struggling, but his arms wouldn't move. His legs wouldn't kick or run. Peter Gabriel sang the last lines of that favorite song. Marta's face was all he could see, all he ever wanted to see.

And then he was under. He was gone. Lance Priest was gone.

Epilogue

Frank Wyrick seldom failed in his assignments. Geoffrey Seibel had entrusted the surveillance expert with dozens, hundreds of assignments in 25-plus years.

It was Wyrick who first looked into a 12-year-old boy named Lance Porter Priest in Fort Worth, Texas. And it was Wyrick who arrived in Tulsa, Oklahoma in 1987 to again delve into a 21-year old candidate.

Wyrick was an expert at gathering information. He used audio, video and was more than adept at examining files and paperwork to ferret out details others missed. He was a gifted spy, even though he didn't officially work for the CIA.

But this assignment, the mission just completed as he walked out the doors of the Central Intelligence Agency headquarters in Langley, Virginia, was different. Seibel tasked Wyrick with something he had never done before. And Frank Wyrick seldom failed.

For this mission, he was not gathering information. Instead, the surveillance pro had been asked, ordered really, to eliminate information. His job this time was to erase, eradicate, wipe out and destroy evidence. Wyrick had done just that.

In the preceding eleven months, Wyrick had traveled thousands of miles, visited hundreds of locations, watched thousands, literally thousands of hours of video, listened to endless audio and read millions of words. Instead of keeping videotape, audiocassettes and reams of paper and storing the data in a secure facility only he and Seibel knew about, Wyrick destroyed each and every piece of evidence. Everything.

Walking out of CIA headquarters just now, Wyrick looked back for a moment before moving on. Behind him, he had pulled up the very last piece of computer data containing information about the subject. He deleted it, and erased the hard drive of the huge computer.

All evidence was gone. CIA operative Lance Porter Priest was gone. Nothing remained. No proof that Lance had ever been associated with, evaluated by, recruited or hired by the CIA remained. Seibel kept most of it off the books the past five years, and before that. But small fragments existed. File entries, security video, telephone recordings and notes provided by a staff psychologist named Braden, had made their way into official CIA records.

But now, eleven months later, Wyrick had completed his mission. It was all gone. Everything. Nothing remained. Lance joined Marta in the black hole that was a unique creation of a genius, evil or otherwise. Seibel required complete control of his universe. And now he had it. He had Lance and his life and future in his hand.

Less than 10 humans knew about his identity as a CIA resource. And Seibel held complete control over these people. He had plans to eliminate many of them. Not just erasing information they possessed, but erasing their lives, their existence in his universe. He had big plans for his ghost agent.

She lived a waking dream. Something scarcely more than dead, but less than alive. She had no will.

Her creator, the one who functioned as a ruthless god in her world, had held her hand when she came to after days, maybe years. He told her the news after she pleaded. Her love, her life was gone. He had tracked and followed Yousef to his destination that morning. He was there when the truck exploded in the underground garage of the World Trade Center.

Lance tried to stop the explosion. He was right next to the truck, when it blew. He was gone. Seibel said the words with pain in his voice and tears in his eyes. He was a liar without peer. Almost.

The nurse's name was Jenni, with an "i." Her mom did that to her. When relatives started shortening her baby daughter's name from Jennifer to Jenni, she insisted it be spelled like that. Not "ie" or "y." Nurse Jenni didn't think about that as she checked patient vitals at 2:30 a.m. in a secret medical facility.

She knew only this patient's first name, per protocol. The woman was Patient Susan, and she was beat to all hell. This patient was brought in yesterday from an undisclosed location. Jenni and the select team at the facility knew from lots of experience not to ask questions. But it was obvious this poor woman had been in a terrible accident. Looked like an explosion of some sort because of the burn marks and array of injuries.

Nurse Jenni noted Patient Susan's heartbeat, blood pressure, oxygen saturation and pulse. None of the numbers were great, but they were stable. She added her 2:30 a.m. data collection to the patient's medical chart hanging at the end of the bed. She flipped a few more pages into the chart to take a look at lab results. The hospital name and information where the lab work was initially done had been redacted, as usual.

Jenni leafed through and found what she was looking for. She might be a trusted, ethical and confidential employee of a classified government medical facility, but Jenni was also a mother. She had two little ones at home. She was trained and excelled at not becoming emotionally involved with patients. But a mother can't help it. Jenni pursed her lips and shook her head when she read the information an ultrasound had confirmed. Too bad. The injuries were too severe.

She looked up from the chart to the sleeping face of Patient Susan. "I'm sorry honey. I'm sure that little angel who was inside you is in heaven now. God bless."

ABOUT THE AUTHOR

So, here is where you read interesting information about Christopher Metcalf. The basics – he's married to the beautiful Diana and they have five, yes five, kids. The family lives in Oklahoma. You can learn more about the author or contact Chris by visiting www.christophermetcalf.com.

Chris really appreciates your time and hopes you enjoyed reading *The Perfect Weapon*. If you haven't read it, *The Perfect Candidate* is the first book in the Lance Priest series. *The Perfect Angel*, the third installment, will be published in late 2012. Preacher has to overcome significant challenges. But no one ever said life, or death, is fair.

THE PERFECT ANGEL

COMING SOON

Lance Priest is dead.

He wouldn't use those exact words. No, Geoffrey Seibel was more delicate, more eloquent. Seated opposite Janet Loomis and her husband Rich, Seibel perfected the image of remorse; his head bowed at the appropriate angle, his eyes smiling, yet glistening with sorrow for their loss.

He had sat here before, in this very room. Seibel had lied to these two people before, one a mother, the other a stepfather. He sat and spoke with them about their son's great achievements as an Army recruit. Their son Lance had earned distinction and honor in Iraq. He was injured, but would be fine. He was a fighter and a soldier. Seibel left out the part about Lance being in Baghdad with a team of CIA operatives and Delta Force specialists to intercept nuclear weapons and try to assassinate Saddam. And he neglected to tell Lance's mother that her son was a spy, a spook, a CIA operative trained to hunt, destroy and kill. And he was the best Seibel had ever seen.

Then, as now, he wore the uniform of a major in the U.S. Army. The uniform was only a partial lie. He was, at one point in his distant past, a distinguished officer in the nation's armed forces. It was a long time ago. Wearing the uniform now was a cover he assumed several times a year. He used the uniform like he did most everything else in life. It was there to help him achieve a goal. It was a prop. Nothing more.

He traveled to Tulsa, Oklahoma this time to personally deliver terrible news to the parents of one of the country's brave soldiers. He could tell by the way they sat holding hands on the sofa across the coffee table from him that they knew he had not come for pleasantries. So he got right to it.

"You both know how proud of Lance the Army and our government are," Seibel nodded his head as he said the words.

"Yes, we all are," Rich spoke for both of them.

"And you know that because of his impressive work in Iraq and other assignments, Lance had been given additional responsibilities." Seibel looked each of them in the eye.

"We don't really know what Lance has been doing the last couple years. He only told us it was a special assignment that required him to travel a lot," Rich squeezed Janet's hand. She sighed; it was painful for Seibel to watch.

"Major Seibel, do you have something to tell us? We are pleased to see you, but why are you here?" Lance's mother had the gift of directness. Seibel liked that.

The CIA legend nodded and sat forward to put his forearms on his thighs. The uniform was a little snugger than it had been the last time he was here two years ago, right after Desert Storm. "Yes Mrs. Loomis, I have something to tell you, to tell you both. For the last two years, Lance was assigned to an anti-terrorism taskforce operated jointly with the FBI. He was tracking several terrorist cells. His gift with foreign languages, especially Arabic, was extremely useful." And with that, he let it slip, gently. He used "was" instead of "is." The past tense of the word had a physical effect on the mother. She inhaled sharply but kept her eyes on Seibel.

"Lance was working with the team tracking the cell responsible for the World Trade Center bombing last week." Seibel paused.

"Go on sir," Rich urged him on and put a hand onto his wife's shoulder.

"Lance was very close, extremely close. He was there, in the building. He was in the parking garage where the explosion took place." Seibel looked down at the hat in his hands. He didn't need to say more. They knew why he was here.

Janet dropped her head and put a closed fist to her mouth. "Is he gone?" She whispered the words.

"Yes ma'am. He was killed in the explosion, along with several others. He served his country well, a hero." Seibel raised his eyes to meet Rich's. Janet could only look at the floor. She had just learned her oldest son was dead. She shook her head slightly as a tear began its journey down her cheek.

"Did you bring him home? Did you bring his body?"

"Yes. I escorted his remains and casket." Seibel nodded. And with that, Janet broke down. Rich took her into his arms. She buried her face in his shoulder. She sobbed. The two men let her.

Minutes later, Janet and Rich stood to thank Major Seibel for coming in person to deliver the news. Rich shook the Major's hand. Janet gave a wet hug. Seibel stood outside the home signaling a white van parked down the street to pull up to the curb. There were plans to make, a funeral to arrange for a fallen hero. Lance had always expressed his desire to be cremated.

Seibel stood beside the van where four uniformed Army personnel stepped out of the vehicle and stood at attention. He turned back to look at the house. He knew a woman stood behind the closed front door. Maybe she had fallen to the floor. Such a terrible blow. To have your child die before you.

Seibel knew that pain as well. But he didn't think about that standing there in front of the grieving home. His face showed nothing but remorse and sorrow. Behind his eyes, there were other feelings. Like always.

Light and dark blurred. Time fell in on itself. Movement, jarring movement, bookended by endless immobilization. Pain was measured in degrees, but not really. There wasn't really any feeling. Not really. There was always something insulating. Something smothering everything else. One thing kept it all from collapsing into blackness. It was Neil Sedaka. *Damn.*

www.ingramcontent.com/pod-product-compliance
Lightning Source LLC
Chambersburg PA
CBHW020819180626
46814CB00001B/35